Our Admirable Betty
A Romance

by

Jeffery Farnol

Our Admirable Betty
A Romance

by Jeffery Farnol

ISBN: 978-93-61157-70-7

Published by

DOUBLE 9 BOOKS

2/13-B, Ansari Road
Daryaganj, New Delhi – 110002
info@double9books.com
www.double9books.com
Tel. 011-40042856

ABOUT THE AUTHOR

From 1907 until his death in 1952, Jeffery Farnol was a British writer who wrote over 40 romance novels, many of which were set in the Georgian Era or English Regency period, as well as swashbucklers. He, along with Georgette Heyer, played a key role in establishing the Regency romance genre. John Jeffery Farnol was born in Aston, Birmingham, England, as the son of Henry John Farnol, a factory-employed brass-founder, and Kate Jeffery. He had two brothers and one sister. He spent his childhood in London and Kent. He went to Westminster School of Art after losing his job at a Birmingham metal-working company. In 1900, he married Blanche Wilhelmina Victoria Hawley (1883-1955), the 16-year-old daughter of renowned New York scenic artist H. Hughson Hawley. They moved to the United States, where he found work as a scene painter. They had a daughter, Gillian Hawley. He returned to England in 1910, settling in Eastbourne, Sussex. He divorced Blanche in 1938, married Phyllis Mary Clarke on May 20, and adopted her daughter Charmian Jane. His nephew was Ewart Oakeshott, a British illustrator, collector, and amateur historian who wrote on medieval arms and armour.

CONTENTS

CHAPTER I
CONCERNING THE MAJOR'S CHERRIES

"The Major, mam, the Major has a truly wonderful 'ead!" said Sergeant Zebedee Tring as he stood, hammer in hand, very neat and precise from broad shoe-buckles to smart curled wig that offset his square, bronzed face.

"Head, Sergeant, head!" retorted pretty, dimpled Mrs. Agatha, nodding at the Sergeant's broad back.

"'Ead mam, yes!" said the Sergeant, busily nailing up a branch of the Major's favourite cherry tree. "The Major has a truly wonderful 'ead, regarding which I take liberty to ob-serve as two sword-cuts and a spent bullet have in nowise affected it, Mrs. Agatha, mam, which is a fact as I will maintain whenever and wherever occasion demands, as in dooty bound mam, dooty bound."

"Duty, Sergeant, duty!"

"Dooty, mam—pre-cisely." Here the Sergeant turning round for another nail, Mrs. Agatha bent over the rose-bush, her busy fingers cutting a bloom here and another there and her pretty face quite hidden in the shade of her mob-cap.

"Indeed," she continued, after a while, "'tis no wonder you be so very— fond of him, Sergeant!"

"Fond of him, mam, fond of him," said the Sergeant turning to look at her with glowing eyes, "well—yes, I suppose so—it do be a—a matter o' dooty with me—dooty, Mrs. Agatha, mam."

"You mean duty, Sergeant."

"Dooty, mam, pre-cisely!" nodded the Sergeant, busy at the cherry tree again.

"See how very brave he is!" sighed Mrs. Agatha.

"Brave, mam?" The Sergeant paused with his hammer poised— "Sixteen wounds, mam, seven of 'em bullet and the rest steel! Twenty and three pitched battles besides outpost skirmishes and the like and 'twere his honour the Major as saved our left wing at Ramillies. Brave, mam? Well—yes, he's brave."

"And how kind and gentle he is!"

"Because, mam, because the best soldiers always are."

"And you, Sergeant, see what care you take of him."

"Why, I try, mam, I try. Y'see, we've soldiered together so many years and I've been his man so long that 'tis become a matter o'——"

"Of duty, Sergeant—yes, of course!"

"Dooty, mam—pre-cisely!" nodded the Sergeant.

"Pre-cisely, Sergeant and, lack-a-day, how miserable and wretched you both are!"

The Sergeant looked startled.

"And the strange thing is you don't know it," said Mrs. Agatha, snipping off a final rose.

The Sergeant rubbed his square, clean-shaven chin and stared at her harder than ever.

"See how monstrous lonely you are!" sighed Mrs. Agatha, hiding her face among her newly-gathered blooms, a face as sweet and fresh as any of them, despite the silver that gleamed, here and there, beneath her snowy mob-cap.

"Lonely?" said the Sergeant, staring from her to the hammer in his hand, "lonely, why no mam, no. The Major's got his flowers and his cherries and his great History of Fortification as he's a-writing of in ten vollums and I've got the Major and we've both got—got——

"Well, what, Sergeant?"

The Sergeant turned and began to nail up another branch of the great cherry tree, ere he answered:

"You, mam—we've both got—you, mam—"

"Lud, Sergeant Tring, and how may that be?"

"To teach," continued the Sergeant slowly, "to teach two battered old soldiers, as never knew it afore, what a home might be. There never was such a housekeeper as you, mam, there never will be!"

"A home!" repeated Mrs. Agatha softly. "'Tis a sweet word!"

"True, mam, true!" nodded the Sergeant emphatically. "'Specially to we, mam, us never having had no homes, d'ye see. His honour and me have been campaigning most of our days—soldiers o' fortune, mam, though there weren't much fortune in it for us except hard knocks—a saddle for a piller, earth for bed and sometimes a damned—no, a—damp bed, mam, the sky for roof——"

"But you be come home at last, Sergeant," said Mrs. Agatha softer than ever.

"Home? Aye, thanks to his honour's legacy as came so sudden and unexpected. Here's us two battered old soldiers comes marching along and finds this here noble mansion a-waiting for us full o' furniture and picters and works o' hart——"

"Art, Sergeant!"

"Aye, hart, mam—pre-cisely—and other knick-knacks and treasures and among 'em—best and brightest——"

"Well, Sergeant?"

"Among 'em—you, mam!" said he; and here, aiming a somewhat random blow with the hammer he hit himself on the thumb and swore. Whereon Mrs. Agatha, having duly reproved him, was for examining the injured member but, shaking his head, he sucked it fiercely instead and thereafter proceeded to hammer away harder than ever.

"But then—you are—neither of you so very—old, Sergeant."

"The Major was thirty-one the day Ramillies was fought and I was thirty-three—and that was ten years agone mam."

"And you are both monstrous young for your age—so straight and upright—and handsome. Y-e-e-s, the Major is very handsome—despite the scar on his cheek—the wonder to me is that he don't get married."

Hereupon the Sergeant dropped the hammer.

"As to yourself, Sergeant," pursued Mrs. Agatha, her bright eyes brimfull of mischief, "you'll never be really happy and content until you do."

Hereupon the Sergeant stooped for the hammer and seemed uncommonly red in the face about it.

"As to that mam," said he, a thought more ponderously than usual, "as to that, I shall never look for a wife until the Major does, it has become a matter o'——"

"Duty, of course, Sergeant!"

"Of dooty, mam—pre-cisely!" Saying which, the Sergeant turned to his work again; but, chancing to lift his gaze to a certain lofty branch that crawled along the wall just beneath the coping, he fell back a pace and uttered a sudden exclamation:

"*Sacré bleu!*"

"Lud, Sergeant!" cried Mrs. Agatha, clasping her posy to her bosom and giving voice to a small, a very small scream, "how you do fright one with your outlandish words! What ails the man—there be no Frenchmen here to fight—speak English, Sergeant—do!"

"Zounds!" exclaimed the Sergeant with his gaze still fixed.

"Sergeant—pray don't oathe!"

"But zookers, mam——!"

"Sergeant—ha' done, I say!"

"But damme, Mrs. Agatha mam, asking your pardon, I'm sure—but don't ye see—he's been at 'em again! The three best clusters on the tree—gone, mam, gone! Stole, Mrs. Agatha mam, 'twixt now and twelve o'clock noon——"

"O Gemini, the wretch!"

"I'll take my oath them cherries was a-blowing not an hour agone, mam, on that branch atop the wall!"

"Who could ha' done it?"

"Not knowing, mam, can't say, but this last week the rogue has captured fourteen squads of our best cherries—off this one tree, and this, as you know, Mrs. Agatha mam, be the Major's favourite tree! So I say, mam, whoever the villain be, I say—damn him, Mrs. Agatha mam!"

"Fie—fie, Sergeant, swearing will not mend matters."

"Maybe not, mam, maybe not, but same does me a power o' good! Egad, when I mind how I've watched and tended them particular cherries Mrs. Agatha I could——"

"Then don't, Sergeant!"

"What beats me," said he, rubbing his square chin with the shaft of the hammer, "what beats me is—how did he do it? Must be uncommonly long in the arms and legs to reach so high unless he used a pole——"

"Or a ladder?" suggested Mrs. Agatha.

"Meaning he did it by escalade, mam? Hum—no, I see no signs of scaling ladders mam and the ground is soft, d'ye see? But a pole now——"

"Or a ladder—on the other side of the wall, Sergeant——"

"B'gad, mam!" he exclaimed. "I believe you're right—though to be sure the house next door is empty."

"Was!" corrected Mrs. Agatha. "Lud, Sergeant, there's a great lady from London been living there a month and more with a houseful of lackeys and servants."

"Ha, a month, mam? Lackeys and servants say you? B'gad, say I, that's them! Must report this to the Major. Must report at once!" and the Sergeant laid down his hammer.

"And where is the Major?"

"Mam," said the Sergeant, consulting a large, brass chronometer, "the hour is pre-cisely three-fourteen, consequently he is now a-sitting in his Ramillie coat a-writing of his History of Fortification—in ten vollums."

"'Twill be pity to wake him!" sighed Mrs. Agatha.

"Wake him?" repeated the Sergeant, staring; whereupon Mrs. Agatha laughed and went her way while he continued to stare after her until her trim figure and snowy mob-cap had vanished behind the yew-hedge.

Then the Sergeant sighed, reached for his coat, put it on, adjusted his tall, leathern stock, sighed again and turning sharp about, marched into the house.

CHAPTER II
INTRODUCING THE RAVISHER OF THE SAME

Major John D'Arcy was hard at work on his book (that is to say, he had been, for divers plans and papers littered the table before him) but just now he leaned far back in his elbow-chair, long legs stretched out, deep-plunged in balmy slumber; perceiving which the Sergeant halted suddenly, stood at ease and stared.

The Major's great black peruke dangled from the chair-back, and his close-cropped head (already something grizzled at the temples) was bowed upon his broad chest, wherefore, ever and anon, he snored gently. The Major was forty-one but just now as he sat lost in the oblivion of sleep he looked thirty; but then again when he strode gravely to and fro in his old service coat (limping a little by reason of an old wound) and with black brows wrinkled in sober thought he looked fifty at the least.

Thus he continued to sleep and the Sergeant to stare until presently, choking upon a snore, the Major opened his eyes and sat up briskly, whereupon the Sergeant immediately came to attention.

"Ha, Zeb!" exclaimed the Major in mild wonder, "what is it, Sergeant Zeb?"

"Your honour 'tis the cherries——"

"Cherries?" yawned the Major, "the cherries are doing very well, thanks to your unremitting care, Sergeant, and of all fruits commend me to cherries. Now had it been cherries that led our common mother Eve into—ha—difficulties, Sergeant, I could have sympathised more deeply with her lamentable—ha—I say with her very deplorable—ha——"

"Reverse, sir?"

"Reverse?" mused the Major, rubbing his chin. "Aye, reverse will serve, Zeb, 'twill serve!"

"And three more squads of 'em missing, sir—looted, your honour's arternoon by means of escalade t'other side party-wall. Said cherries believed to have been took by parties unknown lately from London, sir, not sixty minutes since and therefore suspected to be not far off."

"Why, this must be looked to, Zeb!" said the Major, rising. "So, Sergeant, let us look—forthwith."

"Wig, sir!" suggested the Sergeant, holding it out.

"Aye, to be sure!" nodded the Major, taking and clapping it on somewhat askew. "Now—Sergeant—forward!"

"Stick, sir!" said the Sergeant, proffering a stout crab-tree staff.

"Aye!" smiled the Major, twirling it in a sinewy hand, "'twill be useful like as not."

So saying (being ever a man of action) the Major sallied forth carrying the stick very much as if it had been a small-sword; along the terrace he went and down the steps (two at a time) and so across the wide sweep of velvety lawn with prodigious strides albeit limping a little by reason of one of his many wounds, the tails of his war-worn Ramillie coat fluttering behind. Reaching the orchard he crossed to a particular corner and halted before a certain part of the red brick wall where grew the cherry tree in question.

"Sir," said the Sergeant, squaring his shoulders, "you'll note as all cherries has been looted from top branch—only ones as was ripe——"

"A thousand devils!" exclaimed the Major.

"Also," continued the Sergeant, "said branch has been broke sir."

"Ten thousand——" The Major stopped suddenly and shutting his mouth very tight opened his grey eyes very wide and stared into two other eyes which had risen into view on the opposite side of the wall, a pair of eyes that looked serenely down at him, long, heavy-lashed, deeply blue beneath the curve of their long, black lashes; he was conscious also of a nose, neither straight nor aquiline, of a mouth scarlet and full-lipped, of a chin round, white, dimpled but combative and of a faded sun-bonnet beneath whose crumpled brim peeped a tress of glossy, black hair.

"Now God—bless—my soul!" exclaimed the Major.

"'Tis to be hoped so, sir," said the apparition gravely, "you were swearing, I think?"

The Major flushed.

"Young woman——" he began.

"Ancient man!"

"Madam!"

"Sir!"

The Major stood silent awhile, staring up into the grave blue eyes above the wall.

"Pray," said he at last, "why do you steal my cherries?"

"To speak truth, sir, because I am so extreme fond of cherries."

Here Sergeant Tring gurgled, choked, coughed and finding the Major's eye upon him immediately came to attention, very stiff in the back and red in the face.

The Major stroked his clean-shaven chin and eyed him askance.

"Sergeant, you may—er—go," said he; whereat the Sergeant saluted, wheeled sharply and marched swiftly away.

"And pray," questioned the Major again, "who might you be?"

"A maid, sir."

"Hum!" said he, "and what would your mistress say if she knew you habitually stole and ate my cherries?"

"My mistress?" The grave blue eyes opened wider.

"Aye," nodded the Major, "the fine London lady. You are her maid, I take it?"

"Indeed, sir, her very own."

"Well, suppose I inform her of your conduct, how then?"

"She'd swear at me, sir."

"Egad, and would she so?"

"O, sir, she often doth and stamps at and reviles and rails at me morning, noon and night!"

"Poor child!" said the Major.

"Truly, sir, I do think she'd do me an injury if she didn't care for me so much."

"Then she cares for you?"

"More than anyone in the world beside! Indeed she loveth me as herself, sir!"

"Women be mysterious creatures!" said the Major, sententiously.

"But you know my lady belike by repute, sir?"

"Not even her name."

"Not know of the Lady Elizabeth Carlyon!" and up went a pair of delicate black brows in scornful amaze.

"I have known but three women in my life, and one of them my mother," he answered.

"You sound rather dismal, methinks. But you must have remarked my lady in the Mall, sir?"

"I seldom go to London."

"Now, sir, you sound infinite dismal and plaguily dull!"

"Dull?" repeated the Major thoughtfully, "aye perhaps I am, and 'tis but natural—ancient men often are, I believe."

"And your peruke is all askew!"

"Alack, it generally is!" sighed the Major.

"And you wear a vile old coat!"

"Truly I fear it hath seen its best days!" sighed the Major, glancing down wistfully at the war-worn garment in question.

"O, man," she cried, shaking her head at him, "for love of Heaven don't be so pestilent humble—I despise humility in horse or man!"

"Humble? Am I?" queried the Major and fell to pondering the question, chin in hand.

"Aye, truly," she answered, nodding aggressively, "your humility nauseates me, positively!"

"Child," he answered smiling, "what manner of man would you have?"

"Grandad," she answered, "I would have him tall and strong and brave, but—above all—masterful!"

"In a word, a blustering bully!" he answered gently, grey eyes a-twinkle.

"Aye," she nodded vehemently, "even that, rather than—than a—a——"

"An ancient man, ill-dressed and humble," he suggested and laughed; whereat she frowned and bit her bonnet-string in strong, white teeth, then:

"'Tis a very beast of a coat!" she exclaimed, "stained, spotted, tarnished, tattered and torn!"

"Torn!" exclaimed the Major, glancing down at himself again. "Egad and Sergeant Zebedee mended it but a week since——"

"And the buttons are scratched and hanging by threads!"

"Aye, but they'll not come off," said the Major confidently, "I sewed 'em on myself."

"You sewed them—you!" and she laughed in fine scorn. "Indeed, sir, I marvel they don't drop off under my very eyes!"

"Madam," said he gravely, "among few accomplishments, permit me to say I am a somewhat expert—er—needles-man."

Hereupon the apparition seated herself dexterously on the broad coping of the wall and from that vantage surveyed him with eyes of cold disparagement. And after she had regarded him thus for a long moment she spoke 'twixt curling red lips:

"O, Gemini—I might have known it!"

At this the Major ruffled the curls of his great wig and regarded her with some apprehension. At last he ventured a question:

"And pray madam, what might you have known concerning me?"

"A man who sews on his own buttons is a disgrace to his sex," she answered.

"But how if he have no woman to do it for him?"

"He should be a man and—get one."

"Hum!" said the Major thoughtfully, "a needle is a sharp engine and apt to prick one occasionally 'tis true, and yet a man may prefer it to a woman."

"And you," she exclaimed, drooping disdainful lashes, "you—are a—soldier!"

"I was!" he answered.

"Soldiers are gallant, they say."

"They are kind!" bowed the Major.

"You are, I think, the poor, old, wounded soldier Major d'Arcy who lives at the Manor yonder?" she questioned.

"I am that shattered wreck, madam, and what remains of me is very humbly at your service!" and setting hand to bosom of war-worn coat he bowed with a prodigious flourish.

"And you have never been so extreme fortunate as to behold my Lady Elizabeth Carlyon?"

"Hum!" said the Major, pondering, "what like is she?"

At this slender hands clasped each other, dark eyes upturned themselves to translucent heaven and rounded bosom heaved ecstatic:

"O sir, she is extreme beautiful, 'tis said! She is a toast adored! She is seen but to be worshipped! She hath wit, beauty and a thousand accomplishments! She hath such an air! Such a killing droop of the eyelash! She is—O, she is irresistible!"

"Indeed," said the Major, glancing up into the beautiful face above, "the description is just, though something too limited, perhaps."

The eyes came back to earth and the Major in a flash:

"Then you have seen her, sir?"

"I'm sure of it."

"Then describe her—come!"

"Why, she is, I judge, neither too short nor too tall!"

"True!" nodded the apparition, gently acquiescent.

"Of a delicate slimness— —"

"True—O, most true, sir!"

"Yet sufficiently—er—full and rounded!"

The dark eyes were veiled suddenly by down-drooping lashes:

"You think so, sir?"

"Hair night-black, a chin well-determined and bravely dimpled—

"It hath been remarked before, sir!"

"Rosy lips— —"

"Fie, sir, 'tis a vulgar phrase and trite. I suggest instead rose-petals steeped in dew."

"A nose— —"

"Indeed, sir?"

"Neither arched nor straight and eyes—eyes— —" the Major hesitated, stammered and came to an abrupt pause.

"And what of her eyes, sir? I have heard them called dreamy lakes, starry pools and unfathomable deeps, ere now. What d'you make of them?"

But the Major's own eyes were lowered, his bronzed cheek showed an unwonted flush and his sinewy fingers were fumbling with one of his loose coat-buttons.

"Nought!" said he at last, "others methinks have described 'em better than ever I could."

"Major d'Arcy," said the voice softer and sweeter than ever, "I grieve to tell you your wig is more over one eye than ever. And as for your old coat, some fine day, sir, an you chance to walk hereabouts I may possibly trouble to show you how a woman sews a button on!"

Saying which the apparition vanished as suddenly as it had appeared.

The Major stood awhile deep-plunged in reverie, then setting the crabtree staff beneath his arm he wended his way slowly towards the house, limping a little more than usual as he always did when much preoccupied.

On his way he chanced upon the Sergeant wandering somewhat aimlessly with a hammer in his hand.

"Sergeant," said he slowly, "er—Zebedee—if any more cherries—should happen to—er—go astray—vanish——"

"Or be stole, sir!" added the Sergeant.

"Exactly, Zeb, precisely,—if such a contingency should arise you will—er——"

"Challenge three times, sir and then—"

"Er—no, Sergeant, no! I think, under the circumstances, Zeb, we'll just—er—let 'em—ah—vanish, d'ye see!"

Then the Major limped slowly and serenely into the house and left the Sergeant staring at the hammer in his hand with eyes very wide and round.

"*Ventre bleu! Sacré bleu!* Zookers!" said he.

CHAPTER III
WHICH TELLS HOW THE MAJOR
CLIMBED A WALL

A wonderfully pleasant place was the Major's orchard, very retired and secluded by reason of its high old walls flushing rosily through green leaves; an orchard, this, full of ancient trees gnarled and crooked whose writhen boughs sprawled and twisted; an orchard carpeted with velvety turf whereon plump thrushes and blackbirds hopped and waddled, or, perched aloft, filled the sunny air with rich, throaty warblings and fluty trills and flourishes. Here Sergeant Tring, ever a man of his hands, had contrived and built a rustic arbour (its architecture faintly suggestive of a rabbit-hutch and a sentry-box) of which he was justly proud.

Now Major d'Arcy despite his many battles had an inborn love of peace and quietness, of the soft rustle of wind in leaves, of sunshine and the mellow pipe of thrush and blackbird, hence it was not at all surprising that he should develop a sudden fancy for strolling, to and fro in his orchard of a sunny afternoon, book in hand, or, sitting in the Sergeant's hutch-like sentry-box, puff dreamily at pipe of clay, or again, tucking up his ruffles and squaring his elbows, fall to work on his History of Fortification; and if his glance happened to rove from printed page or busy quill in a certain direction, what of it? Though it was to be remarked that his full-flowing peruke was seldom askew and the lace of his cravat and the ruffles below the huge cuffs of his Ramillie coat were of the finest point.

It was a hot afternoon, very slumberous and still; flowers drooped languid heads, birds twittered sleepily, butterflies wheeled and hovered, and the Major, sitting in the shady arbour, stared at a certain part of the old wall, sighed, and taking up his pipe began to fill it absently, his gaze yet fixed. All at once he sprang up, radiant-eyed, and strode across the smooth grass.

The faded sun-bonnet was not; her black hair was coiled high, while at white brow and glowing cheek silken curls wantoned in an artful disorder, moreover her simple russet gown had given place to a rich, flowered satin. All this he noticed at a glance though his gaze never wandered from the witching eyes of her. Were they blue or black or dark brown?

"Sir," said she, acknowledging his deep reverence with a stately inclination of her shapely head, "I would curtsey if I might, but to curtsey on a ladder were dangerous and not to be lightly undertaken."

Quoth the Major:

"It has been a long time—a very long time since you—since I—er—that is—

"Exactly five days, sir!"

"Why—ah—to be sure these summer days do grow uncommon long, mam—

"Which means, sir, that you've wanted me?"

The Major started:

"Why er—I—indeed I—I hardly know!" he stammered.

"Which proves it beyond all doubt!" she nodded serenely.

The Major was silent.

"Then, sir," she continued gravely, "since 'tis beyond all doubt you wanted me and hither came daily to look for me, as methinks you did—?"

Here she paused expectant, whereupon the Major stooped to survey his neat shoe-buckle.

"Well, sir, did you not come patiently a-seeking me here?"

"Why, mam," he answered, rubbing his chin with his pipe-stem, "'tis true I came hither—having a fancy for——"

"Then, sir, since being hither come you found me not, why, having legs, didn't you climb over the wall and seek me where you might have found me?"

The Major caught his breath and nearly dropped his pipe.

"Indeed it never occurred to me!"

"To be sure the climbing of walls is an infinite trying and arduous task for—ancient limbs," she sighed, shaking her head, "yet—even you, might have achieved it—with care."

The Major laughed:

"'Tis possible, mam," said he.

"And it never occurred to you?"

"No indeed, mam, and never would!"

"Then you lack imagination and a man without imagination is akin to the brutes and—" but here she broke off to utter a small scream and glancing up in alarm he saw her eyes were closed and that she shuddered violently.

"Madam!" he cried, "mam! My lady—good heaven are you sick—faint?"

Regardless of the cherry-tree he reached up long arms and swinging himself up astride the wall, had an arm about her shivering form all in a moment; thus as she leaned against him he caught the perfume of all her warm, soft daintiness, then she drew away.

"What was it?" he questioned anxiously as she opened her eyes, "were you faint, mam? Was it a fit? Good lack, mam, I——"

"Do—not—call me—that!" she cried, eyes flashing and—yes, they were blue—very darkly blue—"Never dare to call me—so—again!"

"Call you what, mam?"

"Mam!" she cried, gnashing her white teeth—"'tis a hateful word!"

"Indeed I—I had not thought it so," stammered the Major. "It is, I believe, a word in common use and——"

"Aye, 'tis common! 'Tis odious! 'Tis vulgar!"

"I crave your ladyship's pardon!" And he bowed as well as his position would allow, though a little stiffly.

"You are marvellous nimble, sir!"

"Your ladyship is gracious!"

"Considering your age, sir!"

"And you, madam, I lament that at yours you should be subject to fits."

"Fits!" she cried in frowning amaze.

"Seizures, then——"

"'Twas no seizure, sir—'twas yourself!"

"Me?" he exclaimed, staring.

"You—and your abominable tobacco-pipe!" Here she shivered daintily.

"Alack, madam, see, 'tis broke!"

"Heaven be thanked, sir."

"'Twas an admirable pipe—an old friend," he murmured.

"O fie, sir—only chairmen and watchmen and worse, drink smoke. 'Tis a low habit, vicious, vain and vulgar."

"Is it so indeed, madam?"

"It is! Aunt Belinda says so and I think so. If you must have vices why not snuff?"

"But I hate snuff!"

"But 'tis so elegant! There's Sir Jasper Denholm takes it with such an air I vow 'tis perfectly ravishing! And Sir Benjamin Tripp and Viscount Merivale in especial—such grace! Such an elegant turn of the wrist! But to suck a pipe—O Gemini!"

"I'm sorry my pipe offends you!" said he, glancing at her glowing loveliness.

And here, because of her beauty and nearness he grew silent and finding he yet held part of his clay pipe, broken in his hasty ascent, he fell to turning it over in his fingers, staring at it very hard but seeing it not at all; whereat she fell to studying him, his broad shoulders and powerful hands, his clean-cut aquiline features, his tender mouth and strong, square chin. Thus, the Major, glancing up suddenly, eye met eye and for a long moment they looked on one another, then, as she turned away he saw her cheek crimson suddenly and she, aware of this, clenched her white fists and flushed all the deeper. "'Tis abominable rude to—stare so!" she said, over her shoulder.

"You are the Lady Elizabeth Carlyon, I think?" he enquired.

"And then, sir?"

"Then you are well used to being stared at, methinks."

"At a distance, sir!"

Here the Major edged away a couple of inches.

"You have heard of such a person before, then?" she enquired loftily.

"I go to London—sometimes, madam, when I must and when last there I chanced to hear her acclaimed and toasted as the 'Admirable Betty'!" said he, frowning.

"I am sometimes called Betty, sir," she acknowledged.

"Also 'Bewitching Bet'!" Here he scowled fiercely at a bunch of cherries.

"Do you think Bet so ill a name, sir?" she enquired, stealing a glance at him.

"'Bewitching Bet'!" he repeated grimly and the hand that grasped his broken pipe became a fist, observing which she smiled slyly.

"Or is it that the 'bewitching' offends you, sir?" she questioned innocently.

"Both, mam, both!" said he, scowling yet.

"La, sir," she cried gaily, "in this light and at this precise angle I do protest you look quite handsome when you frown."

The Major immediately laughed.

"If," she continued, "your chin were less grim and craggy and your nose a little different and your eyes less like gimlets and needles—if you wore a modish French wig instead of a horsehair mat and had your garments made by a London tailor instead of a country cobbler and carpenter you would be almost attractive—by candle light."

"Is my wig so unmodish?" he enquired smiling a trifle ruefully, "'tis my best."

"Unmodish?" White hands were lifted, and sparkling eyes rolled themselves in agonised protest. "There's a new tie-wig come in—*un peu negligée*—a most truly ravishing confection. As for clothes——"

"And needles," he added, "pray what of your promise?"

"Promise, sir?"

"You were to teach me how to sew on a button, I think?"

"Button!" she repeated, staring,

"If you've forgot, 'tis no matter, madam," said he and dropped very nimbly from the wall.

"Ah, my forgetfulness hath angered you, sir."

"No, child, no, extreme youth is apt to be extreme thoughtless and forgetful——"

"Sir, I am twenty-two."

"And I am forty-one!" he said wistfully.

"'Tis a monstrous great age, sir!"

"I begin to fear it is!" said he rather ruefully.

"And great age is apt to be peevish and slothful and childish and fretful and must be ruled. So come you over the wall this instant, sir!"

"And wherefore, madam?"

"'Tis so my will!"

"But——"

"Plague take it, sir, how may I sew on your abominable buttons with a wall betwixt us? Over with you this moment—obey!"

The Major obeyed forthwith.

CHAPTER IV
CONCERNING THE BUTTONS
OF THE RAMILLIE COAT

"Now pray remark, sir," said the Lady Elizabeth Carlyon, seating herself in a shady arbour and taking up her needle and thread, "a woman, instead of sucking her thread and rubbing it into a black spike and cursing, threads her needle—so! Thereafter she takes the object to be sewed and holds it—no, she can't, sir, while you sit so much afar, prithee come closer to her—there! Yet no—'twill never do—she'll be apt to prick you sitting thus——"

"If I took off my coat, madam——"

"'Twould be monstrous indecorous, sir! No, you must kneel down—here at my feet!"

"But—madam——"

"To your knees, sir, or I'll prick you vilely! She now takes the article to be sewed and—pray why keep at such a distance? She cannot sew gracefully while you pull one way and she another! She then fits on her thimble, poises needle and—sews!" The which my lady forthwith proceeded to do making wondrous pretty play with white hand and delicate wrist the while.

And when she had sewn in silence for perhaps one half-minute she fell to converse thus:

"Indeed you look vastly appealing on your knees, sir. Pray have you knelt to many lovely ladies?"

"Never in my life!" he answered fervently.

"And yet you kneel with infinite grace—'tis quite affecting, how doth it feel to crouch thus humbly before the sex?"

"Uncommon hard to the knees, madam."

"Indeed I fear you have no soul, sir."

"Ha!" exclaimed the Major, rising hastily, "someone comes, I think!"

Sure enough, in due time, a somewhat languid but herculean footman appeared, who perceiving the Major, faltered, stared, pulled himself together and, approaching at speed, bowed in swift and supple humility and spoke:

"Four gentlemen to see your ladyship!"

"Only four? Their names?"

The large menial expanded large chest and spake with unction:

"The Marquis of Alton, Sir Jasper Denholm, Sir Benjamin Tripp and Mr. Marchdale."

"Well say I'm out—say I'm engaged—say I wish to be private!"

The large footman blinked, and the Major strove to appear unconscious that my lady held him tethered by needle and thread.

"Very good, madam! Though, 'umbly craving your ladyship's pardon, my lady, your aunt wished me to tell you most express— —"

"Well, tell her I won't!"

"My lady, I will—immediate!" So saying, the large footman bowed again, blinked again and bore himself off, blinking as he went.

"And now, Major d'Arcy, if you will condescend to abase yourself we will continue our sewing lesson."

"But mam— —"

"Do—not— —"

"Your ladyship's guests— —"

"Pooh! to my ladyship's guests! Come, be kneeling, sir, and take heed you don't break my thread."

"Now I wonder," said the Major, "I wonder what your lackey thinks— —"

"He don't, he can't, he never does—except about food or drink or tobacco—faugh!"

Up started the Major again as from the adjacent yew-walk a faint screaming arose.

"Good God!" exclaimed the Major. "'Tis a woman!"

"Nay sir, 'tis merely my aunt!"

"But madam—hark to her, she is in distress!"

"Nay sir, she doth but wail—'tis no matter!"

"'Tis desperate sound she makes, madam."

"But extreme ladylike, sir, Aunt Belinda is ever preposterously feminine and ladylike, sir. Her present woe arises perchance because she hath encountered a grub on her way hither or been routed by a beetle—the which last I do fervently hope."

This hope, however, was doomed to disappointment for very suddenly a lady appeared, a somewhat faded lady who, with dainty petticoats uplifted, tripped hastily towards them uttering small, wailing screams as she came.

"O Betty!" she cried. "Betty! O Elizabeth, child—a rat! O dear heart o' me, a great rat, child! That sat in the path, Betty, and looked at me, child—with a huge, great tail! O sweet heaven!"

"Looked at you with his tail, aunt?"

"Nay, child—faith, my poor senses do so twitter I scarce know what I say—but its wicked wild eyes! And it curled its horrid tail in monstrous threatening fashion! And O, thank heaven—a man!"

Here the agitated lady tottered towards the Major and, supported by his arm, sank down upon the bench and closing her eyes, gasped feebly.

"Madam!" he exclaimed, bending over her in great alarm.

"O lud!" she murmured faintly.

"By heaven, she's swooning!" exclaimed the Major.

"Nay, sir," sighed Lady Betty, "'tis no swoon nor even a faint, 'tis merely a twitter. Dear aunt will be herself again directly—so come let me sew on that button or I'll prick you, I vow I will!"

At this Lady Belinda, opening her languid eyes, stared and gasped again.

"Mercy of heaven, child!" she exclaimed, "what do you?"

"Sew on this gentleman's buttons, aunt!"

"Buttons, child! Heaven above!"

"Coat-buttons, aunt!"

"Mercy on us! Buttons! In the arbour! With a man——"

"Major d'Arcy, our neighbour, aunt. Major, my aunt, Lady Belinda Damain."

Hereupon the Major bowed a trifle awkwardly since Lady Betty still had him in leash, while her aunt, rising, sank into a curtsey that was a wonder to behold and thereafter sighed and languished like the faded beauty she was.

"My undutiful niece, sir," said she, "hath no eye to decorum, she is for ever shocking the proprieties and me—alack, 'tis a naughty baggage—a romping hoyden, a wicked puss——"

"Aunt Belinda, dare to call me a 'puss' again and I'll scratch!"

"And you are Major d'Arcy—of the Guards?"

"Late of the Third, madam."

"Related to the d'Arcys of Sussex?"

"Very distantly, I believe."

"Charming people! A noble family!"

The Major would have bowed again but for my lady Betty's levelled needle; thereafter while her aunt alternately prattled of the joys of Bath and languished over the delights of London, the Major's buttons were rapidly sewn into place and my lady was in the act of nibbling the thread when once again the ponderous menial drew nigh who, making the utmost of his generous proportions, announced:

"Lord Alvaston, Captain West and Mr. Dalroyd——"

"O Betty!" exclaimed Lady Belinda, clasping rapturous fingers, "Mr. Dalroyd—that charming man who was so attentive at Bath and afterwards in London—such legs, my dear, O Gemini!"

"To see the Lady Elizabeth—most express, my ladies."

"Tell them to go—say I'm busy——"

"Betty!" wailed her aunt.

"Say I'm engaged, say——"

"O Bet—Betty—my child," twittered her aunt, "why this cruel coldness—this harsh rigour?"

"O say I'm out—say anything!"

"Which, my lady, I did—most particular and Mr. Dalroyd remarks as how he'll wait till you will—most determined!"

"O the dear, delightful, bold creature! And such a leg, my dear! Such an air and—O dear heart o' me, if he isn't coming in quest of us yonder! The dear, desperate, audacious man! I'll go greet him and do you follow, child!"

And Lady Belinda fluttered twittering away, followed by the ponderous lackey.

The Major sighed and glanced toward the distant ladder.

"You would appear to be in much request, madam," said he, "and faith, 'tis but natural, youth and such beauty must attract all men and——"

"All men, sir?"

"Indeed, all men who are blessed with eyes to see——"

Here chancing to meet her look he faltered and stopped.

"To see—what?" she enquired.

"'Bewitching Bet'!" he answered bowing very low.

"Ah—no!" she cried—"not you!" and turning suddenly away she broke off a rose that bloomed near by and stood twisting it in her white fingers.

"And wherefore not?" he questioned.

"'Tis not for *your* lips," she said, softly.

The Major whose glance happened to be wandering, winced slightly and flushed.

"Aye—indeed, I had forgot," said he, rather vaguely—"Youth must to youth and——"

"Must it, sir?

"Inevitably, madam, it is but natural and——"

"How vastly wise you are, Major d'Arcy!" The curl of her lip was quite wasted on him for he was staring at the rose she was caressing.

"'Twas said also by one much wiser than I 'crabbed age and youth cannot live together.' And you are very young, my lady and—very beautiful."

"And therefore to be pitied!" she sighed.

"In heaven's name, why?"

"For that I am a lonely maid that suffers from a plague of beaux, sir, most of them over young and all of them vastly trying. 'Bewitching Bet'!" This time he did see the scorn of her curling lip. "I had rather you call me anything else—even 'child' or—'Betty.'"

They stood awhile in silence, the Major looking at her and she at the rose: "'Betty'!" said he at last, half to himself, as if trying the sound of it. "'Tis a most—pretty name!"

"I had not thought so," she answered. And there was silence again, he watching where she was heedlessly brushing the rose to and fro across her vivid lips and looking at nothing in particular.

"Your guests await you," said he.

"They often do," she answered.

"I'll go," said the Major and glanced toward the ladder. "Good-bye, my lady."

"Well?" she asked softly.

"And—er—my grateful thanks——"

"Well?" she asked again, softer yet.

"I also hope that—er—I trust that since we're neighbours, I—we——"

"The wall is not insurmountable, sir. Well? O man," she cried suddenly—"if you really want it so why don't you ask for it—or take it?"

The Major stared and flushed.

"You—you mean——"

"This!" she cried and tossed the rose to his feet. Scarcely believing his eyes he stooped and took it up, and holding it in reverent fingers watched her hasting along the yew-walk. Standing thus he saw her met by a slender, elegant gentleman, saw him stoop to kiss her white fingers, and, turning suddenly, strode to the ladder.

So the Major presently climbed back over the wall and went his way, the rose tenderly cherished in the depths of one of his great side-pockets and, as he went, he limped rather noticeably but whistled softly to himself, a thing very strange in him, whistled softly but very merrily.

CHAPTER V
HOW SERGEANT ZEBEDEE
TRING BEGAN TO WONDER

Mrs. Agatha sat just within the kitchen-garden shelling peas—and Mrs. Agatha did it as only a really accomplished woman might; at least, so thought Sergeant Zebedee, who, busied about some of his multifarious carpentry jobs, happened to come that way. He thought also that with her pretty face beneath snowy mob-cap, her shapely figure in its neat gown, she made as attractive a picture as any man might see on the longest day's march—of all which Mrs. Agatha was supremely conscious, of course.

"A hot day, mam!" said he, halting.

Mrs. Agatha glanced up demurely, smiled, and gave all her attention to the peas again.

"You do be getting more observant every day, Sergeant!" she said, shelling away rapidly.

The Sergeant stroked his new-shaven cheek with a pair of pincers he chanced to be holding and stared down at her busy fingers; Mrs. Agatha possessed very shapely hands, soft and dimpled—of which she was also aware.

"But you look cool enough, mam," said he, ponderously, "and 'tis become a matter of——"

"Duty, Sergeant?" she enquired.

"No, mam, a matter of wonder to me how you manage it?"

"Belike 'tis all because Nature made me so."

"Natur', mam—aye, 'tis a wonderful institootion——"

"For making me cool?"

"For making you at all, mam!" Having said which, he wheeled suddenly, and took three quick strides away but, hearing her call, he turned and took three slow ones back again. "Well, mam?" he enquired, staring at the pincers.

"'Tis a hot day, Sergeant!" she laughed. At this he stood silent awhile, lost in contemplation of her dexterous hands.

"Egad!" he exclaimed, suddenly, "'Tis a beautiful finger!"

"Is it, Sergeant?"

"For a trigger—aye mam. To shoot straight a man must have a true eye, mam, but he must also have a shooting-hand, quick and light o' the finger, d'ye see, not to spoil alignment. If you'd been a man, now, you'd ha' handled a musket wi' the best if you'd only been a man— —"

"But I'm—only a woman."

"True, mam, true—'tis Natur' again—fault o' circumstance— —"

"And I don't want to be a man— —"

"Certainly not, mam— —"

"And wouldn't if I could!"

"Glad, o' that, mam."

"O, and prithee why?"

"Because as a woman you're—female, d'ye see—I mean as you're what Natur' intended and such being so you're—naturally formed—I mean— —"

"What d'you mean, pray?"

"A woman. And now, talking o' the Major— —"

"But we're not!"

"Aye, but we are, mam, and so talking, the Major do surprise me—same be a-changing, mam."

"Changing? How?"

"Well, this morning he went— —"

"Into the orchard!" said Mrs. Agatha, nodding.

"Aye, he did. Since I finished that arbour he's took to it amazing—sits there by the hour—mam!" Mrs. Agatha smiled at the peas. "But this morning, mam, arter breakfast, he went and turned out all his—clothes, mam. 'Sergeant,' says he, 'be these the best I've got'—and him as never troubled over his clothes except to put 'em on and forget 'em."

"But you hadn't built the arbour then!" said Mrs. Agatha softly.

"Arbour!" exclaimed the Sergeant, staring.

"You've known him a long time?"

"I've knowed him nigh twenty years and I thought I did know him but I don't know him—there's developments—he's took to whistling of late. Only this morning I heard him whistling o' this song 'Barbary Allen' which same were a damned—no, a devilish—no, a con-founded barbarious young maid if words mean aught."

"True, she had no heart, Sergeant!"

"And a woman without an 'eart, mam——"

"A heart, Sergeant!"

"Aye, mam," said he, staring at the pincers, "a maid or woman without an 'eart is no good for herself or any——"

"Man!" suggested Mrs. Agatha, softly.

"True, mam, and speaking o' men brings us back to the Major and him a-whistling as merry as any grig."

"Grigs don't whistle, Sergeant."

"No more they do, mam, no—lark's the word. Also he's set on buying a noo wig, mam, and him with four brand-noo—almost, except his service wig which I'll grant you is a bit wore and moth-eaten like arter three campaigns which therefore aren't to be nowise wondered at. But what is to be wondered at is his honour troubling about suchlike when 'tis me as generally reports to him when garments is outwore and me as has done the ordering of same, these ten year and more. And now here's him wanting to buy a noo wig all at once! Mam, what I say is—damme!"

"Sergeant, ha' done!"

"Ax your pardon, mam, but 'tis so strange and onexpected. A noo wig! Wants one more modish! Aye," said the Sergeant, shaking his head, "'modish' were the word, mam—'modish'! Now what I says to that is——"

"Sergeant, hush!"

"Why I ain't said it yet, mam——"

"Then don't!"

"Very well, mam!" he sighed. "But 'modish'——"

"And why shouldn't he be modish?" demanded Mrs. Agatha warmly, "he's young enough and handsome enough."

"He's all that, mam, yet——"

"Why should any man be slovenly and old before his time?"

"Aye, why indeed, mam but——"

"There's yourself, for instance."

"Who—me, mam?" exclaimed the Sergeant, hitting himself an amazed blow on the chest with the pincers, "me?"

"Aye, you! Not that you're slovenly, but you talk and act like a Methusalem instead of a—a careless boy of forty."

"Three, mam—forty-three."

"Aye, a helpless child of forty-three."

"Child!" murmured the Sergeant. "Helpless child—me? Now what I says to that is——"

"Hush!" said Mrs. Agatha, severely; but beholding his stupefaction she laughed merrily and taking up the peas, vanished into the kitchen, laughing still.

"Child—me—helpless child!" said the Sergeant, staring after her. "Now what I says is——"

And there being none to hush him, the Sergeant, in English, French and Low Dutch, proceeded to "say it" forthwith.

CHAPTER VI
WHICH DESCRIBES, AMONG
OTHER THINGS, A POACHER

The Major rubbed his chin with dubious finger, pushed back his wig and taking up the letter from the desk before him, broke the seal and read as follows:

"MY VERY DEAR UNCLE:

"Being in a somewhat low state of health and spirits—"

"Spirits!" said the Major. "Ha!"

"—induced by a too close application to my duties—"

"Hum!" quoth the Major, rubbing his chin harder than ever.

"—I purpose (subject to your permission) to inflict myself upon you—"

"The devil he does!"

"—having been ordered rest and quiet and country air."

"Hum! I wonder!" mused the Major.

"Pray spare yourself the fatigue of writing as I leave London at once and well knowing your extreme kindness I hope to have the felicity of greeting you within a day or so,

Your most grateful, humble and obedient nephew,
TOM."

Having read this through the Major fell to profound meditation.

"I wonder?" he mused and pulled the bell.

"Sergeant!" said he, as the door opened.

"Sir?" said the Sergeant advancing three paces and coming to attention.

"Are there any—er—strangers in the village?"

"Last time I chanced to drop into the 'George and Dragon' there was a round dozen gentlemen a-staying there, sir."

"Young gentlemen?"

"Aye, sir, them as I ob-served was, and very fine young gents too—almost as fine as their lackeys, sir."

"A dozen of 'em, Zebedee!"

The Major rubbed his chin again and frowned slightly.

"Then my nephew will make the thirteenth. Tell Mrs. Agatha to have a chamber ready for him to-night."

"The Viscount a-comin' here, sir? Always thought same couldn't abide country!"

"He hath changed his mind it seems or——"

The Major paused suddenly and glanced toward the open window, for, upon the air without was a distant clamour of voices and shouting pierced, ever and anon, by a wild hunting yell. As the uproar grew nearer and louder the Major rose, and crossing to the casement, beheld his lodge-gates swung wide before an insurging crowd, a motley throng, for, among rustic homespun and smock-frock he espied velvet coats brave with gold and silver lace. Before this riot a tall and slender gentleman strode waving a richly be-laced hat in one hand and flourishing a whip in the other.

"Hark away! Hark away!" he yelled, while from those behind came boisterous laughter and shouts of "Yoick!" "Tally-ho!" "Gone away!" and the like.

At the terrace steps the concourse halted and out upon this clamorous throng the quiet figure of the Major limped, his wig a little askew as usual. As he came, the clamour subsided and the crowd, falling back, discovered half-a-dozen stalwart keepers who dragged between them a slender youth, bruised and bloody.

"Ah," said the Major, surveying the scene with interest, "and what may all this be?"

"O demmit, sir!" cried the slender young gentleman, clapping hat to gorgeous bosom and bowing, "Step me vitals, sir—what should it be but a demmed rogue and a rebbit, sir!"

"O, a rabbit?" said the Major.

"And a rogue, sir! Pink me, 'tis the demmdest, infernal, long-leggedest rascal and led us the demmdest chase I promise you! Hill and dale, hedge and wall, copse and spinney, O demn! Better than any fox I ever hunted, there was only Alvaston, Marchdale, your humble and one or two keeper-fellows in at the death—pace too hot, sir—strike me dumb!"

"And pray, sir," enquired the Major, "whom have I the fortune to address?"

"O Ged, sir, to be sure—I'm Alton—very obedient, humble—gentleman yonder blowing his nose like a demmed trumpet is my friend Tony Marchdale of Marchdale—big fellow in the purple coat and nose to match is Sir Benjamin Tripp" (here Sir Benjamin bowed, spluttering mildly) "gentleman with the sparrow-legs is Lord Alvaston" (here his lordship posturing gracefully with his slender legs, bowed, cursing amiably)—"stand-and-deliver gentleman with hook-nose, Captain West of the Guards—die-away gentleman in lavender and gold, Mr. Dalroyd—fat fellow in abominable scratch-wig who looks as if he'd swallowed a lemon the wrong way, don't know—and there we are, sir—demme!"

"And I, gentlemen, am John d'Arcy, at your service. What can I do for you?"

"O egad, sir—strike me everlasting blue, 'tis we have been doing for you! Here we've caught your rogue for you—chased him high—chased him low—here, there and everywhere—bushes, burrs and briers, dirt and dust sir—O demmit!

"If," began the Major, "if you will have the goodness to be a little more explicit——"

But here the short, plump, fierce-eyed gentleman in the scratch-wig, elbowing aside the yokels who stood near strode forward excitedly:

"You are Major d'Arcy?" he challenged.

The Major bowed.

"Why then, sir, give me leave to say we've had the extreme good fortune to catch a poacher on your land. You'll know me of course. I'm Sir Oliver Rington of Chevening."

"No!" said the Major.

"Then you'll have heard of me, to be sure?"

"I fear not."

"Sir, I'm your member—and——"

"I rejoice to know it!"

"And justice o' the peace."

"I felicitate you!"

"As such, sir, 'tis my present endeavour to get an enactment passed making the law more rigorous against poaching——"

"A noble work!" sighed the Major.

"In the which, sir, I am being vigorously supported by the neighbouring gentry. You are a stranger in these parts, I think?"

"I have resided at the Manor precisely a month and two days, sir."

"Then, sir, permit me to say that the quality hereabouts are united against such miserable rogues as this damned poaching rascal."

"You are something in the majority, 'twould seem!" said the Major, glancing from the blood-smeared face of the solitary captive to the shuffling throng.

"We are determined to put down such roguery with a firm hand, sir," answered Sir Oliver, truculently, "I have already succeeded in having four such rascals as yon transported for life, sir."

"For a dem rebbit—O Ged!" exclaimed Lord Alton.

"You forget, Alton," interposed Mr. Dalroyd, languidly, "you forget, the rabbit may be a sheep next week, a horse the next, your purse the next and——"

"And this, sir, was merely a rabbit, I believe, which happens to be mine," said the Major, turning to glance at the speaker.

Mr. Dalroyd was tall and slim and pallidly handsome; from black periwig to elegant riding boots he was *point-de-vice*, a languid, soft-spoken, very fine gentleman indeed, who surveyed the Major's tall, upright figure, with sleepy-lidded eyes. So for a long moment they viewed each other, the Major serene of brow, his hands buried in the pockets of his threadbare Ramillie coat, Mr. Dalroyd cool and leisuredly critical, yet gradually as he met the other's languid gaze, the Major's expression changed, his black brows twitched together, his keen eyes grew suddenly intent and withdrawing a hand from his pocket, he began absently to finger the scar that marked his temple; then Mr. Dalroyd smiled faintly and turned a languid shoulder.

"Gentlemen," said he, "our sport is done, the play grows wearisome—let us be gone."

At this, Sir Oliver Rington approached the Major and in his eagerness tapped him on the arm with his whip.

"With your permission, Major, I'll see this rogue set in the stocks and after safely under lock and key. You'll prosecute, of course."

Very gently the Major set aside Sir Oliver's whip and limped over to the prisoner:

"He looks sufficiently young!" said he.

"A criminal type!" nodded Sir Oliver, "I've convicted many such—a very brutal, desperate rogue!"

"To be sure he's very bloody!" said the Major.

"Aye," growled Sir Oliver, "and serve him right—he gave enough trouble for six."

"And something faint!"

"Aye, feint it is sir—the rascal's shamming."

"And dusty!"

"O, a foul beast!" agreed Sir Oliver.

"And hath a hungry look. So shall he go wash and eat——"

"Wash—eat—how—what in the devil's name, sir——"

"Sergeant!"

"Sir!" answered the Sergeant, very upright and stiff in the back.

"Take the fellow to the stables and when he's washed—feed him!"

"Very good, sir!" Saying which, the Sergeant advanced upon the drooping prisoner, set hand to ragged coat-collar, and wheeling him half-left, marched him away.

"Strike me everlasting perishing purple!" exclaimed the Marquis.

"Damnation!" cried Sir Oliver, his whip quivering in his fist, "d'ye mean to say, sir—d'ye mean——" he choked.

"I mean to say, that since the prisoner stole my property I will dispose of him as I think fit——"

"Fit sir—fit—as you think fit!" spluttered Sir Oliver.

"Or as it pleases me, sir."

"You sir—you!" panted Sir Oliver in sudden frenzy, "and who the devil are you that dare run counter to the law—a beggarly half-pay soldier——"

"O demmit, sir!" exclaimed the Marquis, restraining plump ferocity, "try to be a little decent, I beg, just a little—remember you are not in the House now, sir!"

Sir Oliver sulkily permitted himself to be drawn a little aside, then, halting suddenly, wheeled about and pointed at the Major with his whip.

"Gentlemen all," he cried, "behold a man who hath no respect for the Constitution, for Church, State or King God save him! Behold a—a being who is traitor to his class! A man who—who'd—O damme—who'd—shoot a fox!"

The Major laughed suddenly and shook his head.

"No," said he, "no, I'll shoot neither foxes—nor even fools, sir—if—I say if—it may be avoided. And so, gentlemen, thanking you for your extreme zeal on my behalf in the matter of my poacher, I have the honour to bid you, each and every, good day."

So saying, the Major bowed and turning, limped into the house.

CHAPTER VII
WHICH RELATES HOW THE
POACHER ESCAPED

The rising sun made a glory in the east, purple, amber and flaming gold; before his advent sombre night fled away and sullen mists rolled up and vanished; up he came in triumphant majesty, his far-flung, level beams waking a myriad sparkles on grass and leaf where the dew yet clung; they woke also the blackbird inhabiting the great tree whose spreading boughs shaded a certain gable of the Manor. This blackbird, then, being awake, forthwith prepares to summon others to bid welcome to the day, tunes sleepy pipe, finds himself astonishingly hoarse, pauses awhile to ruminate on the wherefore of this, tries again with better effect, stretches himself, re-settles a ruffled feather and finally, being broad awake, bursts into a passionate ecstasy of throaty warblings.

It was at this precise moment that the Major thrust cropped head from his open lattice and leaned there awhile to breathe in the dawn's sweet freshness and to feast his eyes upon dew-spangled earth. And beholding noble house and stately trees with smiling green fields beyond where goodly farmsteads nestled, all his own far as the eye could see and farther, he drew a deep and joyous breath, contrasting all this with his late penury. Now, as he leaned thus in the warm sun, his wandering eye fell upon a small isolated outbuilding, its narrow windows strongly barred, its oaken door padlocked. Instantly the Major drew in his head and began to dress; which done, he clapped on his peruke and opening the door with some degree of care, stepped forth of his chamber, and, carrying his shoes in his hand, tiptoed along the wide gallery, and, descending the great stairs with the same caution, proceeded to a certain small room against whose walls were birding-pieces, fishing-rods, hunting-crops, spurs and the like. From amid these heterogeneous articles he reached down a great key and slipping it into his pocket, proceeded to furtively unbar, unlock and let himself out into the young morning. Outside he put on his shoes and descending marble steps and crossing trim lawns presently arrived at a forbidding oaken door, which he opened forthwith.

The poacher lay half-buried among a pile of hay in one corner but at the Major's entrance started up, disclosing a pale, youthful face, whose dark, aquiline features were vaguely reminiscent.

"Hum!" said the Major, rubbing his chin and staring, whereat the prisoner, scowling sullenly, turned away.

"Ha!" said the Major. "Sirrah, 'tis a fair day for walking I think, therefore, an you be so minded—walk!"

"D'ye mean you'll let me—go?" demanded the prisoner.

"Aye!"

"Free?"

"There's the door!"

The prisoner sprang to his feet, brushed the hay from his rough and stained garments, glanced from his deliverer to the glory of the morning and stepped out into the sunlight.

"You were wiser to avoid Sir Oliver Rington's neighbourhood, and here's somewhat to aid you on your way."

So saying, the Major strode off and left the poacher staring down at the gold coins in his palm.

The Major wandered thoughtfully along box-bordered paths, past marble fauns and nymphs; between hedges of clipped yew and so to the rose-garden, ablaze with colour and fragrant with bloom. In the midst was a time-worn sundial set about with marble seats and here the Major leaned to muse awhile and so came upon a quaint-lettered posy graven upon the dial which ran as follows:

"Youth is joyous; Age is melancholy:
Age and Youth together is but folly."

"Hum!" said the Major and sighed, and sighing, turned away, limping more than usual, for his meditations were profound. Thus, deep in thought he came back to the isolated building, locked it up again, and wended his way back to the house.

Having replaced the key he sat himself down in his study and tucking up his ruffles, fell to work on his History of Fortification, though, to be sure, his pen was frequently idle and once he opened a drawer to stare down at a rapidly fading rose.

Gradually the great house about him awoke to life and morning bustle; light feet tripped to and fro, maids' voices chattered and sang merrily, dusters flicked, mops twirled and Mrs. Agatha admonished, while, from the kitchens afar came the faint but delectable rattle of crockery while the Major drove parallels, constructed trenches and covered ways and dreamed of the Lady Betty Carlyon, of her eyes, her hair, the dimple in her wilful chin and of all her alluring witchery. And bethinking him of her warm, soft daintiness, as when she had leaned in his clasp for that much-remembered moment, he almost thought to catch again the faint, sweet fragrance of her.

Moved by a sudden impulse he rose, and crossing to a mirror, stood to examine himself critically as he had never done before in all his life.

And truly, now he came to notice, his wig was shabby despite the Sergeant's unremitting care; then his shoes were clumsy and thick of sole, his cotton stockings showed a darn here and there and his coat—!

The Major shook his head and sighed:

"'Tis a very beast of a coat!"

In his heart he ruefully admitted that it was.

Now, as to his face?

The Major stared keenly at well-opened, grey eyes which stared back at him under level brows; at straightish nose, widish mouth and strong, deep-cleft chin; each feature in turn was the object of his wistful scrutiny and he must even trace out the scar that marked his left temple and seek to hide it with the limp side-curls of his peruke. Then he turned away and seating himself at his desk leaned there, head on hand, staring blindly at the written sheets before him.

And behind his thoughts was a line from the posy on the sundial:

"Youth is joyous, Age is melancholy:"

The Major sighed. Suddenly he started and turned as a knock sounded on the door, which, opening forthwith, disclosed the Sergeant, his usually trim habit slightly disordered, his usually serene brow creased and clammy, his eye woeful.

"Ah, Sergeant," said the Major placidly, "good morning, Zeb."

"Sir," said the Sergeant, advancing three steps and coming to attention. "I've come, sir, to report gross dee-reliction of dooty, sir."

"Indeed—whose?"

"Mine, sir. You put prisoner in my charge, sir—same has took French leave, sir, by aid o' witchcraft, hocus-pocus, or the devil, sir, prisoner having vanished himself into thin air, sir — —"

"Remarkable!" said the Major.

"Found the place locked up and all serene, sir, but on opening door found prisoner had went which didn't seem nowise nat'ral, sir. Hows'mever, fell in a search party immediate, self and gardeners, sir, but though we beat the park an' the spinney, sir, owing to spells and witchcraft 'twas but labour in vain, prisoner having been spirited away, d'ye see?"

"Astonishing!" said the Major.

The Sergeant mopped his brow and sighed.

"Prisoner having bolted and altogether went, sir—same being vanished, though suspecting witches and hocus-pocus, must hold myself responsible for same— —"

"No, no, Zeb."

"And feel myself defaulter, sir, owing to which shall stop and deny myself customary ale to-day, sir."

"Very good, Zeb."

"And talking of ale, sir, think it my dooty to report as in the 'George and Dragon' last evening Sir Oliver Rington were talking agin' you, sir—very fierce."

"I'm not surprised, Zeb, his kind must talk."

"Same person, sir, made oncommon free wi' your name, laying thereto certain and divers eppythets, sir, among which was 'vulgar fellow' and 'beggarly upstart' which me overhearing was forced to shout 'damn liar' as in dooty bound, sir. Whereupon his two grooms, wi' five or six other rogues, took me front, flank and rear and run me out into the road. Whereupon, chancing to have pint-pot in my hand, contrived with same to alter the faces o' two or three of 'em for time being, as in dooty bound, sir. All of which has caused more talk which I do truly lament."

"A pint-pot is an awkward weapon, Zebedee!"

"True, sir, same being apt to bend."

"I trust you did no serious hurt, Sergeant?"

"Not so serious as I could ha' wished, sir."

"And I hope it won't occur again."

"I hope so too, sir! Regarding the prisoner, sir— —"

"He has escaped, I understand, Zeb."

"He has so, your honour."

"Then there is no prisoner."

"Why as to that, sir," began the Sergeant, scratching his big chin—

"As to that, Zeb, 'tis just as well for everyone concerned, especially the prisoner, that—er—isn't, as 'twere and so forth, d'ye see, Sergeant?" So saying the Major took up his pen and the Sergeant strode away, though more than once he shook his head in dark perplexity.

CHAPTER VIII
OF PANCRAS, VISCOUNT MERIVALE

The Major's study, opening out of the library, was a smallish chamber, very like himself in that its appointments were simple and plain to austerity. Its furniture comprised a desk, a couple of chairs and a settee, its adornments consisted of the portrait of a gentleman in armour who scowled, a Sèvres vase full of roses set there by Mrs. Agatha, a pair of silver-mounted small-swords above the carved mantel but within easy reach, flanked by a couple of brace of handsomely mounted pistols.

Just now, table, chairs and settee had been pushed into a corner and the chamber rang with the clash and grind of vicious-darting steel where the Major and Sergeant Zebedee in stockinged-feet and shirt-sleeves, thrust and parried and lunged, bright eyes wide and watchful, lips grim-set, supple of wrist and apparently tireless of arm, the Major all lissom, graceful ease despite his limp, the Sergeant a trifle stiff but grimly business-like and deadly; a sudden fierce rally, a thrust, a lightning riposte and the Major stepped back.

"*Touché!*" he exclaimed, lowering his point. "'Tis a wicked thrust of yours—that in tierce, Zebedee!"

"'Twas you as taught it me, sir," answered the Sergeant, whipping his foil to the salute, "same as you taught me my letters, consequently I am bold to fight or read any man as ever drawed breath."

"You do credit to my method, Sergeant Zeb—especially that trick o' the wrist—'tis mine own and I think unique. Come again, we have another ten minutes."

Hereupon they gravely saluted each other, came to the engage and once more the place echoed to rasping steel and quick-thudding feet. It was a particularly fierce and brilliant bout, in the middle of which and quite unobserved by the combatants, the door opened and a young gentleman appeared. He was altogether a remarkable young gentleman being remarkably young, languid and gorgeous. A pale mauve coat, gold of button and rich of braid, its skirts sufficiently full and ample, seemed moulded upon his slender figure, his legs were encased in long, brown riding-boots of excellent cut and finish, furnished with jingling silver spurs, his face exactly modish of pallor, high-nosed and delicately featured, was set off by a great periwig whose glossy curls had that just and nicely-ordered disorder fashion required; in his right hand he held his hat, a looped and belaced affair, two fingers of his left were posed elegantly upon the silver hilt of his sword the brown leathern scabbard of which cocked its silver lip beneath his coat at precisely the right angle; thus, as he stood regarding the fencing bout he seemed indeed the very "glass of fashion and mould of form" and unutterably serene.

"Ha!" exclaimed the Sergeant suddenly, "clean through the gizzard, sir!" and lowering his point in turn he shook his head, "'twould ha' done my business for good an' all, sir." And it was to be noted that despite their exertions neither he nor the Major breathed overfast or seemed unduly over-heated; remarking which the young gentleman animadverted gently as follows:

"Gad, nunky mine, Gad save my poor perishing sawl how d'ye do it— ye don't blow and ye ain't sweating——"

The Major started and turned:

"What—nephew!" hastening forward to greet his visitor, "What, Pancras lad, when did you arrive?"

"Ten minutes since, sir. I strolled up from the 'George and Dragon' and left my fellows to come on with the horses and baggage. Begad, sir, 'tis a cursed fine property this, a noble heritage! Give you joy of it! Here's a change from your trooping and fighting! You grow warm, nunky, warm, eh?"

"'Tis a great change, nephew, and most unexpected. But speaking of change, Pancras, you have grown out of recognition since last I saw you."

"Gad prasper me, sir, I hope so—'tis five long years agone and I'm my own man since my father had the grace to break his neck a-hunting, though 'tis a pity he contrived to break my mother's heart first, sweet, patient soul. Ha, sir, d'ye mind the day you pitched him out o' the gun-room window?"

"He's dead, Pancras!" said the Major, flushing.

"Which is very well, sir, since you're alive and I'm alive and so's the Sergeant here. How goes it Zeb—good old Zeb. How goes it, Sergeant Zeb?" and the Viscount's white, be-ringed hand met the Sergeant's hairy one in a hearty grip.

"Look at him, nunky, look at him a Gad's name—same old square face, not changed a hair since he used to come a-marching back with you from some campaign or other, rat me! D'ye mind, Zeb, d'ye mind how you used to make me wooden swords and teach me how to bear my point—eh?"

"Aye, I mind, sir," nodded the Sergeant, grim lips smiling, "'tis not so long since."

"Talking of fence, sir, give me leave to say—as one somewhat proficient in the art—that your style is a little antiquated!"

"Is't so, nephew?"

"Rat me if it isn't, sir! It lacketh that niceness of finish, that gracious poise o' the bady, that 'je ne sais quoi' which is all the mode."

"So, nephew, you fence—

"Of course, nunky, we all do—'tis the fashion. I fence a bout or so every day with the great Mancini, sir."

"So he's great these days?"

"How, d'ye know him, uncle?"

"Years ago I fenced with him in Flanders."

"Well, sir?"

"I thought him too flamboyant——"

"O, Gad requite me, sir! Had you but felt his celebrated attack—that stoccata! Let me show you!" So saying, the Viscount tossed his hat into a corner, took the Sergeant's foil and fell into a graceful fencing posture.

"Come, nunky, on guard!" he cried. Smiling, the Major saluted. "Here he is, see you, the point bearing so, and before you can blink——"

"Your coat, sir!" said the Sergeant, proffering to take it.

"Let be, Zeb, let be," sighed the Viscount, "it takes my fellow to get me into 't, and my two fellows to get me out on't, so let be. Come, nunky mine." Smiling, the Major fell to his guard and the blades rang together. "Here he is, see you, his point bearing so, and, ere you can blink he comes out of tierce and——

"I pink you—so!" said the Major.

"Gad's me life!" exclaimed his nephew, staring. "What the—how—come again, sir!"

Once more the blades clinked and instantly the Viscount lunged; the Major stepped back, his blade whirled and the Viscount's weapon spun from his grasp and clattered to the floor.

"Gad save me poor perishing sawl!" he exclaimed, staring gloomily at his fallen weapon, "how did ye do 't, sir? Sergeant Zeb, damme you're laughing at me!"

"Sir," answered the Sergeant, picking up the foil, "I were!"

"Very curst of you! And how did he manage Mancini?"

"Much the same as he managed you, sir, only——"

"Only?"

"Not so—so prompt, sir!"

"The devil he did! But Mancini's esteemed one of the best——"

"So were his honour, sir!"

"O!" said the Viscount, "and he didn't puff and he ain't sweating—my sawl!"

"'Tis use, nephew."

"And country air, sir! Look at you—young as you were five years since—nay, younger, I vow. Now look at me, a pasitive bunch of fiddle-strings—appetite bad, stomach worse, nerves—O love me! A pasitive wreck, Gad prasper me!"

The Major's sharp eyes noted the youthful, upright figure, the alert glance, the resolute set of mouth and chin, and he smiled.

"To be sure you are in a—er—a low, weak state of health, I understand?"

"O sir, most curst."

"Poor Pancras!" said the Major.

"No, no, sir, a Gad's name don't call me so, 'tis a curst name, 'twas my father's name, beside 'tis a name to hang a dog. Call me Tam, Tam's short and to the point—all my friends call me Tam, so call me Tam!"

"So be it, Tom. So you come into the country for your health?"

"Aye, sir, I do. Nothing like the country, sir, balmy air—mighty invigorating, look at the ploughmen they eat and drink and sleep and—er——"

"Plough!" suggested the Major, gravely.

"Begad, sir, so they do. And besides, I do love the country—brooks and beehives, nunky; cabbages, y'know, cows d'ye see and clods and things——"

"And cuckoos, Tom."

"Aye, and cuckoos!" said the Viscount serenely.

"Indeed, the country hath a beauty all its own, sir, so am I come to— —"

"Be near her, nephew!"

"Eh? O! Begad!" saying which Viscount Merivale took out a highly ornate gold snuff-box, looked at it, tapped it and put it away again. "Nunky," he murmured, "since you're so curst wide-awake I'm free to confess that for the last six months I've worshipped at the shrine of the Admirable Betty— de-votedly, sir!"

"There be others also, I think!" said the Major, handing his foil to the Sergeant.

"Gad love me, sir, 'tis true enough! The whole town is run mad for her pasitively, and 'tis small wonder! She's a blooming peach, nunky, a pearl of price—let me perish! A goddess, a veritable— —"

"Woman!" said the Major.

"And, sir, this glory of her sex blooms and blossoms—next door. Ha' ye seen her yet?"

"Once or twice, Tom."

"Now I protest, sir—ain't she the most glorious creature—a peerless piece—a paragon? By heaven, 'tis the sweetest, perversest witch and so do my hopes soar."

"Doth she prove so kind, nephew?"

"O sir, she doth flout me consistently."

"Flout you?"

"Constantly, thank Vanus! 'Tis when she's kind I fall i' the dumps."

"God bless me!" exclaimed the Major.

"Look'ee sir, there's Tripp, for instance, dear old bottlenose Ben, she smiles on him and suffers him to bear her fan, misfortunate dog! There's Alton, she permits him to attend her regularly and hand her from chair or coach, poor devil! There's West and Marchdale, I've known her talk with them in corners, unhappy wights! There's Dalroyd— —"

"The 'die-away' gentleman?" said the Major.

"O he's death and the devil for her, he is—a sleepy, smouldering flame, rat me! And she is scarce so kind to him I could wish. But as for me, nunky, me she scorns, flouts, contemns and quarrels with, so doth hope sing within me!"

"Hum!" said the Major, clapping on his wig.

"So I am here in the fervent hope that ere the year is out she may be my Viscountess and—O my stricken sawl!"

"What is't, nephew?"

"Aye, sir, that's the question—what? Faith, it might be anything."

"You mean my wig, Tom?" enquired the Major, laughing, yet flushing a little.

"Wig?" murmured the Viscount, "after all, sir, there is a resemblance— though faint. Sure you never venture abroad in the thing?

"Why not?"

"'Twould be pasitively indecent, sir!"

Here the Major laughed, but the Sergeant, setting the furniture in place, scowled fixedly at the chair he chanced to be grasping.

"Perhaps 'tis time I got me a new one," said the Major, slipping into his coat.

"One!" exclaimed the Viscount. "O pink me, sir—a man of your standing and position needs a dozen. A wig, sir, is as capricious as a woman—it can make a gentleman a dowdy, a fool look wise and a wise man an ass, 'tis therefore a—what the——"

The Viscount rose and putting up his glass peered at his uncle in pained astonishment:

"Sir—sir," he faltered, "'tis a perfectly curst object that—may I venture to enquire——"

"What, my coat, Tom?"

"Coat—coat—O let me perish!" And the Viscount sank limply into a chair and drooped there in dejection. "Calls it a coat!" he murmured.

"'Tis past its first bloom, I'll allow——"

"Bloom—O stap me!" whispered the Viscount.

"But 'twas a very good coat once——"

"Nay sir, nay, I protest," cried the Viscount, "upon a far, far distant day it may have been a something to keep a man warm, but 'twas never, O never a coat——"

"Indeed, Tom?"

"Indeed, sir, in its halcyon days 'twas an ill dream, now—'tis a pasitive nightmare. Have you any other garment a trifle less gruesome, sir?"

"I have two other suits I think, Sergeant?"

"Three, your honour, there's your d'Oyley stuff suit" (the Viscount groaned), "there's your blue and silver and the black velvet garnished with——"

"Sounds curst funereal, Zeb! O my poor nunky! Go fetch 'em, Sergeant, and let me see 'em—'twill distress and pain me I know but—go fetch 'em!"

Here, at a nod from the Major, Sergeant Zebedee departed.

"I—er—live very retired, Tom," began the Major.

"We'll change all that, sir——"

"The devil, you say!"

"O nunky, nunky, 'tis time I took you in hand. D'ye ever hunt now?"

"Why no!"

"Visit your neighbours?"

"Not as yet, Tom."

"Go among your tenantry?"

"Very seldom——"

"O fie, sir, fie! Here's you pasitively wasting all your natural advantages,—shape, stature, habit o' bady all thrown away—I always admired your curst, high, stand-and-deliver air—even as a child, and here's you living and clothing yourself like——"

He paused as the Sergeant re-entered, who, spreading out the three suits upon the table with a flourish, stood at attention.

"I knew it—I feared so!" murmured the Viscount, turning over the garments. He sighed over them, he groaned, he nearly wept. "Take 'em away—away, Zeb," he faltered at last, "hide 'em from the eye o' day, lose 'em, a Gad's name, Zeb—burn 'em!"

"Burn 'em, sir?" repeated the Sergeant, folding up the despised garments with painful care, "axing your pardon, m'lord, same being his honour's I'd rather——"

"Next week, nunky, you shall ride to town with me and acquire some real clothes."

The Major stroked his chin and surveyed the Sergeant's wooden expression!

"Egad, Tom," said he, "I think I will!"

Glancing from the window, the Major beheld a train of heavily-laden pack-horses approaching, up the drive.

"Why, what's all this?" he exclaimed.

"That?" answered the Viscount yawning, "merely a few of my clothes, sir, and trifling oddments— —"

"God bless my soul!"

"Sir," said the Sergeant, tucking the garments under his arm beneath the Viscount's horrified gaze, "with your permission will proceed to warn grooms and stable-boys of approaching cavalry squadron!" and he marched out forthwith.

CHAPTER IX
WHICH IS A VERY BRIEF CHAPTER

"I pr'ythee spare me, gentle boy
Press me no more for that slight toy
That foolish trifle of a heart
I swear it will not do its part
Though thou dost thine——"

The Viscount checked his song and inserting the upper half of his person through the open lattice, hailed the Major cheerily.

"What, uncle, nunky, nunk—still at it? 'Tis high time you went to change your dress."

"O? And why, Tom?"

"I look for our company here in twenty minutes or so."

"What company, may I ask?"

"Lady Belinda and Our Admirable Betty."

"Good God!" ejaculated the Major starting up in sudden agitation. "Coming here—you never mean it?"

"I do indeed, sir!"

"But Lord! Why should they come?"

"As I gather, sir, 'tis because you invited 'em——"

"I? Never in my life!"

"Why, 'tis true sir, I was your mouthpiece—your ambassador, as it were."

"And she—er—they are coming here! Both!"

"Both, sir."

"Lord, Tom, 'tis a something desperate situation, what am I to do with——"

"Leave 'em to me sir! They shan't daunt you!"

"Ha! To you, Tom?"

"And dear old Ben— —"

"O?"

"And Alton— —"

"Indeed!"

"And Marchdale— —"

"Any more, nephew?"

"And Alvaston— —"

"Ah?"

"And Dalroyd and Denholm— —"

"Did I invite 'em all, Tom?"

"Every one, sir!"

"I wonder what made me?"

"Loneliness, sir!"

"D'ye think so, Tom?"

"Aye, you've always been a lonely man, I mind."

"Perhaps I have—except for the Sergeant."

"You are still, sir."

"Belike I am—though I have Sergeant Zeb."

"But we'll change all that in a month—aye, less! You shall grow two or three hundred years younger and enjoy at last the youth you've never known."

"Faith, you'd give me much, Tom!"

The Viscount took out his snuff-box, tapped it, opened it, and forgot his affectations.

"Sir," said he, "there was, on a time, a little, wretched boy, who, hating and fearing his father, grieving in his sweet mother's griefs until she died, found thereafter a friend, very tender and strong, in a big, red-coated uncle— —"

"By adoption, nephew."

"Aye sir, but I found him more truly satisfying to my youthful needs than any uncle by blood, Lord love me! At whose all too infrequent visits my boyish griefs and fears fled away—O Gad, sir, in those days I made of you a something betwixt Ajax defying the lightning and a—wet-nurse, and plague take it, sir, d'ye wonder if I——" Here the Viscount took a pinch of snuff and sneezed violently. "Rat me!" he gasped, "'tis the hatefullest stuff!" Followed a volley of sneezing and thereafter a feeble voice—"The which reminds me sir we must drink tea——"

"But I abominate tea, Tom."

"So do I, sir, so do I—curst stuff! You know the song:

'Let Mahometan fools
Live by heathenish rules
And be damned over tea-cups and coffee—'

But the women dote on it, dear creatures! 'Tis to the sex what water is to the pig (poor, fat, ignorant brute!) ale to the yeoman (lusty fellow) Nantzy to your nobby-nosed parson (roguish old boy) and wine to your man of true taste. So, let there be tea, sir."

"By all means, Tom!"

"And sir—if I may venture a suggestion—?"

"Take courage, nephew, and try!"

"Why then, wear your blue and silver, nunky, 'tis the least obnaxious and by the way, have you such a thing as a lackey or so about the place to get in one's way and to be tumbled over as is the polite custom, sir?"

"Hum!" said the Major thoughtfully, "I fancy the Sergeant has drafted 'em all into his gardening squad—ask Mrs. Agatha, she'll know."

CHAPTER X
INTRODUCING DIVERS FINE GENTLEMEN

"Gentlemen!" said the Viscount, "you have, I believe, had the honour to meet my uncle, Major d'Arcy, for a moment, 'tis now my privilege to make you better acquainted, for to know him is to honour him. Uncle, I present our Ben, our blooming Benjamin—Sir Benjamin Tripp."

"Ods body, sir!" cried Sir Benjamin, plump, rubicund and jovial. "'Tis a joy—a joy, I vow! Od, sir, 'tis I protest an infinite joy to——"

"Ha' done with your joys, Ben," said the Viscount, "here's Tony all set for his bow! Nunky—Mr. Anthony Marchdale!" Mr. Marchdale, a man of the world of some nineteen summers bent languidly and lisped:

"Kiss your hands, sir!"

"I present Lord Alvaston!" His lordship, making the utmost of his slender legs aided by a pair of clocked silk stockings bowed exuberantly.

"Very devoted humble, sir! As regards your poacher, sir, ma humble 'pinion's precisely your 'pinion sir—poacher's a dam rogue but rogue's a man 'n' rabbit's only rabbit—if 'sequently if dam rogue kills rabbit an' rabbit's your rabbit——"

"Stint your plaguy rabbits a while, Bob. Nunky, Captain West."

"Yours to command, sir!" said the Captain, a trifle mature, a trifle grim, but shooting his ruffles with a youthful ease.

"The Marquis of Alton!"

"I agree with Ben, sir, 'tis a real joy, strike me dumb if 'tisn't!"

"Sir Jasper Denholm!"

Sir Jasper, chiefly remarkable for an interesting pallor, and handsome eyes which had earned for themselves the epithet of "soulful," bowed in turn:

"Sir," he sighed, "your dutiful humble! If you be one of this sighful, amorous fellowship that worships peerless Betty from afar, 'tis an added bond, sir, a——" Speech was extinguished by a gusty sigh.

"Od so!" exclaimed Sir Benjamin, hilariously, "do we then greet another rival for the smiles of our Admirable Lady Betty—begad!"

The Major started slightly then smiled and shook his head in denial.

"Nay sir, such presumption is not in me——"

"But, indeed, sir," sighed Sir Jasper, "you must have marked how Cupid lieth basking in the dimple of her able chin, lieth ambushed in her night-soft hair, playeth (naughty young wanton) in her snowy bosom, lurketh (rosy elf) 'neath——"

"Sir!" said the Major, rather hastily, "I have eyes!"

"Enough, sir—whoso hath eyes must worship! So do we salute you as a fellow-sufferer deep-smit of Eros his blissful, barbed dart."

"Od rabbit me, 'tis so!" cried Sir Benjamin. "Here's wine, come, a toast, let us fill to Love's latest bleeding victim—let us solemnly——"

The door opened, a rehabilitated footman announced: 'Lady Belinda Damain, Lady Elizabeth Carlyon,' and in the ladies swept, whereupon the Major instinctively felt to see if his peruke were straight.

"O dear heart!" exclaimed the Lady Belinda, halting with slim foot daintily poised. "So many gentlemen—I vow 'tis pure! And discussing a toast, too! O Gemini! Dear sirs, what is't—relate!"

"I' faith, madam," cried Sir Benjamin, "we greet and commiserate another victim to your glorious niece's glowing charms, we salute our fellow-sufferer Major d'Arcy!"

The Major laughed a little uncertainly as he hastened to welcome his guests.

"Indeed," said he, "what man having eyes can fail to admire though from afar, and in all humility!"

At this, Lady Betty laughed also and meeting her roguish look he flushed and bent very low above the Lady Belinda's hand but conscious only of her who stood so near and who in turn sank down before him in gracious curtsey, down and down, looking up at him the while with smile a little malicious and eyes of laughing mockery ere she rose, all supple, joyous ease despite her frills and furbelows.

"Doth he suffer much, think you, gentlemen?" she enquired, turning towards the company yet with gaze upon the Major's placid face. "Burneth he with amorous fire, think you, wriggleth he on Cupid's dart?"

"O infallibly!" answered Sir Benjamin, "I'll warrant me, madam, he flameth inwardly——

"E'en as unhappy I!" sighed Sir Jasper Denholm.

"And I myself!" said the Captain, shooting a ruffle.

"O Gad!" exclaimed Viscount Merivale, "why leave out the rest of us?"

"Demme, yes!" cried the Marquis, "we are all our divine Betty's miserable humble, obedient slaves to command——"

"'Tis excellent well!" exclaimed my lady gaily, "miserable slaves, I greet you one and all and 'tis now my will, mandate and command that you shall attend dear my aunt whiles I question this most placid sufferer as to his torments. Major, your hand—pray let us walk!"

As one in a dream he took her soft fingers in his and let her lead him whither she would. Side by side they passed through stately rooms lit by windows rich with stained glass; beneath carved and gilded ceilings, along broad corridors, up noble stairways and down again, she full of blithe talk, he rather more silent even than usual. She quizzed the grim effigies in armour, bowed airily to the portraits, peeped into cupboards and corners, viewing all things with quick, appraising, feminine eyes while he, looking at this and that as she directed him, was conscious only of her.

"'Tis a fine house!" she said critically, "and yet it hath, methinks, a sad and plaintive air. 'Tis all so big and desolate!"

"Desolate!" said he, thoughtfully.

"And lonely and cold, and empty and—ha'n't you noticed it, sir?"

"Why, no!"

"I marvel!"

"As for lonely, mam, they tell me I am naturally so, and then I have my work."

"And that, sir?"

"I'm writing a History of Fortification."

"It sounds plaguy dull!"

"So it does!" he agreed. In time they came to the library and study but on the threshold of that small, bare chamber, my lady paused.

"You poor soul!" she exclaimed. The Major looked startled. "'Tis here you sit and write?" she demanded. He admitted it. "And not so much as a rug on the floor!"

"Rugs are apt to—er—encumber one's feet!" he suggested.

"Nor a picture to light this dull panelling! Not a cushion, not a footstool! O 'tis a dungeon, 'tis deadly drear and smells horribly of tobacco—faugh!"

"Shall we rejoin the company?" he ventured.

"So bare, so barren!" she sighed, "so lorn and loveless!" Here she sank down at the desk in the Major's great armchair and shook disparaging head at him: "Why not work in comfort?"

"Is it so lacking?" he questioned, "I was content——"

"With very little, sir!"

"Surely to be content is to be happy?"

"And are you so—very happy, Major d'Arcy?"

"I—think so! At the least, I'm content——"

"Is a man ever content?" she enquired, taking up one of his pens in idle fingers.

The Major fell to pondering this, watching her the while as, with the feather of the pen she began to touch and stroke her vivid lips and he noticed how full and gentle were their curves.

"He is a fool who strives for the impossible!" said he at last.

"Nay, he is a very man!" she retorted. "Are there many things impossible after all, to a man of sufficient determination, I wonder—or a woman?"

The Major, seating himself on a corner of the desk, pondered this also; and now the feather of the pen was caressing the dimple in her chin, and he noticed how firm this chin was for all its round softness.

"'Deed, sir," she went on again, "I feel as we had known each other all our days, I wonder why?"

The Major took up his tobacco-box that lay near by and turned it over and over before he answered and without looking at her:

"I'm happy to know it, madam, very!"

"And my name is Betty and yours is John and we are neighbours. So I shall call you Major John and sometimes Major Jack—when you please me."

"How did you learn my name?" he asked gently; but now he did look at her.

"Major John," she answered lightly, "you possess a nephew."

"Aye, to be sure!" said he and looked at the tobacco-box again, then put it by, rather suddenly, and rose, "which reminds me that the company wait you, mam——"

"Do—not——"

"Madam!"

"Nor that!"

"My lady Betty," he amended, after a momentary pause. "The company—

"Pish to the company!"

"But madam, consider——"

"Pooh to the company! Pray be seated again, Major John. You love your nephew, sir?"

"Indeed! 'Tis a noble fellow, handsome, rich and—young——"

"True, he's very young, Major John!"

"And—er—" the Major glanced a little helplessly towards the tobacco-box, "he—he loves you and, er——"

"Mm!" said Lady Betty, biting the pen thoughtfully between white teeth. "He loves me, sir—go on, I beg!"

"And being a lover he awaits you impatiently."

"And the others, sir."

"And the others of course, and here are you—I mean here am I——"

"You, Major John—but O why drag yourself into it?"

"I mean that whiles they wait for sight of you I—er—keep you here——"

"By main force, sir."

The Major laughed.

"They will be growing desperate, I doubt," said he.

"Well, let 'em, Major John, I prefer to be—kept here awhile. Pray be seated as you were."

He obeyed, though his usually serene brow was flushed and his gaze wandered towards the tobacco-box again, perceiving which, my lady placed it in his hand.

"As regards your nephew——"

"Meaning Tom."

"Meaning Pancras, sir, he plagued me monstrously this morning. I was alone within the bower and he had the extreme impertinence to—climb the wall."

"The deuce he did, mam!"

"It hath been done before, I think, sir!" she sighed. "Being stole into the arbour he set a cushion on the floor and his knees thereon and, referring to his tablets, spoke me thus: 'Here beginneth the one-hundred-and-forty-sixth supplication for the hand, the heart, the peerless body of the most adorable— —' but I spare you the rest, sir. Upon this, I, for the one-hundred and forty-sixth time incontinent refused him, whereupon he was for reading an ode he hath writ me, whereupon I, very naturally, sought to flee away, whereupon a great, vile, hugeous, ugly, monstrous, green and hairy caterpillar fell upon me—whereupon, of course, I swooned immediately."

"Poor child!" said the Major.

"The couch being comfortably near, sir."

"Couch!" exclaimed the Major, staring.

"Would you have me swoon on the floor, sir?"

"But if you swoon, mam— —"

"I swoon gracefully, sir—'tis a family trait. I, being in a swoon, then, Major John, your nephew had the extreme temerity to—kiss me."

The Major looked highly uncomfortable.

"He kissed me here, sir!" and rosy finger-tip indicated dimpled chin. "To be sure he aimed for my lips, but, by subtlety, I substituted my chin which he kissed—O, passionately!"

The Major dropped the tobacco-box.

"But I understand you—but you were swooning!" he stammered.

"I frequently do, Major John, I also faint, sir, as occasion doth demand."

"God bless my soul!" he exclaimed.

"And wherefore this amaze, sir?"

"'Fore Heaven, madam, I had not dreamed of such—such duplicity."

"O Innocence!" she cried.

"Do all fine ladies feign swoons, madam?"

"Major Innocence, they do! They swoon by rote and they faint by rule."

"Thank Heaven there be none to come swooning my way!" said he fervently.

"Dare you contemn the sex, sir?

"Nay, I'm not so bold, madam, or sufficiently experienced."

"To be sure your knowledge of the sex is limited, I understand."

"Very!"

"You have known but three ladies, I think?"

The Major bowed.

"Then I make the fourth, Major John."

"But indeed, I should never learn to know you in the least."

"Why, 'tis very well!" she nodded. "That which mystifies, attracts."

"Do you wish to attract?" he enquired, stooping for the tobacco-box.

"Sir, I am a woman!"

"True," he smiled, "for whose presence several poor gentlemen do sigh. Let us join 'em."

"Ah! You wish to be rid of me!" She laid down the pen and, leaning chin on hand, regarded him with eyes of meekness. "Do you wish to be rid of me?" she enquired humbly. "Do I weary you with my idle chatter, most grave philosopher?" She had a trick of pouting red lips sometimes when thinking and she did so now as she waited her answer.

"No!" said he.

"I could wish you a little more emphatic, sir and much more—more fiercely masculine—ferocity tempered with respect. Could you ever forget to be so preposterously sedate?"

"I climbed a wall!" he reminded her.

"Pooh!" she exclaimed, "and sat there as gravely unruffled, as proper and precise as a parson in a pulpit. See you now, perched upon a corner of the desk, yet you perch so sublimely correct and solemn 'tis vastly annoying. Could you ever contrive to lose your temper, I wonder?"

"Never with a child," he answered, smiling.

Lady Betty stiffened and stared at him with proud head upflung, grew very red, grew pale, and finally laughed; but her eyes glittered beneath down-sweeping lashes as she answered softly:

"'Deed, sir, I'm very contemptibly young, sir, immaturely hoydenish, sir, green, callow, unripe and altogether of no account to a tried man o' the world sir, of age and judgment ripe—aye, a little over-ripe, perchance. And yet, O!" my lady sighed ecstatic, "I dare swear that one day you shall not find in all the South country such a furiously-angry, ferociously-passionate, rampantly-raging old gentleman as Major John d'Arcy, sir!"

"And there's your aunt calling us, I think," said he, gently. Lady Betty bit her lip and frowned at her dainty shoe. "Pray let her wail, sir, 'tis her one delight when there chance to be a sufficiency of gentlemen to attend her, so suffer the poor soul to wail awhile, sir—nay, she's here!"

As the Major rose the door opened and Lady Belinda entered "twittering" upon the arms of Viscount Merivale and Sir Benjamin Tripp.

"Olack-a-day, dear Bet!" she gasped, "my own love-bird, 'tis here you are and the dear Major too! We've sought thee everywhere, child, the tea languishes—high an low we've sought thee, puss. 'Tis a monstrous fine house but vast—so many stairs—such work—upstairs and downstairs I've climbed and clambered, child——"

"Od so, 'tis true enough!" said Sir Benjamin clapping laced handkerchief to heated brow, "haven't done so much, hem! I say so much climbing for years, I vow!"

Here the Viscount, serene as ever, slowly closed one eye.

"Come Betty sweet, tea grows impatient and clamours for thee and I for tea, and the gentlemen all do passion for thee."

"By the way, Tom," said the Major as they followed the company, "I don't see Mr. Dalroyd here."

"No more he is, nunky!" answered the Viscount, "but then, Lord, sir, Dalroyd is something of an unknown quantity, at all times."

CHAPTER XI
IN WHICH LADY BELINDA TALKS

"And pray mam," enquired the Major as they strolled over velvety lawn, "are you and my lady Betty settled in the country for good?"

The Lady Belinda stopped suddenly and raised clasped hands to heaven.

"Hark to the monster!" she ejaculated, "O Lud, Major, how can you? Stop in the country—I? O heaven—a wilderness of cabbages and caterpillars—of champing cows and snorting bulls! Sir, sir, at the bare possibility I vow I could positively swoon away——"

"Don't, mam!" cried the Major hastily. "No, no mam, pray don't," he pleaded.

"I detest the country sir, I——"

"Quite so, quite so," said the Major soothingly, "cows mam, I understand—quite natural indeed!"

"I loathe and abominate the country, sir—so rude and savage! Such mud and so—so infinite muddy and clingy! What can one do in the country but mope and sigh to be out of it?"

"Well, one can walk in it, mam, and——"

"Walk, sir? But I nauseate walking—in the country extremely. Think of the brooks sir, so—so barbarously wet and—and brooky. Think of the wind so bold to rumple one and spiky things to drag at and tear and take liberties with one's garments! Think of the things that creep and crawl and the things that fly and buzz—and the spiders' webs that tickle one's face! No sir, no— the country is no place for one endowed with a fine and delicate nature."

"Certainly not, mam," said the Major heartily. "Then you'll be leaving shortly?"

"I so beseech Heaven on my two bended knees, sir, but alas, I know not! 'Tis Betty—an orphan, sweet child and in my care. But indeed she's so wickedly wilful, so fly-by-night, so rampant o' youth and—and unreason."

"Indeed, mam!"

"And though sweet Bet is an angel of goodness she hath a temper, O!"

"Hum!" said the Major.

"And such—such animal spirits! So vulgarly robust! Such rude health and vigorous as a dairy-maid! And talking of dairy matters, only the other morning I found her positively—milking a cow!"

"Egad and did you so, mam?"

"And this morning such a romping in the dairy and there was she—O sir!"

"What, mam?"

"Arms all naked—churning, sir!

"O, churning?"

"Riotously, sir!"

"Did you—er—swoon, mam?"

"Indeed I could ha' done, dear Major, but—'twixt you and me, though dear Bet hath the best of hearts, she is perhaps a little unsympathetic I'll not deny, and hath betimes a sharp tongue, I must confess."

"Indeed I—I should judge so, mam."

"O you men!" sighed the Lady Belinda, turning up her eyes, "so quick to spy out foibles feminine—la sir and fie! But indeed though I do love my sweet Bet, O passionately, truth bids me say she can be almost shrewish!"

"You have my sympathy, mam!"

"Dear Major, I deserve it—if you only knew! The pranks she hath played me—so wild, so ungoverned, so—so unvirginal!" The Major winced. "I have known her gallop her horse in the paddock—man-fashion!" The Major looked relieved; perceiving which, Lady Belinda, sinking her voice, continued: "And once, sir, O heaven, can I ever forget! Once—O I tremble to speak it! Once——" The Major flinched again. "Once, sir, she actually ventured forth dressed in—in—O I blush!—in—O Modesty! O Purity!—in—O——!"

"Madam, a God's name—in what?"

"Male attire, sir—O I burn!"

The Major did the same.

"Not—you don't mean—abroad, mam, in—in 'em?"

"I do, sir, I do! She swaggered down the Mall, sir ogling the women, and finding me alone and I not knowing her, she did so leer and nudge me that I all but swooned 'twixt fear and modesty, sir!"

"Good God!" ejaculated the Major, faintly, "was she—alone, madam?"

"She was with her naughty brother Charles and methought he'd die of his unseemly mirth. A wild youth, indeed and she hath the same lawless spirit, sir. All their motherless days I have cared for 'em and what with their waywardness and my own high-strung nature—O me!"

"I can conceive your days have not been—uneventful, mam."

"Charles is known to you, of course, sir?"

"No, mam."

"But your nephew Pancras and he are greatly intimate!"

"I've never even heard of him, madam."

"Why then you don't know that poor, naughty, misguided Charles is— hush, they come! Yonder, sir—O Cupid, a ravishing couple!"

Lady Betty and the Viscount were approaching them, quarrelling as usual, she bright-eyed and flushed of cheek, he handsome, debonair and unutterably serene.

"A truly noble pair, dear Major!" sighed Lady Belinda.

"Indeed, yes, mam!"

"'Twould be an excellent match?"

"Excellent!"

"Both so well suited, so rich, so handsome——"

"And so—young, mam!"

"O sir, I yearn to have 'em married!" The Major was silent. "'Twould tame her wildness, I warrant. How think you?"

"Belike it would, madam."

"Then let us conspire together for their good, dear sir! Let us wed 'em as soon as may be—come?"

"But mam, I—er—indeed, madam, I know nought of such things I——"

"Nay sir, never doubt but we shall contrive it betwixt us. 'Tis then agreed—O 'twill be pure! Henceforth we are conspirators, dear Major, O 'tis ravishing! Hush—yonder come the gentlemen to make their adieux, I think—let us meet 'em!"

As one in a dream the Major gave her his hand and together they rejoined the company who took leave of their host with much bowing of backs, flirting of ruffles, flicking of handkerchiefs and tapping of snuff-boxes. As the Major stood to watch their departure my lady Betty beckoned him to her side:

"And pray, dear sir, hath my aunt recounted you all my sins?" she enquired soft-voiced.

"I have learned you can milk a cow and felicitate you——"

"Of course she told you how I wore breeches, sir?"

The Major gasped, and stood before her blushing and mute; perceiving which, she laughed:

"Indeed, they become me vastly well!" she murmured, and sank before him in the stateliest of curtseys. "Au revoir, my dear Major Jack!" she laughed and giving her hand to an attendant adorer, moved away down the drive with all the gracious dignity of a young goddess.

Long after the gay company had vanished from sight Major d'Arcy stood there, head bowed, hands deep-plunged in coat pockets and with the flush still burning upon his bronzed cheek.

CHAPTER XII
THE VISCOUNT DISCOURSES
ON SARTORIAL ART

Viscount Merivale sighed ecstatic.

"Beautiful!" he murmured. "O beautiful, nunky! Here we have perfection of fit, excellence of style, harmony of colour and graciousness of line!"

"Colour," reflected the Major, "is't not a little fevered, Tom, a little—hectic as 'twere?"

"Hectic—O impiety! You are a sentient rhapsody, a breathing poem, sir, blister me!"

The Major regarded his reflection in the mirror dubious and askance; his plum-coloured, gold-braided coat, his gorgeous embroidered waistcoat, his clocked stockings and elegant French shoes; his critical glance roved from flowing new periwig to flashing diamond shoe-buckles and he blinked.

"I find myself something too dazzling, Tom!"

"Entirely *à la mode*, sir, let me perish!"

"A little too—exotic, Tom!"

"Rat me sir—no, not a particle."

"And I feel uncomfortably stiff in 'em——"

"But, sir, reflect on the joy you confer on the beholder!"

"True, I had forgot that!" said the Major smiling.

"You are a joy to the eye nunky, an inspiration, you are, I vow you are. If your breeches cramp you, suffer 'em, if your coat gall you, endure it for the sake o' the world in general—be unselfish, sir. Look at me—on state occasions my garments pinch me infernally, cause me pasitive torture, sir, but I endure for the sake of others, sir."

"You are a martyr, Tom."

"Gad love me, sir, 'tis so, a man of fashion must be. So there you stand as gay a young spark as ever ruffled it——"

"These shoe-buckles, now," mused the Major, "here was an egregious folly and waste of money——"

"Nay, you could afford 'em, sir, and there's nothing can show your true man of taste like an elegant foot."

"Still, considering my age, Tom—

"A man is as old as he looks, sir, and you look no older than thirty-one."

The Major shook his head.

"I could ha' wished myself a little more sombre-clad——"

"Sambre sir—O Gad support me, sambre? Permit me to say, sir, with the greatest deference in the world—tush t'you, sir! Why must ye pine to be sambre? You ain't a parson nor a Quaker, nor yet a funeral! With all due respect, sir—pish! You are as sober clad as any self-respecting gentleman could desire."

"D'ye think so, Tom?"

"Sure of it, sir, 'pon my honour!"

"Hum!" said the Major still a little dubious and reaching for his gold-laced hat, was in the act of setting it on his head when a cry from the Viscount arrested him.

"Gad love me, sir, what are you about with your hat?"

"I am about to put it on, sure, nephew."

"O Lard, sir, never do so, I beg!"

"In heaven's name why not?"

"Because 'tis never done sir. Fie, 'tis a curst barbarian act never committed by the 'ton'!"

"But damme, Tom, what are hats for?"

"To show off one's hand sir, to fan one's self gracefully, to be borne negligently 'neath the arm, to point a remark or lend force to an epigram, to woo and make love with, to offend and insult with, 'tis for a thousand and one things, sir, but never O never to put on one's head—'tis a practice unmodish, reprehensible and altogether damnable!"

"Tom," said the Major, looking a little dazed, "now look'ee, Tom, I'm no town gallant nor ever shall be, to me a hat is a hat, and as such I shall use it——"

"But reflect sir, consider how it will discommode your peruke."

"Tom, well-nigh all my days I have worn a uniform and consequently any other garments feel strange on me—these cursedly so. But since I've bought 'em, I'll wear 'em my own way. And now, since 'tis a fine evening, I'll walk abroad and try to get a little used to 'em."

Saying which the Major clapped on his hat a little defiantly and strode out of the room.

In the wide hall he met Mrs. Agatha and conscious of her glance of surprised approval, felt himself flushing as he acknowledged her curtsey; thereafter on his way out he stepped aside almost stealthily to avoid one of the neat housemaids; even when out in the air he still felt himself a mark for eyes that peeped unseen and hastened his steps accordingly.

And now, as luck would have it, he came upon the Sergeant busied at one of the yew hedges with a pair of shears; checking a momentary impulse to dodge out of sight, the Major advanced and touched him with his gold-mounted cane. The Sergeant turned, stared, opened his mouth, shut it again and came to attention.

"Well, Sergeant?" he enquired. Sergeant Zebedee blinked and coughed. "Sergeant, I—ah—er—O damme, Zeb, what d'ye think of 'em?"

"Sir, being by natur' a man o' few words all I can say is—Zounds!"

"D'ye—d'ye like 'em Zeb?"

"Sir," answered the Sergeant, sloping the shears across his arm and standing at ease, "I've a seen you in scarlet and jacks, I've a seen you in cuirass and buff but—I ain't never a seen you look younger, no, nor better, and that's God's truth amen, your honour."

"I'm glad o' that, Zeb, very!" and the Major glanced full-skirted coat and silk stockings with a kindlier eye. "To speak truth, Zeb, I found 'em a little—er—overpowering at first, as 'twere."

"So they are, sir, as overpowering as ever was!"

"Eh?" said the Major, starting.

"Like the old regiment at Malplaquet, sir, they ain't to be took lightly, nor yet withstood, sir."

"Hum!" said the Major, his eyes travelling up to a patch of fleecy cloud. "And now as regards yourself, Sergeant. Since you refuse to accept more pay——"

"Not a groat, sir! Which ain't to be wondered at when you consider as you've rose me twice since you dropped in for this here fortun'—not a stiver, sir!"

"Just so, Zeb, just so! Therefore I propose to advance you an extra ten guineas a year as—er—a clothes-bounty, as 'twere."

"Clo'es, sir! And me wi' two soots as refuses to be wore out not to mention this here. Take these breeches, for example, they've done dooty noble and true for three years and no sign o' weakness front or rear— —"

"Still, 'tis time they were retired from the active list, Zeb. So at the first opportunity you will proceed to fit yourself out anew—from head to foot. See to it, Sergeant Tring!"

"Very good, sir. Orders is orders."

"And the sooner the better, Zebedee." And the Major nodded and went his way.

"*Nom d'un chien!*" exclaimed the Sergeant looking after his master's tall, elegant figure. "All I says is—Lord—Lord bless his eyes and limbs!"

Reaching the highway the Major turned aside from the village and mounting a stile with due heed to his dainty apparel, followed a footpath that led over a sloping upland, crossed a murmurous rill and led on beside a wood from whose green depths came leafy stirrings and the evening song of thrush and blackbird. As he progressed, the leaping rill grew to a gurgling brook, widened to a splashing stream, hurrying over pebbly bed until it deepened to a slumberous pool spanned by a rustic bridge.

Evening was at hand and the westering sun cast long shadows making of these drowsy waters a pool of sombre mystery. Being upon the bridge the Major paused to look down into these stilly depths and, leaning well over the handrail, to survey himself in this watery mirror—the graceful fall of his lace steenkirk, the flowing curls of his glossy peruke, the cock of his laced hat; all of which he observed with a profound and grave attention. So lost and absorbed was he that he leaned there quite unconscious of one that had halted just within the wood, crouching furtively amid the leaves. A tall, burly, gipsy-looking fellow this, who caressed a knotty bludgeon in hairy fingers and whose narrowed eyes roved over the indolent, lolling figure on the bridge from gemmed cravat to glittering shoe-buckles; once he took a stealthy forward step, the knobby club a-swing in eager hand but, heeding the wide spread of these plum-coloured shoulders, the vigorous length of these resplendent limbs, scowled and crouched back among the leaves again. Presently, the Major, having settled his hat more to his liking, went on across the bridge and along a path that led over a wide sweep of green meadow and so to another stile flanked by high hedges. Here he paused again to watch a skylark hovering against the blue and to catch the faint, sweet ripple of song. And leaning there with gaze aloft, he fell to deep thought, turning over in his mind a problem that had vexed him much of late, a problem he had pondered by day and thought over by night, to wit:—

> Could a feminine being blessed by a bounteous Nature in all the outward attributes most desirable in womanhood, a face beyond compare and goddess-shape, but one who had wantonly exposed that shape to public regard clad in the baser garb of masculinity—could such a one be worthy of a man's humble respect and reverent homage? Would his mother (God rest her sweet soul) have thought her virginal? Would his aunt Clarissa have endured her for a moment?

He sighed heavily and like an echo, came a sob and then another. He started, and guided by these sounds, discovered a very small damsel who wept bitterly, a huddled, woeful little figure in the grassy ditch beneath the hedge.

"Why, child," said he, "what's your sorrow?"

At this she glanced up in sudden fear but, like his voice, the Major's grey eyes were gentle and very kindly; perceiving which she rose, the better to bob him a curtsey, and sobbed forth her woe:

"O sir, 'tis all along of another grand gentleman like you as took away my letter."

Forgetting fine clothes and dignity together, the Major sat down in the ditch, drew the small, woebegone figure beside him and patted her tear-stained cheek.

"Tell me all about it, you very small maid," said he. The little girl hesitated, viewing him with the quick, intuitive eyes of childhood then, checking her sobs, nestled within his velvet-clad arm.

"'Twas a letter, sir, as was gave me by a dirty man as did meet me by the old mill, sir."

"You mean the ruined mill beyond the park wall, child?"

"Yes, please sir."

"And a dirty fellow, was he?"

"Yes sir, only with a clean voice—soft, like yours. And he give me a groat and says I must take the letter to the Lady Carlyon as lives at Densmere Court——"

"Lady Carlyon!" exclaimed the Major staring. "Good Lord! 'Tis strange, very strange. Sure that was the name, child?"

"Sure, sir—the man did say it over and over and how I must give it to only her. So I went 'long the road, sir, but a grand gentleman came up behind me—so fine he was and grand and asked to see the letter and took it and says as how he will give it to my lady and bid me run away and that's all, sir."

"Well, never grieve, my small maid. You've done no harm—come let me dry those pretty cheeks," which the Major with belaced handkerchief did forthwith. "What's your name, child?" he enquired, lifting her to her feet.

"Charity Bent, sir."

"'Tis a pretty name. Many brothers and sisters?"

"No, sir. I do be all father's got to take care o' him."

"So you take care of him, do you, child?"

"When he be at home, sir, he do work at the great house."

"Which is that?"

"The Manor, sir. And now I must go an' cook his supper, he'll be along home soon."

"Eh—cook?" said the Major, staring at the small speaker. "Child, how old are you?"

"Nine, please sir."

"Lord!" exclaimed the Major, and lifting her up he kissed her rosy cheek and, taking off his hat, stood to watch the small figure flit away down the grassy way beyond.

Hat in hand he leaned there once again, revolving in his mind the old problem under a new aspect, thus:

Question: Which is the more worthy, a humble village child of nine who cooks her father's supper or a proud and idle young goddess who wears— —

The Major sighed and put on his hat.

CHAPTER XIII
OF INDIGNATION, A WOOD, AND A GIPSY

It was at this juncture that the Major became aware of a tall, buxom, not to say strapping country-wench approaching down the lane, sun-bonnet on head and large basket on comely arm; one garbed as all maids should be, in simple gown that allowed free play to vigorous, young limbs; one who moved with step blithe and purposeful, doubtless busied upon some useful and womanly duty as all women should be.

So thought the Major as he watched the approach of this rustic lass, comparing her in her naturalness and simplicity to wood-nymphs and dryads and goddesses of groves and fountains, and altogether to the disadvantage of patched and powdered beauties in their coquettish frills and furbelows. Sighing again, he turned to go back.

"God bless your honour and, so please your honour, a humble good day to your honour!" said a voice.

The Major stopped, wheeled, and dropped his cane:

"Betty!" he exclaimed.

"John!" said she. But, meeting his look, flushed and drooped her lashes, whereupon he fell to stammering.

"I—I was but now—'Tis strange but I was——"

"Thinking of me, Major John?"

"Indeed!" he answered.

"Kindly, Major Jack?"

"Pray," he enquired, "pray—er—are you alone?"

"Momentarily!" she sighed. "But Sir Benjamin Tripp is somewhere about, the Marquis is not far hence and Mr. Marchdale mopes at hand——"

"You mean they seek you——?"

"Most pertinaciously, sir, but quite vainly by reason that I can climb."

"Climb?" repeated the Major, staring, "pray what?"

"A wall, sir."

"Wall?" he murmured.

"Two, sir. I had to run away. They're dear creatures, to be sure, but the Marquis persists in recounting pedigrees of horses and dogs, Sir Benjamin rhapsodises in metre and poor Mr. Marchdale, being very young, is so egregiously in love with me that I climb and clamber over walls and here I am. Pray aid me over this stile ere they find me."

The Major's aid was so energetic and prompt that Lady Betty was over the stile and walking beside him, flushed and a little breathless all in a moment.

"You are forgetting your fine cane, sir," said she in a small voice.

"Aye, to be sure!" And flushing, he picked it up rather hastily.

"And now prithee my basket—'twould never suit so fine a gentleman." The Major flushed, seeing which she added: "Though indeed I do like you infinitely so."

"And I," said he impulsively, his keen, bright glance appraising her from head to foot, "I find you infinitely more—more—er—womanly as 'twere—but pray why so large a basket?"

"To carry eggs, sir, and butter and such. Some of your tenants are miserably poor, Major John."

"Hum!" said he, thoughtfully. "And you buy them butter——"

"I make them butter, sir."

"Ha—do you, by Jove!" he exclaimed, his eyes shining.

"I make them butter with the aid of certain polite, perspiring, and I greatly fear, profane gentlemen." The Major's smooth brow grew ruffled.

"Meaning whom, mam?"

"Well, to-day 'twas Sir Benjamin Tripp, the Marquis, Sir Jasper Denholm and Mr. Marchdale. To see Sir Benjamin churning is—O 'tis rare, 'tis killing!" And my lady stood still the better to laugh.

"Sir Benjamin Tripp—churning?" exclaimed the Major.

"So hot—so scant o' breath!" she gurgled. "And his ruffles flip-flopping and his fine peruke all askew. To-morrow 'twill be Lord Alvaston and Captain West and—O 'twill be pure!" and once again she trilled with laughter until, beholding the Major's expression, she stopped breathless and wiping her eyes on the back of slender hand like any rustic lass. "Doth it not strike you as comical?" she demanded.

"O vastly!" said he, and sighed.

"If you had but seen Sir Benjamin, poor, dear, good creature—he did so blow and pant!"

"Extreme diverting!" admitted the Major and sighed again.

"And pray, Major d'Arcy, do you always utter deep-fetched and doleful breathings when amused? Smile, sir, this instant!" The Major obeyed, whereupon she shook critical head: "'Twas much like a grimace caused by an extreme anguish, but 'twill serve for one so preternaturally grave as Major d'Arcy."

"Do I seem so grave, indeed?" he questioned wistfully.

"As the tomb, sir!" The Major blinked: walked a dozen yards or so in silence and sighed deeper than ever, strove to disguise it in a cough and failing, stood rueful. My lady stopped and faced him:

"Major John—Major d'Arcy, sir, look at me. Now prithee why all this windy woe, this sighful sorrow—what evil thought harrows your lofty serenity to-day?"

"I think," said he, hands tight-clenched upon his cane, "I am haunted by a certain evening in the Mall!"

"O? Indeed? The Mall?"

"Aye, my lady, the Mall." Slowly, slowly her red lips curved, her gaze sank beneath his.

"You mean, I think, when I wore——"

"I do!" said he hastily.

"So you have not forgot?"

"Would to heaven I might!"

"And prithee why?"

"'Twas so unworthy your proud womanhood!"

My lady flushed, averted her head and walked on in a dignified silence until they reached the rustic bridge; here she paused to look down into the stilly pool.

"Heigho!" she sighed. The Major was silent and seeing how he frowned with his big chin out-thrust, she bit her lip and dimpled.

"The moon will be at the full to-night!" Still he didn't speak. "And when the moon is full I always feel excessive feminine and vapourish!" The Major, staring into the gloomy water, gloomed also. "And when I feel vapourish, chiding nauseates me and reproaches give me the megrims."

"I would not reproach you, child— —"

"Ancient sir, I am not a child. And you do reproach me—you said 'twas unworthy!"

"Aye, I said so," he admitted, keeping his gaze bent upon the sleepy pool, "I said so, my lady, because I would have you in all things most noble, most high and far removed 'bove fear of reproach. Because I would have you worthy of all reverence."

"Alas!" she sighed, "here is a something trying role for a poor maid who chances to be very human flesh and blood!"

"And yet," said he in his grave, gentle voice, "knowing you flesh and blood, in my thought you were very nigh to divinity also."

"Were?" she questioned softly. "Is my poor divinity lost so soon?" And her arm touched his upon the handrail. The Major sighed and immediately the arm withdrew itself and, before he could speak, she laughed, though her merriment rang a little hollow. "And forsooth is it so deep a sin, so black a crime to have ventured abroad in my brother's clothes? And if it were, pray who is Major d'Arcy to sit in judgment? Am I dishonoured, smirched beyond redemption— —"

"No—no— —" he exclaimed.

"So stained, so steeped in depravity— —"

"Ah no indeed!" he cried, "indeed madam—ah, Betty it was but that it seemed so—so— —"

"So what, sir?"

"So—so—unmaidenly."

My lady Betty caught her breath in a gasp, her cheeks glowed hot and angry and she fronted him with head upflung.

"How dare you—how dare you think me so—speak me so!" Even as she spoke, proud colour ebbed, hot anger was ousted by cold disdain and he blenched before the scorn of her eyes; he grew humble, abject, reached out hands in supplication:

"My lady I—I—God knows I would not hurt you! Indeed I did but mean— —"

"Enough sir, 'tis sufficient!" said she disdainfully. "Major d'Arcy doth pronounce me unmaidenly—O, 'tis all-sufficing!" and, as she turned her back on him, her very garments seemed to radiate scorn unutterable.

"Stay!" he pleaded, as she moved away. "Ah, never leave me so—do but let me explain—hear me!"

"Be silent, sir!" she commanded, speaking over her shoulder, "I've heard enough, aye—enough for a lifetime!" And stepping from the bridge she turned aside into the wood; but there, his hand upon her arm arrested her.

"Child, whither go you?"

"Whereso I will, sir. A fair, good even to you and—good-bye!"

"Not through the wood, madam! There be rough folk about, the Sergeant tells me—gipsies, tramping folk and the like."

"O sir," she sighed, "I may prefer such to Major—Prudery—d'Arcy!" and setting aside a bramble-shoot she went on into the wood, and, when he would have followed, checked him with an imperious gesture. "Come no further, sir, here be thorns to spoil gay finery—and besides," she added, glancing back at him with merciless eyes, "your sober airs annoy me, your lofty virtue is an offence—pray suffer me to go alone!"

The Major flushed painfully, took off his hat and bowed.

"As you will, madam!" said he and, stepping aside, watched her go until the leaves had hidden her from sight. Then, putting on his hat, he took a score or so of slow strides away and as many slow strides back again, until, being come some little way in among the trees, he halted to listen. Faint and far he caught a rustle, a leafy stirring that told where she moved and, guided by this he began to follow into the depths of the wood. Suddenly he paused to listen intently, cane grasped in powerful fist, then hurried on at speed, choosing his way with quick, soldierly eye and making very little sound for all his haste and so reached a little clearing.

She stood, back set to a tree, hands gripping her basket, head erect and defiant but in her wide eyes a sickening fear as she fronted a tall, burly, gipsy-looking fellow who carried a knobby bludgeon and whose eyes, heedful and deliberate, roved over her trembling loveliness and whose hairy lips curled as he slowly advanced. Then the Major stepped out from the leaves, his gait unhurried and limping a little as was usual. But at sight of him my lady, uttering a gasp, let fall her basket almost forgetting shuddering fear in amazement as she beheld the face that looked out between the precise curls of the Major's great periwig. The gipsy fellow saw it also, and, reading its expression aright, sprang immediately to a defensive posture and spoke between a growl and a whine:

"What now, master? There be no harm done, sir—nought but a bit o' pleasantry wi' a country wench!" The Major neither spoke nor altered his leisurely advance until, coming within striking distance, he leapt. Heavy bludgeon whirled, long cane whizzed and the fellow, uttering a hoarse gasp, dropped his weapon and gave back, clutching at useless, dangling limb. But the Major's long arm rose and fell, beating the man to his knees, to his face; even then, as the fellow writhed helpless, those merciless blows rained down tirelessly until a voice cried:

"Don't! Don't! Ah, Major John—you'll kill him!" The Major stepped back, panting a little.

"Kill him," he repeated gently, "why no, mam, no—his sort take a vast deal of killing. I would but give him such a—er—reminder as shall not fade awhile."

"Nay sir, no more, I beg! And see, your cane is broke——"

"Why so 'tis!" said the Major and tossing it aside he picked up the knobby bludgeon, seeing which Lady Betty caught his arm and held it:

"Nay, you are cruel—cruel! You shall not, I say. He has enough!"

"Aye, perhaps he has," said the Major, "and 'twould be distressing for you of course, though when one must fight 'tis as well to be thorough." Saying which he resettled his ruffles, tucked the bludgeon under his arm and bowed. "Pray let us be going, madam!" My lady hesitated and glanced at her assailant's prostrate figure. "A few bruises, mam, he will be well enough in an hour or so—though somewhat sore. And now, with your leave I'll see you out o' the wood, evening falls apace and the Sergeant was right, it seems." Then he picked up her basket and motioning her to lead the way, followed her through the wood.

For once in her twenty-two years of life my lady Betty felt herself at a disadvantage; twice she turned to speak but he, walking behind with head bowed, seemed utterly oblivious of her, wherefore she held her peace and threw up proud head disdainfully. And yet he had saved her and—from what? At this she shivered and disdain was forgotten. Still it is difficult to express gratitude with proper dignity to a man upon a narrow, brier-set path especially when that man keeps himself perseveringly behind one. So my lady waited until they should be out of the hateful wood.

Thus they went in a silence unbroken until they came out in a bye-lane that gave upon the highway. Here, with the glory of the sunset all about her, she paused, quick-breathing, flushed and with witching eyes a-droop and reached out her hands to him; but the Major chanced to be looking just then at a tall gentleman lounging toward them down the shady lane.

"Yonder is Mr. Dalroyd, I think, madam," said the Major, "he shall relieve you of my presence," and into those pleading, outstretched hands he set—the basket.

My lady started away, her lips quivered and, blinded by sudden tears she turned and sped away.

So the Major limped homeward through the afterglow, quite unconscious of the ugly, knobby bludgeon beneath his arm, his mind once more busied with the problem viewed from yet another aspect:

Question: Might it be possible that a true woman can be womanly no matter what she chance to wear?

CHAPTER XIV
SOME DESCRIPTION OF A KISS

Mrs. Agatha, gathering beans and aided by the Viscount's two valets, smiled and dimpled on each in turn while the Sergeant, busied in an adjacent corner with a ladder, cursed softly but with deep and sustained heartiness.

Mrs. Agatha's basket was three parts full and Sergeant Zebedee, having pretty well exhausted the English and French tongues, was vituperating grimly in Low Dutch, when a bell jangled distantly, a faint but determined summons, and immediately after, the Viscount's voice was heard near at hand and imperative:

"Arthur! Charles! Where a plague are the prepasterous dags! Oho, Charles! Arthur!"

The two valets, galvanised to action exceeding swift, started, saluted Mrs. Agatha and betook themselves within doors at commendable speed, and the Sergeant, having at last juggled his ladder into position, vituperated them out of sight and was in the act of mounting when he was aware of Mrs. Agatha at his elbow.

"'Tis surely a lovely day, Sergeant!" said she demurely.

"Is it so, mam?"

"Well, isn't it?"

"Why mam, I ain't had doo time to notice same, d'ye see. But, since you ax me I say no, mam, 'tis a dam—no, a cur—no, a plaguy hot day." Saying which, the Sergeant rolled snowy shirt-sleeve a little higher above a remarkably hairy and muscular arm and mounted one rung of the ladder.

"The house do be very—gay these days, Sergeant."

"O mam! And why?"

"Well, since Viscount Merivale came with his two gentlemen."

"His two what, mam? Meaning who, mam?"

"Lud, Sergeant, his gentlemen for sure, Mr. Arthur and Mr. Charles—so polite, so witty and they never swear!" The Sergeant snorted. "One can never be dull in their company. Mr. Charles has such a flow of talk and Mr. Arthur is a perfect mine of anecdote, ha'n't you noticed?"

"Why no, mam. The only mines as I'm acquainted with is the kind that explodes."

"But indeed, Sergeant, everything seems changing for the better—take his honour the Major, see how young he looks in his fine things—aye, as young as his nephew and handsomer. And now 'tis your turn to change——"

"I ain't given to change, mam."

"A frill to your shirt, say, and your wig powdered——"

"Frills, mam—never! And I haven't powdered my wig since we quit soldiering, why should I? What's a man of forty-three want to go a-powdering of his wig for? Frills, mam? Powder, mam? Now what I say to that is——"

"Ha' done, Sergeant!"

"Very good, mam! Only I leave frills and powder and such to young fly-b'-nights——"

"Powder, and frills, and ruffles at your wrists, Sergeant——"

"And talkin' o' fly-b'-nights, mam, brings me to a question I wish to ax you and meant to ax you afore."

"A—a question, Sergeant?" she repeated faintly, beginning to trace out a pattern on the path with the toe of her neat shoe.

"As I want you to answer prompt, mam, aye or no."

"Very well, Sergeant," said she, fainter than before. "I'm listening."

"D'ye sleep well o' nights, mam?"

Mrs. Agatha started, glanced up swiftly and, for no apparent reason, blushed very red under the Sergeant's direct gaze.

"Lud, Sergeant Zebedee, what's that to do with it—I mean——"

"Everything, mam!"

"And why shouldn't I sleep? I've no bad conscience to wake me, thank God."

"Then ye do sleep well?"

"Ye-es!"

"Then you ain't heard nor seen nothing toward the hour o' midnight—footsteps, say?"

"Footsteps! O Lud—where?"

"Anywhere! You never have?"

"Never!"

"P'r'aps you don't believe in ghostes, mam, spectres, or say—apparations?"

"I—I don't know. Why?"

"You've never happened to see a pale shape a-fluttering and a-flitting by light o' moon?"

"Gracious me—no, Sergeant! You make me all of a shiver! Have you?"

"No, mam!"

"O cruel, to fright one so!"

"But hope an' expect to observe same to-night towards the hour o' midnight or thereabouts and if so, shall immediately try what cold steel can do agin it."

"Gracious goodness, Sergeant, what d'you mean?"

"I mean as I'm a-going to find out what it is as walks o' nights."

"But ghosts don't walk, they glide."

"Maybe so, mam, but this ghost or apparation ain't a glider 'tis a walker, same being observed to leave footmarks. Also Roger Bent the second gardener as lives nigh the old mill has seen it twice—says same haunts the old mill o' moony nights, says—but there's Roger now, he shall tell you!" The Sergeant whistled, beckoned and the second gardener, a young-old, shock-headed man, approached, knuckling his forehead to Mrs. Agatha.

"Roger," said the Sergeant, "tell us what ye saw last night."

"A gobling!" said Roger, "a grimly gobling an' that's what."

"Bless us!" exclaimed Mrs. Agatha, "what was it like?"

"Why," answered Roger, ruffling his shock of hair with a claw-like right hand, "'twere rayther like a phamtom, mam—very much so, that's what!"

"O—where was it?"

"'Twas a-quaking i' the ruin o' the owd mill, mam, dithering and dathering glowersome like."

Mrs. Agatha gasped, noting which, Roger shook his head gloomily. "Always know'd th' owd mill was haunted but never seed nowt afore. I do 'ope as my hens aren't witched from laying, that's what."

"And then you followed it, Roger?"

"Aye, I did so, Sergeant, me 'aving a dried hare's-foot 'ung round my neck d'ye see which same do be a powerful charm, give me by old Betty the witch, a spell as no gobling nor speckiter can abide."

"And where did it go?"

"Along by the spinney, Sergeant, then along the back lane and I see it vanish it-self through th' orchard wall and that's what!"

"And there was its footmarks in the earth this morning, mam, sure enough. All right, Roger."

Hereupon Roger knuckled again to Mrs. Agatha and betook himself back to his duties.

"'Tis dreadful!" exclaimed Mrs. Agatha, clasping her pretty hands.

"'Tis queer, mam, queer—but 'twill be queerer if I don't find out all about it 'twixt now and to-morrow morning."

"Sergeant Zebedee—Zebedee, don't!"

"Mam, I must."

"For—my sake."

"Mam, I—'tis become a matter o' dooty with me."

"Have you any charm to ward off evil, Sergeant?"

"Why no, mam."

"Then I'll give you one," and speaking, she took a ribbon from her white neck, a blue ribbon whereon a small gold cross dangled. "You shall wear this!" said she, blushing a little. "Come, stoop your head!"

"Why, Mrs. Agatha I—I——"

"O pray stoop your head!"

The Sergeant obeyed and it naturally followed that the Sergeant's neat wig was very near Mrs. Agatha's pretty mob-cap, so near, indeed that a tress of her glossy hair tickled his bronzed, smooth-shaven chin; the Sergeant saw her eyes, grave and intent, the oval of a soft cheek, the curve of two lips—full, soft lips, ripely delicious and tempting and so near that he had but to turn his head——

The Sergeant turned his head and for a long, breathless moment lips met lips then:

"Why, Sergeant!" she exclaimed breathlessly. "O Sergeant—Zebedee— Tring!" And turning, she sped away into the house.

Left alone the Sergeant picked up his hammer, stared at it and put it carefully into his pocket; having done which, he laughed, grew solemn, and sighed.

"Well," said he at last, "all I says is——"

But for once he could find no words for it in English, French or Dutch.

CHAPTER XV
WHEREIN IS MUCH TALK BUT LITTLE ACTION

Mr. Marchdale threw down his cards pettishly and swore, Lord Alvaston, sprawling in his chair, surveyed his slender legs with drowsy approval, the Marquis of Alton yawned and Mr. Dalroyd shuffled for a new deal; hard by the Captain and Sir Jasper diced sleepily and in the ingle Sir Benjamin snored outright.

"Sink me!" murmured Lord Alvaston, "sink me if I've touched an ace all the evening!"

"Aye, Dalroyd and Alton have all the luck!" exclaimed Mr. Marchdale with youthful petulance.

"Dem'd queer thing, but I feel dooced sleepy!" yawned the Marquis.

"'S'ffect o' country air," murmured Lord Alvaston, "look at Ben."

"Aye begad, will some one be good enough to stir him up, his dem'd snoring makes me worse——"

"Who's snoring?" demanded Sir Benjamin, sitting bolt upright, broad awake in a moment, and straightening his wig. "Od's body, I do protest I did but close my eyes for a moment——"

"And snored, Ben, damnably—'ffect o' country air——"

"And churning, Ben—eh, Benjamin?" suggested Mr. Dalroyd. "You've taken up dairy-work, I understand."

Sir Benjamin reached for and filled his wine-glass and grew a little more rubicund than usual.

"Od so, sir," said he, "'When in Rome'—od's body! 'do as Rome does.' And we are in the country and—ah—being here 'mid rural things simple and sweet I—hem! I say I——"

"Snore, Ben!" murmured Lord Alvaston, "and very natural too!"

"And churn, Ben!" nodded Mr. Dalroyd, his delicate nostrils quivering in his sleepy smile, "You churn till you sweat, churn till you blow like any grampus, I understand."

Sir Benjamin took a gulp of wine, choked, coughed, and grew purple.

"Eh? What? Ho!" exclaimed the Captain. "A churn? Ben? Split me! Some pretty dairy-wench? Aha! Ben—confess!"

Pompous, dignified, Sir Benjamin rose and took a pinch of snuff with great deliberation and apparent satisfaction.

"Od, gentlemen," said he, lace handkerchief a-flutter, "since you'd have it, I'll freely—hem! freely confess it. But 'twas no rustic charmer, no village beauty, no dainty wench o' the dairy bewitched me—no, no! Od's my life, sirs, I've been beforehand wi' most of ye—body o' me—yes! For 'twas my joy and felicity to—ah—hem! to labour at the delightful art of— ah—buttermaking 'neath the bright and witching eyes of—our Admirable Betty!"

"O sly, Ben!" murmured Lord Alvaston, "O Ben—curst sly, sink me!"

"But—a churn!" said the Captain. "Begad! So fatiguing!"

"I churned, firstly, gentlemen, because 'twas so my lady's will and such is, and ever will be, my law, as the mighty Hercules span for the tender Omphale so did I churn for my lady. I churned, secondly, because the churn is a—hem! a romantic engine—I appeal to Alton!"

"So 'tis," mumbled his lordship, "demme if 'tisn't!"

"And I churned thirdly, because the labour entailed is admirable for the—hem! for tuning up the liver—I refer you to Marchdale."

"Nothing like it!" assented that youthful man of the world, "for liver, megrims or the pip give me a churn—and Betty along with it o' course."

"Ha," said Mr. Dalroyd, his smile growing a little malicious, "and then, having put your liver in tune with the churn you proceeded to put it out again by swallowing deep potations of—rhubarb wine of my lady's own decoction."

Sir Benjamin sat down, his plump features took on a careworn expression and he shuddered slightly.

"Rhubarb!" whispered Lord Alvaston, staring.

"Rhubarb!" muttered the Captain. "O Gad! Poor Ben!"

"Heroic Ben!" said Sir Jasper, his fine eyes more soulful than ever.

"Three glasses!" sighed Sir Benjamin. "Aye—three—she insisted! But, body o' me, sirs, what would you? Beauty is the—hem! the fount, the source, the mainspring of valour, is't not? As in olden days our ancestors were ready and eager to adventure life and limb for the bright eyes of their

fair ladies, surely we, in like manner, should be equally willing to risk our—
hem! our—I say to risk our——"

"Stomachs!" suggested Alvaston, "my own 'pinion precisely! Stomach's only stomach but th' heart's a noble organ—seat o' the 'flections and all that sort o' thing. Which reminds me, not a single ace have I held this game."

"But—split me! Why rhubarb?" demanded the Captain, "Why endeavour t' poison poor Ben? O burn me!"

"'Twas a woman's notion," explained Sir Jasper, "a whim, a fancy. The whole sex, dear creatures, be full of 'em, 'tis what makes 'em so infinite captivating——"

"Not," enquired the Captain, "not rhubarb——"

"No, no—'tis the mystery of 'em—the wonder of their changing moods that makes women so alluring and Bet the most bewitching of 'em all. By Venus, she's elusive as a sunbeam, mysterious as fate, changeable as——"

"Begad," exclaimed the Marquis, "and that's the dem'd truth—that's Betty to a T and that's how I'm coming continual croppers—if she were only a little more like a horse or a dog I should know what to expect and how to treat her——"

"I suggest—precisely the same," smiled Mr. Dalroyd, "and horses one spurs and dogs one whips and my lady would be better for a little of both. Women should be managed, they expect it and they love the strong hand!"

Sir Benjamin gaped, the Captain stared, Sir Jasper rolled his eyes and Mr. Marchdale, furrowing youthful brow, spoke:

"As a man of the world I vow there's wisdom in't. The lovely creatures look for strength in a man—mastery, d'ye see, though a whip——"

"Od sir," ejaculated Sir Benjamin, "'tis rank heresy!"

"Pure savagery!" gasped Sir Jasper.

"Precisely my own 'pinion!" murmured Lord Alvaston. "For if a dog's a dog he's only a dam dog—'sequently whip him when needful. Same with a horse. But a woman being a woman ain't a dog nor a horse, therefore since she is a woman 'stead of whipping, worship——"

"Talking o' whips," said the Marquis, "I should devoutly and vastly desire to see some masterful ass attempt to horsewhip Bet, 'twould be a sight for the gods—she has all her brother's fire and spirit with a cleverer head."

"None the less, Alton," retorted Mr. Dalroyd, "the man who wins her will be the man who masters her."

"No, no, Dalroyd," exclaimed Sir Jasper soulfully, "who shall master a goddess? Who but the humblest of her admirers shall hope to win the queen of women?"

"I'm with you there, Denholm!" said Lord Alvaston heartily, "and talking o' queens, not an ace have I touched this game—I'm done!"

"Same here!" growled Mr. Marchdale. "You've all the luck, Dalroyd. I owe you another fifty, I think?"

"Seventy-five!" murmured Mr. Dalroyd.

"Well, I'm for bed!" yawned his lordship.

"So'm I!" nodded Mr. Marchdale.

"Eh—bed?" cried the Marquis reproachfully. "Bed—and not gone twelve yet—shameful, O dem!"

"'Tis the country air," explained Marchdale, "in London I'm at my best and brightest at three o'clock in the morning as you very well know, Alton, but here I'm different, 'tis the curst country air, I think."

"And the churn!" said the Marquis, "Betty kept you at it, you and Ben, not to mention the rhubarb wine, I escaped that—eh, Ben?"

"You were nearer the window!" sighed Sir Benjamin, rising.

"What, are you for bed too? Nay, stop at least for a nightcap or so—let's have up another half-dozen o' burgundy!"

"Nay, bed for me," yawned his lordship of Alvaston, "we may be set a-digging or a-ploughing or some such, to-morrow—one never can tell——"

"Ha!" exclaimed the Captain, "would lose a hundred—joyfully, to see Alvaston perform on the hoe, begad!"

So amid much laughter and banter the company arose and in twos and threes sauntered up to their various rooms, all save Mr. Dalroyd who, left alone, sat awhile playing idly with the cards that littered the table. At last he slipped a white hand into the bosom of his coat and taking thence a scrap of soiled and crumpled paper, smoothed it out and perused it thoughtfully, and, as he read, his lips curved and his nostrils quivered; then, re-folding this strange missive he put it away and, ringing the bell, demanded his valet.

In due time came a discreet knock and thereafter a discreet person entered, tall, quick-eyed, low-voiced, soft-stepping, he was a very model of a fashionable gentleman's gentleman though his eyes were perhaps a little too close together and their glance a trifle furtive.

"Joseph," said Mr. Dalroyd, surveying his 'gentleman' with a languid interest yet with eyes that seemed to observe his entire person at one and the same time. "Joseph, this afternoon I gave you leave to ramble abroad, well knowing your passion for country roads and cross-roads." Joseph bowed supple back and smiled deferentially, though his eyes appeared somehow to come a little closer together. "Consequently, Joseph, you rambled, I take it?"

"I did, sir!"

"And in your rambles you may have chanced by the old mill, Joseph?"

"Indeed, sir, a charming ruin, very picturesque, the haunt of bats and owls, sir."

"Anything else?"

"No, sir."

"Nothing? Are you sure, Animal?"

"Positively, sir!"

"Were there no signs, Thing?"

"None, sir."

"Did you use your eyes well, Object?"

"Everywhere, sir."

"Have you heard any talk in the village of this ghost lately?"

"Frequently, sir. Three people swear they've seen it."

"How do they describe it?"

"They all agree to horns, sir, and a shapeless head."

"Do you believe in ghosts, Joseph?"

"That depends, sir."

"On what, fool?"

"On who sees them sir."

"You were almost famous for the possession of what is called 'nerves of iron' in your predatory days, if I remember rightly, Joseph?"

The obsequious Joseph started slightly and his bow was servile.

"Consequently you don't fear ghosts?"

"No, sir."

"Neither do I, Joseph, and 'tis nigh upon the witching hour, bring me my hat and cane." And Mr. Dalroyd rose languidly.

"Sir," said Joseph as he handed his master the articles in question, "might I suggest one of your travelling-pistols— —"

"No, Joseph, no, 'twould drag my pocket out o' shape, and ghosts are impervious to pistols or shall we say 'barkers' 'tis the more professional term for 'em, I believe?"

Once again the obsequious Joseph started slightly, observing which, Mr. Dalroyd flashed white teeth in languid amusement. "I may be gone an hour or more, Joseph, remain awake to undress me."

"Very good, sir! And if I might suggest, sir, 'tis said the ghost walks the churchyard o' nights latterly."

"That sounds sufficiently ghostly!" nodded Mr. Dalroyd. "And by the way, let your tongue remain discreetly inactive—for your own sake, Joseph!"

"Very good, sir—certainly!—and may you burn in everlasting fire!" added the obsequious Joseph under his breath as he watched his master's languid figure out of sight—his eyes seeming closer together than ever.

CHAPTER XVI
HOW MR. DALROYD SAW A GHOST AND THE SERGEANT AN APPARITION

Mr. Dalroyd stepped out into a summer night radiant with moonbeams and full of the heady perfume of ripening hay. Far as eye could see the wide road stretched away very silent and deserted, not a light gleamed anywhere, the village had been deep-plunged in slumber hours ago.

Mr. Dalroyd sauntered on, past silent cottages, across a trim green and so to the churchyard gate, beyond which the tombstones rose, phantom-like beneath the moon. For a while he stood to contemplate this quiet scene, then started and glanced up at the church tower as a deep-toned bell began to chime the hour of midnight. One by one he counted the deliberate strokes, waited until the last had boomed and died away, then, opening the gate, stepped into the churchyard and strolled on among the graves, his cane airily a-swing, following the paved walk that led round the church. Thus he presently passed from light into shadow, a gloom all the deeper by contrast with the moon's bright splendour, a gloom in which carved headstone and sarcophagus took on strange and unexpected shapes. Suddenly Mr. Dalroyd's cane faltered in its airy swing, stopped, and he stood motionless, his body rigid, his breath in check, his eyes wide and staring. Before him loomed a great mausoleum, its pallid outline vague in the half-light, but on this side the weatherworn marble was cracked and split and from this yawning fissure a ghastly radiance streamed; then this unholy light vanished and upon the stillness came a ghostly rustling, a soft thud and the sound of heavy breathing. Mr. Dalroyd shrank cowering into the deeper shadow of a buttress and dropping his cane upon the grass groped for the hilt of his small-sword. Then, as he stared unwinking, forth from the tomb a dim form wriggled, crouched awhile fumbling, stood upright, and Mr. Dalroyd saw a vague head, awful and shapeless and crowned with curving horns. This dreadful thing stood awhile as if listening for distant sounds then took a stride forward, floundered over a grave and cursed fluently. Mr. Dalroyd loosed rigid fingers from his sword-hilt, picked up his cane and, keeping well in the shadow, began to follow this strange figure; ghost-like it flitted on among the tombs until, reaching the wall, it leapt nimbly over, stood to listen and glance furtively about, then set off down the road at a smart pace. Mr. Dalroyd, treading with infinite caution for the night was very still, followed whither it led, viewing the shapeless thing with gaze that never wavered. Thus, in a while, they reached a grassy bye-lane flanked on the one side by a thick hedge and on the other by a high wall. Here the figure paused and Mr. Dalroyd, shrinking into the shadow of the hedge, saw it glance up and down the lane, saw it lift long arms and heard a faint scuffling as, mounting this wall it paused awhile athwart the coping ere it vanished on the other side. Looping his cane on his wrist Mr. Dalroyd crossed the lane and drawing himself up peered over the wall in time to see this mysterious figure flit among the trees of an orchard, mount yet another wall and vanish again. Without more ado Mr. Dalroyd in turn clambered up and over the wall and dropping on soft, new-turned earth, continued the pursuit, that is to say he had crossed a smooth stretch of lawn and was in the very act of mounting the other wall when strong hands seized him from behind and a gruff voice said in his ear:

"You ain't no ghost, I'll swear! Right about turn and show us your face!" And Mr. Dalroyd was swung round so violently that his hat fell off. "Zounds!" exclaimed the Sergeant, "'tis nought but one o' these fine London sparks arter all!" Mr. Dalroyd swore. "Sir," said the Sergeant imperturbably, "why and wherefore d'ye trespass, and so late too? Sir, what's the evolution, or shall we say, manoover?"

"Rogue," said Mr. Dalroyd, "pick up my hat!"

"Rogue, is it?" mused the Sergeant.

"Animal, my hat!"

"Animal, now?"

"D'ye hear, vermin?" Mr. Dalroyd stood, his head viciously out-thrust so that the long curls of his peruke falling back from brow and cheek discovered more fully his haughty features, delicately pale in the bright moonlight; and beholding this face—its fine black brows, aquiline nose, fierce eyes and thin-lipped mouth the Sergeant fell back, staring:

"Zounds!" he exclaimed, and gaped.

Something in the Sergeant's attitude seemed to strike Mr. Dalroyd who, returning this searching look, lounged back against the wall, one hand toying with the curls of his wig, and when next he spoke his voice was as languidly soft as usual.

"What now, ass?" The Sergeant drew a deep breath:

"Talking o' ghosts and apparations," said he, "I aren't so sure as you ain't one, arter all."

"Why, worm?"

"Because if you happened to be wearing an officer's coat—red and blue facings, say, and your legs in a pair o' jack-boots, I should know—ah, I'd be sure you was a ghost."

"What d'ye mean?" Mr. Dalroyd's slender brows scowled suddenly, and before the malevolence of his eyes the Sergeant gave back another step.

"What d'ye mean, toad?"

"I mean as you'd be dead! But your coat ain't red, is it, sir? And your jack-boots is buckle-shoes, and you're very much alive, ain't you, sir—so I'll ax you to pick up your property and to get back over the wall yonder and to do it—prompt, sir."

The Sergeant was a powerful fellow, at his hip swung a heavy hanger and in hairy fist he gripped a very ugly, knobby bludgeon, observing which facts, Mr. Dalroyd did as was suggested; but, ere he dropped back into the lane he turned and smiled down at the stalwart Sergeant.

"My very good clod," said he, "one of these fine, sunny days you shall be drubbed for this—soundly, yes, soundly!"

The Sergeant nodded:

"Sir," said he, "same will be welcome, for, though life in the country agrees wi' me on the whole better than expected, things is apt to grow over quiet now and then and any little bit o' roughsome as you can offer will be dooly welcome and do me a power o' good!"

"Be it so!" nodded Mr. Dalroyd and, smiling, he dropped from view.

Then the Sergeant, whistling softly, strode bedwards quite unaware of the shapeless, horned head that watched him as he went.

CHAPTER XVII
HOW MY LADY BETTY WROTE A LETTER

"DEAR MAJOR D'ARCY,

"Burning yet with a natural womanly indignation by reason of your shameless accusations, each and all as cruel, as unmanly, as unwarranted as unjust I— —"

"Pho!" exclaimed Lady Betty and tearing up her unfinished letter, threw it on the floor and stamped on it.

"To MAJOR D'ARCY:

"SIR,

"Though unvirginal, unmaidenly, unwomanly, and lost to all sense of modesty and shame, I am yet not entirely removed from the lesser virtues and amongst them— —"

"Pish!" cried Lady Betty, and rent this asunder also.

"MY DEAR MAJOR D'ARCY,

"By this time of course you are duly sorry and deeply ashamed, for the very many indelicate expressions you gave voice to concerning me. You have perchance passed a sleepless night and such is but your due considering the abandoned and shameful treatment you accorded me. But seeing you saved me from the brutal arms of— —"

"Pshaw!" cried Lady Betty, and this letter shared the fate of its predecessors.

Her black brows frowned, her pink finger-tips were ink-stained, her cheeks glowed, her bosom heaved, her white teeth gnashed themselves, in a word, Lady Betty was in a temper.

"Aunt Belinda, I—hate you!"

"Lud Betty, do you child!" murmured that lady, opening sleepy eyes, "Pray what's amiss now?"

"Why must you tattle of me to Major d'Arcy?"

"I? Tattle? O Gemini!"

"Of me—and breeches?"

"Breeches! La miss and fie! I should swoon to name 'em to a man! So indelicate, so immodest, so——"

"Unvirginal!" cried Betty, and stamped pretty foot more angrily than ever.

"Truly, miss! Indeed such a word has never crossed my lips to one of the male sex and never shall——"

"And when you told him he was duly shocked, I suppose, and rolled up his eyes in a spasm of virtue and lifted his hands in prudish horror?" demanded Lady Betty, kicking savagely at the litter of torn paper.

"Nay, he frowned, I remember, and positively blushed—and no wonder!"

"He blushed!" cried Betty scornfully, "and he a man—a soldier! By heaven he seems more virginal than Diana and all her train! Fie on him, O, 'tis shameful—so big, so strong, so—squeamish! O Lord, how I hate, detest and despise him!"

"Gracious heaven!" ejaculated Lady Belinda, sitting up suddenly, "I do verily believe you're in love with him!"

"In love with—him! I?" cried Lady Betty, "I in love with——" she gasped and stopped suddenly, staring down at the torn paper at her feet and, as she stared, her lashes drooped and up over creamy chin from rounded throat to glossy hair crept a wave of vivid colour.

"O Betty," wailed her aunt, "Betty, is it true—is it love or are you only taken with his—his medieval airs?"

"Aunt Belinda," said Betty, turning her back and staring out through the open lattice, "there are times when I wonder I don't—bite you!"

"He's so much your elder, Betty!"

"And so much my younger, aunt—in some ways, he's a very child! But suppose I do marry him, what then, aunt?"

"Marry him! Heaven above—marry Major d'Arcy? Betty, are you mad? You so young and giddy, he so—so mature and grave——"

"You never saw him climb a wall, aunt!"

"Old enough to be your father, girl! So very sober and reserved! So very serious and quiet——"

"You haven't seen him in his plum-coloured velvet, aunt!"

"But you—O Bet, you never really—love him!"

"Of—course—not! What has love to do with marriage, dear aunt? Love-marriages are so unmodish—'tis like plough-boy and dairy-wench—hugging and kissing—faugh, so vulgar and nauseous! Nay, aunt, I desire a marriage à la mode: 'Good-morrow to your ladyship, I trust your ladyship slept well?' A solemn bow, a kiss upon one extreme finger-tip!' O, excellently, sir, I hope you the same.' A smile and gracious curtsey—and so to breakfast. Now Major d'Arcy is a gentleman, rich, sufficiently handsome, and once a husband would be fairly easy to manage! Indeed I might do worse, aunt!"

"But so much—ah, so very much better, girl. There is the Duke of Nairn——"

"A drunken old reprobate! Charles told me that once, being more tipsy than usual he——"

"Hush, miss! He worshipped you. Then there is His Grace of Hawcastle——"

"An addle-pated popinjay!"

"Fie, Betty! Then there is Lord Alvaston, the Marquis, Viscount Merivale and the rest——"

"Aye, but I can't wed 'em all, aunt, so will I wed none!"

"Lud child, here's scandalous talk! But O Betty, what—what of love?"

"True, dear aunt—what?"

"Ah, child, 'tis fair woman's crowning joy and strong man's consolation sweet——

"'Tis a disease and megrim o' the mind, aunt, the which, I do thank heaven, hath ne'er yet come anigh me——"

"Aye but it will, Betty, it will!"

"Then with pill and purge and bolus I will drive it hence again."

"Nay child," sighed the Lady Belinda, as her niece arose, "talk how you will, but when love comes to thee, as come he will, why then, Ah me! what with thy ardent temperament, thy headstrong spirits, thy bustling health then—O then shall I tremble for thee!"

"Nay, prithee spare yourself, dear aunt, I can tremble for myself when needful." Saying which my lady went out into the garden.

Very slowly she went, her head bowed, her bright eyes grave and troubled; once she stopped to frown at a hollyhock and once to cull a rose only to drop it all unnoticed ere she had gone a dozen yards. Thus thoughtful and preoccupied she came to that secluded corner of her garden where, against a certain wall a ladder stood invitingly: mounting forthwith, she perched herself upon the broad coping and glanced down into the Major's orchard. The hutch-like sentry-box showed deserted but at the foot of the wall and almost immediately below her, Sergeant Zebedee stooped above a new-turned border of earth, busily engaged with a foot-rule. Lady Betty reached softly over and plucking an apricot, dropped it with remarkable accuracy into the very middle of the Sergeant's trim wig.

"*Sacré nom!*" he ejaculated, and starting erect, glanced up into my lady's serene blue eyes.

"'Tis Sergeant Zebedee, I think?" she enquired gravely.

The Sergeant saluted and stood at attention:

"I was so baptised, my lady, and an uncommon awk'ard name I've found it."

"Nay, 'tis a quaint name and suits you. If you have any children——"

"Chil——!" The Sergeant gasped.

"They should be called James and John, of course! So the poor Major passed a sleepless night, did he, Sergeant?"

"O!" said the Sergeant, staring, "Did he, mam?"

"Well, hasn't he?"

"Not as I know of, my lady."

"And when will he come home?"

"Home?" repeated the Sergeant, scratching his wig, "Why, mam, he has, I mean he hasn't, him not having been out, d'ye see."

"He must be a great trial and worry to live with, Sergeant?"

"No, my lady, no—except when he don't take his rations reg'lar—food and drink, d'ye see."

"Ah, doth his appetite languish of late?"

"Never was better, mam! He do seem to grow younger and brisker every day."

"Indeed, 'tis pity he's so wild!"

"Wild, mam? The Major——?"

"So gay, so bold and audacious." The Sergeant could only stare. "His wife will lead a sorry life I fear, poor soul!"

The Sergeant fell back a step opening eyes and mouth together:

"Zooks!" he muttered, "axing your ladyship's pardon but—does your ladyship mean—Zounds! Axing your pardon again, my lady, but—wife! Does your ladyship mean to say— —? Is't true, madam?"

"So 'tis said!" nodded her unblushing ladyship.

"But who, my lady, and—when?"

"Nay, he's very secret."

"Pro-digious!" exclaimed the Sergeant, his eyes shining. "His honour was ever a great hand at surprises—ambuscades d'ye see, madam— ambushments, my lady, sudden onfalls and the like, and for leading a forlorn hope there was none to compare."

"You mean he has fought in a battle, Sergeant?"

"A battle, mam!" The Sergeant sighed and shook reproachful head. "Twenty and three pitched battles, my lady and twelve sieges, not to mention sorties, outpost skirmishes and the like! 'Fighting d'Arcy' he was called, madam! Sixteen wounds, my lady, seven of 'em bullet and the rest steel— —"

"Heavens!" exclaimed my lady, "I marvel there is any of him left!"

"What is left, my lady, is all man! There never was such a man! There never will be."

"'Fighting d'Arcy'!" she repeated. "It sounds so unlike—and looks quite impossible—see yonder!" And she turned towards where, afar off, the object of their talk limped towards them his head bent studiously above an open book from which he raised his eyes, ever and anon, as if weighing some abstruse passage; thus he presently espied my lady and, shutting the book, thrust it into his pocket and hastened towards her. Hereupon the Sergeant saluted, wheeled and marched away, yet not before he had noted the glad light in the Major's grey eyes and, from a proper distance, had seen him clasp my lady's white hand and kiss it fervently. Instantly the Sergeant fell to the "double" until he was out of sight, then he halted suddenly, shook his head, smacked hand to thigh and laughed:

"All I say is, as there ain't, there never was, there never will be a word for it—not one!"

CHAPTER XVIII
HOW MAJOR D'ARCY RECOVERED HIS YOUTH

So the Major kissed my lady's hand, kissed it not "on one extreme finger-tip," but holding it in masterful clasp, kissed it on rosy palm and dimpled knuckles, kissed it again and again with all the ardour of a boy of twenty; and my lady sighed and—let him kiss his fill.

She wore her rustic attire but her simple gown was enriched here and there, with the daintiest of lace as was her snowy mob-cap; and surely never did rustic beauty blush more rosily or look with eyes more shy than she when at last he raised his head:

"Good morrow to your worship!" said she softly, "I trust your honour slept well?"

"No!" he answered, speaking with a strange, new vehemence, "I scarce did close my eyes all night for thought of you——"

"Of me?"

"And of my—my folly! I looked for you this morning—I wished to tell you ... I ... I——" Seeing him thus at a loss, my lady smiled a little maliciously, then hasted to his relief:

"This morning?" said she gently, "I was making more butter for my poor folk—with the aid of my lord of Alvaston, Captain West, and Sir Jasper. But they proved so awkward with the churn that Sir Benjamin must needs show 'em how 'twas done. And after he made much of my rhubarb wine and would have them all taste it and insisted on the Captain drinking three glasses—poor man!"

"Wherefore 'poor'?"

"Why, sir, 'tis truly excellent wine—to look at, but I fear 'tis perhaps a trifle—sourish!" Here she laughed merrily, grew solemn and sighed, glancing shyly at the Major who stood, head bowed, fumbling with one of the gold buttons of the plum-coloured coat.

"I—trust your ladyship is well after your—your fright of yesterday," said he at last.

"My ladyship is very well, sir," she sighed, "though vapourish!"

"Which means?"

"Perhaps I—mourn my lost divinity."

Her tone was light, but he saw that her lips quivered as she averted her head.

"Betty," he cried impulsively, "I was a fool! All night long I've burned with anger at my folly, for I do know you could never be aught but pure and maidenly no matter what you—you chanced to wear. So do I come craving your forgiveness."

"O Major—Major Jack," she sighed, leaning towards him, all glowing tenderness, "first hear me say you spoke me truth, it—it was indeed— unworthy—a hoyden trick! But I have trod a different world to you—a world of careless gaiety and idle chatter, where nought is serious, reverence unknown and love itself a pastime. So I have loved no man—save my brother Charles for we've been lonely all our days—nay, Major John!" for he had caught her hand to his lips again.

"And I dared think you unmaidenly!" he murmured, in bitter self-reproach.

"So would the mother I never knew had she seen me as—as poor Aunt Belinda saw me—and yet—I vow 'twas monstrous laughable!" and my lady hovered between laughter and tears.

"Am I forgiven?" he pleaded.

"Aye, most fully!"

"Why then—to prove it—will you ... would you——"

"Well, your honour?" she questioned humbly.

"Would you permit me to show you the rose-garden?"

"But I have seen it!"

"Aye to be sure, so you have!" he answered, a little dashed. "Though the roses were scarce in bloom then."

"Truly I do love roses, Major Jack——"

"And they are in the full splendour of their beauty——"

"But—this wall?" she demurred. "And ... no ladder!"

He reached up eager arms. "O Major John!" she exclaimed and drew back, blushing as rosily as the shyest maid that ever tripped in dairy. "'Twould be so—so extreme unmaidenly—wouldn't it?" The Major flushed and his arms dropped. "Though indeed I—do love roses!" she sighed. The Major glanced up eagerly. "But 'tis so awkward and someone might see——"

"Not a soul!" he assured her.

"Then ... if you'll turn your head a moment ... and are sure none can spy ... and will be vastly careful ... and are quite, quite sure you can manage——"

It was managed almost as she spoke, he with an assured adroitness, she with such gracious ease that, in the same moment they were walking side by side over the smooth turf, as calm and unruffled as any two people ever were or will be. "'Tis a dear orchard, this!" she sighed, stopping to pat the rough bark of a huge, gnarled apple-tree.

"'Twas here I first saw you," said he.

"Stealing your fruit!" she nodded.

"It seems long ago."

"And yet 'tis but a few short weeks."

Slowly they went on together, past lily-pool asleep in marble basin, through green boskages amid whose leafy shade marble dryads shyly peeped and fauns and satyrs sported; beneath the vast spread of mighty trees across smooth, grassy levels, by shady walks and so at last to the blazing glory of the rose-garden. Here my lady paused with an exclamation of delight.

"Indeed, indeed, 'tis lovely—lovelier than I had dreamed! Are you not proud of it?"

"Yes," he answered, "more especially since I never owned a foot of land till of late—or a roof to shelter me, for that matter."

"You were a soldier!"

"And a very poor one!" he added.

"And they called you 'Fighting d'Arcy!'" said she, looking into the grey eyes she had been wont to think almost too gentle.

"That sounds strange—on your lips," said he with his grave smile, "I perceive the Sergeant has been talking."

"He has been boasting to me of all your wounds, sir!" The Major laughed. "He is greatly proud of you, sir."

"He saved my life more than once."

"You must have been a very desperate soldier to have been wounded so very often, Major John!"

"Why you see, at that time," he answered, handing her down the steps into the garden, "I wished to die."

"To die?" she repeated. "O, prithee why?"

"This was twenty years ago, I was a boy then," he sighed. "To-day I am— —"

"A man, and therefore wiser," said she as they went on together among the roses. "And pray why did you seek death?" she questioned softly.

"Because I had lost the woman I loved."

"So then you—have—loved?"

"As a boy of twenty may," he answered. "She—I was an ensign without influence and prospects and—they forced her to wed a wealthier than I."

"O! And she did?" Lady Betty stopped to stamp an angry foot.

"Indeed they—compelled her— —"

"Major John sir, no woman that is a woman can be compelled in her affections!"

"She was very young."

"Pooh, sir! I am not yet a withered and wrinkled crone, yet no one shall or should compel me!" And here, with a prodigious flutter of her print gown, my lady seated herself on rustic bench beside the sundial.

"No indeed," said he, "you are—are different." At this she flashed him a swift up-glance and, meeting his gaze, dimpled, drew aside her garments' ample folds and graciously, motioned him beside her. The Major sat down.

"And was she happy?"

"No!"

"Which doth but serve her to her deserts!" The Major winced, perceiving which, my lady faced him. "How, do you love her yet?" she questioned.

"My lady, she is dead," he answered. Lady Betty turned and leaning to a rose that bloomed near by, touched it with gentle fingers.

"And—do you—love her yet, Major John?" she asked softly.

"I held her in my memory as the sweetest of all women until a few weeks ago," he answered simply. My lady's caressing fingers faltered suddenly.

"She was the third woman in your life?"

"Yes," he answered, "because of her memory I have lived a hard life and let love go by nor thought of it."

"Not once?"

"Not once, until of late." My lady was silent, and, leaning nearer, he continued: "Twenty years ago I gave my love and, being hopeless, sought for death and never found it. So, hating war, I made of war my life. I became a soldier of fortune and wheresoever battle was, there was I; when one campaign ended I went in quest of others. So I have learned much of men, of foreign countries, and war in every shape, but of women and love—nothing whatever. Indeed I should be fighting yet but for this unexpected legacy. And now——" He sighed.

"And now?" she repeated softly.

"Now I find that youth has fled and left but emptiness behind!"

"Poor, O poor, decrepit, ancient man!" she sighed, "with your back so bent and your arms so feeble! So wrinkled, so toothless, and so blind!" And rising she turned away and leaned round elbows on the sundial. Now presently he came and stood beside her, looking into her lovely, down-bent face then pointed to the legend graven on the stone.

"Read," said he, "read and tell me—is't not wisdom?" And, very obediently, she read aloud:

"Youth is joyous; Age is melancholy:
Age and Youth together is but folly."

"Indeed," she nodded, "'tis a very wise proverb and, like most other proverbs, sayeth very plainly that black is black and white is white. And truly I do think you a great coward, Major 'Fighting d'Arcy'!"

"Betty?" said he, a little breathlessly.

"You may be very brave in battle but in—in other things you are a very coward!"

"My lady—O Betty! Do you mean ... is it possible that such miracle could be... You in the bloom of your youth and beauty, I——"

"So bent with years!" said she in tender mockery, "so feeble and so—very—blind!"

The Major's philosophic calm was shattered, his placid serenity gone all in a moment; he reached out sudden, passionate arms but without attempting to touch her.

"Betty," he cried, "God knows if I'm presumptuous fool or blessed beyond my hopes, but hear me say—I love you, for all your dainty loveliness, your coquette airs and graces, but, most of all, for the sweet, white, womanly soul of you. And 'tis no flame of youthful passion this, soon to fade, 'tis a man's enduring love desiring all, asking nothing.... I mean, Betty, whether you wed me or no, needs must I love you to the end of time!"

"E'en though I should love and wed another?" she questioned softly.

"Aye, truly!"

"Indeed, you are nobler than I—because"—here she paused to trace out the time-worn lettering on the dial with pink finger-tip—"because if you should love, or wed another, then I—should die of rage and jealousy and grief and——"

The Major's long arms were close about her and, stooping, he kissed her again and again, her fragrant hair, her eyes, her tender mouth.

"O Betty," he sighed, "my beautiful Betty, the wonder of it!"

"O John," she sighed tremulously, "O Jack, indeed 'tis a very furious lover you are! You make love as you fight—as if you loved it—nay, show mercy!" He released her instantly and stood back staring down at her with dazzled eyes.

"Am I rough?" he asked anxiously. "Dear, forgive me! But 'tis all so strange, so unexpected, so marvellous beyond belief! There be so many to love you that I——"

"Shall teach you what love truly is," she murmured, "And I—don't mind—a little roughness, Jack dear!"

"God, 'tis marvellous!" said he at last, holding her away to feast his eyes on her glowing loveliness. "'Tis passing wonderful that of all your throng of lovers you should choose such as I—so much older, so much——" his breath caught, the strong hands that clasped her so tenderly quivered suddenly. "Betty," said he hoarsely, "'tis no coquettish whim, this—no youthful fancy? You do love me indeed?" Now seeing the haggard pleading of his eyes, the quiver of his lips and all his shy humility, she uttered a soft cry and drawing him close, pillowed his troubled brow against her soft cheek.

"Ah dearest," she whispered, "why must you doubt? Love for you hath been in my heart from the first I think, though I never guessed 'twas love until to-day. And for your age—O foolish! I would not have thee younger by an hour and—for my love, 'tis here deep within my heart and will but grow with length of days for to know thee more is to love thee more. You think me over-young, I know, light-thoughted, belike and careless, but in her heart a woman is ever older than a man, and, despite my seeming heedlessness your Betty is methinks much the woman you would have her be."

"Aye, truly," he answered, "the sweetest, the loveliest, noblest woman, I do think, in all this big world!" But when he would have caught her to him again she, blushing, laughing, stayed him to straighten lacy mob-cap and pat rebellious curls with hands a little tremulous, then, sitting down, crossed slim feet demurely and motioned him beside her.

"'Deed, sir," she sighed, "you do make love to perfection! And yet—your love is so—so wonderful that I grow a little fearful lest I prove unworthy——"

"Ah, never!" he cried, drawing her hands to his lips.

"Such love doth make me very humble, Jack dear, 'tis all so different, so reverent and yet also 'tis a little—fierce!" she whispered, yielding to his compelling arms.

"Nay, am I so?" he asked, anxiously, his hold relaxing.

"Ele-mentally!" she murmured, pillowing cheek on plum-coloured velvet regardless of lace cap. "Yet methinks I do—love such ferocity!"

"O Betty, when will you wed me?"

"O John, here is a question to ponder. First, when would you have me?"

"To-day! To-morrow! Soon!"

"O impatient youth!" she murmured. "Second, shall your wife enjoy all liberty?"

"So much as she desire," he answered tenderly.

"Third, shall she live in town i' the season, attend balls, theatres, routs, card-parties, masquerades, drums and the like?"

"If she so wish," said he, a little sadly; perceiving which, she nestled closer to him.

"Fourth, will you swear to be a husband *à la mode*?"

"What may that be?" he enquired.

"Will you be very polite to your wife and seldom intrude upon her privacy as is the modish custom, will you keep separate establishments, will you——"

"By heaven—no!" exclaimed the Major; whereat, and very suddenly, she kissed him.

"Indeed I do think you will make almost as good a husband as lover!" she sighed. "And—Major Jack, dear—if you would wed me soon——"

"Nay sweet," he broke in, "here was a selfish thought! You are so young——

"A ripe woman of twenty-two, sir!"

"But youth loveth freedom, my Betty, so shall you enjoy it while you will and come to me—when you will!"

"Nay, dear, foolish John, you do speak as you were a prison! What is maiden freedom compared to—wifehood?" she breathed.

"Wife!" he repeated reverently, "'tis a sweet word, Betty!"

"So is—husband, John."

"My Betty—dear—when?"

"Is three months hence too long?"

"Aye, 'tis very long—but——"

"Six weeks, Jack?"

O never-to-be-forgotten hour! Hour long dreamed and yet expected never, so swift to haste away but whose memory was to blossom, sweet and all unfading.

"Dear," said she at last, "since you are not for marriage '*à la mode*' I shall plague you mightily——"

"God!" he exclaimed softly, "what a life 'twill be!"

But all at once she started from him as, afar off, a faint wailing arose:

"Betty, my love! O Bet—my Betty love!"

My lady frowned and rising, laid rosy finger to lip.

"Not a word yet, my John! Let our secret be ours awhile. Come, let us meet her."'

Slowly they went amid the roses and sighed for the hour that was gone and wondered to see the sun so low; and thus they presently beheld Lady Belinda twittering towards them escorted by the Sergeant and the tall, well-fed menial.

"O naughty Bet!" she cried, "O wicked puss and truant! I've sought thee this hour and more, I've called thee until my poor voice grew languishing and weak! Ah, dear Major, scold her for me, prithee scold!"

"Nay, madam," he answered, bowing, "I fear the blame is mine, I was for showing my lady the roses as 'twere, and—er——"

"La, dear aunt," said my lady, "how warm you look, so red—so flushed and fulsome!"

"'Tis the sun—the sun!" cried Lady Belinda, "I vow I cannot abide the sun, it nauseates me!"

"Then let us into the shade, mam," said the Major, offering his arm. "'Twill be cool on the terrace, a—er—a dish of tea——"

"Nay, nay, sir, alack and no, we have neighbours expected. Sir Oliver and Lady Rington, Mrs. Wadhurst, and Lady Lydia Flyte—and that minds me, naughty Bet, you were to have gone a-riding to-day with Mr. Dalroyd and Sir Jasper—they called expectant and you were not! Then came poor young Mr. Marchdale, in a great taking, to know if you'd object to his rhyming 'Bet' with 'sweat!' The Captain called, too, with dear Sir Benjamin Tripp—so modish—so elegant! But solemn as two owls, though why owls should be solemn I don't know never having seen one near enough! So you see, dear Major, we positively must away!"

The Major, having escorted them to his park gates, stood to watch that slender, shapely form out of sight, then, sighing, limped slowly housewards lost in happy dreams. As he went he remembered with an odd relief that the Viscount was in London and would remain there several days. Presently he came upon the Sergeant who bore a rake "at the trail" much as if it had been a pike: and the Sergeant's face was beaming and his bright eye almost roguish:

"Ha, Zeb," said the Major, halting to view him over, and his own eyes were shining also, "why Zeb, how deuced smart you look!"

"My best clothes, sir, new ones being on order as commanded, sir."

"Aye, but 'tis not your clothes exactly, you seem—younger, somehow."

"Why, sir," said the Sergeant, a little diffidently, "I took the liberty o' powdering my wig,—no objections I hope, your honour?"

"None at all Zeb, no, no! Egad, 'tis like old times!" So saying, the Major smiled and passed on to the house, whistling softly as he went.

CHAPTER XIX
HOW THE MAJOR LOST HIS YOUTH AGAIN

It was a night of midsummer glory; an orbed moon rode high in queenly splendour filling the world with a radiance that lent to all things a beauty new and strange. Not a breath stirred, trees, tall and motionless, seemed asleep, so still were they.

Thus the Major, on his way to bed, paused to lean from the open casement of his study and to gaze, happy-eyed, upon the radiant heaven and to dream of the future as many a man has done before and since. All at once he started and stared to behold Sergeant Zebedee abroad at this witching hour. But the Sergeant was there for other things than dreaming, it seemed, for upon his shoulder he bore a blunderbuss, a broadsword swung at his thigh, and from one of his big side-pockets appeared the heavy, brass-mounted butt of a long-barrelled pistol. Wondering, the Major stepped out through the casement and followed. Sergeant Zebedee marched with elaborate caution and was keeping so sharp a lookout before that he quite overlooked the Major behind him; but all at once a stick snapped, round wheeled the Sergeant, blunderbuss at "the ready" but, seeing the Major, he immediately lowered his weapon and stood easy.

"'S'noggers, sir," said he, "I thought you was it!"

"It, Zebedee?"

"Aye, your honour, it, him, or her. If it ain't a him 'tis a her and if it ain't a her it's an it—or shall us say a apparation, sir. Same being said to walk i' the orchard o' nights lately——"

"An apparition—in the orchard, Zeb? Have you seen it?"

"Why no, sir, not exactly, but what I did see was—hist!"

The Sergeant halted suddenly, crouching in the shadow of a hedge; they were close on the orchard now and, upon the stilly air was a soft rustle, a faint scraping sound and, parting the leafy screen, the Major saw a dark figure silhouetted above the wall, a nebulous shape that seemed to hang suspended a moment ere it vanished over the wall into my lady's garden.

"That weren't no apparation, sir!" whispered the Sergeant, looking to pan and priming, and, hurrying forward, pointed to a footprint in the soft, newly-turned soil. "Never heard as spectres wore shoes, sir." The Major, staring at that slender footprint, felt suddenly cold and sick, and wondered; then, as the Sergeant prepared to climb the wall, checked him:

"Wait—wait you here!" he muttered. "Make way!" Reaching up, the Major swung himself astride the coping and silently mounted the wall. Before him was a flagged walk which, as he remembered, led to the arbour; this walk he avoided and, stepping in among the bushes, began to advance cautiously, eyes and ears on the strain, for the shadows lay dense hereabouts. Thus he was close upon the arbour when he stopped suddenly, arrested by the sound of a man's voice, low and muffled.

"... 'tis you now, Bet, and only you——"

"... Ah God, how may I? And yet ... my own dear, have I ever refused thee ... I've yearned for thee so..." Here the sound of passionate kisses.

It was her voice indeed, but so tender, so full of thrilling gentleness! The Major shivered and a sudden faintness and nausea seizing him, leaned weakly against a tree, and ever, as he leaned thus, their voices reached him—his low and eager, hers a-thrill with tenderness.

The Major turned and, groping like one blind, crept back until he came to the wall and crouching there, his head between his arms, seemed to shake and writhe as with some horrible convulsion.

"That you, sir?" a voice whispered hoarsely. Silently the Major drew himself up and dropped back into his own grounds.

"What was it, sir?"

"Nought, Zeb."

"D'ye mean 'twere a ghost, arter all?"

"Aye!"

"Didn't notice if 'twere a her or a him, sir?"

"No!"

"Why then, did you chance to ob-serve——" but seeing the Major's face, Sergeant Zebedee broke off with a gasp and, dropping his blunderbuss, reached out quick hands: "Good God! Your honour! What's amiss?"

"Let be, Zeb, let be," said the Major wearily, putting by these kindly hands, "'tis nought to worry over—nought to matter, nought i' the world, Zeb. Leave me awhile. Go to bed!"

"Bed, your honour? And leave you alone? Sir, I beg——"

"Sergeant Tring—get you indoors!"

The Sergeant stiffened, saluted, and, wheeling about, marched away forthwith, but, once in the shadows, turned to glance anxiously at the lonely figure so pale and still and rigid under the moon.

Being alone, the Major seemed to shrink within himself, and, limping slowly into the gloom of the hutch-like sentry-box, cast himself face down across the table and lay there; and from that place of shadows came sounds soft but awful. At last he lifted heavy head, and, staring before him, perforce beheld that part of the wall where he had first seen her; and again he writhed and shivered. But, all at once, as the spasm passed, he leaned forward tense and fierce, for in that precise spot a man was climbing the wall. The Major rose and stood with breath in check, watching as the unknown clambered into view, a slender figure that paused for a lingering, backward glance, then leapt down into the orchard; but, doing so, the unknown tripped, lost his hat and cursed softly, and in that moment the Major gripped him in iron hands and stared into the pale, fierce face of Mr. Dalroyd; the long curls of his peruke had fallen back leaving his features fully exposed in the strong moonlight, and now, as the Sergeant had done before him, the Major blenched and drew back, his fingers loosing their hold.

"Effingham!" he gasped, "Effingham—by God!"

Mr. Dalroyd smiled and fingered his curls:

"'Tis Major d'Arcy, I think!" said he gently. "And Major d'Arcy is either drunk or mad, my name, as he very well knows, is Dalroyd much and ever at his service. Though, permit me to say 'tis scarce a—laudable or honourable thing to—spy upon the tender hours of his fair neighbours! 'Tis true I trespass, but love, sir, love——!" Mr. Dalroyd smiled, sighed and picked up his hat. "If you wish to quarrel, sir, you lose your labour for I quarrel with no man—to-night!"

"Sir," said the Major, his voice calm and unshaken, "whoever you are and whatever your name, I advise you to go—now, this instant!"

Mr. Dalroyd surveyed the Major with languid interest, the pallid serenity of his face, the smouldering eyes, the haggard lips, the moist brow, the nervous, clutching fingers, and smiling, went his way leaving the Major to his agony.

For now indeed it seemed that all the fiends of hell had risen up to mock and gibe and torture the quivering soul of him; beneath their obscene hands his reverent love lay shamed and writhing in the dust.

"Betty!" he whispered, "O my love!" Yet even as he spoke he knew that the woman he had worshipped was not and never had been; he had clothed her warm youth and beauty with divinity, had adored and made of her an ideal and now his dream was done, his ideal shattered and by one who wore the cold, satyr-like face of Effingham—Effingham who had died upon his sword-point years ago in Flanders; almost unconsciously his quivering fingers sought and touched the scar upon his temple. And now, remembering her voice as he had heard it, thrilling with ineffable love and tenderness, he alternatively shivered in sick horror and burned with shame, a shame that crushed him to his knees, to his face. That it should be Effingham of all men, or one so hatefully like! So the Major, grovelling there beneath the moon, knew an agony in his stricken soul, deeper, fiercer than flesh may ever know; and thus, towards the dawn-hour, Sergeant Zebedee found him.

"Sir—sir," said he, kneeling beside that prostrate form, "God's love, sir—what's amiss?"

The Major raised himself and stared round about with dazed eyes.

"Ah Zeb," said he, slowly, "I do think I must ha' slept of late and dreamed, Zeb, a fair sweet dream that later changed to nightmare—but 'twill pass. I've lived awhile i' the paradise of fools!"

"Nay sir, here's spells and witchcraft! 'Tis an ill place and an ill hour—come your ways wi' me, sir."

"Aye, 'tis witchcraft—spells and enchantments, as 'twere, Zeb, but 'twill pass. Lend me your arm." So saying the Major rose and began to limp towards the house. But, as they went thus, side by side, he paused to glance up at the waning moon. "'Tis a fair night, Zeb, I've never seen a fairer. What o'clock is it?"

"Nigh on to three, your honour."

"So late! How time doth flee a man once youth be gone. We've kept many a night-watch together ere now, Zeb, but the hours never sped so fast in those days, we were younger then, Zebedee, so much younger, d'ye see."

Being come into his study the Major stood beside his desk staring down at his orderly papers and documents, vacant-eyed.

"You'll come to bed now, sir?" enquired the Sergeant anxiously.

"Nay Zeb, 'tis so late I'll e'en sit and watch the dawn come."

"Why then sir, you'll take something to eat and drink? Do now!"

The Major shook his head:

"I want nought, Zeb, save to be—alone."

Sergeant Zebedee sighed heavily, shook doleful head and going out, shut the door softly behind him.

"That it should be Effingham of all men, or one so hatefully like!"

The Major clenched his hands and began to pace restlessly back and forth. And now came Memory to haunt him—her sweet, soft voice, the droop of her black lashes, the way she had of pouting red lips sometimes when thoughtful, her eyes, her hands, her quick, light feet, and all the infinite allurement of her. And now——!

"That it should be—Effingham!"

Here again he was seized of faintness and nausea, fierce tremors shook him and sinking into his elbow-chair he sat crouched above the desk, his face bowed between clutching hands. Sitting thus, the great house so still and silent all about him, he must needs remember how she had called it a "desolate" house. And, in truth, so it was and must be for him now until the end. The end?

Once more he rose and took to his restless pacing. What end was there for him now but a succession of dreary days, while old age crept upon him bringing with it loneliness and solitude—a great, empty house and himself a solitary, loveless old man. And he had dreamed of others perchance to bear his name! God, what a life it might have been! And now, this was the end; he had walked in a "fool's paradise" indeed.

Pausing in his tramping he lifted haggard eyes to the pistols on the wall; with fumbling hands he opened a certain drawer in his desk, and, taking thence a brown wisp that once had been a fragrant rose, looked down at it awhile with eyes very tender, then let it fall and set his foot upon it, and leaning back in his chair stared down at all that remained. Long he sat thus, chin on breast, his drawn face half buried in the gay curls of his glossy peruke, but now his gaze had wandered back to the pistols on the wall. The candles, guttering in their sockets, burned low and lower, flickered and went out, but he sat on, motionless and very still; at last he sighed, stirred, rose from his chair, reached groping hand up to the wall and stood suddenly rigid.

"Major John, dear, some of your tenants are miserably poor, Major John!"

It was as if she had uttered these words again, the small room seemed to echo her soft voice, the darkness seemed full of her fragrant presence. The Major sank back in the chair and covered his face with twitching fingers;

but, little by little, upon the gloom about him stole a faint glow, a tender radiance, an ever-brightening glory and lo, it was day. And presently, beholding this gladsome light, he lifted drooping head and glanced about him.

"Betty!" he whispered, "O sweet woman of my dream, though the dream vanish memory abideth and in my memory I will hold thee pure and sweet and fragrant everlastingly!"

Then he arose and heeding no more the pistols on the wall, went forth calm-eyed into the golden, joyous freshness of the dawn.

CHAPTER XX
HOW THE MAJOR RAN AWAY

Larks, high in air, carolled faint and sweet, birds chirped joyously from fragrant hedgerows, a gentle wind set leaves dancing merrily, and the Major's big bay mare, being full of life and the joy of it, tossed her shapely head and beat a tattoo with her four round hoofs; but the Major rode with shoulders drooping and in gloomy silence, wherefore the Sergeant trotting behind on his stout cob, stared at the woebegone figure and shook anxious head:

"She's a bit skittish, sir," he hazarded at last as the powerful bay pranced sideways toward the hedge, "a bit wilful-like, your honour!"

"She's so young, Zeb," answered the Major absently, "so young, so full of life and youth that 'tis but to be—eh, what the devil are you saying, Sergeant Zebedee?"

"Why your honour, I——"

"Hold your tongue, sir!"

"But sir," began the Sergeant, wondering to see his master's face so red all at once, "I did but——"

"Be silent!" said the Major and, giving his mare the rein, rode on ahead while the Sergeant trotted after staring in turn at the blooming hedges, the white road, the blue sky and the Major's broad back.

"'Sniggers!" he exclaimed at last under his breath,

Presently the road narrowed between high, sloping banks clothed with brush and bramble from amid which tangle a man rose suddenly, a tall, dark, gipsy-looking fellow, at whose unexpected appearance the Major's bay mare swerved and reared, all but unseating her rider; whereat the fellow laughed vindictively, the Sergeant swore and the Major soothed his plunging steed with voice and hand. Breathing fierce anathemas and dire threats, the Sergeant was in the act of dismounting when the Major stopped him peremptorily.

"But sir, 'tis a rogue, 'tis a plaguy rascal, 'tis a——"

"'Tis no matter, Zeb."

"But damme sir, same do be a-shaking his dirty fist at your honour this moment! Sir, I beg——"

"'Tis very natural, Zeb."

"Nat'ral sir, and wherefore?"

"I—er—had occasion to—ha—flog the fellow."

"Flogged him, sir?"

"And broke my—ha—very modish cane a-doing it!"

"Cane, sir?" repeated the Sergeant, jogging alongside again. "Ha, and brought home his bludgeon instead, I mind, not so ornymental—but a deal handier, your honour."

Here the Major fell again to gloomy abstraction, observing which the Sergeant held his peace until, having climbed a steepish ascent, they came where stood a finger-post at the parting of the ways and here the Sergeant ventured another question:

"And wherefore flog same, sir?"

"Eh?" said the Major, starting, "O, for a good and sufficient reason, Zeb, and——" He broke off with a sudden breathless exclamation and the Sergeant, following the direction of his wide gaze, beheld three people approaching down a shady bye-road.

"Why sir," he exclaimed, "here's my Lady Carlyon as——"

The Major wheeled his big bay and, clapping in spurs, galloped off in the opposite direction.

"*Sapperment!*" exclaimed the Sergeant. He was yet staring in amazement after his master's rapidly retreating figure when he became aware that my lady had reined up her horse beside him.

"Why Sergeant," she questioned, "O Sergeant, what is't? Why did he spur away at sight of me?"

"Bewitchment, mam—black magic and sorcery damned, my lady!" answered the Sergeant, shaking rueful head. "Last night, your ladyship, he see the devil, same being in form of a apparation——"

"Sergeant Zebedee, what do you mean?"

"A gobling, mam—a ghost as vanished itself away into your garden, my lady—we both see same and his honour followed it."

"Into—my garden?" she questioned quick-breathing, her eyes very bright, her slender hand tight-clenched upon her riding-switch.

"Aye mam, your garden. Since when he's been witched and spellbound, d'ye see."

"How—how?"

"Why, a tramp—tramping in his study all night long and groaning to himself—right mournful, mam."

"Groaning?"

"And likewise a-sighing—very dismal. And this morning I took the liberty of observing him unbeknownst—through the window, d'ye see—me not having had a wink o' sleep either—and when he lifted his head——"

"Well?" she said faintly.

"'Twas like—like death in life, mam."

My lady's head was bowed but the Sergeant saw that the hand grasping the whip was trembling and when she spoke her voice was unsteady also:

"I—I'm glad you—told me, Sergeant. I—O I must see him! Get him home again—into the orchard. I—must speak with him—soon!"

"But mam, he's set on riding to Inchbourne—means to look over the cottages as Jennings has let go to rack and ruin, and when he's set on doing a thing he'll—do it."

"He ran away at sight of me, Sergeant?"

"He did so, mam, by reason of the black art and——"

"And he shall run away again—I'll ride to Inchbourne ahead of you and frighten him back home——"

"Zounds!" exclaimed the Sergeant.

"And when he reaches home contrive to get him into the orchard——"

"Zooks!" exclaimed the Sergeant.

Here Mr. Dalroyd, who had been chatting with the Marquis hard by but with his gaze ever upon my lady's lissom figure, urged his horse up to them.

"The Major would seem in a hurry this morning," said he, smiling down into my lady's pensive face, "or is it that his horse bolted with him?"

The Sergeant snorted but, before he could speak, Lady Betty's gloved hand was upon his arm.

"Sergeant Zebedee," said she gently, "I—trust to you and you won't fail me, I know!" Then, smiling a little wistfully she turned and rode away between her two cavaliers.

"Now all I says is," said the Sergeant, rasping his fingers across his big, smooth-shaven chin, "all I says is that look o' hers has drove the word 'fail' clean off the field wi' no chance o' rallying. All I asks is—How?" Having questioned himself thus and found no answer, he presently set off in pursuit of the Major, as fast as his stout cob would carry him.

The Major sat his fretting mare beneath the shadow of trees, but despite this shade he looked hot and uncomfortable.

"You've been the deuce of a while, Zebedee," said he, fidgeting in his saddle.

"No help for it, your honour," answered the Sergeant, saluting, "her ladyship having halted me, d'ye see."

"Ha—what did she say, Zeb?"

"Demanded wherefore you bolted, sir."

"And—what did you tell her?"

"Explained as 'twere all on account o' witchcraft and sorcery damned, sir."

"Then be damned for a fool, Zebedee!" The Sergeant immediately saluted. "Then—er—what did she say?"

"Stared, sir, and cross-examinationed me concerning same, and I dooly explained as you did see a apparation in form of the devil—no, a devil in form of a——" The Major uttered an impatient ejaculation and rode on again. And after they had ridden some distance in silence the Sergeant spoke.

"Begging your pardon, sir, but you're wrong!"

"I think not, Zeb,'" sighed the Major, "'tis for the best."

"But sir, 'tis the wrong way to——"

"On the contrary 'tis the only way, Zeb, the only way to save her pain and vexation. I couldn't bear to see her shrink—er—ha, what a plague are you saying now, in the fiend's name, Sergeant?"

"Why sir, I only—"

"Be silent, Zebedee!"

"Very good, your honour, only this be the wrong way to Inchbourne."

"Egad!" exclaimed the Major, staring. "Now you mention it, Zeb, so 'tis!" And wheeling his horse forthwith, the Major galloped back to the cross-roads. Being come thither he halted to glance swiftly about and seemed much relieved to find no one in sight.

"Zebedee," said he suddenly as they rode on, knee to knee, "tis in my mind to go a-travelling again."

"Thought and hoped our travelling days was done, sir."

"Aye, so did I, Zeb, so did I—but," the Major sighed wearily, "none the less I'm minded to go campaigning again, leaving you here to—er—look after things for me, as 'twere, Zeb."

"Can't and couldn't be, your honour! You go and me stay? Axing your pardon, sir—Zounds, no!"

"Why not, pray?"

"Well first, sir, what would your honour do without me?"

"Truly I should—miss you, Zeb——"

"So you would, sir, so why think of going? Secondly, here's me been hoping—ah, hoping right fervent as you'd bring it off, sir, wi' colours flying and drums a-beating as gay as gay."

"Bring what off, Zeb?"

"Wedlock, sir." The Major flinched, then turned to scowl:

"Be curst for a presuming fool, Zebedee!" The Sergeant immediately saluted. "Whom should I marry at my time of life, think you?"

"Lady Elizabeth Carlyon, sir."

The Major's bronzed cheek burned and he rode awhile with wistful gaze on the distance.

"I shall—never marry, Zebedee!" said he at last.

"Why sir, asking your pardon, but that depends, I think."

"Depends!" repeated the Major, staring. "On what?"

"The Lady Elizabeth Carlyon, your honour."

Here ensued another long pause, then:

"How so, Zeb?"

"Sir, when some women makes up their mind to a man it ain't no manner o' good that man a-saying 'No'!"

"Pray what d'you know of women, Sergeant Zebedee?"

"That much, sir!"

"Hum!" said the Major. "Nevertheless I shall never wed, Zebedee!"

Here he sighed again and the Sergeant did likewise.

"Which I do sadly grieve to hear, sir, for your honour's sake, her ladyship's and—my sake!"

"And why yours, Zeb?"

"Sir, if you was to wed my lady and vicey-versey, the which I did hope, why then belike I might do the same with Mrs. Agatha and versey-vicey."

"God—bless—my soul!" exclaimed the Major.

"She's a pro-digious fine figure of a woman, your honour!"

"She is so, Zeb, she is indeed. But I had no idea——"

"Nor did I, sir, till a few days ago and then it came on me—ah, it come on me like a flash, your honour, quick as a musket-ball!"

"Then, if she's willing, Zeb, marry by all means and before I go I'll——"

"Begging your pardon, sir, can't be done—not to be thought on—if you wed why then I wed, if so be as she'll have me, sir, and vicey-versey, but if you don't, I don't and versey-vicey as in dooty bound, sir."

"But, if you love each other—why not, Zeb?"

"Because sir, you a bachelor, me a bachelor now and for ever, amen!"

"A Gad's name—why?"

"Your honour, 'tis become a matter o' dooty wi' me d'ye see."

"You're a great fool, Sergeant, aye—a fool, Zebedee, but a very faithful fool, Zeb!"

"Aye sir! And yonder's Inchbourne!" said the Sergeant, pointing to a hamlet bowered amid trees in the valley below them.

The thatched cottages of Inchbourne village stood upon three sides of a pleasant green and in this green was a pool shaded by willows and fed by a rippling brook.

"'Tis a mighty pretty place!" said the Major.

"Aye, sir—to look at—from a distance, but there ain't a cottage as aren't damp, nor a roof as don't leak like a sieve. Still 'tis pretty enough I'll not deny, though 'tis an ill-conditioned folk lives there, your honour, hang-dog rascals, poachers and the like——"

"And small wonder if things be so bad, ill-conditions beget roguery, Zeb, I marvel what Jennings can have been doing to let things come to such a pass!"

"Co-lecting rents mostly, sir!"

"You've no particular regard for Mr. Jennings, Zebedee."

"I never said so, your honour."

"He complained of you once, Zebedee— —"

"Sir, the same month as you and me come a-marching into this here estate said Jennings turned old Bet Seamore out of her bit o' cottage whereupon I dooly ventured a objection— —"

"Hum!" mused the Major, staring down at the peaceful hamlet. "He will be awaiting us— —"

"At the d'Arcy Arms!" nodded the Sergeant.

"Jennings was agent here in my uncle's time and bears an irreproachable character, Zeb— —"

"Character!" quoth the Sergeant. "Sir, his character worries him to that degree he's a-talking of it constant. Says he to me, old Betty a-sobbing over her bits o' furniture as was a-lying there in the road, 'no rent no roof!' says he, ''tis my dooty to look arter Squire's interests,' says he, 'and dooty's part o' my character. I was born with a irreproachable character,' says he, 'and such I'll keep same,' he says. 'Why then,' says I, 'since I can't kick your character, I'll kick you instead,' I says, which I did forthwith, wherefore complaint to you as aforesaid, sir."

"Ha!" said the Major, frowning. "'Twas wrong in you to assault my agent, Zeb, very wrong, but— —I must enquire into the matter of the eviction. You should have told me before." Saying which, he gave his mare the rein and they began to descend the hill.

"They call old Betty a witch, sir," continued the Sergeant, his keen gaze roving expectantly among the scattered cottages, "aye, a witch, sir, and now owing to Mr. Jennings' character d'ye see she do live in the veriest pigsty of a place which is the reason as my Lady Carlyon has took to riding over and a-visiting of her constant— —"

"Has she, Zeb, has she?" said the Major, his voice very gentle.

"Aye sir, folks hereabouts know her well—she stays wi' 'em hours sometimes and—Zounds, there she is!"

"Where?" demanded the Major, reining his mare upon its haunches.

"Yonder, sir, see, she's a-going into old Bet's cottage now and— —"

But the Major had wheeled about and was already half-way back up the hill.

"Sir," cried the Sergeant as they reached the brow of the hill, "what about that there Mr. Jennings as is a-waiting— —"

"He must wait awhile — we'll come back later, Zeb."

"No manner o' use, sir, my lady'll stop a couple of hours and by that time he'll be drunk, d'ye see. Best get home, sir — —"

"Why?"

"Well first there's your great History o' Fortification in ten vollums a-waiting to be wrote, and secondly you can come here another day — —"

"So I can, Zeb, so I can!" agreed the Major and straightway fell into a profound meditation while Sergeant Zebedee began to turn over in his mind various ways and means of achieving the second part of my lady Betty's so urgent request, pondering the problem chin in hand, his fierce black brows close-knit in painful thought. Suddenly he smiled and slapped hand to thigh.

"What now?" enquired the Major, starting.

"Why sir, there do be some evolutions as a man ain't so nat'rally adapted for as a fe-male so, thinks I sir, I'll ask Mrs. Agatha — —"

CHAPTER XXI
OF CRIMINATIONS

"Zebedee," said the Major, staring down at his empty desk, "what's become of my manuscript and papers?"

"I' the orchard, sir."

"The orchard—why there?"

"Why sir, seeing the day s'fine, the sun s'warm and the air s'balmy I took 'em out into the arbour, your honour."

"And who the plague told you to?"

"Mrs. Agatha, sir, and seeing 'tis quiet there wi' none to disturb, d'ye see, I took same, hoping what wi' the sun so warm and the air so balmy and your History o' Fortification in ten vollums you might—capture a wink or so o' sleep, p'r'aps, you not having closed a optic all last night, your honour."

"Ha!" growled the Major and, limping to the open casement, scowled out upon the sunny garden.

"And you was ever fond o' the orchard, sir."

"Damn the orchard!"

"Heartily, sir, heartily if so commanded, though 'tis for sure a pleasant place and if you, a-sitting there so snug and secluded, could nod off to sleep for an hour or so, what with the sun so warm and the air so balmy, 'twould do you a power o' good, sir, you being a bit—strange-like to-day, d'ye see."

"Strange? How?"

"Your temper's a leetle shortish and oncertain-like, sir."

"Aye," nodded the Major grimly, "belike it is, Zeb." He turned and limped slowly to the door but paused there, staring down at the polished floor. "Zebedee," said he suddenly, without lifting his frowning gaze, "what a plague gave you to think there was—there could be aught 'twixt my lady and me?"

"Observation, sir." The Major's scowl grew blacker:

"And—Mrs. Agatha?" he enquired, "does she know?"

"Being a woman, sir, she do—from the very first."

"Ha!" exclaimed the Major bitterly, "and the maids—I suppose they know, and the footmen, and the grooms, and the gardeners and every peeping, prying——"

"Sir," said the Sergeant fervently, "I'll lay my life there's no one knows but Mrs. Agatha and me—her by nat'ral intooitions and me by observation aforesaid."

"Do I——show it so——plainly, Zeb?"

"No, sir, but Mrs. Agatha's a remarkable woman—and I've learned to know you in all these years, to know your looks and ways better than you know 'em yourself, sir, wherefore I did ventur' to put two and two together and made 'em five, it seems. For (I argufies to myself) it ain't nowise good for man to live alone seeing as man be born to wedlock as the sparks do up'ard fly and what's bred i' the bone is bound to be. Moreover man cleaveth to woman and vicey-versey, your honour. Furthermore (argues I) wedlock is a comfortable institootion—now and then, sir, and very nat'ral 'twixt man and maid whereby come heirs o' the body male and female, your honour. And furthermore (I argues) you're a man and she's a maid and both on you apt and fit for same, therefore, if so—why not? Moreover again (thinks I) if two folk do love each other and there ain't any kind o' just cause nor yet impedimenta—why then (says I) wherefore not obey Natur's call and—— your honour——d'ye see——there y'are, sir!" Here the Sergeant stopped and stood at attention, breathing rather hard, while the Major, who had averted his head, was silent awhile; when at last he spoke his voice sounded anything but harsh.

"You're a good soul, Sergeant Zeb, a good soul. But that which is—— impossible can—er—can never be.

'Youth is joyous; Age is melancholy:
Age and Youth together is but folly.'

"'Tis a true saying, Zeb," he sighed, "a true saying and not to be controverted."

"Certainly not, sir," answered the Sergeant, "and you'll find your History o' Fortification a-laying on the table in the arbour, sir, also pens and ink, also pipe and tobacco, also tinder-box, also——"

"Why then, Zeb, since as you say the sun is so warm and the air so balmy I'll go out and sit awhile and dream I'm young again, for to youth all things are possible—or seem so." And, sighing, he limped forth into the sunshine. But now, as he went slowly towards the orchard, he smiled more than once, and once he murmured:

"God bless his honest heart!"

Thus, slow and listless of step, he came at last into the pleasant seclusion of the orchard and, with head bowed and shoulders drooping like one that is very weary, entered the cool shadow of the hutch-like sentry-box and started back, trembling all at once and with breath in check.

She sat looking up at him, great-eyed and very still, yet all vigorous young life from the glossy love-lock above white brow to her dainty riding-boot.

"Why John," said she softly, "do I fright you? Will you run from me again you great, big, 'Fighting d'Arcy'?" And now, because of his look, over snowy neck and cheek and brow crept a rosy flush, her lips quivered to a shy smile, never had she seemed so maidenly or so alluring; the Major clenched his fists and bowed his head. "John," she commanded tenderly, "come you hither to me!" and she patted the seat beside her with white hand invitingly. Major d'Arcy never stirred, so she reached out and catching him by the skirt of his coat, drew him near and nearer until he was seated beside her.

"And now," she questioned, "why do you tramp to and fro sleepless all night? Why do you gallop away at sight of me? Why are your poor cheeks so pale and your eyes so heavy with pain? Why do you sit and stare mumchance? Why? Why? Why?"

Now looking down into these bright eyes that met his so unflinchingly, hearkening to her soft and tender voice, his own eyes blenched and putting up his hands he covered his face that he might not see all the beauty of her and when he spoke his voice was hoarse and broken.

"My lady—why are you here—after last night? Dear God!"

"Because you need me, John, to comfort you, 'twould seem. If indeed you are bewitched by cruel fancies I am here to drive them away."

"Would to God you might," he groaned, "or that I had died before last night!"

"John," said she gently, "John—look at me! Do I seem changed, less worthy your love?"

"No, no, and yet—God help me—I saw, I heard!"

"What did you hear?"

"Your words of love—last night—in the arbour—your kisses."

At this, she started but her glance never wavered.

"What did you see?"

"I saw—him—damn him—leap back over the wall—Dalroyd!"

"Dalroyd!" she gasped, "Dalroyd—are you sure?"

"I had him in my grip! I looked into his evil face— —"

"Dalroyd!" she whispered, and with the word her proud head drooped and he saw her hands were shaking.

"Betty," said he hoarsely, "O Betty, 'tis not that my dream of possessing you is done, but—dear heaven—that it should be—such a man! For if I do guess aright he is one so vile, so— —"

"John!" she cried, "O think you 'twas to meet—him, I was there?"

"Aye, I saw him—fresh from your embraces—the damnable rogue boasted of it and I was minded to strangle him—but—for your sake— —"

"My sake?"

My lady rose and stood very pale and still, looking down at the Major's agony.

"And you think," she questioned softly, "you believe I was there to meet—him, at such an hour?"

"Betty—Betty—God help me—what am I to think?"

"What you will!" she answered. "Therein shall be your punishment!" And turning she would have left him, but he caught at her habit.

"My lady," he pleaded, "for God's sweet sake be merciful and deny it. Tell me I dreamed—say that my eyes saw falsely, tell me so in mercy and I'll believe."

"No!" she said dully, "No! Were I to swear this on my knees yet deep within your heart this evil doubt would still rear its head— —"

"Nay, nay—I vow—I swear!"

"You have been so swift to spy out evil in me from the first," she went on in the same passionless voice, "first you thought me a wild hoyden, then unvirginal, now—now, a sly wanton! So will I make your evil thoughts so many whips to scourge you for all your cruel doubt of me!"

Saying which, she broke from him and crossing the orchard on flying feet reached the ladder set for her there by the Sergeant's willing hands, she mounted, then paused to glance back over her shoulder but seeing how the Major remained meekly where she had left him, his head bowed humbly between clasping hands, she frowned, bit her lip, then gathering up the voluminous folds of her riding-habit climbed back very dexterously over the wall, frowned at him again, shook her head at him and vanished.

But then—ah then, being hid from all chance of observation she leaned smooth cheek against the unfeeling bricks and mortar of that old weather-beaten wall and fell to a silent passion of grief.

"O John!" she whispered, "O foolish, blundering, cruel John dear—I wonder if you'll ever know—how much I yearned—to kiss your dear, sad, tired eyes!"

Then, drying her tears, she lifted proud head and walked with much dignified composure into the house.

CHAPTER XXII
WHICH RELATES HOW SERGEANT ZEBEDEE TRING QUELLED SCANDAL WITH A PEWTER-POT

The tap-room of the ancient "George and Dragon" Inn is a long, low, irregular chamber full of odd and unexpected corners in one of which, towards the hour of three, sat Sergeant Zebedee Tring as was his wont so to do. A large tankard of foaming Kentish ale stood before him from which he regaled himself ever and anon the while he perused a somewhat crumpled and ragged news-sheet. But to-day, as the Sergeant alternately sipped and read he paused very often to frown across the length of the room towards a noisy group at the farther end; a boisterous company, whose fine clothes and smart liveries proclaimed their gilded servitude and who lounged, yawned, snuffed, sipped their wine or spirits and lisped polite oaths and fashionable scandal all with as fine, as correct and supercilious an air as either of their several masters could have done or any other fine gallants in St. James's. Moreover it was to be noticed, that each of them had modelled himself, in more or less degree, upon the gentleman who happened to rejoice in his service; hence man was faintly reminiscent of master.

"Josh, my nib," said an extremely languid individual, sticking out a leg and looking at it with as much lazy approval as my Lord Alvaston might have regarded his own shapely limb, "Josh, my sunbeam, there's something up—stap my vital organ!"

"Up, sir, up?" enquired a stoutish, pompous person, inhaling a pinch of snuff with all the graceful hauteur of Sir Benjamin himself, "Up, William—up what, up where? Od, sir—pronounce, discover."

"Josh, my bird, here's my guv'nor—here's Alvaston been a-sweating and swearing, writin' o' verses—poetical verses all the morning—which same is dooced queer, Josh, queer, fishy and highly disturbing—burn my neck if t'ain't."

"Od!" exclaimed the dignified Josh, "Od, sir, I protest 'tis a amazing co-in-seedence, here's mine been doing the actool same—I found Sir Benjamin up to the same caper, sir—ink all over 'imself—his ruffles—'oly heaven. And poitry too, William, s'elp me!"

"Egad! My eye!" exclaimed a pale youth remarkable for a long nose and shrill voice, "O strike me pale blue, 'tis a plague o' po'try and they've all been and took it. Here's Marchdale rings me up at three o'clock in the morning and when I tumbled up, here's him in his nightcap and a bottle o' port as I thought I'd put safe out of his reach, a-staring doleful at a sheet o' paper. 'Horace,' says he, fierce-like, 'Give me a rhyme for "Bet,"' says he. 'Sir, I hasn't got e'er a one about me,' I says. 'Then find one this instant,' says he. 'Why then sir, 'ow about "debt?"' I says and he—ups and throws the bottle at me!"

"'Twas a poetical frenzy, Horace," explained a horsey-looking wight, winking knowingly, "most poits gets took that way when they're at it—Alton does, only 'twas his boot which me ducking—went clean through the winder."

"Pink my perishing soul!" ejaculated the languid William in sleepy horror, "so they're all at it!"

"'Od refuse me, gentlemen," said Josh, smiting plump fist on table, "we must look into this before it goes too far— —"

"I'm with you, Josh," piped the shrill Horace, "a bottle at your head ain't to be took smiling—nor yet to be sneezed at, strike me pink! Besides I ain't drawed to po'try—it ain't gentleman-like, I call it damned low, gentlemen, eh?"

"Low?" repeated the solemn Josh musingly, "why no, it's hardly that, sir, there's verse, ye see, and there's poetry and t'other's very different from which—O very."

"And what's the diff, my flower?"

"Why, there's poetry, William, and there's verse, now verse is low I grant you, 'od sir, verse is as low as low, but poetry is one o' the harts, O poetry's very sooperior, a gentleman may be permitted to write poetry when so moody and I shan't quarrel with him, but—writing it for—money! Then 'tis mere verse, sir, and won't do not by no means. Verse is all right in its place, Grub Street or a attic, say, but in the gilded halls of nobility—forbid it, heaven—it won't do, sir, it ain't the thing, sir—away with it!"

"Ah, but we ain't in the gilded halls, we're in the country, sir, and the country's enough to drive a man to anything—even poetry, Josh, my tulip! Nothing to see but grass and dung hills, hedges and haystacks—O damme!"

"And a occasional dairymaid!" added Horace, laying a finger to his long nose, "Don't forget the dear, simple, rural creeters!" At this ensued much loud laughter and stamping of feet with shouts of: "A health, Horace is right! A toast to the rural beauties!"

Hereupon the Sergeant lowered the crumpled news-sheet and his scowl grew blacker than ever.

"Dairymaids?" exclaimed the languid William, turning the wineglass on his stubby finger, "Dairymaids—faugh, gentlemen! Joe and me and Charles does fly at higher game, we do, I vow. We've discovered a rustic Vanus! Rabbit me—a peach! A blooming plum—round and ripe—aha! A parfect goddess! Let me parish if London could boast a finer! Such a shape! Such a neck! Such dem'd, see-doocing, roguish eyes, egad!"

"Name—name!" they roared in chorus, "Spit out her name, William!"

"Her name, sirs, begins with a A and ends with another on 'em." Here the Sergeant sat up suddenly and laid aside the crumpled news-sheet. "Begins with a A, sirs," repeated William, still busy with his wineglass, "and ends with a A and it ain't Anna. And—aha, such a waist, such pretty wicked little feet, such——"

"Name!" chorused the others, "Name!"

But, at this juncture the door opened and a man entered rather hastily: his dress was sedate, his air was sedate, indeed he seemed sedateness personified, though the Sergeant, scowling at him over his tankard, thought his eyes a little too close together. He was evidently held in much esteem by the company for his entrance was hailed with acclaim:

"What, Joe! Joey—ha, Joseph," cried the pompous Josh, "you do come pat, sir, pat—we'm just a-discussing of the Sex—Gad bless 'em!"

"Dear creeters!" added Horace, fingering his long nose.

"Woman—divine Woman for ever!" said Joseph, "Woman, sirs, man's joy and curse, his woe and consolation!"

"Sweet creeters!" added Horace. "But William here tells us of a rural beauty—a peach and a Vanus as you and him's got your peepers on, Joe, so we, being all friends and jolly dogs, demands the fair one's name."

"One minute and I'm with you," answered the sedate and obsequious Joseph, "business first, pleasure after!" So saying he beckoned to a man who had followed him in from the road, a tall dark, gipsy-looking fellow at sight of whom the Sergeant clenched his fists and murmured "Zounds!" The obsequious Joe having brought the fellow into an adjacent corner remote from the noisy company, broke into soft but fierce speech:

"So you'll follow me—even here, will you?"

"Why for sure, Nick, for sure I'll follow you to——"

"My name's Joe, curse you!"

"Then 'Joe' we'll make it, Nick. And I foller ye for the sake o' past merry days, Joey, and—a guinea now and then, pal."

The Sergeant, who had risen, sat down again.

"Blackmail, eh?" snarled Joseph.

"Don't go for to be 'arsh, Joey lad—a guinea, come! Or shall I ax 'ee, here afore your fine pals to pipe us a chaunt o' the High Toby——"

"Hold your dirty tongue you——"

"A guinea, pal—say a guinea, come!"

"Take it and be damned!"

"Thank 'ee kindly, Joey, and mind this—now as ever I'm your man if you should want anyone——" here the fellow made an ugly motion with his thumb, nodded, winked, and crossing to the door, took himself off.

Sergeant Zebedee was about to follow when he checked himself and clenched his fists again.

"Begins with a A and ends with another A?" cried one of the company. "Question remains—who, Joey, who? Speak up, Joseph."

The sedate Joseph had crossed to his companions and now stood glancing sedately round the merry circle.

"Well, since you ask," he answered, "who should it be but Mistress Agatha—pretty Mrs. Agatha at the Manor House."

The Sergeant's nostrils widened suddenly and his grim jaws closed with a snap.

"Such a shape!" repeated the languid William. "Such a waist! Such dem'd, see-doocing, roguish eyes, begad!"

"Ah, and she knows it too!" piped Horace, "not a civil word for e'er a one on us, let alone a kiss or a sly squeeze! And why——?"

"Because," drawled Joseph, shaking sleek head, "because—since you ask me, I answer you as she is meat for her betters—her master, belike—the Major with the game leg—Squire d'Arcy of the Manor."

The Sergeant glanced into his tankard, found therein a few frothy drops, spilled them carefully upon the floor and hurled the empty vessel at the last speaker. Fortunately for himself the discreet Joseph moved at that moment and the heavy missile, hurtling past his ear, caught the long-nosed Horace in the waistcoat and floored him. Whirling about, Joseph was amazed to see the Sergeant advancing swiftly and with evident intent, and the next moment all was riot and uproar. Over crashed the table, chairs and their occupants were scattered right and left and there rose a cloud of dust that grew ever thicker wherein two forms, fiercely-grappled, writhed and smote and twisted.

And, after some while, the dust subsiding a little, the startled company beheld Sergeant Zebedee Tring sitting astride his antagonist who writhed feebly and groaned fitfully. Seated thus the Sergeant proceeded to re-settle his neat wig which had shed much of its powder, to tuck up his ruffles and to dust the marks of combat from his garments; having done which to his satisfaction and recovered his wind meantime, he addressed the gaping company.

"One o' you sons o' dirt bring me my hat!" The article in question being promptly handed to him, he put it on, with due care for the curls of his wig and glared round upon each of the spectators in turn:

"Now if," said he at last, "if there's any other vermin-rogue has got aught to say agin his betters, two in particular, I shall be happy to tear his liver out and kick same through winder! Is there now?"

Ensued a silence broken only by a faint groaning from the obsequious Joe; whereupon the Sergeant proceeded:

"You will all o' you notice as I'm sitting on this here piece o' filth as is shaped like a man—I don't like to, but I do it because he won't stand up and fight, if he would—ah, if he only would, I'd have his liver so quick as never was, d'ye see, because he spoke dirt regarding two o' the sweetest, noblest folk as brightens this here dark world. Further and moreover I, now a-sitting on this piece o' rottenness, do give warning doo—warning to all and sundry, to each and every—that if ever a one o' you says the like again—ah, or whispers same, in my hearing or out, that man's liver is going to be took out and throwed on the nearest dung-hill where same belongs. Finally and lastly, if there's ever a one o' you as feels inclined to argufy the point let him now speak or for ever hold his peace and be damned! Is there now?"

As no one breathed a word, the Sergeant sighed, rose from the moaning Joseph and, crossing the room, picked up his battered tankard and shook gloomy head over it; then, handing it to the round-eyed landlord, sighed again:

"That'll be the second tankard I shall ha' paid for in the last six weeks, Jem," said he, "I do seem oncommon misfort'nate with pewter-ware!"

So saying, he nodded and turning his back on the silent and chastened company, marched blithely homeward.

Now presently as he went, he was surprised to see the Major, who stood beside the way, his hands crossed upon his crab-tree staff, his laced hat a little askew, his grey eyes staring very hard at a weatherbeaten stile. As the Sergeant drew near, he started, and lifting his gaze, nodded.

"Ha, Zeb," said he, thoughtfully, "I'm faced with a problem of no small magnitude, Zeb—a question of no little difficulty!" and he became lost in contemplation of a lark carolling high overhead.

"Nothing serious I hope, your honour?"

"Serious, why—no Zeb, no. And yet 'tis a matter demanding a nice judgment, a—er—a reasoned deliberation, as 'twere."

"Certainly, sir!"

"Yet for the life of me I can come to no decision for one of 'em is much like t'other after all save for colour, d'ye see, Zeb, and serve the same purpose. Yet to-morrow—to-morrow I would look my very best and—er— youngest as 'twere, Zeb."

"Meaning which and who, sir—how and where, your honour?"

"Come and see, Zeb."

Herewith the Major turned and strode away, the Sergeant marching exactly two paces in his rear and without another word until, reaching the study in due course, the Major carefully closed the door and pointed with his crab-tree staff to some half-dozen of his new suits of clothes disposed advantageously on table and chairs.

"There they are, Zeb," said he, "though egad, now I look at 'em again they don't seem exactly right, somehow——"

"Why, sir, you've only got 'em mixed up a bit—this here dove-coloured coat goes wi' these here breeches and vicey-versey—this mulberry velvet wi'—

"Aye, to be sure, Zeb, to be sure. Now I see 'em so, I rather think we'll make it the mulberry, though to be sure the pearl-grey hath its merits— hum! We must deliberate, Zeb! 'Twill be either the mulberry or the grey or the blue and silver or t'other with the embroidery or—hum! 'Tis a problem, Zeb, a problem—we must think—a council of war!"

"Aye, sir!" answered the Sergeant, staring.

"Anyway, 'twill be one of them, Zeb—to-morrow afternoon. To be sure I rather fancy the orange-tawney, and yet the blue and silver—hum!"

Here the perplexed Major crossed to the mullioned window and standing there drew a letter from his pocket and unfolding it with reverent fingers read these words:

"DEAR AND MOST CRUEL MAJOR JOHN,

To-morrow is to be an occasion, therefore to-morrow I do invite you to come at four of the clock, or as soon after as you will, to look upon the sad, pale and woeful face of

deeply wronged,
much abused,
cruelly slandered,
ELIZABETH.

To Major ill-thinking, vile-imagining, basely-suspecting d'Arcy—these."

CHAPTER XXIII
DESCRIBES A TRIUMPH AND A DEFEAT

Lady Belinda leaning back upon her cushioned day-bed, glanced up from the open book before her and surveyed her niece's lovely, down-bent head with curious solicitude.

"Betty, love," said she at last, "Bet, my sweet witch, you're vapourish! So will I read to thee—list to this," and lifting her book, Lady Belinda read as follows: "'It must be granted that delicacy is essential to the composition of female beauty and that strength and robustness are contrary to the idea of it.' Alack, Betty, dear child and my sweet, I do fear you are dreadfully robust and almost repulsively strong! Hearken again: 'The beauty of women is greatly owing to their delicacy and weakness'—O my love, how just! I myself was ever most sincerely delicate and weak! How very, very true!" Here Lady Belinda paused, eyeing her niece expectantly, but, in place of indignant outburst, was silence; Betty sat apparently lost in mournful reverie.

"You like Mr. Dalroyd, I think, aunt?" she enquired suddenly.

"Indeed—a charming man! So elegant! Such an air—and such—O my dear—such a leg!"

"Major d'Arcy has a leg also, aunt—two of 'em!"

"And limps!" added Lady Belinda, "Limps woefully at times!"

"'Tis a mark of distinction in a soldier!" exclaimed Betty, flushing.

"True, dear Bet, very true—a mark of distinction as you say, though it quite spoils his grace of carriage. Still, despite his limp, the Major hath admirable limbs—a leetle robust and ultra-developed perhaps, child, doubtless due to his marching and counter-marching, whatever that may be. None the less, though I grant you his leg, Bet—he limps! Now Mr. Dalroyd, on the other hand— —"

"Leg, aunt!"

"Lud, child— —!"

"His leg, dear aunt, keep to his leg!"

"Gracious me, miss—what under heaven— —"

"Legs, aunt, legs!"

"Mercy on us, Betty, what of his legs?"

"They are bearing him hither at this moment, dear aunt."

"O Gemini!" wailed the Lady Belinda, starting up from her cushions. "Heaven's mercy, Bet, how can you! And me in this gown—behold me—so faded and woebegone— —"

"Nay, dear aunt, a little rouge— —"

"I meant my garments, miss—look at 'em! And my hair! Ring the bell—call the maids! I vow I shall swoon an' he catch me so— —"

"Nay, aunt, you do look very well and Sir Benjamin— —"

"He too!" shrieked Lady Belinda, "I faint! I'm all of a twitter—I— —

"And Lord Alvaston, aunt, and the Marquis, and Mr. Marchdale, and Major d'Arcy— —" but Lady Belinda had fled, twittering.

Left alone, Betty grew restless, crossed to the open lattice and frowned at the flowers on the terrace, crossed to her harp in the corner and struck a discord with petulant fingers, took up her aunt's discarded book, frowned at that, dropped it; finally she sat down and propping white chin on white fist, stared down at her own pretty foot.

"I wonder if you'll come?" she murmured. "Major John, O John, you cruel Jack, I wonder if—all night long—you lay wakeful, too? I wonder—ah, I wonder if— —"

A tapping at the door and, starting up, she stood bright-eyed, rosy lips apart, all shy expectancy from head to foot then, sighing, sank gracefully upon the day-bed and took up her aunt's discarded book as the door opened and the large menial announced:

"Mr. Dalroyd!"

My lady rose majestically and never had she greeted Mr. Dalroyd with such a radiant smile.

"You are come betimes, sir!" she said gently as he bowed to kiss her hand.

"Is that so great matter for wonder?" he enquired, his ardent gaze drinking in her loveliness. "You know full well, sweet Lady Coquetry, 'tis ever my joy and constant aim to—be alone with you, to touch this white hand, to kiss— —"

"Fie, sir!" she sighed, but provocation was in the droop of eyelash, the tremulous curve of lip and in all the soft, voluptuous languor of her.

Mr. Dalroyd's usually pale cheek glowed, his long, white hands twitched restless fingers and he seated himself beside her.

"Betty," he murmured, "O Betty, how delicious you are! From the first moment I saw you I——"

"'Twas at Bath, I think, sir, or was it at Tunbridge?"

"Nay, my lady, since we're alone, have done with trifling——"

"But indeed, sir, 'tis a trifling matter since you and I are but trifles in a trifling world. And 'tis a trifling day—and mine is a trifling humour so, since we're alone, let us trifle. And speaking of trifles—have you writ me the trifling ode I did command, sir?"

"Faith no, madam, there are so many to do that and I would fain be exempt. Where others scribble bad verses to your charms I would feast my sight upon them. Look you, Betty," he continued, leaning nearer, his languid eyes grown suddenly wide, his thin nostrils quivering. "I'm no tame dog to run in leash like the rest of your train of lovers, to come at your call and go when you are weary—content with a word, a glance—treasuring a rose from your bosom, a riband from your hair and seeking nought beyond—no, by God! 'tis you I want—fast in my arms, close on my heart, panting 'neath my kisses——" As he spoke he drew yet nearer until his hot breath was upon her cheek, wherefore my lady put up her fan and, leaning there all gracious ease surveyed him with clear, unswerving gaze, his ill-restrained ferocity, his clutching fingers, his eyes aflame with passionate desire; and beholding all this, my lady dazzled him with her smile and nodded lovely head:

"O excellently done!" she laughed lightly. "Indeed, sir, now you do trifle to admiration!"

"Trifle?" he exclaimed hoarsely, "Trifle is it? Not I, by heaven—ah Betty—maddening witch——" His arms came out fiercely but, before he could clasp her, she had risen and stepped back out of reach, looking down at him with the same steady gaze, the same bewildering smile.

"Nay, sir," she said gently, "though in this trifling world you are but a trifle, 'tis true, yet your trifling offends me like your neighbourhood!" and crossing to the open lattice she leaned there, staring out into the sunny garden. Mr. Dalroyd watched her awhile beneath drooping lids then, rising, sauntered after her.

"And pray, madam, why this sudden, haughty repugnance?" he demanded softly, "you know and have known from the first, that I love you."

"Why then, 'tis an ugly thing, your love!"

"'Tis very real, Betty, I live but to win you and—win you I shall."

"You are vastly confident, sir."

"Truly," he smiled, "'tis so my nature. And I am determined to possess you—soon or late, Betty."

"Even against my will?" she questioned.

"Aye, against your will!" he murmured.

"Even supposing that I—despised you?"

"'Twould but make you the more adorable, Betty."

"Even though you knew I—loved another man?"

"'Twould make you the more desirable, Betty."

At this she turned and looked at him and, under that look, Mr. Dalroyd actually lowered his eyes; but his laugh was light enough none the less.

"Betty," he continued softly, "I would peril my immortal soul to possess you and, despite all your haughty airs and graces—win you I will——"

"Enough, sir!" she retorted, "Am I so weak of will, think you, to wed where I so utterly—despise?" And, viewing him from head to foot with her calm gaze, she laughed and turned from him as from one of no account. For one breathless moment Mr. Dalroyd stood utterly still then, stung beyond endurance, his modish languor swept away on a torrent of furious anger, he came close beside her and stood striving for speech; and she, leaning gracefully at the open casement, hummed the lines of a song to herself very prettily, heeding him not at all.

"Madam!" said he, thickly, "By God, madam, none hath ever scorned me with impunity—or ever shall! Hark'ee madam——"

My lady gazed pensive upon the sunny garden and went on humming.

"Ha, by heaven!" he exclaimed, "I swear you shall humble yourself yet—you shall come to me, one o' these days soon and leave your pride behind. D'ye hear madam, d'ye hear my will shall be your law yet——"

Now at this she turned and laughed full-throated and ever as she laughed she mocked him:

"Indeed, sir, and indeed? Shall I run humbly to your call? Must I creep to you on lowly knees——"

"Aye—by God, you shall!" he cried, his passion shaking him.

"And must I plead and beg and sue, must I weep and sigh and moan and groan? And to you—you, of all trifling things? I wonder why?"

"For your brother's sake!" he answered between white teeth, stung at last out of all restraint.

"My brother—my Charles? What can you know of him—you?"

"Enough to hang him!"

Once again her laughter rang out, a joyous, rippling peal:

"O Mr. Dalroyd!" she cried at last, dabbing at her bright eyes with dainty handkerchief, "O, indeed, sir, here is trifling more to my mind—nay, prithee loose my hand!"

Mr. Dalroyd obeyed and stepped back rather hastily as the door opened and the footman announced:

"Major d'Arcy!"

The Major advanced a couple of strides then halted, fumbled with his laced hat and looked extremely uncomfortable; next moment my lady was greeting him gaily:

"Welcome, dear Major! You know Mr. Dalroyd, I think—so gay, so witty! Just now he is at his very gayest and wittiest, he is about telling me something extreme diverting in regard to my brother, my dear, wilful Charles—but you have never met my brother, I think, Major d'Arcy?"

"Never, madam!" he answered, bowing over her hand and dropping it rather as if it had stung him.

"Why then, sir," she laughed, "Mr. Dalroyd shall tell you all about him. Pray proceed, Mr. Dalroyd."

But hereupon Mr. Dalroyd having acknowledged the Major's stiff bow, stood fingering the long curls of his peruke and, for once in his life, felt himself entirely at a loss; as for the Major, he stood in wondering amazement, staring at my lady's laughing face as if he had never seen it before in all his days.

"Come, sir, come!" she commanded, viewing Mr. Dalroyd's perplexity with eyes very bright and malicious, "Charles is for ever playing some naughty trick or other, tell us his latest."

"Faith, madam," said Mr. Dalroyd at last, "I, like Major d'Arcy, have never had the good fortune to meet your brother."

"But you have seen him and very lately, I think—yes, I'm sure you have—confess!"

"Nay indeed, my lady, how—where should I see him——"

"Why with me of course, sir, last night—in the arbour."

Mr. Dalroyd recoiled a slow step, his heavy eyelids fluttered and fell, then happening to glance at the Major, he saw his face suddenly transfigured with a radiant joy, beholding which, Mr. Dalroyd's delicate nostrils twitched again and his long white fingers writhed and clenched themselves; then he turned upon my lady, seemed about to burst into passionate speech but bowed instead and strode from the room.

Left alone, the Major dropped his hat and my lady turning back to the casement, leaned there and began to sing softly to herself, an old, merry song:

"A young cavalier he rode on his way
Singing heigho, this loving is folly."

"Betty," said the Major humbly, "O Betty—forgive me!"

"And there met him a lady so frolic and gay
Singing, heigho, all loving is folly."

"Betty, I—O my dear love—my lady," he stammered, "I know that my offence is great—very heinous. I have wronged you in thought and in word—I should have known you were the sweet soul God made you. But I—I am only a very ordinary man, very blind, very unworthy and, I fear but ill-suited to one so young—but indeed I do love you better than my life so may Love plead my forgiveness. But if I have sinned too grievously, if forgiveness is impossible then will I very humbly—

"So he lighted him down and he louted him low
Singing heigho, be not melancholy,
And he kissed her white hand and her red mouth also
Singing heigho, love's quarrels are folly."

She stood waiting—waiting for the swift tread of feet behind her, for the masterful passion of his clasping arms, for his pleading kisses; instead, she heard him sigh and limp heavily to the door. Then she turned to face him and, being disappointed, grew angry and disdainful.

"Major d'Arcy," she cried, "O Major d'Arcy—what a runaway coward you are!"

He paused and stood regarding her wistfully and lo! as he looked her mocking glance wavered and fell, her lip quivered and almost in that instant he had her in his arms; but now, even now, when she lay all soft and tremulous in his embrace, he must needs stay to humbly plead her forgiveness, and then—Sir Benjamin Tripp's voice was heard in the hall beyond:

"Od's body, I do protest Dalroyd can be almost offensive at times!"

When the door opened Major d'Arcy stood staring blindly out of the window his clenched fists thrust deep into the pockets of the dove-coloured coat, and my lady, seated afar, frowned at her dainty shoe; next moment she had risen and was greeting the company all smiles and gaiety.

"Dear my lady," cried Sir Benjamin, bowing over her white hand with elaborate grace, "your most submissive humble! Major d'Arcy sir—yours! Sweet Madam, most beauteous Queen of Hearts, you behold us hither come, rivals one and all for your sweet graces, yet rivals united in hem! in worship of Our Admirable Betty!"

At this was a loud hum of approval with much graceful bending of backs, shooting of ruffles and tapping of snuff-boxes.

"Here in bowery Westerham," continued Sir Benjamin, laced handkerchief gracefully a-flutter, "here in this smiling countryside celebrated alike for hem! for beauty—I say for beauty and—and—

"Beer!" suggested his lordship sleepily.

"No, no, Alvaston—'od, no sir—tush! Egad you quite put me out! Where was I? Aye—the smiling country-side famous alike for beauty of scene, of womenkind, of——"

"Horses!" said the Marquis.

"A plague o' your horses, sir!"

"But Ben——"

"I say I'll have none of 'em, sir! Here, dear lady, within these Arcadian solitudes we exist like so many Hermits of Love, passing our days immune from strife political and the clash of faction, remote from the joys of London—its wose, its hem! I say its——"

"Dust!" sighed Sir Jasper.

"Aye, its dust, its——"

"Watchmen!" quoth Mr. Marchdale.

"Watchmen?" repeated Sir Benjamin doubtfully. "Y—es, its watchmen, its woes, its——"

"Smells!" yawned Lord Alvaston.

"Smells?" gasped Sir Benjamin, "'Od requite me sir—smells, sir!"

"What smells?" enquired Lady Belinda, pausing abruptly on the threshold with hands clasped. "Not fire? O Gemini, I shall swoon! Sir Benjamin, your arm pray, positively I languish at the bare idea—fire?"

"No, no, madam," exclaimed Sir Benjamin, supporting her to a chair, "here is no fire save the flames engendered of love, madam, for as I was saying—

"Stay, dear Sir Ben," laughed Betty, "first tell me, have you all writ me your odes?"

"'Od support me, yes faith, madam, we have writ you, rhymed you and versified you to a man, and it hath been agreed betwixt us, one and all, that hem! before these same odes, sonnets, triolets, vilanelles, rondeaus, chants-royal, ballades and the like be humbly submitted to you, we their authors shall hem! Shall——"

"Hold, my Benjamin, hold!" exclaimed Lord Alvaston. "Too much beating 'bout bush, Ben my boy. Dear Lady Bet, what poor Ben's been trying t' say, wants t' say, but don't know how t' say 's simply this—that having wrote odes 'n' things, we're minded t' read 'em t' each other and pass judgment on 'em, 'n' whoever has—

"Clapped the firmest saddle on Pegasus," continued the Marquis, "will be given——"

"He means whoso hath writ the best, Betty," Mr. Marchdale explained with youthful gravity.

"Shall be given three laps and a fly-away start in the Wooing Handicap," the Marquis continued.

"'Od—'Od's my life!" ejaculated Sir Benjamin indignantly, "We're not in the stables now, Alton! Suffer me to explain clearly——"

"But—wooing handicap?" repeated Betty, wrinkling her brows in puzzlement.

"Matrimonial Stakes, then," continued the irrepressible Marquis. "You see, Bet, we are all riding in this race for you and it has been ruled that——"

"My lady," sighed the soulful Sir Jasper, "it hath been agreed that whoso indites the worthiest screed to your beauty, he whose poor verses shall be judged most worthy shall be awarded three clear days wherein to plead his suit with thee, to humbly sigh, to sue, to——"

"A clear field and no favour, my lady!" the Marquis added.

"And," sighed Sir Jasper, "thrice happy mortal he who shall be privileged to call thee 'wife'!"

"Indeed, indeed," laughed my lady, "'tis vastly, excellently quaint— —"

"My idea!" said the Captain, shooting his ruffles. "Came to me—in a moment—like a flash!"

"Though truly," she sighed, "I do begin to think I ne'er shall wed and be doomed to lead apes in hell as they say—unless for a penance I marry Mr. Dalroyd or—Major d'Arcy! But come," she continued, smiling down their many protests and rising, "let us into the garden, 'tis shady on the lawn, we'll act a charade! Sir Jasper, your hand, pray." Thereupon, with a prodigious fluttering of lace ruffles, the flash of jewelled sword-hilts and shoe-buckles, the sheen of rich satins and velvets, the gallant company escorted my lady into the garden and across the smooth lawn.

"'Tis a pert and naughty puss!" exclaimed Lady Belinda, studying the Major's downcast face, "Indeed a graceless, heartless piece, sir!"

"Er—yes, mam," he answered abstractedly.

"A very wicked and irreverent baggage, Major!"

"Certainly, mam."

"Indeed, dear sir, what with her airy graces and her graceless airs I do shudder for her future, my very soul positively—shivers!"

"Shiver, mam?" enquired the Major, starting. "Shiver? Why 'tis very warm, I think— —"

"Nay, this was an inward shiver, sir, a spasmic shudder o' the soul! Indeed she doeth me constant outrage."

"Who, mam?"

"Why Betty, for sure." Here the Major sighed again, his wistful gaze wandered back to the open lattice and he fell to deep and melancholy reverie the while Lady Belinda observed him sharp-eyed, his face leanly handsome framed in the glossy curls of his great peruke, the exquisite cut of his rich garments and the slender grace of the powerful figure they covered, his high-bred air, his grave serenity mingled with a shy reserve; finally she spoke:

"Major d'Arcy, your arm pray—let us go sit out upon the terrace."

"Your—er—pardon madam," he answered a little diffidently, "I was but now thinking of taking—er—my departure— —"

"Go sir—O no sir! Tut Major and fie! What would Betty think of your so sudden desertion? Besides, I feel talkative—let us sit and tattle awhile, let us conspire together to the future good of my naughty niece and your wild nephew—Pancras. Though, by the way, sir, I didn't know Pancras had an uncle."

"Nor has he, mam," answered the Major, escorting her out upon the terrace and sitting down rather unwillingly, "I am but his uncle by—er—adoption, as 'twere."

"Adoption, sir?"

"He adopted me years ago—he was but a child then, d'ye see, and something solitary."

"Mm!" said Lady Belinda thoughtfully, viewing the Major's courtly figure again, "Indeed you are looking vastly well to-day, sir—grey is such an angelic tint—so spiritual! And young—I protest you look as young as Pancras himself!" The Major flushed and shifted uneasily on his seat. "And pray why doth Pancras tarry so long in London?"

"He writes that he is stayed by affairs of moment, mam."

"Then I vow 'tis most provoking in him! Here are you and I both a-burning to marry him to Bet—aren't we, dear Major?"

"Why as to that, mam—er—ah——" The Major grew muffled and incoherent.

"And here's Betty so carelessly rampageous—so, so lost to all sense of feminine weakness, alack!"

"Weakness?" murmured the Major.

"And so masculinely audacious! O dear sir, the vain hours I have spent trying to instil into her a little ladylike languor, a soft and feminine meekness! But alas! Betty is anything but meek—now is she?"

"Why—ah—perhaps not, mam—not exactly meek, as 'twere—and yet——"

"And she fears nought i' the world, living or dead, but a mouse!"

"But pray, mam, what should she fear?"

"La sir, what but your naughty, wicked sex. I vow, ere to-day, I've swooned at the merest sight of a man!"

"You—you've conquered the habit, I trust, mam?" enquired the Major a little anxiously.

"Indeed no, dear Major, I fear I never shall!"

"You don't feel any—inclination—now, mam?"

"Nay sir, unless you give me cause——"

"Egad, mam, I won't! Trust me——"

"Trust a man? Never, sir, 'tis a naughty sex. But talking of Bet, her head is quite turned, she suffers constantly from a surfeit of worshipping wooers, her will is their law, her merest glance or gesture a command—see her yonder, surrounded by her court yet must she have you also—see how she summons you!"

"Summons me—me, mam?" enquired the Major, a little breathlessly. "Nay, I see no summons!"

"With her eyes, sir!"

"Indeed she doth but glance this way."

"I know that trick o' the eyelash, sir! But as I say, Bet hath been spoiled by a too implicit masculine obedience, she groweth more imperious daily. If she but had someone to thwart her a little, cross her occasionally, 'twould do her a world of good."

"Certainly, mam!" he answered, all his attention centred upon that lovely, animated form on the lawn below.

"See—now she beckons you!"

"Egad, so she does!" he exclaimed, his eyes suddenly joyous. "Your pardon, mam, I must—" he gasped, for, attempting to rise, he found himself held and to his horror, perceived Lady Belinda's fingers twisted firmly in the silver-laced lapel of his coat-pocket. "Madam," he exclaimed in great agitation, "I beg—for the love of——"

"Sit still, sir—'twill do her a world of good!"

"But she needs me——"

"Sir, she hath six stalwart gentlemen to do her commands, let them suffice."

"But madam, I must——"

"Remain quiescent, sir—'twould be a sad pity to tear so fine a coat. Bide quiet, dear Major, and work a miracle."

So perforce the Major sat there miserably enough, while, unseen by the gay throng around her my Lady Betty continued to flash him knowledge of her indignant surprise, anger and contempt, even while her laughter rippled gaily to some ponderous witticism of Sir Benjamin.

"It works!" nodded Lady Belinda. "But, O Gemini, never follow her with such sheep's-eyes, Major, nor look so unutterly forlorn or you'll spoil all! Learn this, sir—what we humans strive for is always the thing withheld and—Betty is very human. And that reminds me she hath lately taken to whistling and walking in her sleep——"

"God bless my soul, mam, walking——"

"And whistling—both truly disquieting habits, sir! Morning, noon and night I cannot set foot above stairs but she falls a-whistling—extreme shrill and unpleasant! Lud, only last night, the place being hushed in sleep and everything so weird and churchyardy, sir, I heard a stealthy foot—that crept! I froze with horror! None the less I seized my candle, opened my door and—there was Betty—*en déshabille*, her hair streaming all about her and a loaf——"

"God bless my soul, mam!"

"Clasped to her bosom with one hand, sir, a platter in the other and her eyes—O sir, so wide and sightless! And her motion—so horridly ghostlike and glidy! My blood congealed instantly! But I followed, and she led me upstairs and she led me downstairs and she led me round about until I shivered 'twixt fright and weariness. At last I ventured to touch her—never so lightly, sir, and—O peaceful Heaven!"

"What, mam?"

"Scarce had I done so than she—O——"

"She did what, mam, what—a Gad's name, what?"

"Awoke sir, shrieked and dropped the loaf! Then I shrieked and the maids woke up and they shrieked and we all shrieked—O 'twas gruesome!"

"I can well believe it, mam!"

"And when she'd recovered me with burnt feathers—very noxious! it seemed 'twas all occasioned by a foolish dream—vowed she dreamed she was poor Jane Shore doing penance in Cheapside—though why with a loaf heaven only knows—and here she comes at last with Mr. Marchdale—'tis a case of Mahomet and the mount! Poor, dear young gentleman, see how he languishes! And his eyes! So dog-like!"

Sure enough Lady Betty was approaching in animated converse with her attendant swain but as she passed, the fan she had been using fell and lay unnoticed within a yard of the Major's trim shoe. Stooping, he picked it up, turned it over in reverent fingers then, seeing Betty had passed on, laid it tenderly upon the table whence Lady Belinda immediately took it and unfolding it, fanned herself complacently.

"I protest the sun is very warm here, Major," she sighed, "shall we walk?"

Obediently he rose and presently found himself treading smooth turf and vaguely aware of Lady Belinda's ceaseless prattle; chancing to lift his eyes he was surprised to see Betty strolling before him, this time with Lord Alvaston. As he watched, her dainty lace handkerchief fluttered to the grass.

"Aha!" murmured Lady Belinda. Instantly the Major stepped forward but Sir Jasper, who chanced to be near, reached it first, and lifting it tenderly, pressed it to lips, to bosom, and sighing, gave it to Betty's outstretched hand. The Major frowned and heartily wished himself back in his quiet study; Lady Belinda, watching him behind her fan, laughed softly:

"Major d'Arcy," said she, "I am thinking—deeply!"

"Indeed, mam!"

"I'm thinking that, after all, 'twill mayhap be as well if we agree to wed Betty to yourself——" The Major gasped. "Since you worship her so devotedly!"

"Mam—madam!" he stammered, "how did you learn——"

"I have sat beside you for quite twenty minutes, dear sir, and in all my days I never saw such a pitiful case of humble worship and dog-like devotion."

"Indeed mam, I—had begun to—to hope——"

"Hope still, sir. In two months, then. Yes, two months should be quite soon enough. How think you?" The Major was mute and before he could find an answer there came a burst of laughter from the adjacent shrubbery, a chorus of merriment that grew to a roar.

"Now I wonder—?" exclaimed Lady Belinda, halting suddenly, "This way, sir." Following whither he was led the Major soon came upon the merry company. Before them stood my lady Betty; in one hand she grasped the Major's gold-mounted cane, upon her raven hair was perched the Major's gold-laced hat, and now, squaring her shoulders, she began to limp to and fro—a limp there was no mistaking. She bowed and postured, mimicking to the life the Major's grave air, his attitude, his diffidence, the very tones of his voice.

"Egad mam! Good-day mam and how d'ye do, mam? You behold in me a philosopher, hence my gloom and spectre-at-the-feast air, as 'twere, d'ye see. Despite the silvered splendour of my coat and youthful trappings I am of antiquity hoary, mam, full o' years and wisdom, with soul immune and far above all human foibles and frailties, and vanities vain, as 'twere. Vices have I none, save that I do suck tobacco through pipe o' clay——"

Lord Alvaston, beholding the Major, choked suddenly in his laughter, Sir Benjamin started and dropped his snuff-box, the Marquis gasped and stared up at the sky and Lady Betty, turning about, found the Major within a yard of her; and seeing his look of sudden pain, his flushing cheek and the gentle reproach of his eyes, she stood motionless, struck suddenly speechless and abashed. But now, because of her embarrassment, he hastened to her and, to cover her distressed confusion, laughed lightly and stooping, caught her nerveless fingers to his lips:

"Dear my lady," said he, smiling down into her troubled eyes, "till this moment ne'er did I think this awkward, halting gait o' mine could seem so—so graceful as 'twere. I doubt 'twill irk me less, hereafter."

Then, gently possessing himself of hat and cane, he faced the dumb-struck company smiling and serene and, saluting each in turn, limped tranquilly away.

When he was gone, Lady Betty laughed shrilly, rent her laced handkerchief in quick, passionate hands and throwing it on the grass stamped on it; after which she flashed a glance of withering scorn upon the flinching bystanders and—sobbed.

"I detest, despise myself," she cried, "and you—all of you!"

Then she turned and sped, sobbing, into the house.

And the Major?

Reaching his study, he seized that exquisite, that peerless dove-coloured coat in merciless hands and wrenching it off, hurled it into a corner and rang for the Sergeant who came at the "double."

"Zebedee," said he between his teeth, pointing to that shimmering splendour of satin and silver lace, "take that accursed thing and burn it— bury it—away with it and bring me my Ramillie coat."

CHAPTER XXIV
DEALS, AMONG OTHER THINGS,
WITH TREASONABLE MATTERS

"Mrs. Agatha, mam," said the Sergeant, rubbing his square chin with the handle of the shears he had just been using, "he aren't been the same since that there night in the orchard! He be a-fading, mam, a-fading and perishing away afore my very eyes. He aren't ate this day so much as would keep a babe alive let alone a man like him, six foot and one inch, mam. Consequently, this morning I did feel called upon to re-monstrate as in dooty bound mam, and he said—so meek, so mild—so gentle as any bleating lamb, he says to me, says he——"

The Sergeant paused to heave a sigh and shake gloomy head.

"What did he say, Sergeant?"

"Mam, he says, says he—'Damn your eyes, Sergeant Zeb!' says he—but so mild and meek as any sucking dove——"

"Doves don't suck, Sergeant—at least I don't think so, and they never swear, I'm sure!"

"But, Mrs. Agatha mam, so meek he said it, so soft and mournful as my 'eart did bleed for him—his honour as could curse and swear so gay and hearty when needful! He says to me 'Zeb,' says he 'damn your eyes!' he says so sweet as any piping finch, mam." Here the Sergeant sighed heavily. "What's more, mam, he do talk o' marching off campaigning again."

"You mean to fight in more wars and battles?" she enquired with a catch in her voice.

"Aye mam, I do, and if he goes—I go as in dooty bound." Here fell a silence wherein Mrs. Agatha stared down at her basketful of roses and the Sergeant stared at her and rubbed his chin with the shears again. "Mam," said he suddenly, "a fortnight ago, being the thirtieth ultimo, towards three o'clock in the arternoon you did give me a little gold cross which is with me now and shall be hereafter living and dead Amen!"

"O Sergeant!" she said softly; and then "I'm glad you haven't lost it!"

"A fortnight ago mam," continued the Sergeant, "also towards three o'clock in the arternoon I—kissed you and the—the memory o' that kiss is never a-going to fade mam. You'll mind as I kissed you, mam?"

"Did you, Sergeant?"

"Ha' you forgot, mam?"

"Almost!" she answered softly, whereupon the Sergeant took a swift pace nearer, halted suddenly and turning away again, went on speaking:

"I kissed you for three reasons, same being as hereunder namely and viz. to wit, first because I wanted to, second because your pretty red lips was too near and too rosy to resist and third because I did mean to beg o' you to—to be—my wife."

"Did you—Zebedee?"

"I did so—then, but now I—I can't——"

"Why not—Zebedee?"

"Dooty mam, dooty forbids."

"You mean 'duty,' Sergeant," she corrected him gently.

"Dooty mam, pre-cisely! 'Tis his honour the Major, I thought as he were set on matrimony 'stead o' which I now find he's set on campaigning again, he talks o' nothing else o' late—and if he goes—I go. And if I go I can't ask you to wed—'twouldn't be fair."

"And why does he want to go?"

"Witchcraft, mam, devils, sorcery, black magic, and damned spells. Mrs. Agatha I do tell you he are not been his own man since he saw—what he saw i' the orchard t'other night."

"And what was that?" enquired Mrs. Agatha, glancing up bright-eyed from her fragrant basketful of roses.

"A apparition in form o' the dev—no, the devil in form of a apparation, mam."

"Fiddlededee!" exclaimed Mrs. Agatha. The Sergeant jumped and stared.

"Mam!" said he in gentle reproach, "don't say that—ghosts is serious and——"

"A fiddle-stick for your ghost! 'Twould take more than a shade to put his honour off his food, Sergeant Zebedee Tring! The question is, who was your ghost? What was he like?"

"Why since you're for cross-examinating me, I'll confess I caught but a glimpse of same, same having vanished itself away afore my very eyes."

"Where to?"

"Into my Lady Carlyon's garden, mam, and it dissolved itself so quick——"

"Tut!" exclaimed Mrs. Agatha,

"Tut is very well, mam, and—vastly fetching as you say it but none the less——"

"Ha' done Sergeant and let me think! Tell me, the night you went ghost-seeking did you catch ever a one—a man, say?"

"Aye, I did so, mam—one o' these London sparks and very fierce he were too!"

"Which one? What like was he!" With the aid of the shears Sergeant Zebedee described the trespasser very fully as regards face, costume and behaviour.

"That," said Mrs. Agatha, nodding her pretty head, "that should be Mr. Dalroyd—

"Zounds!" exclaimed the Sergeant, "how d'ye know this, mam?"

"Well, Sergeant, I do chance to have eyes, also ears and I do use 'em. This fine gentleman was your ghost t'other night, I'll swear."

"But what o' the hoofs and horns, mam, what o' the stink o' brimstone?"

"Have you seen ever a one yourself, Sergeant, or smelt the brimstone?"

"No mam, but Roger Bent has."

"Fiddlededee again, Sergeant!"

"Eh mam?"

"Roger Bent would see or smell anything. The question is what was Mr. Dalroyd after? Since you can't find out—I will."

"As how, mam?"

"By wagging my tongue, Sergeant."

"At—who, mam?"

"Well, to begin with there is his solemn servant, Mr. Joseph——"

The Sergeant swore fiercely.

"No mam," said he frowning, "not him nor any like him. He aren't fit for you to walk on—'twould dirty your pretty shoes——"

"But I don't mean to walk on him, nor spoil my shoes."

"Then don't hold no truck with him, mam—if you do——" the Sergeant set his grim jaw fiercely.

"Well—what?"

"I shall be compelled to—out with his liver mam, that's all!"

"Lud, Sergeant Tring."

"Bound to do it, Mrs. Agatha, so—keep away from same——"

"Sergeant, don't be a fool! I must use him to find out and why do you think I want to find out?"

"Being a woman—curiosity belike?"

"Being a blockhead you must be told!" cried Mrs. Agatha, her eyes flashing, "I want to find out the Major's trouble to make an end of the Major's trouble because I would keep him here at home. And I would keep him at home because then he won't go a-marching off to the wars, and if he don't go marching to the wars, why then—then——"

"Yes, yes mam—then?"

"Then—find out!" cried Mrs. Agatha her cheeks very red all at once; and she sped away into the house leaving the Sergeant to stare after her and rub his chin with the shears harder than ever. He was so engaged when he was aware of the approach of rapid hoofs and, glancing down the drive, beheld a cavalier swing in at the open gates and come thundering towards him.

The Viscount rode at his usual speed, a stretching gallop; on he came beneath the long avenue of chestnuts, horse hoofs pounding, curls flying, coat-skirts fluttering, nor checked his pace until he was almost upon the Sergeant, then he reined up in full career and was himself on terra firma almost in the same instant.

"Ha, Zeb," he sighed, drooping in modish languor, "split me, but I'm glad to see that square phiz o' thine, 'tis positive tanic after London, I vow! How goeth rusticity, Zeb?"

"As well as can be expected, my lord!"

"And the Major?"

"As well as can be hoped, sir, what with devils, apparations, witchcraft, magic, sorcery and hocus-pocus, m' lud!"

"Gad save my perishing soul!" exclaimed the Viscount, "What's it all mean, Zeb?"

"Well, Master Pancras sir, it do mean—nay, yonder cometh his honour to tell you himself, mayhap." Saying which, Sergeant Zebedee led the Viscount's horse away to the stables while his lordship, knocking dust from his slender person, went to greet the Major.

"Sir," said he as they clasped hands, "'tis real joy to see you again, but pray discover me the why and wherefore of the gruesome nightmare?" and he shook reproachful head at the Ramillie coat.

"'Tis easy, Tom, old and comfortable, d'ye see, while my new ones are so—so plaguy fine and overpowering as 'twere, so to speak, that I feel scarce worthy of 'em. So I—I treasure 'em, Tom, for—for great occasions and the like——"

"A grave fallacy, nunk! Modish garments must be worn whiles the prevailing fashion holds—to-day they are the mode, to-morrow, the devil! Fashion, sir, is coquettish as woman or weathercock, 'tis for ever a-veering, already there is a new button-hole."

"Indeed, Tom! Egad you stagger me!"

"Cansequently sir, being a dutiful nephew, I took thought to order you three more new suits—

"The devil you did!"

"Having special regard to this new button-hole, sir——"

"These will make nine o' them!" sighed the Major.

"Your pardon, sir, exactly thirty-one, neither more or less!"

"Good God, Tom!" ejaculated the Major, halting on the terrace-steps to stare h is amazement, "Thirty-one of 'em? How the deuce——"

"Cut aslant, d'ye see, nunky, and arabesqued with lace of gold or silver——"

"But, nephew—a Gad's name, what am I to do with so many—d'ye take me for a regiment? 'Tis 'gainst all reason for a man to wear thirty-one suits of——"

"Sir, I allude to button-holes!"

"Thank heaven!" murmured the Major.

"Moreover sir, there is, late come in, a new cravat—a poorish thing with nought to commend it save simplicity. It seems you throw it round your neck, get your fellow to twist it behind till you're well-nigh choked to death, bring the ends over your shoulders, loop 'em through a brooch and 'tis done. I propose to show you after supper."

"Hum!" said the Major dubiously. "Meantime a bottle won't be amiss after your long ride, I judge? Come in, Tom, come in and tell me of your adventures."

"Thank'ee, sir, though t' be sure I drapped in at the "George" on my way hither—left my two rogues there with my baggage. Which reminds me I have a letter for you." Diving into his coat-pocket he brought forth the missive in question and tendered it to the Major who took it, broke the seal and read.

"To Major d'Arcy these:

We, the undersigned, do solicit the honour of your company
this night, to sup with Bacchus, the Heavenly Nine, and

Yours to command:

B. TRIPP.
ALVASTON.
A. MARCHDALE.
H. WEST, CAPT.
ALTON.
J. DENHOLM."

"I don't see Mr. Dalroyd's name here, Tom!" said the Major, thoughtfully, as he led the way into the house.

"Nay sir, I protest Dalroyd's a queer fish! But as to this cravat I was describing, 'tis a modification of the Steenkirk——" and the Viscount plunged into a long and particular account of the article, while in obedience to the Major's command, bottle and glasses made their appearance.

"But surely 'tis not a question of clothes hath kept you in London this week and more, Tom?"

"Nay sir, I've been on a quest. London, O pink me 'tis a very dog-hole, 'tis no place for a gentleman these days unless he chance to be a Whig or a damned Hanoverian——"

"Hold, Tom!" said the Major, his quick eyes roving from door to lattice. "Have a care, lad!"

"Nay sir, I know I'm safe to speak out here and to you, Whig though you be. Of late I've perforce kept such ward upon my tongue 'tis a joy to let it wag. Indeed, nunky, London's an ill place for some of us these times, party feeling high. 'Tis for this reason you find Alvaston and Ben and Alton and the rest of 'em rusticating here, not to mention—my lady Bet."

"Ah!" exclaimed the Major. "You don't mean that she—she is not——?"

"No sir! But there is her brother, poor Charles is bit deep, he crossed the Border with Derwentwater last year."

"I feared so!" sighed the Major, frowning at his half-emptied glass. "And you, Tom, you're not——?"

"Sir, my rascally father, as you'll mind, was a staunch Whig and Hanoverian, naturally and consequently I'm Tory and Jacobite——"

"Softly, Tom, softly!" said the Major, his keen eyes wandering again.

"Well, sir!" continued the Viscount, leaning across the table and lowering his voice, "When Charles and young Dick Eversleigh rode for the Border last year I had half a mind to ride with 'em. But Betty was in London and London's the devil of a way from Carlisle. Yesterday, sir, I walked under Temple Bar and there was poor Eversleigh's head grinning down at me.... Like as not mine would ha' been along with it but for Bet. As for Charles, 'twas thought he'd got safe away to France with Mar and the others, but now word comes he was wounded and lay hid. And sir, though I've sounded every source of news in London and out, not another word can I hear save that he's a proscribed rebel with a price on his head and the hue and cry hot after him. Sir, poor Charles is my childhood's friend—and lieth distressed, hiding for his life somewhere 'twixt London and the Border, the question is—where?"

"Here, Tom!" answered the Major softly, "Here in this village of Westerham!"

The Viscount half rose from his chair, fell back again and quite forgot his affectations.

"Sir—d'ye mean it? Here?"

"Three nights ago he was with my lady Betty—in her garden!"

"With Betty—good God!" exclaimed the Viscount and, springing from his chair, began to pace up and down. "'Twill never do, uncle, 'twill never do—he must be got away at all hazards. Charles hath been cried 'Traitor' and 'Rebel'—his property is already confiscate and himself outlaw—and 'none may give aid or shelter to the King's enemies' on pain of death. He must be got away—at once! Should he be found 'neath Betty's care she would be attainted too, imprisoned and belike—Sir, you'll perceive he must be got away at once!"

"True!" said the Major, fingering his wine-glass.

"There none knoweth of his presence here, I trust, uncle—none save you and Betty?"

"None! Stay!" The Major leaned back and began to drum his fingers softly on the arms of his chair. "Tom," he enquired at last, "who is Mr. Dalroyd?"

"Dalroyd is—Dalroyd, sir. Everyone knows him in town—at White's, Lockett's, the Coca Tree, O Dalroyd is known everywhere."

"What d'you know of him, personally?"

"That he's reputed to play devilish high and to be a redoubtable duellist with more than one death on his hands and—er—little beyond. But Ben knows him, 'twas Ben introduced him, ask Ben, sir. But what of him?"

"Just this, Tom, if there is another person in the world who knows of my Lord Medhurst's present hiding-place 'tis Mr. Dalroyd and if there is one man in the world I do not trust it is—Mr. Dalroyd."

The Viscount sat down, swallowed a glass of wine and stared blankly at the toe of his dusty riding-boot.

"Why then, sir," said he at last, "this makes it but the more imperative to have Charles away at once. I must get him over to my place in Sussex, 'tis quiet there, sir—God! I must contrive it one way or another and the sooner the better, but how sir, how?"

"'None may give aid or shelter to the King's enemies on pain of death,' Tom," quoted the Major, gently.

The Viscount flicked a patch of dust from the skirts of his coat.

"Sir," said he, "Charles is my friend!"

"And—my lady's brother, Tom!"

"Perfectly, sir! I shall endeavour to get him to my Sussex place and hide him there until I have arranged for him to cross safely into France."

"Precisely, Tom!"

"The question is—how? All the coast-roads are watched of course!" said the Viscount in deep perplexity. "Ben would help, so would Alton or Alvaston but 'twould be asking them to put their heads in a noose and I can't do it, sir!"

"Certainly not, Tom! 'Tis an awkward posture of affairs and—therefore you may—er—count upon my aid to the very uttermost, of course."

The Viscount took out his snuff-box, tapped it, opened it, and shut it up again.

"Uncle," said he at last, "nunky—sir—" suddenly he rose and caught the Major's hand, gripping it hard: "Gad prasper me sir, I think—yes I think, I'd better—step upstairs and rid me of some o' this Kentish dust."

As he spoke the Viscount turned and strode from the room leaving the Major deep in anxious thought.

CHAPTER XXV
IN WHICH THE GHOST IS LAID

My Lady Elizabeth Carlyon, seated upon a rickety chair among a pile of other lumber high under the eaves, kicked her pretty heels for very triumph as she watched the tatterdemalion eat and drink the dainty meal she had just set before him.

"O Charles—'tis all so vastly romantic!" she exclaimed.

My Lord of Medhurst, chancing to have his mouth rather full, spluttered and lifted handsome head indignantly; thus the likeness to his twin sister was manifest, the same delicate profile and regularity of features, bright, fearless eyes and firm set of mouth and chin, the same proud and lofty carriage of the head.

"Romantic be damned, Bet—saving your presence!" said he, "I've led a very dog's life——"

"My poor, poor boy!" she sighed, touching his thin cheek with gentle, loving fingers which he immediately kissed; thereafter he fell to upon the viands before him with renewed appetite and gusto.

"Egad, Bet," he mumbled, "this is better than a diet of raw turnips and blackberries or eggs sucked warm from the nest——"

"O Charles, hath it been so bad as that?"

"Aye—and worse! Lord, Bet—lass, I've begged and thieved my way hither from the Border. Heaven only knows how oft I've sat i' the stocks for a ravished hen, been kicked and cuffed and stoned out o' villages for a vagrant, consorted with rogues of all kinds, hidden in barns, slept in hayricks and hedges, been abused by man, and stormed at and buffeted by the elements and, on the whole—am the better for it. Nay, sweet lass, no tears!"

Down went knife and fork with a clatter and his ragged sleeve was about her. "No tears, Bet," said he consolingly, "damme, I'll not endure 'em!"

"But O my dear, to think what you have suffered and I—so careless, while you, Charles, you——"

"Learned the meaning of life, Bet! Learned to—to be a man, for I do protest the beggar is a better man than ever was his idle scatterbrain lordship. A year ago when I had all and more than I needed, I was a discontented fool a—a very ass, Bet. To-day, though I've lost all, I've found—I've learned— Egad, I don't know just how to put it but you—you get me, Bet?"

"I understand, dearest boy!"

"Y'see, Bet lass, hardship makes a man either a rogue or a—very man. And, though I'm a beggar, I'm no rogue. 'Twas a great adventure, Bet, a noble effort brought to red ruin by—ah well—'tis finished! I was wounded, as I told you, and had to lie hid for weary weeks. When I ventured abroad at last, 'twas to learn poor Derwentwater was executed and Eversleigh too— poor old Dick! And the rest either in prison with Nithsdale or scattered God knoweth where. So there was I, destitute and with none to turn to of all my friends—for, as you know, 'tis prison or death to shelter such as I, and so in my extremity I—I came to you, Betty——"

"Thank God!" she whispered fervently, giving him a little squeeze.

"But only to beg money enough to carry me beyond seas, dearest! To-night or to-morrow at latest I must be gone——"

"Pho—'tis preposterous, foolish boy! 'Twere madness, dear Charles! I say you shall remain here safe hid until you are fully recovered of your sufferings!"

"Nay Bet, I'll be curst if I do! How, skulk here 'neath your petticoat and let you run the risk of sheltering a 'rebel'? No, no, I'll be——"

"You'll be ruled by me, dear Charles, of course! As for danger, I am your sister and proud to share it with you——" Hereupon he kissed her heartily and sitting down on the floor beside her made great play with knife and fork again.

"In three or four days at most I should reach the sea, Betty. And I'm determined on making the attempt within a night or so. As for risk—bah! I'm become so adept at skulking and hiding I'd elude a whole regiment! And with money in my pocket and no need to thieve or poach—Egad! Talking of poaching, I should be on my way to the plantations at this minute but for a neighbour of yours——"

"Neighbour, Charles?"

"Aye—tall, keen-eyed, soft-spoken and dev'lish placid; true-blue 'spite his limp and infernal old coat——"

"Ah," said Betty softly, "you mean Major d'Arcy, of course!"

"That was the name, I believe, and 'tis thanks to him——"

"Tell me all about it, Charles."

"Well, I'd poached a rabbit, Bet. Keeper saw me, knocked keeper down and bolted. Other keepers headed me off but I ran like a hare and bursting through a hedge, came full tilt upon three be-ruffled exquisites lounging down that quiet bye-lane for all the world as it had been St. James's—and Bet, who should they be but Alton, Marchdale and Alvaston! Seeing me in my rags and the keepers in full cry, Alton yells a 'view hallo' and after me they came on the instant. And a dev'lish fine run I gave 'em, egad! O Betty, I mired 'em in bogs and tore 'em finely in brambles and things before they ran me to earth—even then I doubled up Alton with a leveller, thumped Alvaston on the ear and Marchdale on the nose. Finally the keepers dragged me before a little pompous fellow with a scratch wig and red face, called himself Rington. By this time a crowd had collected and though I was minded to get word to Alvaston 'twas too late, Rington's keepers and the yokels were all about me. So they marched me off in triumph to the Squire, Major d'Arcy, who, smiling mighty affable, threatened to shoot Rington, sent the crowd off with a flea in their ear, as you might say, and me to the kitchen to bathe my hurts and eat a meal, and so to the lock-up. Next morning he woke me very early, bestowed on me some useful advice, a couple o' guineas and my liberty and limped serenely off."

Here my Lord Medhurst proceeded to finish what remained of his supper while Betty sat, chin in hand, staring at the dormer window just now glowing with sunset.

"To-morrow there's no moon. I shall start to-morrow, Bet."

"Faith and you'll not, Charles!"

"Aye, but I will. Look'ee Bet, I'm determined——"

"See here, Charles—so am I!"

"Pish, girl!" said he, looking dignified.

"Tush, boy!" said she, kissing him.

"Nay but, dear Bet, I've your safety at heart and therefore——"

"But, dearest Charles, you've no money in your pocket—and therefore!"

"Egad and that's true enough!" said he ruefully.

"So you'll be ruled by me, boy, and stay here until I think you are fit for travel."

"What o' the servants?"

"This part of the house is empty and—I'll manage the servants!"

"There's Aunt Belinda, she's an infernal sharp nose, Bet."

"Nay, I'll manage Aunt Belinda."

"Why then, what of this Dalroyd?"

"O!" said my lady, knitting black brows, "I'll manage him also."

"Look'ee Bet, I'll allow you've a head, but this fellow's dangerous."

"How so, Charles?"

"Well, he's not afraid o' ghosts for one thing——"

"Ghosts?"

"Y'see Bet, when I reached Westerham my difficulty was to get word with you and for the first night and day or so I lay hid in the ruined mill. And having nought better to do, I started to haunt the place and by means of an old sack and a pair of ram's horns I contrived to be a sufficiently convincing ghost——" Here his lordship chuckled.

"'Twas madness, Charles."

"So 'twas and yet, I vow——" His lordship chuckled again.

"But what of Mr. Dalroyd, Charles?"

"Faith, he took such a plaguy interest in the haunted mill that I left it and took to haunting the churchyard instead—used to hide in a mouldy vault——"

"Charles!" cried Lady Betty and shuddered.

"Finally he and his fellow hunted me out o' that and here I am. Haunting hath its drawbacks and 'twould have saved me much of discomfort had you received the letter I writ you and sent by the little girl."

"Tell me again what was in it, Charles."

His lordship scratched his head and wrinkled youthful brow.

"So far as I remember, Bet, I writ you these words: 'Meet me at midnight in your garden with fifty guineas for your loving and misfortunate fugitive, Charles.'"

Lady Betty set her chin on white fist and stared at her brother so fixedly that he choked upon his last mouthful of supper and remonstrated:

"Gad, Bet, why d'ye fix a man so wi' such great eyes? What might ye be thinking this time?"

"That we are grown more like each other than ever, dear—'tis marvellous! Aye, 'tis marvellous," she continued absently, "though your voice will never do!"

"Voice, Bet? Egad, what's in your mind now?"

"Mr. Dalroyd, Charles, for one thing."

"Aye, and what of the fellow?"

"Would he were choked with a flap-dragon. But—meanwhile——"

"What, Betty?"

"Hark, there's aunt wailing for me, I must go. You are free of all the upper chambers of this wing, but mind, if I whistle you must get you into hiding at once."

So saying, she shook portentous finger at him, smiled and vanished.

CHAPTER XXVI
OF BACCHUS AND THE MUSES

Seldom or never, in all its length of days, had the great dining room of the ancient hostelry of the "George and Dragon" glowed with such sartorial splendour or known such an elegant posturing of silk-clad legs, such a flirting of ruffles, such a whirl of full-skirted coats; coats, these, of velvet, of worked satin and rich brocade, coats of various colours from Sir Benjamin's pink and gold to Lord Alvaston's purple and silver; the light of many candles scintillated in jewelled cravat and shoe-buckle, shone upon crested buttons and on the glossy curls of huge periwigs, black, brown and gold. In the midst of this gorgeous company stood a short, stoutish gentleman, his booted legs wide apart, his sun-burned face nearly as red as his weatherbeaten service coat, a little man with a truculent eye.

"Od's my life, my lord Colonel!" exclaimed Sir Benjamin, wringing his hand, "I know not what propitious zephyr hath wafted George Cleeve into these Arcadian solitudes, but hem! being hither I do protest you shall this night sit the honoured guest of good-Fellowship, Bacchus and the Muses, shedding upon our poetical revels the—the effulgence of your hem! your glories, gracing our company with, I say with the——"

"Hold, Ben!" sighed my Lord Alvaston, making graceful play with his slender legs, "hold hard, Ben, an' get your wind while I 'splain. Sir, what poor Ben's been tryin' t' tell you 'n' can't tell you is—that we shall rejoice if you'll sup with us. And so say we all——"

"Strike me dumb if we don't!" added the Marquis.

"Haw!" muttered the Captain. "B'gad! So we do!"

"Gentlemen," said the Colonel, "I protest ya' do me too much honour, 'tis curst polite in ya' and I take it kindly, rot me, kindly!"

"Od's body, sir," cried Sir Benjamin, "the honour is completely ours, I vow, your exploits in Flanders and Brabant sir, your notable achievements on the stricken fields of Mars, the very name of Colonel Lord George Cleeve coruscates with hem! with glory, shines like—like—a——"

"Star," suggested the Captain. Hereupon Lord Cleeve bowed, the company bowed, shot their ruffles, fluttered their handkerchiefs and snuffed with one another.

"Hem!" exclaimed Sir Benjamin with an air of ponderous waggery, "as I was saying when my Lord Cleeve dropped upon us so happily, 'tis then agreed that Alton and I shall see the Major home at peep o' day!" Here Sir Benjamin grew so waggish that he very nearly laid plump finger to nose but checked himself in time and coughed instead. "I vow 'twill be an honour, for, foxed or no and despite his hem! his rusticity, Major d'Arcy is a gentleman, a——"

"Ha!" exclaimed the Colonel suddenly. "Do ya' mean Jack d'Arcy o' the Third, sir—d'Arcy of Churchill's regiment?" Sir Benjamin bowed and smiled:

"You know him, my lord? A simple, quiet, kindly soul——"

His lordship stared, laughed a short, hoarse bellow and, becoming immediately solemn, nodded:

"That's Jack to a hair, simple, quiet and dev'lish deadly! 'Twas so he looked, I mind, when he killed the greatest rogue and duellist in the three armies. Simple and quiet! Aye, 'twas so he seemed when he led us to the storming of the counterscarp at Namur in '95, as he was when he rallied our broken ranks at Blenheim and, after, when we turned the French right at Oudenarde. He was my senior in those days and where he went I followed and they called him 'Fighting d'Arcy' though a simple soul, sir, as ya' say. I was behind him when he led us against the French left at Ramillies and broke it too. I saw him dragged, all blood and dust, out o' the press at Malplaquet. 'Done for at last,' thought I—but Gad, sirs, they couldn't kill Fighting d'Arcy for all his quiet looks and simple ways! Aye, I know Jack, we were brothers, and like brothers we drank together, slept, quarrelled, and fought together—he seconded me in my first affair of honour!"

"Od's my life!" ejaculated Sir Benjamin. "Our rustic philosopher turns out a very Mars, a thundering Jove, a paladin——"

"True blue, damme!" added the Marquis.

"And yonder he comes," said Mr. Marchdale at the window, "and Merivale with him."

"Nunky," said the Viscount as they entered the hospitable portal of the "George and Dragon," "Ben and Alvaston are set on seeing you comfortably faxed to-night."

"Foxed? Ah, you mean drunk, Tom?"

"Perfectly sir, all in the way of friendship and good-fellowship of course, still I thought I'd let you know."

"For the which I am duly and humbly grateful, Tom," answered the Major as, opening the door, the Viscount bowed and stood aside to give him precedence.

The Major's appearance was hailed with loud cheers and cries of "Fighting d'Arcy," drowned all at once in a hoarse roar as, with a tramp and jingle of heavy, spurred boots, Colonel Lord George Cleeve ran at him, thumped him and clasped him in a bear's hug:

"'Tis the same Jack Grave-airs!" he cried, "the same sedate John! Ha, damme, man-Jack, be curst if I don't joy to see thee again!"

"Why George!" exclaimed the Major, patting the Colonel's back with one hand and gripping his fist with the other, "why Georgie, I do protest thou'rt growing fat!"

"Burn thee for a vile-tongued rogue to say so, Jack! Ha, Jack, do ya' mind that night in the trenches before Maastricht when we laid a trap for young Despard of Ogle's and caught the Colonel? 'Twas next day we stormed and ya' took a bayonet through your thigh——"

"And you brought me down from the breach George——"

"And cursed ya' heartily the while, I forget why but ya' deserved it!"

"Stay, George, supper is served I think, and let me introduce Viscount Merivale"; which done he saluted the company and they forthwith sat down to table.

And now corks squeaked and popped, servants and waiting-men bustled to and fro, glasses clinked, knives and forks rattled merrily to the hum of talk and ring of laughter.

"By the way, sir," said the Major, addressing his neighbour the Marquis, "I don't—er—see Mr. Dalroyd here to-night."

"No more you do sir, strike me dumb! And for the sufficient reason he ain't here. Dalroyd's a determined hunter o' feminine game sir, O dem! To-night he's in full cry, I take it—joys o' the chase, sir—some dainty bit o' rustic beauty—some shy doe——"

"I wonder who?" enquired the Viscount, stifling a yawn.

"Dalroyd's dev'lish close," answered Lord Alvaston, "close as 'n oyster 'sequently echo answers 'who?'"

"Gentlemen all," cried Sir Benjamin, "I rise to give you a name—to call the toast of toasts. I give you Betty—our bewitching, our incomparable, Our Admirable Betty!"

Up rose the company one and all and the long chamber echoed to the toast:

"Our Admirable Betty!"

Ensued a moment's pause and every empty glass shivered to fragments on the broad hearth. But now, as the clatter and hum and laughter broke out anew, the Major, frowning a little, glanced across at the Viscount and found him frowning also.

Courses came and went and ever the talk and laughter waxed louder and merrier, glasses brimmed and were emptied, bottles made the circuit of the table in unending procession; gentlemen pledged each other, toasts were called and duly honoured; in the midst of which the Major feeling a hand upon his shoulder glanced up into the face of the Viscount.

"Nunky," he murmured, "certain things considered, I'm minded for a walk!" and with a smiling nod he turned and vanished among the bustling throng of servants and waiting-men, as Sir Benjamin arose, portentous of brow and with laced handkerchief a-flutter:

"Gentlemen," said he, glancing round upon the brilliant assembly, "gentlemen, or should I rather say—fellow-martyrs of the rosy, roguish archer——"

"Haw!" exclaimed the Captain. "Prime, Ben!"

"Hear, hear!" nodded Alvaston. "Good, Ben—doocid delicate 'n' the bottle's with you, Jasper!"

"We are here, sirs," continued Sir Benjamin, bowing his acknowledgments, "to sit unitedly in hem! in judgment upon the individual compositions of the—the——"

"Field!" suggested the Marquis.

"Gang?" murmured Alvaston.

"Amorous brotherhood!" sighed Sir Jasper.

"Company, gentlemen, of the company. Versification affords a broad field for achievement poetic since we have such various forms as the rondel, ballade, pantoum—"

"O burn me, Ben," ejaculated Alvaston, "you're out there! What's verses t' do with phantoms——"

"I said 'pantoum,' sir—besides which, gentlemen, we have the triolet, the kyrielle, the virelai, the vilanelle——"

"O dem!" cried the Marquis, "sounds curst improper and villainous, too, Ben." Cries of "Order, Ben, order——"

"And likewise O!" added Lord Alvaston.

"Eh?" exclaimed Sir Benjamin, "I say what——"

"None o' your French villainies, Ben," continued the Marquis, "we want nothing smacking o' the tap-room, the stable or the kennel, Ben, 'twon't do! We must ha' nought to cause the blush o' shame——"

"No, Ben," added Alvaston, "nor yet t' 'ffend th' chastest ear——"

"Od sir, od's body—I protest——"

"So none o' your villainies Ben," sighed Alvaston, "no looseness, coarseness, ribaldry or bawdry——"

"Blood and fury!" roared the exasperated Sir Benjamin, "I hope I'm sufficiently a man of honour——"

"Quite, Ben, quite—the very pink!" nodded his lordship affably. "And talkin' o' pink, the bottle stands, Marchdale! Fill, gentlemen. I give you Ben, our blooming Benjamin and no heel-taps!"

The health was drunk with acclaim and Sir Benjamin, once more his jovial and pompous self, proceeded:

"In writing these odes and sonnets we have all, I take it, depended upon our mother—hem! our mother-wit and each followed his individual fancy. I now take joy to summon Denholm to read to us his—ah—effort."

Sir Jasper rose, drew a paper from his bosom, sighed, languished with his soulful eyes and read:

> "Groan, groan my heart, yet in thy groaning joy
> Since thou'rt deep-smit of Venus' blooming boy;
> Till Sorrow's flown
> And Joy's thine own
> Groan!"

"Haw!" exclaimed the Captain, "very chaste! Doocid delicate!"

Sir Jasper bowed and continued:

> "Pant, pant my heart, yet in thy panting ne'er
> Let Doubt steal in to slay thee with despair;
> But till Love grant
> All heart doth want
> Pant!"

"Gad!" said the Marquis, "you're doing a dem'd lot o' panting, Jasper!"

"I vow 'tis quaintly mournful!" nodded Sir Benjamin. "'Tis polished and passionate!"

Again Sir Jasper bowed, and continued:

"Sob, sob my soul, sobs soul— —"

"Hold hard, Denholm!" quoth Alvaston. "There's too many sobs f'r sense. I don't object t' you groaning, I pass y'r pants, but you're getting y'r soul damnably mixed wi' y'r sobs."

"Nay, 'tis a cry o' the soul, Alvaston," sighed Sir Jasper, "a very heart-throb, faith. Listen!"

"Sob, sob my soul sobs soulful night and day
Till she in mercy shall thy pain allay
Till all she rob
And for thee throb
Sob!"

"Curst affecting!" said the Captain, applauding with thumping wine-glass.

"Od gentlemen," cried Sir Benjamin as Sir Jasper sank back in his chair, "I do protest 'tis very infinite tender! It hath delicacy, pathos and a rhythm entirely its own. Denholm, I felicitate you heartily! And now, Alvaston, we call upon you!"

His lordship arose, stuck out a slender leg, viewed it with lazy approval, and unfolding a paper, recited therefrom as follows:

"Let the bird sing on the bough
Th' ploughboy sing an' sweat
But, while I can, I will avow
Th' charms o' lovely Bet.
Let— —"

"Hold!" commanded Sir Benjamin.

"Stop!" cried the Marquis. "Strike me everlastingly blue but I've got 'sweat' demme!"

"'S'heart, so have I!" exclaimed Mr. Marchdale with youthful indignation.

"Burn me!" sighed Alvaston, "seems we're all sweating! 'S unfortunate, curst disquietin' I'll admit, though I only sweat i' the first verse. Le' me go on:"

"Let the parson— —"

"Hold!" repeated Sir Benjamin. "Desist, Alvaston, I object to sweat, sir!"

"An' very natural too, Ben—Gad, I'll not forget you at th' churn! But to continue:"

"Let the parson pray— —"

"Stay!" thundered Sir Benjamin. "Alvaston, sweat shall never do!"

"Why, Ben, why?"

"Because, first 'tis not a word poetic— —"

"But I submit 'tis easy, Ben, an' very natural! Remember the churn Ben, the churn an' le' me get on. Faith! here we're keepin' my misfortunate parson on his knees whiles you boggle over a word! 'Sides if my 'sweat' 's disallowed you damn Alton and Marchdale unheard!"

Hereupon, while Sir Benjamin shook protesting head, his lordship smoothed out his manuscript, frowned at it, turned it this way, turned it that, and continued:

"Let the parson pray and screech— —"

"No, demme, 'tisn't 'screech'—here's a blot! Now what th' dooce—ha, 'preach' t' be sure— —"

"Let the parson pray and preach
And fat preferments get
But, so long as I have speech—
I'll sing the charms o' Bet.

"Let the— —"

"By th' way I take liberty t' call 'tention t' the fact that I begin 'n' end each canto wi' the same words, 'let' 'n' 'Bet.'"

"Let th' world go—round an' round
The day be fine or wet,
Take all that 'neath th' sun is found
An' I'll take lovely Bet."

"Bravo Bob! Bravo! Simple and pointed! Haw!" quoth the Captain, hammering plaudits with his wine-glass again.

"'Tis not—not utterly devoid o' merits!" admitted Sir Benjamin judicially.

"Thank'ee humbly, my Benjamin!"

"Nay, but it hath points, Alvaston, especially towards the finality, though 'tis somewhat reminiscent of Mr. Waller."

"How so, sweet Ben?"

"In its climacteric thus, sir:"

"Give me but what this ribband bound
Take all the rest the sun goes round."

"Egad Ben, I've never read a word o' the fool stuff in my life, so you're out there, burn me! And the bottle roosts with you, Alton. Give it wings. Major d'Arcy sir—with you!"

"Marchdale," said Sir Benjamin, "our ears attend you!"

Mr. Marchdale rose, coughed, tossed back his love-locks, unfolded his manuscript and setting hand within gorgeous bosom read forth the following:

"Chaste hour, soft hour, O hour when first we met
O blissful hour, my soul shall ne'er forget
How, 'mid the rose and tender violet,
Chaste, soft and sweet as rose, stood lovely Bet,
Her wreath-ed hair like silky coronet
O'er-wrought with wanton curls of blackest jet
Each glistered curl a holy amulet;
Her pearl-ed teeth her rosy lips did fret
As they'd sweet spices been or ambergret,
While o'er me stole her beauty like a net
Wherein my heart was caught and pris'ner set
A captive pent for love and not for debt,
A captive that in prison pineth yet.
A captive knowing nothing of regret
Nor uttering curse nor woeful epithet.
I pled my love, my brow grew hot, grew wet,
While sweetly she did sigh and I did sweat."

"Sweat, Tony?" exclaimed the Marquis. "O dem! What for?"

"Because 'twas the only rhyme I had left, for sure!"

"Od, od's my life!" cried Sir Benjamin, "here we have poesy o' the purest, in diction chaste, in expression delicate, in——"

"Nay, but Tony sweats too, Ben!" protested Alvaston.

"No matter, sir, no matter—'tis a very triumph! So elegant! Od's body Marchdale, 'tis excellent—sir, your health!"

"Burn me, Ben, but if Tony may sweat why th' dooce——"

"Major d'Arcy sir, I charge to you!" Hereupon Sir Benjamin filled and bowed, the Major did the same, and they drank together.

"But Ben," persisted Alvaston, "if Tony——"

"West, the floor and our attention are yours, sir!"

The Captain rose, shot his ruffles, squared his shoulders and read:

"Warble ye songsters of the grove—haw!
Warble of her that is my love
Where'er on pinions light ye rove
Haw!
Ye feathered songsters—warble.

"Warble ye heralds of the—haw!—the air
Warble her charms beyond compare
Warble here and warble there
Haw!
Ye feathered songsters—warble.
Warble, warble on the spray
Warble night and warble day
Warble, warble whiles ye may
Haw!
Ye feathered songsters—warble."

"A pretty thing!" nodded Sir Benjamin, "'tis light, 'tis graceful—easy, flowing, and full of——"

"Warbles!" murmured Alvaston.

"'Tis a musical word, sir, and what is poesy but word-music? I commend 'warble' heartily—we all do, I think."

Here a chorus of approval whereupon the Captain bowed, shot his ruffles again, said 'Haw!' and sat down.

"Alton, 'tis now your turn!"

Up rose the Marquis, tossed off his glass, fished a somewhat crumpled paper from his pocket and incontinent gave tongue:

"A song I sing in praise of Bet
I sing a song o' she, sirs
O let the ploughboy curse and sweat
But what is that to me, sirs?
My bully boys, brave bully boys
But what is that to me, sirs?"

"Here's that misfortunate ploughboy sweating again!" sighed Alvaston, while Sir Benjamin choked with wine and indignant horror:

"Hold, od's my life—Alton, hold!" he gasped. "Heaven save us, what's all this? 'Twill never do——"

"Sink me, Ben—why not?"

"Because it sounds like nothing in the world but a low drinking catch, sir, mingled and confused with a vulgar hunting-snatch."

"Nay, you'll find it betters as it goes—heark'ee!"

"I love the pretty birds to hear;
The horn upon the hill
But when my buxom Bet appear
Her voice is sweeter still
Brave boys!
Her voice is sweeter still!

"The fish that doth in water swim
Though burnished bright he be
Doth all his scaly splendours dim
If Bet he chance to see.
Brave boys!
If Bet he chance to see.

"There's joy——"

"Ha' you got much more, Harry?" enquired Alvaston mournfully.

"O demme yes, when I get my leg over Pegasus, Bob, 'tis hard to dismount me."

"There's joy in riding of a horse
That bottom hath and pace
But better still I love of course
Bet's witching, handsome face.
Brave boys!
Bet's witching, handsome face!

"E'en as the——"

"Hold a minute, Harry! You're givin' us a treatise on natural hist'ry, sure?"

"How so, Bob?"

"Well, you've sung 'bout a bird, 'n' fish, 'n' beast—why ignore the humble reptile? If you've got any more you might give us a rhyme 'bout vermin——"

"Demme, Bob, so I have! Heark'ee:"

"E'en as the small but gamesome flea
On her white neck might frisk, sirs
Could I be there—then, e'en as he
My life, like him, I'd risk, sirs.
My bully boys, brave bully boys
My life, like him, I'd risk, sirs!"

Pandemonium broke forth; bottles rolled, glasses fell unheeded and shivered upon the floor while the long room roared with Gargantuan laughter, rising waves of merriment wherein Sir Benjamin's indignant outburst was wholly drowned and his rapping was lost and all unheeded. Howbeit, having broken two glasses and a plate in his determined knocking, he seized upon a bottle and thundered with that until gradually the tempest subsided and a partial calm succeeded.

"Gentlemen!" he cried, his very peruke seeming to bristle with outraged decorum, "gentlemen, I move the total suppression of this verse—" Here his voice was lost in shouts of: "No, no! Let be, Ben! Order!" "I say," repeated Sir Benjamin, "it must and shall be suppressed!"

"O why, my Ben, why?" queried Alvaston, feeble with mirth.

"Because 'tis altogether too—too natural! Too—ah intensely, personally intimate——" Here the rafters rang again while drawers, ostlers and waiting-maids peeped in at slyly-opened doors. Silence being at last restored Sir Benjamin arose, snuffed daintily, flicked himself gracefully and bowed:

"Gentlemen," said he, "after the hem! brilliant flights o' fancy we have been privileged to hear, I allude particularly to Sir Jasper's soulful strophes and to—to——"

"Alton's gamesome flea?" suggested Alvaston, whereat was laughter with cries of "Order."

"And to Marchdale's delightful lyric," continued Sir Benjamin. "I do confess to no small diffidence in offering to your attention my own hem! I say my own poor compositions and do so in all humility. My first is a trifle I may describe as an alliterative acrostic, its matter as followeth."

> "**B**ewitching Bet by bounteous Beauty blessed
> **E**ach eager eye's enjoyment is expressed
> **T**hat thus to thee doth turn then—thrilling thought;
> **T**hou, thou thyself that teach may too be taught,
> **Y**ea, you yourself—to yearn as beauty ought."

"I' faith, gentlemen," said he, bowing to their loud applause, "I humbly venture to think it hath some small ingenuity. My next is a set of simple verselets pretending to no great depth of soul nor heart-stirring pathos, they are hem! they are—what they are——"

"Are ye sure o' that, Ben?" demanded Alvaston earnestly.

"Sure sir, yes sir—od's my life, I ought to be—I wrote 'em!"

"Then let's hear 'em and judge. But look'ee, Ben, if they ain't what they are they won't do—not if you were ten thousand Benjamen!"

Sir Benjamin stared, rubbed his chin, shook his head, sighed and read:

"Venus hath left her Grecian isles
With all her charms and witching wiles
And now all rustic hearts beguiles
In bowery Westerham!

"Ye tender herds, ye listening deer
Forget your food, forget your fear
Our glorious Betty reigneth here
In happy Westerham!

"Ye little lambs that on the green
In gambols innocent are seen
In gleeful chorus hail your queen
Sweet Bet of Westerham!

"Ye feathered——"

"Stop!" exclaimed Alvaston. "Your lambs'll never do, Ben!"

"Od sir, I say egad, why not?"

"Because lambs don't hail 'n' if they could hail their hail would be a 'baa' and being a baa Bet would ha' t' be a sheep t' understand 'em which Gad forbid, Ben! An' the bottle's with——"

"A sheep sir, a sheep?" spluttered Sir Benjamin. "Malediction! What d'ye mean?"

"I mean I object t' Betty being turned int' a sheep either by inference, insinuation or induction—I 'ppeal t' the company!"

Here ensued a heated discussion ending in his lordship's objection being quashed, whereupon Sir Benjamin, his face redder than ever and his elegant peruke a little awry, continued:

"Ye feathered songsters blithely sing
Ye snowy lambkins frisk and spring
To Betty let our glasses ring
In joyous Westerham!"

Sir Benjamin sat down amidst loud acclaim, and there immediately followed a perfervid debate as to the rival merits of the several authors and finally, amid a scene of great excitement, Mr. Marchdale was declared the victor.

And now appeared a mighty bowl of punch flanked by pipes and tobacco at sight of which the company rose in welcome.

"Gentlemen," said Sir Benjamin, grasping silver ladle much as it had been a sceptre, "the Muses have departed but in their stead behold the jovial Bacchus with the attendant sprite yclept Virginia. Gentlemen, it hath been suggested that we shall drink glass and glass and——"

"Damned be he who first cries 'hold enough'!" murmured Alvaston.

"Gentlemen, the night is young, let now the rosy hours pass in joyous revelry and good-fellowship!"

So the merry riot waxed and waned, tobacco smoke ascended in filmy wreaths, songs were sung and stories told while ever the glasses filled and grew empty and the Major, lighting his fifth pipe at a candle, turned to find Lord Cleeve addressing him low-voiced amid the general din across a barricade of empty bottles.

"—don't like it Jack," he was saying, "no duty for a gentleman and King's officer, we're no damned catchpolls ... word hath come in roundabout way of a Jacobite rebel in these parts.... Two o' my captains out with search parties ... poor devil!"

Slowly the clamour of voices and laughter died away, the candles burned low and lower in their sconces and through a blue haze the Major espied Sir Benjamin asprawl in his chair, his fine coat wine-splashed, his great peruke obscuring one eye, snoring gently. Hard by, Alvaston lay forward across the table, his face pillowed upon a plate, deep-plunged in stertorous slumber while the Colonel, sitting opposite, leaned back in his chair and stared up solemnly at the raftered ceiling. Candles were guttering to their end, the long chamber, the inn itself seemed strangely silent and the broad casement already glimmered with the dawn.

"Jack," said the Colonel suddenly, "'tis odd—'tis devilish odd I vow 'tis, but place feels curst—empty!" The Major glanced around the disordered chamber and shivered. "Jack, here's you and here's me—very well! Yonder's Sir Benjamin and Lord Alvaston—very well again! But question is—where's t'others?"

"Why I think, I rather think George, they're under the table."

Hereupon the Colonel made as if to stoop down and look but thought better of it, and stretching out a foot instead, touched something soft and nodded solemnly:

"B'gad Jack—so they are!" said he and sat staring up at the rafters again while the pallid dawn grew brighter at the window.

"Man Jack," he went on with a beaming smile, "'tis a goodish spell since we had an all-night bout together. Last time I mind was in Brabant at——"

The Colonel sat up suddenly, staring through the casement where, in the sickly light of dawn, stood a figure which paused opposite the window to stare up at the sleeping inn, and was gone.

"Refuse me!" exclaimed the Colonel, still staring wide of eye, "Jack—did ye see it?"

"Aye, George!"

"Then Jack if we're not drunk we ought to be—but drunk or no, we've seen a ghost!"

"Whose, George?"

"Why, the spirit of that ravishing satyr, that black rogue you killed years ago in Flanders—Effingham, by Gad!"

"Ah!" sighed the Major.

CHAPTER XXVII
HOW THE SERGEANT RECOUNTED
AN OLD STORY

Viscount Merivale sat alone in the hutch-like sentry-box; his handsome face was unduly grave, his brow care-worn and he bit at his carefully tended nails, which last was a thing in him quite phenomenal.

All at once he clenched his fist and smote it softly on the table:

"Damn him!" he muttered and sat scowling at his torn nails. "Ha, madam, it seems you are like to be the death o' me yet! ... O Woman! ... Howbeit, fight him I will!" Here, chancing to lift his frowning gaze, he saw the Sergeant approaching with a spade on his shoulder.

"What, Zebedee!" he called. The Sergeant glanced round, wheeled and, halting before the arbour, stood at attention. "Ha, Zeb, good old Zeb, come your ways. Sit down, yes, yes, here beside me. I'm beset by devils, Zeb, devils damned of deepest blue, your honest phiz shall fright 'em hence, mayhap—stay though!" The Viscount rose and drew his sword: "That lunge o' yours in tierce, Zeb, 'tis a sweet stroke and sufficiently deadly, show me the 'haviour on't. 'Twas somewhat on this wise as I remember." And falling into a graceful fencing posture, the Viscount made his long, narrow blade flash and dart viciously while Sergeant Zebedee, taking himself by the chin, watched with the eye of a connoisseur. "'Twas so, I think, Zeb?" The Sergeant smiled grimly and shook his head.

"You've got same all mixed up wi' fashionable school-play, Master Pancr—Tom, my lud, which though pretty ain't by no means the real thing."

"How so, Zebedee?"

"Why sir, this here posturing and flourishing is well enough a-'twixt fine gentlemen as happens to draw on each other after a bottle or to wipe out an ill word in a drop or so o' blood—yes. But 'tis different when you're opposite a skilled duellist as means to kill. His honour the Major now, he learned in a hard school and his honour learned me."

"He's had several affairs I think, Zeb?"

"Twenty and two, sir!"

"Ha!" sighed the Viscount, "I've had one and got pricked in the thigh! Here, show me the way on't, Sergeant." So saying, he turned weapon across forearm and bowing in true academic manner, proffered the jewelled hilt to the Sergeant who took it, tested spring and balance of the blade with practised hands, saluted and fell to the "engage"; then he lunged swiftly and recovered, all in a moment.

"'Tis a stroke hard to parry, sir!" said he.

"Gad love me!" sighed the Viscount, "do't again Zeb—slowly man and with explanations."

"Why look'ee sir, 'tis a trick o' the wrist on the disengage. You are in tierce—so, your point bearing so—very good! You play a thrust, thus d'ye see, then—whip! up comes your point and you follow in with a lunge—so! Try it, my lud."

"Hum!" said the Viscount, taking back his sword.

But having "tried it" once or twice with very indifferent success, he shook his head and, sheathing his weapon, sat down again and grew more despondent than ever. "Sit ye down, Zeb," said he, "the blue devils have me sure."

"Devils, Master Tom sir," said the Sergeant, seating himself on the bench his own hands had contrived, "I aren't nowise surprised, same do haunt the place o' late, this here orchard being 'witched d'ye see and full o' hocus-pocus."

"'Tis hard to believe, Zeb, what with the sky so blue and the grass all dappled with sunlight. Nay 'tis a fair world, Zeb, and hard to leave. Life's a desirable thing and hard to lose! Save us! What a world 'twould be if all women were sweet as they seemed and men as true!"

"Sure there's a deal o' roguery i' the world Master Pancras—Tom, sir! As witness—last night!"

The Viscount winced, muttered between clenched teeth and scowled at his fist again:

"Is the Major come home yet?" he enquired.

"Yes, sir. Come in along with Lord Cleeve, same as served under his honour years agone."

"How were they, Zeb?"

"His honour oncommon solemn and my lord oncommon talkative—wouldn't nowise part wi' his boots, threatened to shoot the first man as dared touch same. Last night must ha' been—a night, sir!"

"Aye!" nodded the Viscount absently. "You told me last night you actually caught the fellow one night—in the orchard here?"

"Fellow, my lud?"

"Mr. Dalroyd."

"I so did, sir—same being in the act o' scaling wall—taking my lady's garden by escalade as ye might say."

"'Twas Dalroyd, you're—quite sure, Zeb?"

"If 'twasn't—'twere a ghost sir."

"What d'ye mean?"

"The ghost of an officer of Ogle's as his honour killed in Flanders in a duel, Master Tom."

"Ah!" said the Viscount thoughtfully. "A duel!"

"Aye, sir, only this man's name were Effingham."

"A duel!" repeated the Viscount. "'Twas over a woman of course?"

"Aye sir, and an evil tale it is and I'm a man o' few words—but if so be you've a mind for't——"

"I have, Zeb—proceed——"

"Well, it seems this Captain Effingham with his company had took prisoner a French officer in his own chateau, d'ye see, and meant to shoot same in the morning for a spy. But to Captain Effingham comes the officer's wife—young she was and very handsome, and implored the Captain to mercy, which he agreed to if she'd consent to——"

"I take you, Zeb!"

"'Twas for her husband's life and she was very young, sir—I chanced to see her arterwards. So the Captain had his way. Next morning, very early, comes a roll o' musketry. She leaps out o' bed, runs to the lattice and there's her husband being carried by—dead! So she falls distracted and kills herself wi' the Captain's sword and arter comes his honour the Major and kills the Captain. 'Twas a pretty bout, sir, for the Captain was a master at rapier-play and famous duellist—laid his honour's head open from eye to ear at the first pass and, what wi' the blood-flow and heavy boots I thought his honour was done for more than once—and if he had been, well—I had finger on trigger and 'twould ha' been no murder—him!"

"The Major killed him?"

"Dead as mutton, sir."

"Did you bury the villain?"

"No time, sir, we were a flanking party on a forced march, d'ye see."

"And you say Dalroyd is like him?"

"As one musket-ball to another, Master Tom."

"And she was young and beautiful, Zeb?"

"About my lady Betty's age sir, and much such another."

"Ah!" murmured the Viscount and scowled at his fist again. "Look'ee Zeb, 'tis my fancy to master that thrust, every morning when you've done with the Major you shall fence a bout or so with me, eh?"

"'Twill be joy, Master Tom."

"But, mark this Zeb, none must know of it—especially my uncle. I—I'm minded to surprise him. So not a word and——"

On the warm, sunny air rose a woman's voice rich, sonorous and clear, singing a plaintive melody. The Viscount rose, flicked a speck from velvet coat-skirts and, crossing the orchard, swung himself astride the wall. My lady Betty was gathering a posy; at the Viscount's sudden appearance she broke off her song, swept him a curtsey then, standing tall and gracious, shook white finger at him.

"Naughty lad!" said she. "Since when have you taken to philandering in country lanes after midnight?"

The Viscount actually gasped; then took out his snuff-box, fumbled with it and put it away again.

"I—I—Gad preserve me, Bet!" he stammered, "what d'ye mean?"

"I mean, my poor Pancras, since when ha' you taken to spying on me?"

The Viscount's cheek flushed, then he leaned suddenly forward his hands tight-clenched:

"Betty," said he, his voice sunk almost to a whisper, "O Bet, in God's name why d'you meet a man of Dalroyd's repute—alone and at such an hour?" My lady's clear gaze never wavered and she laughed gaily:

"Dear Pancras," she cried, "your tragical airs are ill-suited to the top of a wall! Prithee come down to earth, smooth that face of care, dear creature, and let us quarrel agreeably as of yore!"

The Viscount obeyed slowly and looking a little grim:

"Look'ee Bet," said he as they trod the tiled walk together, "I have lived sufficiently long in this world to know that the mind of a woman is beyond a man's comprehension and that she herself is oft-times the sport of every idle whim— —"

"'Tis a Daniel come to judgment! O excellent young man!'" she mocked. Whereat the Viscount became a little grimmer as he continued:

"Yet, because my regard for you is true and sincere, I do most humbly implore you to forego this madcap whim— —"

"Whim, Viscount Merivale, my lord?"

"Aye—whim, fancy, mischief—call it what you will! 'Tis impossible you can love the fellow and not to be thought on."

"Dear Pan," she sighed, "I vow there are times I could kiss you as I used, when we were children."

"Trust me instead, dear Bet! Confess, the fellow hath a hold over you? Have you met him often at night?"

"Twice!"

"Shall you meet him again?"

"Thrice!"

"Alone? And—at midnight? Alone, Betty?"

"Quite alone."

"God!" he exclaimed, "what will the world think?"

"The world will be asleep."

"But how if you should be seen as I saw you—in the lane?"

"'Tis small chance," she answered, brushing her roses across red lips a-pout in thought. "'Tis why I choose a spot so remote and so late an hour."

"But alone—at midnight—with Dalroyd! By heaven, Betty, you run greater and more ugly risks than you know."

"I think not, Pan."

"But I tell you, and God forgive me if I misjudge the fellow—from what I know—from what I hear he's a very satyr—a— —"

"Indeed I think he is!" she sighed. "So do I go prepared."

"How—how?" he demanded. "I say no maid should run such risk, willingly or no— —"

"Pancras!" She turned and faced him suddenly. "You never doubt me— you?"

"Never Bet, never, I swear. But 'tis only that I've known you all your days and because I know you commit this folly and risk these dangers for Charles's sake. But Betty, in God's name what will the end be?"

"An end shall justify the means!"

"The means—the means! Aye, but there are some means so shameful that no end may ever justify—you never think to sacrifice yourself to——"

My lady laughed; then seeing the anxiety of his face, the tremor of his clenched fist, she took that fist in her soft, cool fingers and drawing him within the arbour made him sit beside her.

"Pan dear," she said gently, "O rest secure in this:—'tis true I love my brother but no tender martyr am I so brave or so unselfish, even for his dear sake, to yield myself up to—the beasts. This body of mine I hold much too precious to glut their brutish appetite."

"Why then, Bet, promise me this folly shall cease, you'll see Dalroyd no more, at least at such an hour—promise me."

"No, Pancras."

"Ha! And wherefore not?"

"Because 'tis so my whim."

"Why then you leave me but one alternative, Betty."

"Prithee—what?"

"I'll stop it in despite of you."

"Cry you mercy, sir—how?"

"Very simply."

"Ah, Pancras, you mean a—duel? No no, not that—you shall not—I forbid such folly!" The Viscount smiled. "He'd kill you, Pan, I know it—feel it!" The Viscount's smile grew a little rueful.

"None the less, 'twould resolve the problem—at least for me," he answered.

"But, Pancras, see how clumsily! O Lud, these meddling men!" she sighed.

"Heavens, these wilful women!" he retorted.

"Still, Sir Wiseacre, being a woman I'll meet and outwit the beast with a woman's weapons. So now prithee let there be no thought of such clumsy weapons as this!" and tapping the ornate hilt of the Viscount's sword, she rose. "Come," said she, reaching him her hand, "take me within-doors and I will stay thee with flagons."

Now as they crossed the broad lawn together the balmy air was suddenly pierced by a shrill and flute-like whistle.

"Aha!" exclaimed the Viscount, stopping suddenly to glance about.

As he stood thus he was amazed by an object which, hurtling from on high, thudded upon the grass, and stepping forward he picked up a much worn and battered shoe. From this sorry object his gaze, travelling aloft, presently discovered a figure which had wriggled itself half out of a small dormer window beneath the eaves and, despite this perilous position, was beckoning to him vigorously.

"Oho!" exclaimed the Viscount, turning to my lady Betty. "So you have him here, 'tis as I thought!" But when he would have waved and saluted his lordship of Medhurst in return, Betty stayed him with a gesture.

"The servants, Pan—" she warned him.

"You'll take me up, Bet, you'll let me see the old lad?" the Viscount pleaded. "I've been scheming out ways and means of getting him first to my place in Sussex and then over seas——"

"Phoh!" exclaimed my lady. "And yourself and him dungeoned in the Tower within the week. How should you know he was hereabouts—'twas that Major d'Arcy, I'll vow!"

"True, he mentioned the matter and moreover——"

"Ha!" cried my lady stamping her foot, "so he must be talking already!"

"Aye—to me, Bet, why not i' faith! And—though a Whig——"

"A flapdragon!" exclaimed my lady.

"I say though a Whig he is as ready to aid Charles into safety as you or I. Nay, he hath even proffered to harbour him in his own house."

"Mm!" said my lady, smiling down at her roses, "I wonder why a Whiggish soldier should run such risk for Charles, a stranger?"

"Because the Major chances to be the best, the bravest, the most unselfish gentleman I have the honour to know!" replied the Viscount.

"Dear Pancras!" she sighed, "an you would talk with Charles, you shall, so come your ways and be silent—Pancras dear!"

So she brought him into the house and, finger on lip, led him up back stairways and along seldom used passages to a door small but remarkably strong; here she paused to reach a key from a dark corner, a key of massive proportions at sight of which the Viscount whistled.

"You see, Pan," she explained, fitting it to the lock, "Charles is quite determined to get away at once for my sake, but I'm quite determined he shall stay for his own sake, until I judge him sufficiently recovered, and — hark to him, Pan, hark to my naughty child!" She laughed as an impatient fist thumped the stout door from within and a muffled voice reached them. "Be silent, sir!" she commanded. Followed a sulky muttering, the door swung open and my lord of Medhurst appeared, petulant and eager:

"What Pan!" he cried. "What Tom—Tommy lad! Y'see how she treats me!"

"Hush!" exclaimed my lady, closing the door.

"Gad, Charles!" exclaimed the Viscount as they embraced, "you're thin and pale, is't your wound?"

"Nay—nay, I vow I'm well enough, Tom——"

"But I protest art worn to a shadow——"

"A shadow—aha!" His lordship laughed gaily. "Say a shade, Tom, a ghost and you're in the right with a vengeance. But tell me the latest town news, Tommy, who's in and who's out? Stands London where it did——"

"Nay first, Charles, I'm here to smuggle you away to my Sussex place there to keep you hid until I can arrange for you to cross into France. 'Twill be the simplest matter i' the world, Charles, I'll have a couple of fast horses in the lane at midnight, we shall reach my place by dawn or thereabouts. How say you?"

"Why I say, dear lad, 'tis all very well but you forget one thing."

"And that?"

"Your own risk, Pan."

"Tush!" exclaimed the Viscount.

"Quite so, Tom," nodded my lord, "but d'ye dream I'd ever shelter myself behind thy faithful friendship? How say you, Bet?"

"Spoken like my own Charles!" she answered and clasping her arm about him set her cheek to his, and the Viscount, glancing from one face to the other, fell back in staring surprise.

"Gad love me!" he exclaimed. "'Tis years since I saw you out of a peruke, Charles and now I do—I vow your likeness to Bet is greater than ever—faith 'tis marvellous! Same features, same gestures, same height——"

"Nay I swear I'm taller by a good inch, Tom——"

"But the similarity is wonderful——"

"Except for his voice!" sighed my lady, "and that—hush! 'Tis the coach returned, aunt is back from Sevenoaks already!" So saying, she crossed to the window and leaned out. "Heavens!" she cried, "aunt must ha' driven home galloping, the horses are all in a lather o' foam. I wonder——"

"Betty!" cried a voice, "O Betty!"

"Save us!" ejaculated my lady, crossing to the door and turning the key, "she's coming up!"

"Betty!" cried Lady Belinda from the landing without, "O Betty, let me in—let me in!" Here the strong door was shaken by eager hands. "Let me in, Betty, O I know who's there—I've known for days. Let me in for O Lud—I've such terrible news—quick, open the door!"

Instantly Betty obeyed and Lady Belinda tottered in, closed it again and leaned there breathless.

"Charles!" she cried. "My wicked wanderer! My wayward boy! O I shall faint—I swoon!" But Lady Belinda did neither, instead she caught the earl to her bosom, kissed him tenderly and spoke. "My dears, there are soldiers at Sevenoaks seeking our fugitive—they may be here at any time!"

"The devil!" exclaimed the fugitive.

"We must do something!" said the Viscount.

"We will!" nodded my lady.

CHAPTER XXVIII
THE MAJOR COMES TO A RESOLUTION

Colonel Lord George Cleeve sat perched astride a chair on the desk in the corner and watched where the Major and Sergeant Zebedee fronted each other for their wonted morning's fencing-bout:

"You'll find me a little sluggish as 'twere after last night, Zeb," said the Major, taking his ground.

"Why there have been other nights, sir, and I never found you so yet," answered the Sergeant, as, returning the Major's salute, he came to his guard, and, with a tinkle and clash of steel, they engaged, the Major, light-poised and graceful, the Sergeant balanced upon stockinged feet, cunning, swift and throbbing with vigorous strength. Now as their play became closer it seemed that the weapons were part of themselves, this darting, twining steel seemed instinct with life and foreknowledge as lightning thrust was met by lightning parry; while the Colonel, craning forward in his chair, cursed rapturously under his breath, snorted and wriggled ecstatic. It was a long, close rally ending in a sudden grinding flurry of pliant blades followed by a swift and deadly lunge from the Sergeant met by an almost miraculous riposte, and he stepped back to shake his head and smile; while the Colonel slapped his thigh and roared for pure joy of it.

"Sir," said the Sergeant, "'tis me is sluggish it seems! Clean through my sword-arm!"

"Faith, Zeb, I saw it coming in time."

"Joy!" cried the Colonel, sprinkling himself copiously with snuff, "O man Jack 'tis a delight t' the eye, a balm t' the soul, a comfort t' the heart! Rabbit me, Jack, Sergeant Zeb is improved out o' knowledge."

"Aye, George, Zeb is an apt pupil. Come again, Sergeant."

At this moment the door opened and the Viscount lounged in, but seeing what was toward, seated himself on a corner of the desk as the foils rang together again. Before the next venue was decided the Colonel was on his legs with excitement and the Viscount's languor was forgotten quite, for, despite their buttoned foils, they fought with a grim yet joyous ferocity, as if death itself had hung upon the issue. Their blades whirled and clashed, or grinding lightly together seemed to feel out and sense each other's attack; followed cunning feints, vicious thrust or lunge and dexterous parry until, at last, the Major stepped back and lowered his point:

"'Tis your hit, Zeb—here on my wrist!"

"Why 'twas scarce a hit, your honour."

"Most palpable, Zeb!"

"Gad love me!" murmured the Viscount, "and they don't sweat and they ain't panting!"

"Music!" snorted the Colonel, bestriding his chair again, "poetry, pictures—bah! Here you have 'em all together! A fine 'ooman's a graceful sight I'll allow, but sirs, for beauty and music, poetry and grace all in one, give me a couple o' well-matched small-sworders!"

"Parfectly, sir!" bowed the Viscount. "Though, nunky, if I may venture the remark and with all the deference in the world, your play is perhaps a trifle austere—lacking those small elegancies and delicate refinements——"

The Colonel rolled truculent eye and sprinkled himself with snuff again.

"Master Tom sir—Pancras my lud," said the Sergeant, "I were thinking p'r'aps you'd play this third venue with his honour?"

"Gad, nunky, 'twould be a joy," murmured the Viscount. So saying he took the Sergeant's foil. "You'll mind sir, how you disarmed me last time——"

"'Twas but a trick, Tom, and you were all unsuspecting."

"At least, sir, this time I shall play more cautious." And the Viscount saluted and fell to his guard, one white hand fanning the air daintily aloft. The foils crossed and, as the bout progressed, the Viscount's self-assurance grew, he even pressed the Major repeatedly and twice forced him to break ground; time and again his point missed by inches while the Sergeant watched between a smile and a frown and the Colonel wriggled on his chair again:

"Faith!" cried he, as the foils were lowered by common consent. "The lad hath a wrist, Jack, and a quick eye for distance—he should make a fencer one o' these days—with pains——"

"Gad so, sir!" exclaimed the Viscount, a little huffed, "I rejoice to know it!"

"And though his point wavers out o' the line like a straw i' the wind and his parade is curst inviting and open, still——"

"Let me perish, what d'ye mean, my lord?"

"Come again, Tom and I'll show you!" said the Major.

"Those are fairly large buttons on your waistcoat. I'll take the top four. On guard, Tom!"

Again the foils met and almost immediately the Major's blade leapt and the Sergeant counted "One—two!" The Viscount broke ground, then lunged in turn and the Sergeant counted again, "Three—four!" The Viscount stepped back, pitched his foil into a corner and stared at the Major in rueful amaze, whereupon Lord Cleeve laughed, and, clambering from the table, clapped him on the shoulder:

"Never be discouraged, Viscount," said he, "never be peevish, sir, in your place I should ha' fared little better. Few may cope with d'Arcy o' the Buffs—or Sergeant Zebedee for that matter!"

"Gad love me sir," answered the Viscount smiling, "'twould seem so."

"And now, man Jack, I'm for Sevenoaks on small matter o' business, moreover 'tis like my lady Carlyon will be thereabouts and young Marchdale promised to make me known to 'Our Admirable Betty.' Will ye ride with me, Jack?"

"Why thank'ee George, no—there's my chapter on the Defects of Salient Angles d'ye see, for one thing——"

"Devil burn your salient angles!"

"But here's Tom now. Tom might join you," suggested the Major with a meaning glance at his nephew.

"'Twould be a joy, sir!" murmured the Viscount dutifully.

"Why then I'll go get into my boots," nodded the Colonel and strode from the room.

"Nunky," said the Viscount, rearranging his cravat before the mirror with scrupulous care, "there are soldiers at Sevenoaks and the man they seek lieth hid—next door, if I mistake not!"

"Art sure, Pancras?"

"I spoke with Charles himself a while since, and my lady Belinda saw the soldiers to-day. Question, what's to do, sir?"

"'Tis a problem, nephew, and one requiring a nice judgment. Let me think! Sergeant, I'll thank you for my Ramillie coat. And she hath him hid?" enquired the Major, getting into the garment in question.

"Under lock and key, nunky. Charles would have been away ere this for her sake, but she'd locked him in. You see he is still scarce recovered of his wound and hardships, and Betty is determined to keep him till he be quite strong again."

"To be sure!" nodded the Major, fingering the tarnished buttons of his old campaigning coat. "And she locked him in—'twas like her! As for the soldiers, Tom, having traced him so far, they will be here next 'tis sure and her house will be searched first, of course."

"Gad sir!" exclaimed the Viscount, striding to and fro in sudden perturbation. "You take it devilish calm and serene! If they search there they'll find him beyond doubt——"

"Not so, Tom, I'll see to that."

"You sir—how?"

"He shall come here."

"Here nunky—here in this house—with Colonel Cleeve your guest?"

"Precisely, Tom—I must hide him under old George's honest nose. 'Tis irregular, as 'twere—aye, 'tis vastly irregular, and yet——" Here there rose a distant roaring, a hoarse and intermittent clamour.

"Gad love us!" exclaimed the Viscount, starting, "what's here?"

"'Tis only George roaring for thee, Tom."

"And the horses are at the door, my lud!" added the Sergeant, glancing from the window.

"So begone, Tom and——"

"No no, sir, I'll stay and aid you with——"

"Nay, look'ee Tom, you ride to Sevenoaks with George. You learn precisely when the soldiers march for Westerham and, if need be, you make your excuses and ride back to warn me of their coming. Your dapple-grey is the fastest thing on four legs and—ah, George—I do but stay my nephew to give him certain commissions and, as I was saying, his big dapple-grey is the fastest——"

"Ha—rot me, Viscount, we'll see that—we'll see that!" nodded the Colonel pulling on his gauntlets. "Now, if you're ready, sir?"

"Quite, my lord, quite!" smiled the Viscount, and, taking hat, gloves and whip from Sergeant Zebedee, he bowed and followed the Colonel out. Thereafter rose the clatter of their horse-hoofs which died rapidly away until they were lost altogether.

"Zeb," said the Major, sinking heavily into his chair and leaning head on hand, "Sergeant Zebedee, I go about to do a thing I never thought to do. We fought and bled for England and Queen Anne Zeb, you and I, and after for King William and then for King George, and now, it seems, I must forget my loyalty for the sake of a youth I've never seen, a Jacobite fugitive, Zeb, whose life is held forfeit—but, he is the brother of one—one I hold—very dear, Zeb. And for her sake I am about to be false to the oath I swore as an officer, I am about to give aid and shelter to an enemy of my king. This is a grief to me, Zeb, a great grief, since honour was very dear to me, but she—is dearer still! So shall I do this thing gladly—aye, even though it lose me all as well as honour—even life itself because 'tis for—her." Here the Major paused to sigh and the Sergeant finding nothing to say, saluted. "But as for you yourself, Zeb, all these long, hard years you've served faithfully and kept your record clean, and God forbid I should smirch it. So, Zebedee, you will take a week's leave—you will get you to London or——"

"Which, saving your presence, can't nowise be, your honour!" answered the Sergeant. "King George is very well and I say, God bless same. But then King George and me don't chance t' have fought for England together side by side, nor yet have saved each other's life, sir—very good! But, says I, in action or out, wheres'ever you've led I've folleyed most determined, and I'm too old to change my tactics, sir. So, your honour, I'm with you in this, in that, or in t'other, heretofore, now and hereafter, so be it, amen!" Having said which, the Sergeant saluted again and stood at ease.

"You risk your neck, Zeb!"

"I've risked every member I possess afore now, like your honour."

"I mean there is a danger that——"

"Dangers has been our daily meat and drink, sir, and perils our portion. Consequently if dangers and perils should threaten your honour 'tis only nat'ral I should share same, besides 'tis become a matter o' dooty wi' me, d'ye see, sir?"

"Zeb," said the Major, rising, "Zebedee—ha—Sergeant Tring, give me your hand! And now," he continued, as their hands gripped and fell apart, "bring me my hat and cane, Zeb, I'll to my lady." These being produced, the Major clapped on laced hat, took ebony cane in hand and crossed to the door; but there the Sergeant stayed him:

"Sir," said he in gentle remonstrance, "you'll never go in your old coat?

"And wherefore not, Zeb?"

"'Tis not in keeping wi' your brave new hat, your honour!"

"Maybe not, Zeb," sighed the Major, "but then 'tis in most excellent keeping with my—my limp, d'ye see. So let be, Zeb, let be!"

And so the Major went forth upon his errand and, being a little perturbed as to his possible reception, fell to planning himself a line of conduct for the forthcoming interview and forming stern resolutions that should govern him throughout. Thus, as he walked, head a-droop and deep-plunged in thought, his limp was rather more pronounced than usual.

CHAPTER XXIX
TELLS HOW LADY BETTY DID THE SAME

And so my Lady Carlyon sitting in her arbour, lovely head bent above a book on surgery, presently espied the Major's tall figure advancing towards her; and beholding the familiar features of the Ramillie coat, its threadbare seams, its tarnished braid and buttons, she had the grace to blush, and felt her breath catch unwontedly.

The rosy flush still mantled her cheeks as she rose to greet him, quick to heed the courtly grace of his stately bow and his air of gentle aloofness.

"Madam—my lady, pray pardon this unwarranted intrusion, but——"

"O sir," she murmured, eyes a-droop, "most fully."

"I am come on account of your brother, my Lord Medhurst."

"Ah!" she sighed, "you mean my dear rebel—will't please you to sit, sir?"

"Thank you, I had—rather stand," he answered gently.

"And pray sir, what of my brother?"

"My lady, it seems the soldiers—a search-party have reached Sevenoaks and may be on their way hither, and your house would prove but a dangerous hiding-place, I fear. They would naturally search there first and very thoroughly."

"And you are here to warn me?"

"I am here to offer him the more secure shelter of the Manor."

Here my lady sighed, glanced swiftly up at his averted face and made room for him beside her on the rustic bench.

"Will you not—sit down, sir?" she asked softly.

"Thank you but I—am very well here!" he answered; whereupon my lady frowned at her book and fluttered its pages with petulant fingers.

"Can it be sir," she questioned, "can it possibly be that Major John d'Arcy so—so sternly orthodox and——and Whiggish is willing to give shelter to a Jacobite rebel?" The Major bowed. "And you are a—loyal soldier?"

"I—was!" he answered, sighing so deeply that she glanced at him again and beholding his troubled face, her petulant fingers were stilled, her frown vanished and her voice grew suddenly pleading and tender.

"Prithee, Major John will you not—sit awhile?" and she drew aside the folds of her gown invitingly.

"Indeed I—I had—rather not!" he answered, drawing back a step.

My lady's round bosom heaved tempestuous and she glanced at his averted face with eyes of scorn.

"Sir," said she, "the soldier who shelters the enemies of his king is a—traitor!" The Major winced. "And traitors are sometimes—hanged, sir!"

"Or shot, or beheaded!" he murmured.

"And you, Major d'Arcy, you are willing to run all these risks and wherefore?" The Major prodded diligently at a patch of moss with his cane, while, chin on hand, she watched him, waiting his answer.

"Need you ask?" he muttered.

"I do ask, sir," said she, her watchful gaze unwavering; and he, conscious of this intent look, flushed, grew uneasy, grew abashed; finally he raised his head and returned her look and in his eyes was that which called imperious to all her womanhood, that before which her own eyes fell though his voice was very tender as he answered:

"My lady you know well 'tis—for you. You know my love is one that counteth not risk, now or—or ever."

At this, my lady having seen and heard all she had desired, bowed shapely head and was silent awhile, staring down at the page before her headed: "Quartern Ague." When at last she spoke her voice quavered oddly and he flinched, believing that she laughed at him again.

"Your coat is more—more threadbare and—woebegone than—ever, John!" Here he sighed, still thinking that she mocked him but, as he turned away, he saw something that fell sparkling upon the page before her, followed by another and another. The Major stood awe-struck.

"My lady!" he exclaimed, "mam——"

"Do—not——" my lady sobbed but stamped her foot at him none the less.

"Madam," he corrected hastily.

"Nor that, sir! I'll not be 'madam-ed' or 'my lady-ed'—by you—any longer."

"Betty! O Betty!" he cried yearningly.

"John!" she sighed, "Jack!" And lifting her head she looked at him with eyes brimful of tears, tears that would not be winked away, so she dabbed at them with her handkerchief and sobbed again. The Major stepped hastily into the arbour.

"Betty?" he questioned in awed wonderment.

"Yes—I'm weeping, sir," she confessed. "I'm shedding—real tears and 'tis not a custom of mine, sir—consequently 'tis not so easy as to faint or—swoon. I hate to—sob and weep, and I—despise tears—besides they hurt me, John." He came a quick step nearer. "O 'tis very cruel to make a poor maid weep—how can you, John dear?"

"I?" he exclaimed aghast, "I—make you weep?"

"Indeed you—you! O cruel!"

"In heaven's name, how—what have I done?"

"Heaped coals of fire, John! Burnt me! Scorched me!"

The Major stared, utterly at a loss and fumbled with one of his tarnished buttons; then, seeing his bewilderment, she laughed through her tears and, choking back her sobs, rose and stretched out her arms to him.

"John," she murmured, "you dear, noble, generous Jack—ah, don't you see? When I made a public mock of you the other day, you hid your pain for my sake—and to-day, O to-day you come ready and willing to aid my brother heedless of risks and dangers. And now—now you—stand so—far off! John dear, if—if you won't sit down—prithee come a little nearer for me—just to—touch you."

Now hearing the thrill in her voice, beholding the melting tenderness of her look, his doubts were all forgotten and his stern resolutions swept clean away; so he came near, very near and, sitting down, clasped her yielding loveliness to the shabby, war-worn Ramillie coat.

"My dear, brave, noble John," she sighed, "and I such a beast to thee! To make a mock of thee for fools to laugh at—but none so great a fool as I—yes, Jack I repeat——" But here the Major closed her self-accusing lips awhile. "Yes, dear John," she continued, "I was a positive beast—though 'tis true you did anger me vastly!"

"How?" he questioned, drawing her yet nearer.

"You would not heed my signals—my fan, my handkerchief, both unregarded."

"Fan?" he repeated. "Handkerchief? You mean—Egad!" His fervent arms grew suddenly lax and he sighed. "Dear," said he, shaking rueful head, "I fear you do find me very obtuse, very dull and stupid, not at all the man— —"

"The only man!" she whispered.

"But to think I could be so dense, such an unutterable blockhead, such a— —" Here my lady in her turn stopped his self-reproaches and thereafter, taking him by two curls of his great periwig, one either side, nodded lovely head at him.

"Though indeed, 'tis true sir, I was a little put out— —"

"And no wonder!" he agreed. "Any other man would ha' known and understood. But I, being nought but a simple— —" Again she sealed his lips, this time with one white finger.

"Nay, Major John sir—I do protest your grave simplicity hath a potent charm in a wilderness of wits and beaux! 'Twas that same, methinks did first attract me, for dear John, hear me confess, I have loved thee from our first meeting—to-day I honour thee also. Dost mind that first hour—when you caught me stealing your cherries? Dost remember, John?"

"Aye, truly," he answered, "'twas in that hour happiness found me—a happiness I had never thought to know!" Here, meeting his ardent gaze, she flushed and drooped her lashes, yet nestled closer.

"John," she whispered, "thou'rt so placid as a rule, so serene and calm yet, methinks there might come a time when I—should—fear thee—almost. Our love is not politely *à la mode*, John!"

"Nor ever could be!" he answered.

"'Tis thing so wondrous great John, that I do tremble—and you—you too, John! Ah prithee loose me awhile. Love is so vastly different from what I dreamed—'tis methinks a happiness nigh to pain. And yet our love hath not run so smooth dear, there have been doubts, and fears, and misconceptions and—mayhap John, there shall be more."

"Heaven forefend, sweet. For indeed thou art my light, without thee this world were place of emptiness and gloom and I a lonely wanderer lost and all foredone. Ah Betty, since love looked at me through thine eyes life hath become to me a thing so precious— —"

"Yet you would peril it, John, and with thy life my happiness."

"Nay, but my Betty— —"

"Aye, but my John, this shall not be! Think you I'll permit that you hazard yourself— —"

"But, dear heart, I have a plan very excellent——"

"So have I, John, a plan more excellent, nay—most!"

"But sweeting, I am here to——"

"To listen to me, of course, my Jack. See now, Charles is my brother and if danger come I, as his sister, am proud and willing to share it with him or to—endure much for his sake. But dear, whiles I live none other shall jeopardise life or fortune in his behalf, on this I am determined and he also. Besides, I have a plan, a wondrous plan, John, shall save my dear Charles from all the soldiers 'twixt here and London town. If they will search my house—let them, but they shall not find him. And after, when he's strong enough, he shall win to France and none to give him let or stay. Moreover John I shall be very sweetly avenged in certain trifling matter. Nay—no questions sir, only meddle not in this and, beyond all, have faith in thy Betty."

The sun had set long since, evening deepened into night but, when he would have gone, she stayed him with gentle hands, with sighs and plaintive murmurs.

"'Tis not yet late ... life holdeth so few hours the like of this ... and John dear, I do feel troubles are nigh us ... doubts, John ... sorrows belike... And yet surely our love is too great... But if you should ... hear aught of evil ... or ... should see——"

"Betty—O Betty, alas, alas!" It was Lady Belinda's voice and in it a note that brought Betty to her feet, suddenly pale and trembling. "Betty, O Betty!" With the cry on her lips Lady Belinda appeared in the half-light hurrying towards them distractedly and wringing her hands as she came: "Alas, Betty!"

"Yes, aunt—dear heaven, what's amiss?"

"'Tis Charles—our dear Charles!"

"What—what of him?"

"O Betty, he's—gone!"

"Gone? But aunt 'tis impossible, his door was locked——"

"Aye, but the window—the window! He's gone, Betty—ropes and things—bed-clothes and what not. O my heart! There they are—dangling from the window—to and fro. But poor, naughty, wilful Charles is gone!"

CHAPTER XXX
CONCERNING CHARLES, EARL OF MEDHURST

If my lady Betty was of a determined temper, my lord of Medhurst was no less so; being set on ridding his sister of his dangerous presence he contrived, so soon as her back was turned, to effect his exit through the window by means of his bed-clothes and sundry odds and ends of rope and cord he had found in the attics.

Darkness having fallen, the frantic search for him being over and the coast at last clear, the earl proceeded to squirm and clamber out of the disused water-butt that had been his hiding-place, knocked the dust and cobwebs from his person (dressed somewhat roomily in a suit of Viscount Merivale's clothes) and glided away into the shadows of the garden swift and silent as any ghost. Reaching the wall he scaled it lightly, paused to sweep off his hat and to blow a kiss towards his sister's window, then dropped into the lane; followed it a little way and, turning aside into the fields set off at a smart pace. Very soon he reached a small wood and had advanced but a little way in among the trees when his quick ears warned him that others were here before him; a bush rustled at no great distance and he caught the sound of a voice hoarse and subdued:

"... heard someone behind us I say!"

"'Twere a bird Joe, wood be full of 'em. 'Taren't our man, he'll come by th' field-path—hist! What's yon?" My lord's eyes sparkled as, settling his hat more firmly, he loosened sword in scabbard and stepped daintily into the open. Then came a sudden rustling of leaves, the muffled thud of hasty feet, and, by light of the rising moon, his lordship saw a tangle of vague forms, that twisted and writhed, and arms that rose and fell viciously; out came his steel and with the long, narrow blade a-glitter he leapt forward shouting blithely as he ran. He was close upon the combatants when one staggered and fell, another was beaten to his knees and then the earl was upon them. Now a light small-sword is an awkward weapon to meet the swashing blows of heavy bludgeons; therefore his lordship kept away, avoiding their rushes and fierce strokes by quickness of foot and dexterity of body; twice his twinkling point had darted vainly but his third thrust was answered by a snarling cry of pain and incontinent his two assailants took to their heels, whereupon his lordship uttered a joyous shout and leapt in pursuit but was staggered by a blow from behind and, reeling aside, saw his third assailant make off after the others. My lord feeling suddenly faint and sick, cursed feebly and dropped his sword then, hearing a groan near by, staggered across to the fallen man.

Thus Sergeant Zebedee presently opening his eyes looked up into the face above him, a face pallid in the moonlight and with a dark smear of blood on the cheek. Hereupon the Sergeant blinked, sat up and stared.

"Zounds!" he exclaimed. "If you ain't the poacher as vanished into air all I say is—Zooks!" His lordship nodded and smiled faintly.

"How goes it, Sergeant?" he questioned, swaying strangely from side to side as he knelt.

"A woundy rap o' the nob d'ye see lad, and more o' the same front and rear, but no worse thanks t'you and now—Gog and Magog, hold up lad! What, ha' they got you too?" His lordship tried to laugh but failing, smiled instead:

"Got me—aye!" he mumbled, "I—almost think—I'm going——" The words ended in a sigh and my lord Medhurst slipped limply to the ground and lay there. Muttering oaths in English, French and Dutch the Sergeant set hands to throbbing head and staring blankly about spied the sword near by; took it up, examined the point instinctively and nodding grimly contrived to set it back in scabbard. Then taking the inert figure in practised hold lifted him to broad shoulder and trudged sturdily off; but as he went the throbbing in his head seemed like hammer-strokes that deafened, that blinded him; yet on he strode nor paused nor stayed until the welcome lights of the Manor gleamed before him. As he plodded heavily on, he became aware of a voice hailing him above the thunderous hammer-strokes and he paused, reeling:

"Zeb, Sergeant Zebedee!"

"Here, sir!" he gasped hoarsely. Next moment the Major was beside him:

"Suffer me, Zebedee," said he, and taking the insensible form in his powerful arms, led the way into the house and so to the library, the Sergeant plodding doggedly in his rear. Laying his inert lordship upon a settee, the Major summoned Mrs. Agatha, who, seeing the Sergeant bruised and bloody screamed once, below her breath, and immediately became all womanly dexterity. Softly, swiftly she bustled to and fro; first came cordials and glasses, thereafter a bowl of water, sponges and soft linen and very soon beneath her able and gentle ministrations the earl sighed, opened languid eyes and sitting up, stared about him while Mrs. Agatha promptly turned her attention to the battered Sergeant.

"Faith, sir," said my lord apologetically, "I—I fear I was so foolish as to swoon——"

"But saved my life first, your honour," added the Sergeant, dodging Mrs. Agatha's sponge to say so, "and winged one o' the rogues into the bargain."

"Then sir," said the Major, "my deepest gratitude is yours. Sergeant Zebedee is—is an old comrade of mine a—a comrade and—and so forth as 'twere, my lord Medhurst."

Here the Sergeant blinked and opened his mouth so wide that Mrs. Agatha felt impelled to promptly fill it with the sponge.

"I trust sir," continued the Major, "you feel yourself a little recovered of your hurts?"

"O infinitely sir—quite, quite!" answered the earl and getting to his feet, staggered and sat down again. "A small vertigo sir, a trifling dizziness," he explained, more apologetically than ever, "but 'twill soon pass."

"Meantime," suggested the Major, viewing his pallor with sharp eyes, "I will, with your permission, send and notify my lady Carlyon of her brother's welfare."

Here, by reason of astonishment and Mrs. Agatha's sponge the Sergeant spluttered and choked:

"As to that sir," answered the earl, fidgeting, "I—faith! I had rather you didn't. And indeed, since you know who I am, 'twill be immediately apparent to you that the farther I am from Betty and the sooner I quit your roof, the better for all concerned——"

"On the contrary, sir," said the Major, "'tis for that very reason I offer you the shelter of my roof until——"

A rush of flying feet along the passage without, a fumbling knock and the door flying open discovered one of the maids her eyes round and staring in fearful excitement:

"Soldiers!" she cried, "O sir—O Mrs. Agatha—'tis the soldiers—all round the house—lanthorns and guns—I do be frighted to death!"

Mrs. Agatha dropped the sponge and uttering no word, pointed one plump finger at the frightened girl and stamped her foot; and before that ominous finger the trembling maid shrank and turning about incontinent fled, slamming the door behind her. For a breathless moment none moved. Then Medhurst rose a little unsteadily, glancing round rueful and helpless.

"So then—'tis ended!" he sighed. "My poor, sweet Bet! And you sir—you—my God, I must not be taken here for your sake!" and he sprang towards the window.

"Stay sir," said the Major gently, "'tis no use, the house is surrounded of course. Aye, I thought so——!" He nodded as in the dark beyond the curtained windows came the measured tramp of feet, a hoarse command and the ring of grounded muskets.

"Sir—sir," exclaimed Lord Medhurst, "God forgive me that I all unwitting as I was, should bring you to this black hazard."

"Nay, my lord," answered the Major, smiling into the earl's troubled face, "grieve not yourself on my account, 'twas I brought you hither knowing who you were, so do not reproach yourself, 'tis but the fortune of war. Hark, they are here, I think——"

"Then I'll go meet 'em!" said his lordship, "I'll give myself up—they shall never—take me!"

"Well said, sir," nodded the Major, his brow unruffled and serene, "we'll go together! Pray, Sergeant, open the door!"

"Don't, Sergeant, don't!" panted Mrs. Agatha, "wait—O—wait!" Thus, speaking, she sped across the room and, kneeling before the great fireplace, seemed to feel along the carved foliage of the mantel with frenzied fingers, then uttered a gasp of satisfaction: "Quick—quick my lord!" she panted. And even as she spoke the great hearthstone sank down endwise turning upon itself and disclosing a narrow flight of steps. The earl uttered a sound between a laugh and a sob, turned aside to take up hat and sword and, descending into the gloomy depths, glanced up blithe of eye and waved his hand as the stone swung back into place above him.

Then Mrs. Agatha rose, dusted her silken gown with her pretty white hands and curtseyed:

"Your honour," said she, "with your leave, I'll run out to my poor, silly, frighted maids!" and taking up bowl and sponges while the Sergeant opened the door, she rustled away. With the door still in his hand, Sergeant Zebedee turned to stare at the Major and found the Major staring at him.

"Sir," said he at last, "sir, she's—a——" here he paused to shake solemn head, "sir, she's the—sir—she—is—a—woman!"

"Zeb," answered the Major, sinking into a chair, "she—most—undoubtedly—is!"

But now the house was full of strange stir and hubbub, the tread and tramp of heavy feet, the clatter of accoutrements, and the ring of iron-shod muskets on stone-flagged hall.

"Sir," questioned the Sergeant, putting on his wig and re-settling his rumpled garments, "shall I go out to 'em?"

"Do so, Zeb, and bring the officer to me—here, in the library."

The officer in question, a tall and languid exquisite, found the Major at his desk, who, setting aside his papers, rose to give him courteous greeting.

"Ged, sir," he exclaimed returning the Major's stately bow, "you'll f'give this dem'd intrusion I trust—I'm Prothero, Captain o' Cleeve's, your very dutiful humble. You are Major d'Arcy, I think?"

"The same, sir, and yours to command."

"Let me perish, sir, 'tis an honour to meet you I vow and protest. Colonel Cleeve hath spoke of you—I've heard of you in Flanders also. All o' which doth but make an unpleasant duty—dem'd unpleasant. Regarding the which I may tell you that my lord Colonel is so put out over the business that he hath absented himself until our search here shall be over. But this Jacobite f'low is known to be i' these parts and my orders are to search every house— —"

"And orders are to be obeyed!" smiled the Major. "Let your men search, sir, and meantime a glass or so of Oporto perhaps— —?"

"Ged sir, your kindness smites me t' the heart I vow."

The bottle having duly been brought and the glasses filled the Captain rose and proposed:

"Sir, I give you 'Our Admirable Betty!' 'Tis a health much discussed in these parts o' late I believe, sir," said he, "aye and in London too. And the dem'dest strangest part on't is the man we hunt is her own brother—no less, sir! And since he is so here's wings to his heels say I, curst Jacobite though he be. But when a man is blessed with such a sister damn his politics, say I. And O Cupid, sir, what a crayture! Her shape! Her air! Her pretty, little, dem'd demure foot! I give you her foot, sir. And the pride of her! The grace of her! The dem'd bewitching enchanting entirety of her. I vow 'tis the dem'dest, charmingest piece o' feminine loveliness that ever lured mankind t' demnition. Demme sir, she's the sort o' goddess-crayture that gets into a f'low's blood—goes t' f'low's head like wine sir, makes a f'low forget duty, kindred, country, honour and even himself."

"You have searched my lady's house, I take it?" enquired the Major.

"Faith we have so, sir,—and herself to light us up-stairs and down. So gracious sir! *So très debonnaire!* So smiling and altogether dem'd sedoocing—O Lard!"

On this wise the Captain held forth until the wine was all gone, and his corporal came to announce that the house had been duly and thoroughly searched from cellar to attic, without success: whereupon the Captain rose, shook the Major's hand—babbled forth more apologies in melting, mellifluous accents, roared at his men and finally marched them out of the house and away.

CHAPTER XXXI
WHICH DESCRIBES SOMETHING OF
MY LADY BETTY'S GRATITUDE

The Major, leaning back somnolent in his great elbow-chair, fingers joined and head bowed, listened lethargically to the Sergeant who, sitting bolt upright, read aloud from the manuscript he held.

"'Vauban, in his instructions on the siege of Aeth, giveth notice of sundry salient angles all fortified, the most open by bastions, the others, and those of at least ninety degrees, by demi-bastions——'"

Here the Major snored but so gently that the Sergeant, whose whole attention was centred on the written words, was proceeding all unaware when a small, roundish object hurtled across the room, smote the Major softly upon the cheek and fell to the floor; hereupon the Major opened sleepy eyes.

"Certainly, Zeb!" said he. "Egad you're in the right on't—er—I fear my attention was wandering as 'twere—though I listen very well with my eyes shut!"

The Sergeant lowered the manuscript to stare, round-eyed:

"Anan, sir?" he enquired.

"Go on again, Zeb—this chapter on Salient Angles must be clear and concise as possible. Proceed, Zebedee—we'd got as far as the siege of Aeth, I think." Saying which, the Major closed his eyes again and Sergeant Zebedee, nothing loth, went on:

"'—the most open by bastions, the others, and those of at least ninety degrees, by demi——'"

Once again a small missile flew with unerring aim, struck the Major on the chin and rebounded on to the desk.

The Major started, rubbed his eyes and sat up.

"What now, Zeb?" he enquired. The Sergeant, lowering the manuscript again, stared harder than ever.

"Sir?" he enquired.

"Something—er—touched me I think Zeb!"

"Touched you, sir! Zounds, here's but you and me, your honour!"

"Strange!" mused the Major, rubbing his chin, "very strange, Zeb, I must ha' dreamed it, though I distinctly felt——" He leaned forward suddenly and picked up from the desk before him a half-opened moss rosebud. With this in his fingers he turned towards the open casement behind the Sergeant's chair and beheld a face, all roguish witchery and laughter, and two white hands held out to him.

"Help me in, John—help me in!" she commanded. In an instant the Major was across the room, had clasped those slender hands and my lady, mounting the low sill, stood a moment framed in the heavy moulding of the long window, a very picture of vigorous young womanhood; then leaping lightly down with flashing vision of dainty feet and ankles, she crossed to where the Sergeant stood, very erect and upright, and setting her two hands upon his broad shoulders, smiled up at him radiant-eyed.

"Sergeant Zebedee," said she, "dear Sergeant Zebedee you must be vastly strong to have carried my brother so far. Stoop down!"

Wondering, the Sergeant obeyed and immediately felt the pressure of two warm, soft lips on his smooth-shaven cheek; whereupon he flushed, blinked and stood at attention. "Did you like it, Sergeant?" she enquired.

"My lady, all I can say is—mam I—I did, your ladyship."

"Then stoop again, Sergeant!" With an apologetic glance towards the Major he obeyed and my lady kissed his other cheek. Then she turned and looked at the Major with glistening eyes. "O!" she cried, "I am come overflowing with gratitude to you all for my dear brother's sake. I owe you his life—but for you he—he would be——" Her deep bosom swelled and she bowed her head. "Charles is very—very dear to me and—you saved him to me. O pray, John, may I see Mrs. Agatha?"

Here, at a sign from the Major, Sergeant Zebedee strode from the room shutting the door carefully behind him: and as it closed they were in each other's arms.

"Jack!" she murmured. "My noble John!"

"Nay, beloved," he sighed, "dream not 'twas I. Sergeant Zebedee found him and but for Mrs. Agatha——"

"O my scrupulous man, art afraid lest I do think too well of thee? Art frighted lest I give thee more gratitude than thy just due? Indeed but

Charles hath told me all and I do know 'twas these arms bore him 'neath thy roof, 'twas thy brave heart sheltered him and was ready to face ignominy with him. But indeed if you have no—no will to—kiss me——" The Major kissed her until she sued for mercy. Thereafter, throned in his great chair, she surveyed the bare chamber with gentle eyes: "'Tis a great house, John," she nodded, "and this, a barren corner—and yet, meseemeth, 'tis not so—so outrageously desolate as it was."

"My Betty," he answered, "I do but live for the time when it shall be brightened by thy sweet presence, its floors know the light tread of these dear feet, its walls the music of thy voice and—thy love make it 'home' for me at last."

"'Deed John but you do grow poetical—though perchance thy style might not please Sir Benjamin or Sir Jasper or—O John how I have laughed and laughed——"

Here came a gentle rapping on the door and being bidden enter, Mrs. Agatha appeared demure and smiling, dropped a curtsey to the Major, another to my lady and then she was caught in gentle embrace and kissed.

"Why Mrs. Agatha!" exclaimed my lady, "dear Mrs. Agatha, how pretty you are! 'Tis seldom wit and beauty go together! Thank you, my dear, for a brother's life. For service so great there are no words—nought to repay. But take this and wear it in memory of a sister's gratitude!" And speaking, my lady took a necklet from her own white throat and clasped it about Mrs. Agatha's neck. "But for you," she sighed, "but for you I should have lost my only brother and—" my lady faltered, then, meeting Mrs. Agatha's gentle glance, threw up proud head, "and one I love—beyond all!"

"My lady—O my lady!" cried Mrs. Agatha, "Heaven send you happiness now and ever—both!" Then stooping, she kissed my lady's hand and was gone.

My lady crossed the room and seated herself in the Major's great elbow-chair while he, sitting on a corner of the desk gazed down at her with eyes of rapture.

"Well, Major John?"

"How—beautiful you are!" he sighed and she actually blushed and bowed her head.

"O—John!" she whispered.

"Surely many have told you so before?"

"Hosts, of course, dear Major!" she nodded.

"Aye, I fear I'm not very original," he sighed, "I'm awkward, I know, tongue-tied and mute when I would speak; but dear, my love doth 'whelm me so—poor, futile words are lost——"

"'Deed, sir," she answered demurely, "I find no fault with your powers of converse more especially when you grow personal. That remark, now, 'beautiful' was the word I think, being a woman such will never tire me—as you say them."

"Yet I do but echo what others have said before me."

"Aye, but you say it as no other man ever did—you speak it so sincerely and reverently as it had been a prayer, John."

"God knoweth I'm sincere, Betty."

"So do I, John," and taking the rosebud from the desk she began to open its petals with gentle fingers. So the Major sat gazing at her, wishing that she would lift her eyes and she, knowing this, kept them lowered of course.

"John," said she at last.

"Betty?"

"Sometimes you do seem almost—afraid to—touch me."

"I am."

"And wherefore?"

"Because even now there are times when I scarce can credit my wondrous happiness, scarce believe you can really love—such as I——"

"None the less I shall convince you once and for all—one day, Master Humility!"

And now she lifted her head at last and looked at him, and, thrilling to the revelation of that look, he leaned swiftly down to her, but then she put up gentle hand and stayed him.

"John," she murmured, "dear, when you look at me so you are not a bit humble, I know not if I fear you or—love you most. Stay, John, if my hair should come down and anyone see I—O then quick, John—there's aunt calling! Let us join the company ere we are fetched like truants. She is out on the terrace with Pancras and Mr. Marchdale who is a trifle trying at times being over-youthful and very soberly adoring. 'Chaste hour, soft hour, O hour when first we met!'" she quoted. "Indeed," she laughed, "'tis a very worshipful, humble youth so very unlike——"

"Mr. Dalroyd!" said the Major thoughtfully.

My lady started, the rosebud fell from relaxed fingers and she glanced up with a look in her eyes that might have been mistaken for sudden fear.

"Why—why do you name—him?" she questioned dully; but before he could answer came a knock at the door and Mrs. Agatha appeared to say that "tea was a-drinking on the terrace!"

They found Lady Belinda seated on the terrace before a tea equipage with Mrs. Agatha and a footman in attendance while beside her sat the Viscount, one arm in a sling, dutifully sipping a dish of tea and making wry faces over it.

"Gad love me, 'tis the washiest stuff!" he sighed.

"O dear Major, hark to the naughty wanton!" cried Lady Belinda as the Major bowed over her hand, "First he nigh breaks his neck knocking at fences and now miscalleth tea!"

"Knocks at fences, aunt?"

"Truly, he tells me his horse budged, took off something or other, was very short about it, knocked at a fence and fell—which is not to be wondered at."

"Faith, Viscount," said Mr. Marchdale looking puzzled "'tis a fierce and dangerous beast that grey o' yours but I don't quite see——"

"Nay," smiled the Viscount, "'twas that stiffish fence beyond Meadowbrook Bottom—the Colonel put his Arab at it and cleared but my grey balked, took off short, rapped, came down on his head and I came by a sprained arm and shoulder."

"'Twas all that Colonel Cleeve's fault, I dare swear," cried Lady Belinda, "he's a wild soul, I fear!"

"On the contrary, Aunt Belinda, he's a very noble fellow. And he bade me be sure carry you his humble duty." Here Lady Belinda blushed quite becomingly and perceiving the Viscount had contrived to swallow his tea, forthwith filled him more despite his expostulations.

"Drink it, Pancras," she commanded, "'tis soothing and sedative and good for everything—see how healthy the Chinamen are—so polite too and placid, I vow!"

"I'd no idea, mam," said the Major, "no idea that you and my old friend George were acquaint."

"It happened yesterday sir, in Sevenoaks, Sir Benjamin made us known."

"Talking of the Colonel," said Mr. Marchdale, "the village is all agog over the soldiers—they searched your house as well as my lady's I understand, sir?"

"They did!" nodded the Major.

"Consequently everybody is wondering what i' the world they wanted."

"Why Charles for sure!" answered Lady Betty, "they seemed to think we had him in hiding."

"Charles!" exclaimed Mr. Marchdale opening his mouth and staring, "O—Egad they—they didn't find him, of course!"

"No, and I pray God they never will, wherever he may be."

"Have you seen or heard from him since he rode for Scotland?" enquired Mr. Marchdale. "Because I——"

"More tea, Mr. Marchdale?" demanded Lady Belinda. Mr. Marchdale's feeble refusals were overruled and he was treated beside to a long exordium on the beneficent qualities of the herb, the while he gulped down the beverage to the Viscount's no small satisfaction. As for the Major, he was looking at Betty and she at him, and the Viscount's quick glance happening to rove their way and noting the look in the Major's eyes and the answering flush on her smooth cheek the Viscount's own eyes opened very wide, he pursed his lips in a soundless whistle and thereafter studiously glanced another way.

"Major d'Arcy sir," said Mr. Marchdale, gulping his tea and blinking, "I am come with an embassage to you, Tripp and the rest of us present their service and beg you'll join us at cards this evening—nothing big, a guinea or so——"

"Aye, go, nunky," nodded the Viscount, "I'm going over to try some new songs with Betty." Here Mr. Marchdale sighed heavily.

All too soon for the Major the ladies arose to take their departure.

"We are hoping, dear Major," said Lady Belinda, "that you will come in to supper one evening soon, you and Pancras——"

"With Colonel Cleeve, if he chance to be here still," added Betty.

The gentlemen bowed, the ladies curtseyed, and descended the terrace steps all stately dignity and gracious ease.

Left alone the Major stood awhile to enjoy the beauty of the sunset-sky and to sigh over the past hour; then slowly went into the house.

In the study he found Sergeant Zebedee who stood tentatively beside the desk.

"I was thinking, sir," said he, "that seeing the company is gone we might contrive to get through your chapter on Salient Angles at last!"

"A happy thought, Zeb—by all means."

So they sat down together then and there and the Sergeant took up the manuscript. It was then that the Major spied the fallen rosebud and glancing at the Sergeant stooped and picked it up almost furtively though all the Sergeant's attention was focussed, like his eyes, upon the foolscap in his hand; so, leaning back in his chair the Major raised the bud to reverent lips watching Sergeant Zebedee the while, who, clearing his throat with a loud "Hem!" began to read forthwith:

"'Vauban, in his instructions on the siege of Aeth, giveth notice of sundry salient angles all fortified, the most open by bastions, the others, and those of at least ninety degrees, by demi-bastions...'"

CHAPTER XXXII
FLINT AND STEEL

The Major, puffing thoughtfully at his pipe and hearkening to Sir Benjamin's ponderous witticisms, kept his sharp eyes on the card-players opposite, Mr. Marchdale flushed and eager, the Marquis smiling and good-humoured, Lord Alvaston sleepy as usual and Mr. Dalroyd blandly imperturbable.

"Then, my dear sir, I gather you judge well o' that little flight o' mine t'other night?" enquired Sir Benjamin, "I mean the acrostic alliterative, how did it go——"

'Bewitching Bet, by bounteous beauty blessed' —

you think well on't, Major, eh?"

"Indeed sir, 'twas very ingenious."

"Od's body, sir, I think you've a judgment to be commended, I venture to opine it was ingenious—and therewith not lacking in wit, sir?"

"By no means, Sir Benjamin."

"To be sure the last line might be bettered, though it cost me a world o' thought. 'Twas if I remember:

'Yea you, yourself to yearn as beauty ought.'

Yet od's my life sir! I fail to see how it should be bettered. Y is an awkward, stubborn, damned implacable letter at best, sir."

"Truly a most awkward letter, Sir Benjamin."

Here Mr. Marchdale slammed down his cards petulantly.

"So!" he exclaimed, "that makes another fifteen guineas!"

"Twenty-five, my dear Marchdale!" smiled Mr. Dalroyd, taking up a new pack.

"How much ha' you lost, Alton?"

"Nothing much Tony, only ten or so."

"And you, Alvaston?"

"Nay I'm 'n odd guinea or so t' th' good, s' far," yawned his lordship.

"May I perish," exclaimed Mr. Marchdale, "but you and Dalroyd have all the luck, as usual!"

"I—I in luck?" exclaimed Alvaston, his sleepy eyes wider than usual, "stint y'r dreams and babble not, Tony! Whoe'er saw me win? Never had any measure o' luck since I was breeched, or before. And talking o' luck, Major, how goeth Merivale, how's poor Tom since his spill yesterday?"

"Bruised and sore, sir, but no worse, thank God. He'll be about again in a day or so."

"Tom rides like—like the devil, strike me blue if he don't!" said the Marquis.

"And just as reckless!" added Dalroyd.

"Aye, but here was none o' that. His horse balked a fence, rapped and went down with him. Brute'll kill him yet, damme if he don't!"

"Talking o' luck," pursued Alvaston, sorting his cards lazily, "never had any measure of it yet, either with cards, dice, horses or the sex. An' talkin' o' the sex, Tony my lad, what of its brightest and most particular, what of Bet, how speeds th' wooing?" Mr. Marchdale swore earnestly. "Oho!" murmured Alvaston, "doth she prove so cold and indifferent——"

"Neither one nor t'other, but I must ha' more time."

"Three days must suffice, Tony, 'twas so agreed. After you comes Ben and after Ben, Jasper and then after Jasper, West, with poor Ned and me left nowhere."

"Aye, but damme," quoth the Marquis, "what o' Dalroyd here?"

"Aye, where d'you come, Dalroyd?" queried Alvaston.

Mr. Dalroyd's nostrils worked and his white teeth gleamed. "I come nowhere, anywhere or everywhere," he answered, surveying his hearers beneath lowered eyelids. "A free-lance in love, I—to woo precisely how and where and—when, I choose." Here for an infinitesimal space of time his keen eye rested on the Major.

"You always were such a dem'd dumb dog!" quoth the Marquis.

"Close as 'n oyster!" murmured Alvaston.

"And he's lucky in cards and love, which ain't fair," grumbled Mr. Marchdale. "I've heard whispers of a handsome farmer's daughter not a hundred miles hence—eh, Dalroyd?"

"'Tis your turn to lead, Marchdale!" said Mr. Dalroyd, his lips a little grim.

"My fellow swears he saw you only t'other night—dev'lish late—with an armful o' loveliness——"

"You should kick your fellow for impertinence, Marchdale, and 'tis your turn to lead!"

"I'll be curst if I know what, then!" he exclaimed, slapping down a card at random. "There's Bet, now—and but one more day to win her! Who might win such a goddess in a day, 'tis preposterous——"

"I've heard," smiled Mr. Dalroyd, "yes, I've heard of women being won in less. And as to goddesses, Endymion sighed not vainly nor over long."

"Why as to that I progress—O I progress!" nodded Mr. Marchdale with youthful assertiveness, "she's all witching laughter and affection——"

"Unhappy wight!" exclaimed Mr. Dalroyd.

"Eh?" exclaimed Mr. Marchdale, wine-glass at lip, "How so?"

"Kind Venus save me from affection feminine!" smiled Dalroyd, "Where affection is passion is not. So give me burning love or passionate hate and she is mine."

"Od Dalroyd," interposed Sir Benjamin indignantly, "I say od's my life, sir, here's wooing most unorthodox, most unseemly i' faith!"

"But natural, Ben," retorted Dalroyd, "women love or hate as the wind bloweth. Your loving woman is very well though apt to cloy, but your hater—O Ben! Besides, all women love a little force—to force 'em willing is child's play, to force 'em hating—ah Ben, that methinks is man's play."

"Out on you, sir!" exclaimed Sir Benjamin. "Is it thus you'd win our incomparable, Our Admirable Betty?" Mr. Dalroyd threw down his cards and leaning back in his chair surveyed the indignant Sir Benjamin with his fleeting smile.

"She is a woman, Ben, and therefore to be won one way or t'other." And here once again his keen gaze rested momentarily on the Major's passive figure. As for Sir Benjamin, his face grew purple, his great peruke seemed to bristle again.

"Enough sir!" he cried, "Are we satyrs, hairy and unpolished, to creep, to crouch, to win by forceful fury what trembling beauty would deny? I say no sir—I say the day of such is long gone by I—I appeal to Major d'Arcy!"

The Major, being thus addressed, blew forth a cloud of smoke, fanned it away with his hand and spoke in his measured, placid tones:

"I fear sir, even in these days satyrs walk among us now and then though indeed they have covered their hairy and unpolished hides 'neath velvets and fine linen and go a-satyrizing delicately pulvilled. Yet woman, I take it, hath been granted eyes to see the brute 'neath all his dainty trappings."

Here there fell a moment's silence, for the company, quick to sense the sudden tenseness in the air, sat in rapt expectation of what was to be; perceiving which Mr. Dalroyd smiled again and the Major went on smoking. At last, when he judged the silence had endured long enough, Mr. Dalroyd spoke:

"Major d'Arcy, Ben's simile is perchance a little harsh, for he would have us all satyrs, in that at some time or other, every man doth seek, pursue and hunt the lovely sex to his own selfish end. Even you yourself, I dare swear, have dreamed dreams, have beheld a vision of some dainty beauty you would fain possess. I have, I do confess. Now, doth she yield—well and good! Doth she fly us, we pursue. And do we catch her—well, hate and love are kindred passions, nay indeed, hate is love's refinement, though both are passing moods. Indeed some women are preferable in the hating moods— to know the woman in one's arms hates one, there, sir, so 'tis said, is the very refinement of pleasure."

"Sir," said the Major gently, "I heard one say as much in Flanders years agone and I did my best to kill him and thought I had succeeded, but of late I have begun to entertain grave doubts and never more so than at this minute." Here fell a silence absolute.

Mr. Dalroyd's white lids flickered and into his eyes came a bodeful glare as he met the Major's placid but unswerving gaze and as they fronted each other thus, there fell a silence so absolute that the tick of a clock in distant corner sounded uncannily loud—a chair creaked, a foot scraped the floor, but save for this was silence, threatening and ominous, while Mr. Dalroyd glared at the Major and the Major, leaning back in his chair, stared at Mr. Dalroyd as if he would read the very soul of him. All at once came a whirr of springs and the clock began to chime midnight whereupon was sudden relaxation, chairs were moved, arms and legs stretched themselves.

"Od's my life—midnight already!" exclaimed Sir Benjamin in very apparent relief.

"Aye, faith!" yawned Alvaston, "Now is the witching hour when graveyards yawn——"

"No, no, Bob!" laughed Dalroyd, "Now is the witching hour when beauty coy doth flush and furtive steal to raptures dreamed by day. Now is the witching hour when satyrs in compelling arms— —" he yawned, smiled and rose. "Howbeit sirs, I am summoned hence— —"

"Ah—ah!" nodded Marchdale, "The farmer's daughter—the beauty o' the blue cloak—ha, lucky dog!"

"A blue cloak!" repeated Mr. Dalroyd, "Egad, your fellow's too infernally observant, Marchdale, you should really kick him a little." So saying, Mr. Dalroyd crossed to the corner and took up his sword, "Adieu gentlemen," said he, "I go, shall we say, a-satyrizing—no, 'twould shock our Ben, none the less I—go. Gentlemen, I salute you!" And bowing to the room Mr. Dalroyd sauntered away.

"Burn me!" exclaimed Alvaston, "the wine's near out, let's order up 'nother dozen or so an' make a night on't." This being agreed, the bottles presently made their appearance, glasses clinked and the company began to grow merry. But after two or three toasts had been called and honoured, the Major arose, made his excuses, and calling for his hat, sword and cane, presently took his departure.

CHAPTER XXXIII
DESCRIBING SOMETHING OF COQUETRY AND A DAWN

It was a glorious summer night, the moon riding high in a cloudless heaven, a night full of a tranquil quietude and filled with the thousand scents of dewy earth. Before him stretched the wide road, a silver causeway fretted with shadows, a silent road where nothing moved save himself.

Thus, joying in the beauty of the night, Major d'Arcy walked slowly and took a roundabout course, and a distant clock chimed the hour of one as he found himself traversing a small copse that abutted on his own property.

In this place of light and shadow a nightingale poured forth his liquid notes rilling the leafy mysteries with ecstatic song; here the Major paused and setting his back to a tree, stood awhile to hearken, lost in a profound reverie.

And into this little wood came two who walked very close together and spoke in rapt murmurs; near they came and nearer until the Major started and looking up beheld a woman who wore a blue cloak and whose face, hidden beneath her hood, was turned up to the eager face of him who went beside her. The Major, scowling and disgusted thus to have stumbled upon a vulgar amour and fearing to be seen, waited impatiently for them to be gone. But they stopped within a few yards of him, half screened from view behind a tangle of bushes. Hot with his disgust, the Major turned to steal away, heard a cry of passionate protest, and glancing back, saw the woman caught in sudden fierce arms, viciously purposeful, and drawn swiftly out of sight.

"Mr. Dalroyd," said my lady gently, lying passive in his embrace, "pray turn your head." Wondering, he obeyed and stared into the muzzle of a small pocket pistol. "Dear Mr. Dalroyd—must I kill you?" she smiled; and he, beholding the indomitable purpose in that lovely, smiling face, gnashed white teeth and loosing her, stood back as the Major appeared.

For a tense moment no one moved, then with an inarticulate sound Mr. Dalroyd took a swift backward step, his hand grasping the hilt of his small-sword; but the Major had drawn as quick as he and the air seemed full of the blue flash and glitter of eager steel. Then, even as the swift blades rang together, my lady had slipped off her cloak and next moment the murderous points were entangled, caught, and held in the heavy folds.

"Shame sirs, O shame!" she cried. "Will you do murder in my very sight? Loose—loose your hold, both of you—loose, I say!" Here my lady, shaking the entangled blades in passionate hands, stamped her foot in fury. The Major, relinquishing his weapon, stepped back and bowed like the grand gentleman he was; then Mr. Dalroyd did the same and so they stood facing each other, my lady between them, the bundled cloak and weapons clasped to her swelling bosom; and it was to be remarked that while Mr. Dalroyd kept his ardent gaze bent upon her proud loveliness, the Major, tall and stately, never so much as glanced at her.

"Sir," said he, "our quarrel will keep awhile, I think?"

"Keep—aye sir!" nodded the other carelessly, "you'll remark the farmers in these parts beget goddesses for daughters, sir."

"Major d'Arcy," said my lady, "take your sword, sir."

The Major, keeping his eyes averted, sheathed the weapon and forthwith turned his back; and as he limped heavily away was aware of Dalroyd's amused laughter. He walked slowly and more than once blundered into a tree or tripped over manifest obstacles like one whose eyesight is denied him, and ever as he went Mr. Dalroyd's triumphant laughter seemed to ring in his ears.

Thus at last he came out of the shadow of the little wood, but now was aware of the tread of quick, light feet behind him, felt a hand upon his arm and found my lady at his side. Then he stopped and drawing from her contact glanced back and saw Mr. Dalroyd watching them from the edge of the coppice, his arms folded and the smile still curling his lips; my lady saw him also and with a passionate gesture bade him begone, whereupon he flourished off his hat, laughed again, and bowing profoundly, vanished amid the trees. Then they went on side by side, my lady quick-breathing, the Major grim and stately—a very grand gentleman indeed.

At last they reached a lane whose high banks sheltered them from all chance of observation; here my lady paused.

"O John," she murmured, "I'm so—so weary, prithee don't hurry me so!" The Major, mute and grim, stared straight before him. "John?" said she tenderly. At this he turned and looked at her and before that look my lady cried out and cowered away. "John!" she cried in frightened wonderment.

"Madam," said he, "why are you here, I sought you not? If you are for dallying, go back—back to your——" He clenched his teeth on the word and turned away. "If mam, if you are—for home to-night I'll see you so far. Pray let us go." And he strode impatiently forward, but presently, seeing her stand where he had left her, pale and forlorn, frowned and stood hesitating.

Here my lady, feeling the situation called for tears, sank down upon the grassy bank beside the way and forthwith wept distractingly; though had any been there to notice, it might have been remarked that her eyes did not swell and her delicate nose did not turn red—yet she wept with whole-hearted perseverance.

The Major grew restless, he looked up the lane and he looked down the lane, he turned scowling eyes aloft to radiant moon and down to shadowy earth; finally he took one long pace back towards her.

"Madam!" said he.

My lady sobbed and bowed her lovely head. The Major approached another step.

"My lady!" he remonstrated.

My lady gasped and crouched lower. The Major approached nearer yet.

"Mam!"

My lady choked and sank full length upon the mossy turf. The Major stooped above her.

"Betty!" said he anxiously. "You—you're never swooning?"

"O John!" she said in strangled voice.

"Great heavens!" he exclaimed. "Art ill—sick——?"

"At—at heart, John!" she murmured, stealing a look at his anxious face. The Major stood suddenly erect, frowning a little.

"Madam!" said he. A deep sigh. "My lady—mam——"

"Do not—call me so!"

"You'll take a rheum—a cold, lying there—'tis a heavy dew!"

"Why then I will—let me, John."

"Pray get up, mam—my lady."

"Never, John!"

"Why then——" said he and paused to look up the lane once more.

"What, John?"

"You force me to——" He paused and glanced down the lane.

"To—what, John!"

"To carry you!"

"Never, John! For shame! Besides you couldn't. I'm a vast weight and——"

The Major picked her up, then and there, and began to carry her down the lane. And after they had gone some distance she sighed and with a little wriggle disposed herself more comfortably; and after they had gone further still he found two smooth, round arms about his neck and thereafter a soft breath at his ear.

"Pray don't be angry with your Betty, John dear." The Major stopped and stared down at her in the brilliant moonlight. Her eyes were closed, her rosy lips just apart, curving to a smile; he drew a sudden deep breath, and stooping his head, kissed her. For a long moment he held her thus, lip to lip, then all at once he set her down on her feet.

"Gad!" he cried, "what kind of woman are you to lure and mad me with your kisses——"

"Your woman, John."

"And yet—for aught I know——" the Major clenched his fists and pressed them on his eyes as if to shut out some hateful vision—"ah God, for aught I can be sure——"

"What, John?"

"He—he hath kissed you too, this night——"

"But he hath not, John—nor ever shall."

"Yet I saw you in his arms——" My lady sighed and bowed her head.

"The beast is always and ever the beast!" she said.

"How came you with him in a wood—after midnight?"

"For sufficient reasons, John."

"There never was reason sufficient—nay, not even your brother——"

"Nay dear John, I think different——"

"To peril that sweet body——" The Major choked.

"Nay, I'm very strong—and—and I have this!"

The Major scowled at the small, silver-mounted weapon and turned away.

"There is your maiden reputation— —"

"That is indeed mine own, and in good keeping. Grieve not your woeful head on that score."

"Ah Betty, why will you run such hazard— —"

"Because 'tis so my will, sir." The Major bowed.

"'Tis long past midnight, madam."

"Aye, 'tis a sweet hour—so still and solitary."

"Shall we proceed, madam?"

"At your pleasure, sir." So they went on side by side silently awhile, the Major a little grim and very stately.

"I do think John thou'rt very mannish at times."

"Mannish, madam?"

"Blind, overbearing and apt to be a little muddled."

The Major bowed. "For instance, John, methinks you do muddle a woman of will with a wilful woman." The Major bowed. "Now if, John, if in cause so just I should risk—not my body but my name—my fame, who shall stay me seeing I'm unwed and slave to no man yet—God be thanked." The Major bowed lower than ever and went beside her with his grandest air. "'Deed John," she sighed, "if you do grow any more dignified I fear you'll expire and perish o' pride and high-breeding."

The distant clock struck two as, turning down a certain bye-lane, the Major paused at a rustic door that gave into my lady's herb-garden. But when he would have opened it she stayed him.

"'Tis so late, John— —"

"Indeed 'tis very late, madam!"

"Too late to sleep this night. And such a night, John—the moon, O the moon!"

"What o' the moon, madam?"

"John d'Arcy I do protest if you bow or say 'madam' again I—I'll bite you! And the moon is—is—the moon and looks vastly romantic and infinite appealing. So will I walk and gaze upon her pale loveliness and sigh and sigh and—sigh again, sir."

"But indeed you cannot walk abroad—at this hour— —"

"Having the wherewithal I can sir, and I will, sir."

"But 'tis after two— —"

"Then sir, in but a little while it will be three, heigho, so wags the world—your arm pray, your arm."

"But my lady pray consider—your health—your— —"

"Fie sir and fiddlededee!"

"But the—the dew, 'tis very— —"

"Excellent for the complexion!" and she trilled the line of a song:

'O 'tis dabbling in the dew that makes the milkmaids fair.'

"But 'tis so—unseasonable! So altogether—er—irregular, as 'twere— —"

"Egad sir and you're i' the right on't!" she mocked. "'Tis unseasonable, unreasonable, unwomanly, unvirginal and altogether unthinkable as 'twere and so forth d'ye see! Major d'Arcy is probably pining for his downy bed. Major d'Arcy must continue to pine unless he will leave a poor maid to wander alone among bats and owls and newts and toads and worms and goblins and other noxious things— —"

"But Betty, indeed— —"

"Aye, John—indeed! To-night you did look on me as I had committed— as I had been—O 'twas a hateful look! And for that look I'll be avenged, and my vengeance is this, to wit—you shall sleep no wink this night! Your arm sir, come!"

Almost unwillingly he gave her his arm and they went on slowly down the lane; but before they had gone very far that long arm was close about her and had swept her into his embrace.

"Betty," he murmured, "to be alone with you thus in a sleeping world 'tis surely a foretaste of heaven." He would have drawn her yet nearer but she stayed him with arms outstretched.

"John," said she, "you ha' not forgot how you looked at me to-night, as I were—impure—unworthy? O John!" The Major was silent. "It angered me, John but—ah, it hurt me more! O Jack, how could you?" But now, seeing him stand abashed and silent, her repelling arms relaxed and she came a little nearer. "Indeed John, I'll allow you had some small—some preposterously pitiful small excuse. And you might answer that one cannot come nigh pitch without being defiled. But had you said anything so foolish I—I should ha' sent you home to bed—at once!" Here the Major drew her a little nearer. "But John," she sighed, "you did doubt me for awhile—I saw it in your eyes. Look at me again, John—here a little closer—here where the light falls clear—look, and tell me—am I different? Do I seem any less worthy your love than I was yesterday?"

"No," he answered, gazing into her deep eyes. "O my Betty, God help me if ever I lost faith in you, for 'twould be the end of hope and faith for me."

"But you did lose faith to-night, John—for a little while! And so you shall sue pardon on your knees, here at my feet—nay, 'tis damp, mayhap. I'll sit yonder on the bank and you shall kneel upon a fold of my cloak. Come!"

So the Major knelt to her very reverently and taking her two hands kissed them.

"Dear maid that I love," said he, "forgive the heart that doubted thee. But O love, because I am a very ordinary man, prithee don't—don't put my faith too oft upon the rack for I am over prone to doubts and jealous fears and they—O they are torment hard to bear." Now here she leaned forward and, taking him by two curls of his long periwig, drew him near until she could look into his eyes:

"Jack dear," she said, very tenderly, "I needs must meet this man again—and yet again——"

"Why?" he questioned, "Why?"

"Because 'tis only thus my plan shall succeed. Will you doubt me therefore?"

"No!" he cried hoarsely, "not you—never you, sweet maid! Tis him I doubt, he is a man, strong, determined and utterly ruthless and you are a woman——"

"And more than his match, John! O do but trust me! Do but wait until my plan is ripe——"

"Betty, a God's name what is this wild plan?"

"Nay, that I may not tell thee——"

"Could I not aid?"

"Truly—by doubting me no more, John. By trusting me—to the uttermost."

The Major groaned and bowed his head:

"Ah Betty!" he sighed, "yet must I think of thee as I saw thee to-night—alone with that—that satyr and nought to protect thee but thy woman's wit. God!" he cried, his powerful form shaking, "God, 'tis unthinkable! It must not be—it shall not be!" here he lifted face to radiant heaven, "I'll kill him first—I swear!"

Now seeing the awful purpose in that wild, transfigured face, she cried out and clasping him in tender arms, drew him near to kiss that scowling brow, those fierce, glaring eyes, that grim-set, ferocious mouth, pillowing his head upon her bosom as his mother might have done.

"O my John," she cried, "be comforted! Never let thy dear, gentle face wear look so evil, I—I cannot bear it."

"I'll kill him!" said the Major, the words muffled in her embrace.

"No, John! Ah no—you shall not! I do swear thee no harm shall come to me. I will promise thee to keep ever within this lane when—when we do meet o' nights——" Here the Major groaned again, wherefore she stooped swiftly to kiss him and spoke on, her soft lips against his cheek; "Meet him I needs must, dear—once or twice more if my purpose is to succeed—but I do vow and swear to thee never to quit this lane, John. I do swear all this if thou too wilt swear not to pursue this quarrel."

"He will insist on a meeting, Betty—and I pray God soon!"

"And if he doth not, John—if he doth not, thou wilt swear to let the quarrel pass?"

"Art so fearful for me, Betty?"

"O my John!" she whispered, her embrace tightening, "how might I live without thee? And he is so cold, so—deadly!"

"Yet art not afraid for thyself, Betty!"

"Nor ever shall be. So promise me, John—O promise me! Swear me, dear love!" And with each entreaty she kissed him, and so at last he gave her his promise, kneeling thus his head pillowed between soft neck and shoulder; and being in this fragrant nest his lips came upon her smooth throat and he kissed it, clasping her in sudden, passionate arms.

"John!" she whispered breathlessly. "O John!"

Instantly he loosed his hold and rising, stood looking down at her remorsefully.

"Dear—have I—angered you?" he questioned in stammering humility.

"Angry—and with thee?" and she laughed, though a little tremulously.

"Betty, I do worship thee—revere thee as a goddess—and yet——"

"You tickle me, John! You are by turns so reverent and humble and so—so opposite. I do love your respect and reverent homage, 'tis this doth make me yearn to be more worthy—but alack! I am a very woman, John, especially with thine arms about me and—and the moon at the full. But heigho, the moon is on the wane, see, she sinketh apace."

"Dawn will be soon, Betty."

"Hast seen a many dawns, John?"

"Very many!"

"But never one the like of this?"

"Never a one."

"O 'tis a fair, sweet world!" she sighed, "'tis a world of faerie, a dream world wherein are none but thou and I. Here is neither doubt nor sorrow, but love and faith abiding. Come let us walk awhile in this our faerie kingdom."

Slowly they went beneath the fading moon, speaking but seldom, for theirs was a rapture beyond the reach of words. So at last they came to a stile and paused there to kiss and sigh and kiss again like any rustic youth and maid. Something of this was in my lady's mind, for she laughed soft and happily and nestled closer to him.

"My Master Grave-airs," she murmured, "O Master Grave-airs where is now thy stately dignity, where now my fine-lady languor and indifference? To stand at a stile and kiss like village maid and lad—and—love it, John! How many rustic lovers have stood here before us, how many will come after us, and yet I doubt if any may know a joy so deep. Think you paradise may compare with this? Art happy, John?"

"Beloved," he answered, "I who once sought death boldly as a friend now do fear it like a very craven——"

"Ah no!" she cried, "speak not of death at such an hour, my Jack."

"Betty," said he, "O Betty, thou art my happiness, my hope, my very life. I had thought to go wifeless, childless and solitary all my days in my blindness and was content. But heaven sent thee to teach me the very joy and wonder of life, to—to——"

"To go beside thee henceforth, John, my hand in thine, learning each day to love thee a little more, to cherish and care for thee, men are such children and thou in some things a very babe. And belike to quarrel with thee, John—a little——" At this he laughed happily and they were silent awhile.

"See John, the moon is gone at last! How dark it grows, 'tis the dawn hour methinks and some do call it the death hour. But with these dear arms about me I—shouldn't fear so—very much."

Slowly, slowly upon the dark was a gleam that grew and grew, an ever waxing brightness filling the world about them.

"Look!" she whispered, "look! O John, 'tis the dawn at last, 'tis the dayspring and hath found me here upon thy breast!"

Thus, standing by that weatherbeaten stile that had known so many lovers before them, they watched day's majestic advent; a flush that deepened to rose, to scarlet, amber and flaming gold. And presently upon the brooding stillness was the drowsy call of a blackbird uncertain as yet and hoarse with sleep, a note that died away only to come again, sweeter, louder, until the feathered tribe, aroused by this early herald, awoke in turn and filled the golden dawn with an ecstasy of rejoicing.

Then my lady sighed and stirred:

"O John," said she, "'tis a good, sweet world! And this hath been a night shall be for us a fragrant memory, methinks. But now must I leave thee— take me home, my John."

So he brought her to the rustic gate that opened upon the lane and setting it wide, stooped to kiss her lips, her eyes, her fragrant hair and watched her flit away among the sleeping roses.

When she had gone he closed the door and trod a path gay with dewy gems; and hearkening to the joyous carolling of the birds it seemed their glad singing was echoed in his heart.

CHAPTER XXXIV
HOW MR. DALROYD MADE A PLAN
AND LOCKED HIS DOOR

Mr. Dalroyd kicked the obsequious Joseph soundly and cursed him soft-voiced but with a passionate fervour; yet such violence being apt to disarrange one's dress and to heat and distort one's features, Mr. Dalroyd reluctantly checked the ebullition and seating himself before the mirror surveyed his handsome face a little anxiously and with glance quick to heed certain faint lines that would occasionally obtrude themselves in the region of eye and mouth.

"Positively, I'm flushed!" he panted, "and for that alone I'd kick you downstairs, my poor worm, were it not that 'twould disorder me damnably. As 'tis I'll restore you to the hangman for the rogue you are!"

"Sir," said Joseph, bowing obsequious back and keeping his eyes humbly abased, "you ask a thing impossible——"

"Ask, animal? I never ask, I command!"

"But indeed—indeed sir I cannot even though I would——"

"Think again, Joseph, and mark this, Joseph, I saved you from the gallows because I thought you might be useful, very good! Now the instant you cease to be of use I give you back and you hang—so think again, Joseph."

"Lord—Lord help me!" exclaimed Joseph, writhing and wringing his hands but keeping his eyes always lowered. "Sir, 'tis impossible, 'tis——"

"In your predatory days, Joseph, you were of course well acquainted with other debased creatures like yourself, very good! You will proceed forthwith to get together three or four such—three or four should suffice. You will convene them secretly hereabouts. You will form your plans and next Saturday you will escort my lady Carlyon to a coach I shall have in waiting at the cross-roads."

"Abduct her, sir?"

"Precisely, Joseph! You and your—ah—assistants will bear her to the coach——"

"By force, sir?"

"Force! Hum, 'tis an ugly word! Say rather by gentle suasion, Joseph, but as silently as may be—there must be no wails or shrieking——"

"You mean choke her quiet, sir?" enquired Joseph gently, his eyelids drooping more humbly than ever.

Mr. Dalroyd turned from his toilet and smiled, "Joseph," said he softly, "if I find so much as a bruise or a scratch on her loveliness I'll break every bone in your rogue's carcass. So, as I say, you will see her conveyed silently into the coach, you will mount the rumble with your weapons ready in case of pursuit and upon arrival at our—destination I disburse to you certain monies and give you—quittance of my service."

"Abduction is a capital offence, sir."

"Egad, I believe it is. But you have run such chances ere now——"

"True sir. There was your uncle, since dead——"

"Ha!" exclaimed Mr. Dalroyd and, soft though his voice was, Joseph blenched and cowered.

"I—I've served you faithfully hitherto, sir!" said he hastily.

"And will again, grub!" nodded Mr. Dalroyd. "You will take two days' leave to make your necessary arrangements and on second thoughts I will give you two hundred guineas; one half as earnest-money you shall take with you in the morning—now go. I'll dispense with your services to-night. Begone, object! You shall have the money and further instructions in the morning."

Joseph took a hesitating step towards the door, paused and came back.

"Sir, how if—our scheme fail?"

"The—scheme will not fail."

"Sir, how if I make off with the money?"

"Why then, Joseph, there is your bedridden mother you have so great a weakness for—she cannot abscond."

Here Joseph raised his eyes at last and Mr. Dalroyd happening at that moment to glance into the mirror saw murder glaring at him, instantly Joseph's gaze abased itself, yet a fraction too late, Mr. Dalroyd's hand shot out and catching up a heavy toilet-bottle he whirled about and felled Joseph to his knees.

"Ha!" he exclaimed softly, staring down at the fallen man who crouched with bloody face hidden in his hands, "I've met and mastered your like ere this! Out, vermin—come out!"

And stooping, he seized the cowering form in strong, merciless hands, dragged him across the floor and kicked him from the room. Then, having closed the door Mr. Dalroyd surveyed himself in the mirror again, examined eye and mouth with frowning solicitude and proceeded to undress. Being ready for bed, he took up the candle, then stood with head bent in the attitude of one in thought or like one who hearkens for distant sounds, set down the candle and opening a drawer took out a silver-mounted pistol and glanced heedfully at flint and priming; with this in his hand he crossed the room and slipping the weapon under his pillow, got into bed and blew out the candle. But, in the act of composing himself to sleep, he started up suddenly, and sat again in the attitude of one who listens; then very stealthily, he got out of bed and crossing to the door felt about in the dark and silently shot the bolt.

CHAPTER XXXV
HOW THE SERGEANT TOOK
WARNING OF A WITCH

Sergeant Zebedee having pinked the Viscount in every vital part of his aristocratic anatomy, lowered his foil, shook his head and sighed while the Viscount panted rueful.

"You reached me seven times I think, that bout, Zeb?"

"Eight, sir!"

"Ha, the dooce! How d'ye do it?"

"'Tis your own self, m' lud. How can I help but pink you when you play your parades so open and inviting?"

"Hm!" said the Viscount, frowning.

"And then too, you're so slow in your recoveries, Master Pancras—Tom, sir!"

"Anything more, Zeb?"

"Aye, m' lud. Your hand on your p'int's for ever out o' the line and your finger-play——" The Sergeant shook his head again.

"Devil burn it, Zeb! I begin to think I don't sound over-promising. And yet—Gad love me, Sergeant, but you've no form, no style, y' know, pasitively none! In the schools they'd laugh at your play and call it mighty unmannerly."

"Belike they would, sir. But 'tis the schools as is the matter wi' you and so many other modish gentlemen, same be all froth and flourish. But flourishes though taking to the eye, is slow m' lud, slow."

"Nay, I've seen some excellent fencing in the schools, Zeb, such poise o' bady, such grace——"

"Grace is very well, m' lud—in a school. But 'tis one thing to play a veney wi' blunted weapons and another to fight wi' the sharps."

"True, Zeb, though La Touche teacheth in his book——"

"Book!" exclaimed the Sergeant and snorted.

"Hm!" said the Viscount, smiling, "howbeit in these next three days, I'd have you teach me all you can of your—unmannerly method."

"And wherefore three days, sir?"

"Why as to that Zeb—er—Lard save me, I'm to ride with the Major to Sevenoaks, he'll be waiting! Here, help me on with this!" And laying by his foil, the Viscount caught up his coat.

"Three days, Master Tom, and wherefore three?" enquired the Sergeant as Viscount Merivale struggled into his tight-fitting garment.

"Take care, Zeb, 'tis a new creation."

"And seems much too small, sir!"

"Nay, 'twill go on in time, Zeb, in time. I shall acquire it by degrees. Ease me into it—gently, gently—so!"

"And wherefore three days, sir?" persisted the Sergeant, as the coat being "acquired" its wearer settled its graceful folds about his slender person.

"Why three is a lucky number they say, Zeb," and with a smiling nod the Viscount hasted serenely away.

"Three days!" muttered the Sergeant, looking after him. "Zounds—I wonder!" So saying, he put away the foils and taking a pair of shears set himself to trim one of the tall yew hedges, though more than once he paused to rub his chin and murmur: "Three days—I wonder?"

This remark he had just uttered for perhaps the twentieth time when, roused by a hurried, shambling step, he glanced up and saw Roger, one of the under-gardeners who, touching an eyebrow, glanced over right shoulder, glanced over left, and spoke:

"Sergeant I do ha' worked here i' the park an' grounds twenty-five year man an' boy, an' in all that length o' days I never knowed it to happen afore, an' now it 'ave happened all of a shakesome sweat I be, hares-foot or no— an' that's what!"

"What's to do, Roger?"

"'Tis the eyes of 'er, Sergeant! 'Tis 'er mumping an' 'er mowing! 'Tis all the brimstoney look an' ways of 'er as turns a man's good flesh to flesh o' goose, 'is bones to jelly an' 'is bowels to water—an' that's what!"

"Nay, but what is't, Roger man?"

"'Ere's me, look'ee, trimming them borders, Sergeant, so 'appy-'earted as any bird and all at once, I falls to coldsome, quakesome shivers, my 'eart jumps into my jaws, my knees knocks an' trembles horrorsome-like, an' I sweats——"

"Zounds!" exclaimed the Sergeant.

"Then I feels a ghas'ly touch o' quakesome fingers as shoots all through my vitals—like fire, Sergeant and—there she is at my elber!"

"Who, Roger?"

"And 'er looks at me doomful, Sergeant, an' that's what!"

"Aye, but who, Roger, damme who?"

"'Tis th' owd witch as do be come for 'ee an' that's what!"

"Name of a dog!" exclaimed the Sergeant. "For me?"

"Aye," nodded Roger, glancing over his shoulder again, "'I want the Sergeant,' says she roupysome and grim-like, 'bring me the fine, big, sojer-sergeant,' she says."

"And what's her will wi' me?" enquired the Sergeant, glancing about uneasily.

"Wants to blast 'ee belike, Sergeant," groaned Roger. "Or mayhap she be minded only to 'witch 'ee wi' a bloody flux, or a toothache, or a windy colic or—Angels o' mercy, there she be a-coming!"

Turning hastily the Sergeant beheld a bowed, cloaked figure that hobbled towards them on a stick. The Sergeant let fall the shears and thrusting hand into frilled shirt, grasped a small, gold cross in his sinewy fingers.

Being come up to them the old creature paused and showed a face brown, wrinkled and lighted by glittering, black eyes; then lifting her staff she darted it thrice at the trembling Roger:

"Hoosh! Scow! Begone!" she cried in harsh, croaking voice, whereupon Roger forthwith took to his heels, stumbling and praying as he ran while the Sergeant gripped Mrs. Agatha's gold cross with one hand while he wiped sweat from his brow with the other as he met her piercing eyes.

"Good morrow, mam!" said he at last. The old woman shook her head but remained silent, fixing him with her wide-eyed stare. "Mam," he ventured again, "what would ye wi' me? Are you in trouble again, old Betty? If so—speak, mam!"

The old woman, bowed upon her staff, viewed his tall figure up and down with her bright eyes and nodded:

"'Tis my tall, fine sojer!" she said at last, and her voice had lost its shrill stridency. "'Tis my kind sojer so like the one I lost long and long since. I'm old: old and knew sorrow afore the mother as bore ye. Sorrow hath bided in me all my woeful days. Pain, pain, and hardship my lot hath been. They've hunted me wi' sticks and stones ere now, I've knowed the choking water and the scorch o' cruel fire. I mind all the pain and evil but I mind the good—aye, aye! There's been many to harm and few t' cherish! Aye, I mind it all, I mind it, the evil and the good. And you was kind t' old Betty because your 'eart be good, so I be come this weary way to warn 'ee, my big sojer."

"Warn me—of what, mam?"

"A weary way, a woeful way for such old bones as Betty's!"

"Why then come sit ye and rest, mam. Come your ways to the arbour yonder." Moaning and muttering the old woman followed whither he led, but seeing how she stumbled he reached out his hand, keeping the other upon his small gold cross and so brought her into the hutch-like sentry-box. Down sat old Betty with a blissful sigh; but now, when he would have withdrawn his hand, her fingers closed upon it, gnarled and claw-like and, before he could prevent, she had stooped and touched it to her wrinkled cheek and brow.

"'Tis a strong hand, a kindly hand," she croaked, "'tis a sojer's hand—my boy was a sojer but they killed him when the world was young. I'm old, very old, and deaf they say—aha! But the old can see and the deaf can hear betimes, aha! Come, ope your hand, my dear, come ope your hand and let old Betty read. So, here's a big hand, a strong hand—now let us see what says the big, strong hand. Aha—here's death——"

"Zounds!" exclaimed the Sergeant, starting. "You're something sudden mam, death is our common lot——"

"Death that creeps, my dear. Here's ill chances and good. Here's sorrow and joy. Here's love shall be a light i' the dark. But here's dangers, perils, night-lurkers and creepers i' the gloom. Death for you and shame for her."

"Ha—for her!" cried the Sergeant, his big hand clenching on the feeble, old fingers. "D'ye mean—Mrs. Agatha, mam?"

"No, no, my dear, no no!" answered old Betty, viewing his stern and anxious face with her quick bright eyes. "'Tis not her you love, no, no, 'tis one as loveth him ye serve. 'Tis one with a soul as sweet, as soft and white as her precious body, 'tis one as is my namesake, 'tis——"

"*Sapperment!*" exclaimed the Sergeant. "You never mean my lady Betty, my lady Carlyon— —"

"Aye, aye my dear—'tis she!"

"And in danger, d'ye say? Can ye prove it, mam?"

"Come ye to-morrow t' my cottage at rise o' moon and I'll show ye a thing, ye shall see, ye shall hear. Bring him along o' you him—ssh!" The old woman's clutch tightened suddenly, her bowed figure grew more upright, and she stared wide of eye: "Come," she cried suddenly, in her shrillest tones, "you as do hearken—come! You in petticoats—aha, I can see, I can hear! Come forth, I summon ye!"

A moment's utter silence, then leaves rustled and Mrs. Agatha stood in the doorway, her eyes very bright, her cheeks more rosy than usual.

"Sergeant Tring," she demanded, "what doth the old beldam here?"

Old Betty seemed to cower beneath Mrs. Agatha's look, while the Sergeant fidgeted, muttered "Zounds" and was thereafter dumb. "'Tis an arrant scold and wicked witch," continued Mrs. Agatha, "and should to the brank, or the cucking-stool— —"

"No, no!" cried the old woman, shivering and struggling to her feet. "Not again a God's love, mistress—not again! I'll be gone! Let me go!"

"Nay, not yet mam," said the Sergeant gently as he rose; "you are weary, sit ye and rest awhile. Mrs. Agatha mam, you speak woman-like— —"

"Aye, aye," nodded old Betty, "'tis ever woman is cruellest to woman!"

"As you will, Zebedee Tring!" nodded Mrs. Agatha. "Yonder is Roger Bent shook with a shivering fit at sight of her while you sit here and let her scrabble your hand, but as you will!" and crossing her arms over opulent bosom Mrs. Agatha would have turned away but old Betty stabbed at her with bony finger.

"Woman," she croaked, "I'm here t' save the man you love. Come sit ye and list to my telling." Mrs. Agatha faltered, whereupon the Sergeant caught her hand, drawing her into the arbour: and there, sitting beside the old woman they hearkened to her story.

"Mam," said the Sergeant, "ha' ye told my lady Carlyon aught o' this?"

"Nay, nay," answered old Betty, "I had a mind to—but they wouldna let me see my lady—the footmen and lackeys laughed at poor old Bet and turned her from the door—so I did come to tell my brave sojer-sergeant."

"'Tis just as well, mam," nodded the Sergeant, "for now you shall come wi' us to his honour, the Major will hear you, I'll warrant me, so come your ways, mam."

"Aye," said Mrs. Agatha, "and you shall eat and drink likewise and after the Sergeant shall drive you back to Inchbourne an he will."

Thus Roger Bent, busied in the herb-garden, chancing to lift his head, stood suddenly upright, staggered back and fell into a clump of parsley; and propped upon an elbow, stared, as well he might, for into the sacred precincts of her stillroom went Mrs. Agatha and the Sergeant but between them tottered the bowed form of old Betty the witch.

"Lord!" exclaimed Roger, ruffling up his shock of hair. "My eyes is sure a-deceiving of me—an' that's what!"

CHAPTER XXXVI
HOW THEY RODE TO INCHBOURNE

"And what time doth the moon rise, Zebedee?" enquired the Major as they swung their horses into the high road.

"Ten forty-five about, your honour,"

"Then we've no need for hurry. And egad Zeb, it sounds a wild story!"

"It do so, sir, cock and bullish as you might say."

"To abduct my lady, Zeb!"

"On Saturday night next as ever was, your honour."

"And this is Friday night!" said the Major thoughtfully.

"Which do give us good time to circumvent enemy's manoover."

"How many of the rogues will be there, think you?"

"Can't say for sure, sir. 'Twas three on 'em as ambushed me t'other night."

"Why as to that Zeb, as to that I imagine you brought that drubbing on yourself by your somewhat frequent and indiscriminate—er—pewter-play as 'twere."

"Mayhap sir, though if so be rogues were same rogues I should ha' knowed same, though to be sure 'twere a darkish night and they were masked. Howsobe, my Lord Medhurst pinked one of 'em, his point was prettily bloodied."

"Are you armed, Zeb?"

"Nought to speak of, sir."

"What have you?"

"A sword sir, and a brace o' travelling-pistols as chanced to lay handy which, with your honour's, maketh four shot, two swords and a bagnet."

"Lord, Zeb, we're not going up against a troop!" said the Major, smiling in the dark, "and why the bayonet?"

"'Tis the one I used for to carry when we were on outpost duty at night, sir—the one as I had shortened for the purpose, your honour. You'll mind as there's nought like a short, stiff bagnet when 'tis a case o' silence. And as for a troop you ha'n't forgot the time as we routed that company o' Bavarian troopers, you and me, sir, thereby proving the advantages o' the element o' surprise?"

"Aye, those were desperate times, Zebedee."

"Mighty different to these, sir."

"Aye, truly, truly!" said the Major, gently.

"But if there is to be a little bit o' cut and thrust work to-night, your honour, 'tis as well to be prepared."

"You think old Betty is to be relied on, Zeb?"

"Aye sir, I do."

"None the less I'm glad my lady Carlyon knoweth nought o' the matter, 'tis best, I think, to keep it from her—at least until we are sure, moreover 'tis like enough she—" the Major paused to rub his chin dubiously, "'tis very like she would only——"

"Laugh, your honour?"

"Hum!" said the Major.

"Lord sir, but she's a woundy fine spirit!" exclaimed the Sergeant.

"True, Zeb, very true!" The Major nodded. "Yet I would she were a thought less venturesome and—ah—contrary at times as 'twere, Zeb——"

"Contrairy, sir? Lord love me, there you have it! Woman is a contrairy sect, 'tis born in 'em! Look at Mrs. Agatha, contrairiness ain't no word for same!"

"How so, Zeb?"

"Why, d'ye see sir, when thinking I'd soon be under marching orders—you then talking o' campaigning again—there's me don't venter to open my mind to her touching matrimony though her a-giving me chances for same constant. To-day here's me—you being settled and wi' no wish for foreign fields—here's me, d'ye see, looking for chances and occasions to speak wedlock and such constant and her giving me no chances what-so-ever. And that's woman, sir!"

They rode at a gentle, ambling pace and with no sound to disturb the brooding night-silence except the creak of their saddles and the thudding of their horses' hoofs dulled and muffled in the dust of the road. A hushed and windless night full of the quivering glamour of stars whose soft effulgence lent to hedge and tree and all things else a vague and solemn beauty; and riding with his gaze uplifted to this heavenly host, the Major thought of Life and Death and many other things, yet mostly of my lady Elizabeth Carlyon, while Sergeant Zebedee, gazing at nothing in particular, dreamed also.

"'Tis as well she should learn nought of the ugly business!" said the Major at last.

"But sir, Mrs. Agatha— —"

"I mean her ladyship, Zebedee."

"Aye, aye for sure, sir, for sure!"

"And if there be indeed villainy afoot—if there is, why then egad, Sergeant Zeb, I'll not rest until I know who is at the bottom on't!"

"Aye—who, sir? 'Tis what we're a-going to find out to-night I do hope. And when we do find out, sir—how then?"

"Why then, Zeb—ha, then—we shall see, we shall see!"

After this they rode on in silence awhile, the Major staring up at the glory of the stars again.

"If so be we should be so fortuned as to come in for a little bit o' roughsome to-night, your honour," said the Sergeant thoughtfully, "you'd find this here bludgeon a vast deal handier than your sword and play very sweet at close quarters, sir."

"By the way, Zebedee, I think you once told me you surprised—er—Mr. Dalroyd i' the orchard one night?"

"I did so, your honour."

"And did you chance to—ah—to see his face, to observe his features clear and distinct, as 'twere, Zeb?"

"Aye, sir."

"Well?"

"Aye, very well, sir!"

By this time they had reached the cross-roads and here the Major checked his horse suddenly, whereupon Sergeant Zebedee did likewise.

"Sergeant!"

"Sir?"

The Major leaned from his saddle until he could peer into the Sergeant's eyes.

"Did Mr. Dalroyd remind you of—of anyone you have ever seen before?"

"Of Captain Effingham as your honour killed years agone."

"Ah!" said the Major and sat awhile frowning up at the stars. "So you likewise marked the resemblance, did you, Zeb?"

"I did so, sir."

"And what did you think——"

"Why sir, that Captain Effingham having been killed ten years agone, is very dead indeed, by this time!"

"Supposing he wasn't killed—how then, Zeb?"

"Why then sir he was alive arter all—though he looked dead enough."

"'Twas a high chest-thrust you'll mind, Zeb."

"Base o' the throat, sir."

"Why have you never mentioned your suspicions, Zebedee?"

"Because, your honour, 'tis ever my tactics to let sleeping dogs lie—bygones is bygones and what is, is. If, on t'other hand Mr. Dalroyd's Captain Effingham which God forbid, then all I says is—what is, ain't. Furthermore and moreover Mr. Dalroyd would be the last man I'd ha' you cross blades with on account o' the Captain's devilish sword-play—that thrust of his in carte nigh did your honour's business ten years ago, consequently to-day I hold my peace regarding suspicions o' same."

"D'ye think he'd—kill me, Zeb?"

"I know 'twould sure be one or t'other o' ye, sir."

"And that's true enough!" said the Major and rode on again. "None the less, Zeb," said he after awhile, "none the less he shall have another opportunity of trying that thrust if, as I think, he is at the bottom of this vile business."

But now they were drawing near to Inchbourne village and, reining up, the Major glanced about him:

"What of our horses, Zebedee?" he questioned. "'Twill never do to go clattering through the village at this hour."

"No more 'twill, sir. Old Bet's cottage lieth a good mile and a half t'other side Inchbourne, d'ye see. Further on is a lane that fetcheth a circuit about the village—this way, your honour." So they presently turned off into a narrow and deep-rutted lane that eventually brought them out upon a desolate expanse with the loom of woods beyond.

"Yonder's a spinney, sir, 'tis there we'll leave our horses."

Riding in among the trees they dismounted and led their animals into the depths of the wood until they came to a little dell well hidden in the brush. Here, having securely tethered their horses they sat down to wait the moonrise.

"Sir," said the Sergeant, settling pistols in pockets, "this doth mind me o' the night we lay in such another wood as this, the night we stormed Douai, you'll mind I was wounded just arter we carried the counterscarp— —"

"By a pike-thrust meant for me, Zeb."

"'Twas a pretty fight, sir, 'specially the forcing o' the palisadoes—'twere just such another night as this— —"

"Only we were younger then, Zeb, years younger."

"Why as to that, sir, I've been feeling younger than e'er I was, of late— and yonder cometh the moon at last! This way, sir!"

CHAPTER XXXVII
OF ROGUES AND PLOTS

The moon was fast rising as they left the shadow of the trees and crossing a meadow presently saw before them the loom of a building which, on near approach, proved to be a very tumble-down, two-storied cottage. The Sergeant led the way past a broken fence through a riotous tangle of weeds and so to a door whereon he rapped softly; almost immediately it was opened and old Betty the witch stood on the threshold peering into the dimness under her hand.

"Mam," said the Sergeant, "'tis us—we've come!"

"Aha!" she croaked. "'Tis you—'tis my big sojer—my fine sojer-sergeant an' the lord squire o' the Manor! Come your ways—come your ways in—'tis an ill place for fine folk but 'tis all they've left me. Come in!" Following Sergeant Zebedee's broad back the Major stumbled down three steps into a small, dim chamber, very close and airless, lighted by a smoky rushlight. Old Betty closed the door, curtseyed to the Major and clutching at Sergeant Zebedee's hand, stooped and kissed it, whereupon he glanced apologetically at the Major and saluted.

"'Tis her gratitood, sir," he explained, "on account o' Mr. Jennings me having kicked same, as dooly reported."

"An ill place for the likes o' your honour," croaked the old woman, "an evil place for evil men as will be here anon—the rogues, the fools! They think old Betty's blind and deaf—the rogues! Come, dearies, the moon's up and wi' the moon comes evil so get ye above—yonder, yonder and mum, dearies, mum!" As she spoke old Betty pointed to a corner of the dingy chamber where a rickety ladder gave access to a square opening above. "Go ye up, dearies and ye shall see, ye shall hear, aha—but mum, dearies, mum!"

Forthwith they mounted the ladder and so found themselves in a small, dark loft full of the smell of rotting wood and dank decay. Above their heads stars winked through holes in the mouldering thatch, beneath their feet the rotten flooring showed great rents and fissures here and there through which struck the pallid beams of the twinkling rushlight in the room below.

"God bless my soul!" exclaimed the Major, "does this pestiferous ruin belong to me, Zeb?"

"Well, I don't rightly know, your honour, 'tis a mile and a half out o' the village d'ye see, and hath stood empty for years and years they do tell me, on account of a murder as was done here, and nobody would live here till old Betty come. Folk do say the place is haunted and there be few as dare come nigh the place after dark. But old Betty, being a powerful witch d'ye see sir, aren't nowise afeard of any ghost, gobling nor apparation as ever—ssh!"

Upon the night without, was a sound of voices that grew ever louder, the one hoarse and querulous the other upraised in quavering song:

"O 'tis bien bowse, 'tis bien bowse,
Too little is my skew.
I bowse no lage, but one whole gage
O' this I'll bowse to you— —"

"Stow the chaunting, Jerry!" growled the hoarse voice, "close up that ugly gan o' yourn. Oliver's awake— —"

"Oliver? Aye, so 'tis with a curse on't! The moon's no friend o' mine. Gimme a black night, darkmans wi' a popper i' my famble and t'other in my cly and I'm your cull, ecod!" Here the door of the cottage swung open and two men entered, the one a tall, wild, gipsy-looking fellow, the other a shortish man in spurred boots and long riding-coat from the side-pockets of which protruded the brass-heeled butts of a pair of pistols.

"What, Benno, my lad—what Benno," he cried, scowling round the dismal room beneath the cock of his weatherbeaten hat, "blind me, but here's a plaguy dog-hole for a genty-cove o' the high-toby!"

"O, the high pad is a delicate trade
And a delicate trade o' fame
We bite the cully of his cole
And carry away his game
Oho, and carry away— —"

"Quit, Jerry, quit!" growled the man Benno. "Hold that dasher o' yourn won't 'ee— —"

"No, Benno my cove, if I do ha' a mind for t' sing, I'll sing and burn all, says I!"

"I keep my prancer and two pepps
A tattle in my cly.
When bowsing— —"

"Keep your chaffer still, won't 'ee!" snarled the other. "'Swounds, a pal can't hear hisself! Ha, Bet!" he roared, "old Bet—what grannam, oho—lights, more lights here!"

"Lights—aye," nodded Jerry, "lights inside's well enough but lights outside's the devil! Look at Oliver, look at th' moon, well—curse th' moon says I and—O ecod! What's yon i' the corner? A ladder as I'm a roaring boy—a ladder! Well, here's to see what's above. A doxy, aha, a dimber-dell, oho—"

"When my dimber-dell I courted
She had youth and beauty too— —"

As he sang he whipped a pistol from his pocket and lurched towards the ladder; and Sergeant Zebedee, watching through one of the many crevices, smiled happily and drew his bayonet. Jerry had one foot on the ladder when his companion caught his shoulder and swung him roughly away.

"How now?" he demanded. "What's your ploy?"

"Look'ee Benno, if you're a-hiding of some dimber mort aloft there I'm the cove to— —"

"Ah, you're lushed, Jerry, foxed t' your peepers, sit down—sit down and put away your popp—afore I crack your mazzard!"

Sulkily enough Jerry obeyed and seating himself at the table turned, ever and anon, to view the ladder with a drunken stare.

"Lushed am I?" he repeated. "Drunk hey? Well, so I am and when lushed 'tis at my best I am, my lad. And look'ee a ladder's meant for to climb ain't it? Very well then—I'm the cove to climb it! And look'ee, what's more 'tis a curst dog-hole this for a genty-cove o' the high pad and— —" But here his companion roared again for "Old Bet" and "Lights" until the old woman hobbled in.

"Eh, eh?" she whimpered, blinking from one to the other. "Did ye call, dearie?"

"Aye—bring more glims, d'ye hear— —"

"Candles, dearie, eh—eh?"

"Aye, candles! And I'm expecting company, so bring candles and get ye to bed, d'ye hear?"

"Aye, aye, I hear, dearie, I hear—candles, candles," and muttering the word she hobbled away and presently was back again and stood, mowing and mumbling, to watch the candles lighted.

"Now get ye to bed," cried Benno, "to bed, d'ye hear?"

"Dead, dearie?" she croaked. "Who's dead now? Not me, no, no, nor you—yet. No no, but 'tis coming, aha—'tis coming—dead oho!"

The man Benno fell back a step, eyes wide and mouth agape, then very suddenly made a cross in the air before him, while Jerry, getting on his feet, did the same with unsteady finger on the table.

"The evil eye! 'Tis the evil eye!" he muttered, while old Betty nodded and chuckled as her quick, bright eyes flashed from one to the other.

"I said 'bed'!" roared the gipsy-looking fellow clenching his fists fiercely but falling back another step from old Betty's vicinity, "bed was the word——"

"Aye, aye, dearie!" she nodded, "some in bed an' some out—dead, aye, aye, some by day and some by night—all go dead soon or late, you an' me and all on us—one way or t'other—dead, dearie, dead!"

So saying old Betty hobbled out of the room closing the door behind her.

"A curst old beldam, a hag, a damned witch as I'm a roarer!" exclaimed Jerry shaking his head, while his companion wiped sweat from his brow. "O rot me, a nice dog-hole this and wi' a ladder look'ee, leading devil knoweth where, but I'm the cove to see——"

"Sit still—sit still and take a sup o' this, Jerry!" And crossing to a corner Benno brought thence a stone jar and a couple of mugs and brimming one unsteadily he tossed it off; then sitting down at the rickety table they alternately drank and cursed old Betty.

"Come now, Benno my dimber cove," cried Jerry at last, "what's the game? What ha' ye brought me here for? Tip us the office!"

"Why then we're on the spiriting lay—a flash blowen—a genty mort, Jerry."

"Aha, that should mean shiners, plenty o' lour, Benno?"

"Fifty apiece near as nothing."

"Here's game as I'm a flash padder. What more, cove, what more? Let's hear."

"Not me, Jerry—there's one a-coming as will tip you the lay—an old pal, Jerry, a flaming buck o' the high pad, a reg'lar dimber-damber, a—hist! 'Tis him at last, I think, but ha' your popps ready in case, Jerry."

Here Benno arose and crossing a little unsteadily to the door stood there listening: after a while came a knock, a muffled voice, and, opening the door, he admitted three men. The first a great, rough fellow who bore one arm in a sling, the second a little man, *point-de-vice* from silvered spurs to laced hat, yet whose elegant appearance was somewhat marred by a black patch that obscured one eye; the third was the obsequious Joseph, but now, as he stood blinking in the candle-light, there was in his whole sleek person an air of authority and command, and a grimness in the set of smooth-shaven jaw that transfigured him quite.

At sight of him Jerry sprang up, nearly upsetting the table, and stood to stare in gaping astonishment.

"'Tis Nick!" he cried at last, "Galloping Nick, as I'm a hell-fire, roaring dog! 'Tis Nick o' the High Toby as hath diddled the nubbing-cheat arter all, ecod! Ha, Nick—Nicky lad, tip us your famble and burn all, says I!"

Joseph suffered his hand to be shaken and nodded.

"Drunk as usual, Jerry?"

"Ecod and so I am! Drunk enough t' shoot straight—drunk as I was that night by the gravel-pits on Blackheath. You'll mind that night, Nick and how you——"

"Bah, you're talking lushy, Jerry! Here's Captain Swift and the Chicken so—let's to business."

"Aye, to business, my cullies!" cried Jerry saluting them in turn. "To business—'tis the spiriting of a genty mort, eh Nick?"

"A fine lady, aye!" nodded Joseph. "There's two hundred guineas in't, which is fifty for me and the rest atween you, share and share."

"Which is fair enough, rabbit me!" said the Captain.

"Now hark'ee all," continued Joseph beckoning them near and lowering his voice. "You, Jerry and the Captain will come mounted and meet us at the cross-roads beyond——"

"Cross-roads?" hiccoughed Jerry, "not me, Nick, no, no—there's cross-roads everywhere hereabouts I tell'ee, and I don't know the country hereabouts—no meetings at cross-roads, Nicky, burn my eyes no——" Here Joseph cursed him and fell to biting his nails.

"Why not meet here?" suggested Benno.

"No, nor here!" snarled Jerry, "I don't like this place, 'tis a dog-hole and wi' a ladder look'ee a ladder leading devil knoweth where look'ee—a ladder as is meant to climb and as I'm a-going to c-climb——" But as he rose unsteadily Joseph's heavy hand dragged him down again.

"There's the mill then," said he, "the ruined mill beyond Westerham, we'll meet there. We all know it——"

"I don't," growled Jerry, "and don't want— —"

"The Captain does and you'll ride with him. At the ruined mill then to-morrow night a half after ten—sharp."

"And what then, Nick—ha?" enquired the Captain, taking a pinch of snuff.

"Why then— —" Here Joseph sunk his voice so low as to be inaudible to any but those craning their necks to listen.

"'Tis a simple plan and should be no great matter!" nodded the Captain. "Aye, rat me, I like your plan, Nick— —"

"Aye, but the genty mort," demurred Jerry, "now if she squeal and kick—burn me I've had 'em scratch and tear d-damnably ere now— —"

"Squeeze her pretty neck a little," suggested the Captain.

"Or choke her with her furbelows," grinned Benno.

"No!" said Joseph, scowling, "there's to be no strangling—no rough work, d'ye take me—it's to be done gentle or— —"

"Gentle, ho—gentle, is it!" cried Jerry fiercely. "And how if she gets her claws into me—the last one as I culled for a flash sportsman nigh wrung my ear off—gentle? 'Tain't fair to a man it don't give a man a chance, it d-don't— —"

"And that's all now!" said Joseph, rising. "To-morrow night at the ruined mill—I'll give you your last instructions to-morrow at half after ten. Now who's for a glass over at the inn—landlord's a cull o' mine." At this everyone rose excepting Jerry who lolled across the table scowling from one candle to another.

"Ain't you a-coming, Jerry?" enquired the gipsy-looking fellow, turning at the door.

"No—not me!" snarled Jerry. "Bones do ache—so they do! 'S-sides I've drunk enough, and I—I'm a-going—to climb—that ladder an' burn all, says I."

"Then climb it and be damned!" said the other and strode away after his companions, slamming the door behind him. Jerry sat awhile muttering incoherently and drew a pistol from his pocket; then he rose and steadying himself with infinite pains against the rickety table, fixed his scowling gaze upon the ladder and lurched towards it. But the liquor had affected his legs and he staggered from wall to wall ere, tripping and stumbling, he finally reached the ladder that shook under the sudden impact. For a long moment he stood, weapon in hand, staring up into the blackness above, then slowly and with much labour began the ascent rung by rung, pausing very often and muttering hoarsely to himself; he was already half-way up and the Sergeant, crouched in the shadow, was waiting to receive him with upraised pistol-butt, when he missed his hold, his foot slipped and pitching sideways he crashed to the floor and lay still, snoring stertorously. Almost immediately old Betty appeared, crossed to the outstretched body, looked at it, spat at it and spoke:

"'Tis all well, dearies—he be nice and fast what wi' drink and fall. Come down, my dearies, come down and get ye gone."

The Major followed Sergeant Zebedee down the ladder and crossing to the old woman, removed his hat.

"Mam," said he, "'tis like enough you have saved a great wrong being committed and I am deeply grateful. Words are poor things, mam, but henceforth it shall be my care to see your remaining days be days of comfort. Meantime pray accept this and rest assured of the future." Saying which the Major laid a purse upon the table, then turned rather hastily to escape old Betty's eager, tremulous thanks and stepped from the cottage.

"Zebedee," said he as they led their horses out of the coppice, "I recognised two of these rascals. One is the tramping gipsy I broke my cane over and the other——"

"The other is Mr. Dalroyd's man Joe, sir."

"Ha! Art sure o' that, Zeb?"

"I am so, sir!"

"Excellent!" said the Major, swinging to saddle. "Our expedition to-night hath not been in vain, after all."

"Where now, sir?" enquired the Sergeant, gathering up his reins.

"Home!"

"What—ha' we done, your honour?"

"Until to-morrow night—at the ruined mill, Zeb."

"To-morrow night—zounds, sir!" chuckled the Sergeant as they broke into a trot. "'Twill be like old times!"

"'Twill be five to two, Zebedee!" said the Major thoughtfully.

"Warmish, sir—warmish! Though t' be sure the big rascal bore his arm in a sling, still, 'tis pretty odds, I allow."

"There must be no shooting, Zeb."

"Why your honour, pistols are apt t' be a trifle unhandy for close work, d'ye see. Now, a bagnet——"

"And no steel, Zeb. We'll have no killing if it can be avoided!"

"No steel sir?" gasped the Sergeant. "No steel—!"

"Bludgeons will be best if it should come to fighting," continued the Major thoughtfully, "though I hope to effect their capture without any undue violence——" The Sergeant turned to stare:

"What, is there to be no violence now, your honour?" he sighed.

"Violent methods are ever clumsy, Zeb, I propose to use the element of surprise."

"Ah!" exclaimed the Sergeant and smiling grimly up at the moon he slowly closed one eye and opened it again.

After this they rode some time in silence, the Sergeant's mind preoccupied with the "Element of Surprise" as applied to the odds of five to two, while the Major, looking round about on the calm beauty of the night, dreamed ever of my lady Elizabeth Carlyon as had become his wont and custom.

In due time they reached a certain quiet bye-lane and here the Major checked his horse.

"Sergeant," said he, "'tis a fair night for walking what with the moon—er—the moon d'ye see and so forth——"

"Moon, sir?"

"Aye, the moon!" said the Major, dismounting. "Do you go on with the horses, I've a mind for walking." So he handed Sergeant Zebedee the reins of his horse and turned aside down this quiet bye-lane.

This lane that led away between blooming hedges, that wandered on, haphazard as it were, to lose itself at last in a little wood where nightingales sang; this bye-lane wherein he had walked with her that never-to-be-forgotten night and stood with her to watch the world grow bright and joyous with a new day; this leafy sheltered lane that held for him the sweet magic of her presence and was therefore a hallowed place.

Thus as he walked, his slow steps falling silent on soft mosses and dewy grass, the Major took off his hat.

Bareheaded and with reverent feet he wandered on dreaming of those joys that were to be, God willing, and turning a sharp bend in the lane stopped all at once, smitten to sudden, breathless immobility.

She sat upon the wall, dainty foot a-swing, while below stood Mr. Dalroyd who seized that shapely foot in irreverent hands, stooped and covered it with kisses that grew more bold and audacious until she, stifling laughter in her cloak, freed herself with a sudden, vigorous kick that sent Mr. Dalroyd's hat flying—

The Major turned and hurried away looking neither right nor left; becoming conscious of the hat in his hand, he laughed and crammed it on his head. So he went with great strides until he reached a stile beside the way and halting, he leaned there, with face bowed upon his arms. Long he stood thus, silent and motionless and with face hidden. At last he raised his head, looked up at heaven and round about him like one who wakes in a new world, and limped slowly homewards.

"Sir," said the Sergeant, meeting him at the door, "Colonel Cleeve is here."

"O!" said the Major, slowly. "Is he, Zeb? That is well!"

"A-snoring in the library, sir!"

"Aye, to be sure—to be sure!" said the Major vaguely.

"Y' see 'tis getting late, your honour," continued Sergeant Zebedee, viewing the Major's drawn features anxiously.

"Why then—go you to bed, Zebedee."

"Can I get you aught first, sir—a bite o' something—a bottle or so?"

"No, Zeb, no—stay! Bring me my Ramillie coat."

CHAPTER XXXVIII
HOW THE MAJOR MADE HIS WILL

Colonel Lord George Cleeve, blissfully slumbering in deep armchair beside the library fire, choked upon a snore and, opening his eyes, perceived the Major opposite in another deep chair; but the Major was awake, his frowning gaze was bent upon the fire and ever and anon he sighed deeply.

"Refuse me, Jack!" exclaimed the Colonel, "to hark to you one would think you in love and—er—damnably forlorn, you sigh, man, you sigh, aye, let me perish, you puff grief like any bellows."

"And you snore, George, you snore man, aye, egad, like a very grampus! None the less I joy to see thee, George," said the Major, rising and extending his hand. "When did you arrive?"

"Some half-hour since. And snore, did I? Well, 'tis late enough, o' conscience. Faith Jack, Sir Benjamin brews a devilish strong punch—I supped with the company at the George. Then strolled over with Tom to visit ya' charming neighbours. Man Jack, she's a damned fine creature—ha?"

"She is!" sighed the Major.

"And with an air, Jack—an air." The Major sighed and seemed lost in thought. "I say an air, Jack."

"An air George, as you say."

"Full up o' womanly graces and adornments feminine."

"True, George."

"And thoroughbred, Jack!" The Major stared pensively into the fire. "I say all blood and high breeding, Jack."

"Aye, true George, true!"

"Well then, a man might do worse—ha?" The Major started. "How think ye, Jack? I'm not a marrying man, Jack, as you know, the sex hath never been a weakness o' mine but I'm touched at last, Jack—aye touched with a curse on't!"

"God—bless—my—soul!" exclaimed the Major, staring harder than ever.

"'Fore Gad, man Jack, it came on me like a charge o' cavalry. Like you I meant to live and die a free man and now—O Gad! 'Tis her eyes, I think, I see 'em everywhere—blue, you'll mind, Jack, blue as—as—well, blue."

"Aye, they're blue!" nodded the Major, all grave attention at last.

"Well, 'tis her eyes, Jack, or else her dooced demure airs, or her languishing graces, or her feet, or her shape, or the way she smiles, or—O damme! Howbeit I'm smitten, Jack—through and through—done for and be curst to it!"

"You too!" sighed the Major and stared into the fire again.

"Aye—and why not i' faith? I'm a man sound in wind and limb and but few years ya' senior—why the devil not? She's free to wed and if she's willing and I've a mind for't who the devil's going to stay me—ha?" The Major sighed and shook his head. "Save us, Jack, but ya're curst gloomy, I think!"

"Why as to that, as to that, George, I fear I am. Perhaps if we crack a bottle before we go to bed—how say you?"

"With all my heart!" So the Major brought bottle and glasses and, having filled to each other, they sat awhile each staring into the fire. "And now," continued the Colonel, "what's to stop me a-marrying, Jack, if I'm so minded, come?"

"Is she likely to—to make you happy, George?"

"Rabbit me—and why not?"

"Well," said the Major hesitatingly, "her age——"

"Dooce take me, she's none so old——"

"Old!" repeated the Major, "nay indeed I——"

"She's no filly I'll allow, Jack, but then I shed my colt's teeth long ago. Nay, she's rather in her blooming prime, summer—er—languishing to autumn——"

"Autumn!" murmured the Major, staring.

"No—I see nought against it unless—O smite me, Jack!" The Colonel set down his glass and stared at the Major who stared back at him.

"Unless what, George?"

"Unless y'are bitten too." The Major frowned into the fire again. "If y'are, Jack, if y'are, why then damme I'll not come athwart ya'—no, no—old friends—Gad, no! I'll ride away to-morrow and give you a clear field."

"I shall never marry—never, George!" said the Major and sighed deeper than ever. The Colonel refilled his glass, raised it to his lips, sighed in turn and put it down again.

"Love's a plaguy business!" he groaned. "How old are ye, Jack?"

"Forty-two, almost."

"And I'm forty-five—quite. And i' faith, Jack, when the curst disease plagues men of our age 'tis there to stay. None the less, man Jack, if ya' love her, why then Belinda's not for me——"

"Belinda!" exclaimed the Major.

"Aye, who else? What the dooce, man?"

"I—egad, George, I thought—"

"What did ya' think?"

"'Twas Lady Betty you had in mind."

"Lady Bet——!" The Colonel whistled. "So-ho!" he exclaimed and turned, full of eager questions but seeing how the Major scowled into the fire again, sipped his wine instead and thereafter changed the subject abruptly.

"Ya'r Viscount's a fine lad, Jack!" The Major's brow cleared instantly.

"Aye, indeed, Tom's a man, 'spite all his modish airs and affectations, a man! Where is he, by the way?"

"Went to bed hours since and very rightly, seeing what's toward."

"As what, George?"

"His forthcoming duel with Dalroyd." The Major sat suddenly upright.

"A duel with—Dalroyd!"

"What, didn't ya' know?"

"Not a word."

"Why true, it only happened this evening."

"And when do they fight?"

"That's the curst queer thing about the affair. I don't know, he don't know—nobody knows but Dalroyd. 'Tis a black business, Jack, a black business and looks ill for the lad!"

"Aye!" said the Major, rising and beginning to pace to and fro. "Pray tell me of it, George."

"Well, i' the first place, 'tis a hopeful youth, your nephew, Jack, a lovely lad. Smite me, I never saw an affront more pleasantly bestowed nor more effectively! Such a polished business with him and pure joy for the spectators, he insulted his man so gracefully yet so thoroughly that their steel was out in a twinkling. But the place was cluttered with chairs and tables, so Alvaston and Tripp fell upon Dalroyd and I and Captain West on the Viscount and parted 'em till the matter could be arranged more commodiously for 'em. Well, we cleared the floor and locked the door, they seeming so eager for one another's blood and then—damme, Dalroyd refuses to fight. 'No, gentlemen,' says he, smiling but with death aglare in his eyes, 'I grant Viscount Merivale a day or so more of life, when it suits me to kill him I'll let him know,' and off he goes. 'Tis a vile black business, for if ever I saw a killer, 'tis this Dalroyd. Though why the lad goes out of his way to affront such a man, God only knows. And talking of the affront I've told the story plaguy ill. Here sits Dalroyd, d'ye see, at cards, Jack, and along comes my fine young gentleman and insults him beyond any possibility o' doubt. 'Ah,' says Dalroyd, laying down his cards, 'I believe, I verily believe he means to be offensive!' 'Gad love me, sir,' smiles the Viscount, 'I'm performing my best endeavour that way.' 'You mean to quarrel, then,' says Dalroyd. ''Twill be pure joy, sir!' bows the Viscount. 'Impossible!' sneers Dalroyd. 'Why then, sir,' beams the Viscount, 'perhaps a glass of wine applied outwardly will make my intention quite apparent, because if so, sir, I shall be happy to waste so much good wine on thing of so little worth.' O Jack, 'twas pure—never have I seen it better done. But 'tis an ill business all the same, for when they meet 'twill go ill with the lad, I fear—aye, I greatly fear!"

"Why then, they shan't meet!" said the Major gently.

"Eh—eh?" cried the Colonel. "Damme, Jack—who's to prevent?"

"I, of course, George."

"Aye, but how, a Gad's name?"

"First, I do know Dalroyd a rogue unworthy to cross blades with the Viscount——"

"I doubt 'twill serve, Jack, I doubt."

"Secondly, I intend to cross blades with Dalroyd myself."

"You Jack—you? O preposterous! Smite me, 'tis most irregular."

"Indeed and so it is, George, but——" the Major smiled, and knowing that smile of old the Colonel shrugged his shoulders. "I will but ask you to be here in this room to-morrow night at—say twelve o'clock—alone, George."

"When you use that tone, Jack, I know you'll do't. But how you'll contrive thing so impossible is beyond me. And talking of Dalroyd the resemblance is strong, he's very like——"

"Ah, you mean like Effingham."

"Aye, like Effingham—and yet again he's—different, Jack, and besides 'tis impossible!"

"Ten years must needs alter a man," said the Major thoughtfully. "George, I'd give very much to know if Dalroyd bears a certain scar."

"Impossible, Jack—quite, your thrust was too sure."

"Hum!" said the Major, "howbeit I cross blades with Dalroyd as soon as possible, which reminds me I've made no will and 'tis best to be prepared, George, and you shall witness it if you will."

So the document was drawn up, blunt and soldier-like, and duly attested.

"A will, Jack," said the Colonel throwing down the pen, "is a curst dust to dust and dry bones business, let's ha' another bottle."

"Egad, and so we will!" answered the Major. "And drink success to thy wooing, George."

CHAPTER XXXIX
WHICH IS A QUADRUPLE CHAPTER

I

My lady Betty opened the bedroom door and sneezed violently:

"Aunt Bee," she gasped, "O!"

"Heavens, child, how you pounce on one!" cried Lady Belinda, starting and dropping her powder puff. "What is't?"

"Snuff, aunt—O!"

"Snuff—O Lord! Where? Who?"

"Your Colonel—Cleeve, aunt—O!"

"Colonel Cleeve? Here again? O Heavens!" cried Lady Belinda, flushing.

"He's been waiting below and sprinkling me with his dreadful snuff this half-hour and more, as you know very well, aunt!"

"Indeed miss, and how should I know?" cried Lady Belinda indignantly, stealing a glance at her reflection in the mirror.

"You saw him come a-marching up the drive of course, dear aunt. O he uses the dreadfullest snuff I vow—'tis like gunpowder—and scatters it broadcast! 'And pray how's your lady aunt?' says he, sprinkling it over the window-seat and me. 'O sir, in excellent health I thank you,' says I, 'twixt my sneezes. 'I trust she finds herself none the worse for her walk last night, the air grows chill toward sunset,' says he through a brown cloud. 'Indeed sir,' I choked feebly, 'aunt enjoys the evening air hugely.' 'Then,' says he, speaking like Jove in the cloud, 'I'm bold to hope that she perhaps—this afternoon——' 'I'll go and see,' I gasped, and staggered from the room strangling. 'Tis a dear, shy soul, aunt, for all his ogreish eyes and gruff voice."

"Betty!" exclaimed Belinda clasping her hands, "when I think of him downstairs and our poor, dear Charles abovestairs I could positively swoon——"

"Nay, aunt, the Colonel's presence here is Charles' safeguard surely, and the Colonel's a true soldier, a dear, gentle man 'spite all his bloodthirsty airs and ferocious eyes— —"

"Do you think them so—so fierce, Betty?" questioned Lady Belinda wistfully.

"Go down and see for yourself, aunt." Lady Belinda crossed to the door, but paused there, fumbled with the latch and then, all at once, sobbed, and next moment Betty had her close in her arms.

"Why, aunt!" she whispered. "My dear, what's your grief?"

"O Betty!" whispered Lady Belinda, trembling in those strong young arms, "O my dear I'm—so—old— —"

Betty's eyes filled and stooping she kissed that humbly bowed head:

"Aunt Belinda," she murmured, "Love is never old, nor ever can be. If Love hath come to thee when least expected, Love shall make thee young. Thy years of waiting and unselfish service these have but made thee more worthy—would I were the same. There, let me dry these foolish tears, so. Now go, dear, go down and may'st thou find a joy worthy of thy life of devotion to thy Betty who loveth thee and ever will. I'll upstairs to Charles!"

II

"Now look'ee Bet," my Lord of Medhurst was saying five minutes later, "I'll not endure it another week—I'll not I say. To lie mewed up here, to creep out like a very thief—'tis beyond my endurance— —"

"And mine too, Charles—almost," sighed Betty. "To have to live a hateful lie, to be forced to meet one I despise, to endure his looks, his words, his touches—O!"

"God forgive me, Bet—I'm a beast, a graceless, selfish beast!" cried his lordship, clasping her in his arms. "When I think of all you've done for me I could kick this damned carcass o' mine—forgive me! But ha!" his lordship chuckled boyishly, "Deuce take me Bet, but I avenged you to some extent last night. I sat on the wall, Bet, as coyly as you please and true to a minute along comes my gentleman and kisses my hand and I more demure and shy than e'er you were. 'Betty,' says he, low and eager, 'by heaven, you're more bewitching than ever to-night!' His very words, Bet, as I'm a sinner!" Here my lord chuckled again, laughed and finally fell to such an ecstasy of mirth that he must needs gag and half-choke himself with his handkerchief, while Betty laughed too and thereafter gnashed white teeth vindictively:

"What more?" she questioned, her eyes bright and malevolent.

"Why then, Bet, the fool falls to an amorous ecstasy—pleads for a taste o' my lips—damn him! and finally catches me by the foot and falls to kissing that and I bursting with laughter the while! So there he has me by the foot d'ye see and I nigh helpless with suppressed joy, but when I wished to get away he did but hold and kiss the fiercer. So Bet, I—full of prudish alarms as it were—bestowed on him—a kick!" Here his lordship found it necessary to gag himself again while Betty, leaning forward with hands clasped, watched him gleefully.

"You kicked him!" she repeated. "Hard?"

"Fairly so—enough to send his hat flying, and Bet, as luck would have it who should chance along at that precise moment but Major d'Arcy and——"

Uttering an inarticulate cry my lady sprang to her feet.

"Did he see—did he see?" she demanded breathlessly, "Charles—O Charles—did he see?"

"Begad, I fear he did—why Bet—Betty—good God—what is it?" For, covering her face, Betty had cowered away to the wall and leaned there.

"What will he think!" she murmured. "O what will he think of me?"

My lord stood speechless awhile, his delicate features twitching with emotion as he watched her bowed form.

"Betty dear," said he tenderly at last, "doth it matter to thee—so much?"

"Charles!" she cried, "O Charles!" and in that stricken cry and the agony of the face she lifted, he read her answer.

"Dearest," said he after awhile, clasping his arm about her, "here is no cause for grief. I'll go to him in—in these curst floppy things—he shall see for himself and I'll tell him all——"

"No!" said she rising and throwing up proud head. "I'll die first! We will go through with it to the end—nobody shall know until you are safe—none but you and I and Aunt Belinda. To speak now were to ruin all. So, my Charles, whatsoe'er befall you shall not speak—I forbid it!"

"Forgive me, Bess," he pleaded, "wilt forgive me for jeopardising thy—thy happiness so?"

"Aye to be sure, dear boy!" she answered, kissing him. "Only now I must go!"

"Go, Betty?"

"To him!" she sighed. "I must find out—just how and what he thinks of me."

"Gad's my life, Bet!" sighed his lordship ruefully as he followed her to the door, "I do think thou wert ever the braver of the two of us."

III

"Consequently Tom, dear lad," the Major was saying as he walked the rose-garden arm in arm with the Viscount, "feeling for thee as I do and because of the years that have but knit our affections the closer, I am bold to ask thee what hath moved thee to run so great a risk o' thy life—a life so young and promising."

"Why nunky," answered the Viscount, pressing the arm within his own affectionately, "in the first place I'll confess to a pronounced distaste for the fellow."

"Yes, Tom?"

"His air of serene assurance displeases me."

"Quite so, Tom."

"His air of cold cynicism annoys me."

"Well, Tom?"

"In fine sir, not to particularise, Mr. Dalroyd, within and without and altogether, I find a trifle irksome."

"And so, Tom, for these trivialities, you picked a quarrel with a man who is a notorious and deadly duellist?

"I believe I objected to his method of dealing cards, among other things, sir."

"And now, Tom," said the Major, sitting down beside the sun-dial and crossing his legs, "may I suggest you tell me the real reason—your true motive?"

The Viscount began to pull at and arrange the rich lace of his steenkirk with gentle fingers.

"Gad save my poor perishing soul!" he sighed, "but you're a very persistent nunky!"

"Tom," said the Major softly, "you—you love my lady Betty, I think?"

The Viscount, sitting beside him, was silent a moment, still pulling gently at the lace of his cravat.

"And—and always shall, sir," he answered at last.

"This," said the Major, staring straight before him, "this brings me to a matter I have long wished to touch upon—and desired to tell thee, Tom. For I also thought—that she ... I ... we..."

"Love each other, sir," said the Viscount gently.

"You knew this, Tom?"

"Sir, I guessed it a few days since."

The Major bowed his head and was silent awhile.

"Pancras," said he at last, "'twas none of my seeking. I thought myself too old for love—beyond the age. But Love stole on me all unbeknown, Love gave me back my vanished youth, changed the world into a paradise wherein I, dreaming that she loved me, found a joy, a happiness so great no words may tell of it. And in this paradise I lived until—last night, and last night I found it but the very paradise o' fools, dear lad——"

"Last night!" exclaimed the Viscount, "last night sir?"

"I chanced to walk in the lane, Tom."

The Viscount clenched white hand and smote it on his knee:

"Damn him!" he cried, "he must ha' bewitched her in some infernal manner! That Betty should act so—'tis incredible! Yet 'twas none so dark! And I saw! 'Twas shameless—a vulgar country-wench would never——"

"Hush, Tom, hush!" cried the Major, flushing. "She's—after all she's so young, Tom, young and a little wilful—high-spirited—and—and—young, as 'twere——"

"Betty's no child, sir, and 'fore heaven——"

"'Tis strange I missed you, Tom," said the Major a little hastily.

"The lane makes a bend there sir, and when I saw I stopped——"

"So here's the true cause of your quarrel, Tom?"

"Nay, sir, I've known Betty from childhood, I've honoured and loved her but—'twas not so much on her account——"

"Then whose, Tom?"

"Why sir I—knew you loved her too——"

"God bless thee, lad!" said the Major and thereafter they sat awhile staring studiously away from each other.

"The vile dog hath bewitched her somehow!" explained the Viscount suddenly at last, "I've heard tell o' such cases ere now, sir."

"Heaven send he bewitch none other sweet soul!" said the Major fervently.

"He sha'n't—if I may stop him!" said the Viscount scowling.

"I don't think—no, I don't think he ever will, Tom!"

"Gad love us!" exclaimed the Viscount suddenly in altered tone. "Nunky—sir—look yonder! 'Tis Betty herself and she's seen us! O Lard, sir—she's coming!"

Glancing swiftly round, the Major sat with breath in check watching where my lady was descending the steps into the rose-garden, as fresh, as fair and sweet as the morning itself. With one accord they rose and, side by side, went to meet her.

"Heavens!" she cried as they came up. "How glum you look—and the sun so bright too! Ha' you no greeting for me?"

"Madam," said the Viscount with a prodigious bow, "I was but now relating how, last night, I saw you in a lane, seated upon a wall."

"Was I, Pan?"

"Indeed, my lady!" he answered, taking out his snuff-box.

"And did you see me, too?"

"Who else should see you?" questioned the Viscount staring.

"I thought 'twas only Major d'Arcy—thought to see."

"I saw you also, madam."

"Art sure, Pan?"

"O positive, madam!"

"And prithee—what saw you?"

"'Tis no matter——"

"What saw you, Pan—Tom?"

"I saw that Dalroyd fellow—brutalise your foot."

My lady's cheek grew rosy and her delicate nostrils expanded suddenly, but her voice was smooth and soft as ever.

"Will you swear it, Pan?"

"On oath!" he answered.

"Alack!" she sighed. "On what slender threads doth woman's reputation hang! And if I say I was not there?"

"Then, my lady, I am blind or, having eyes, see visions——"

"Was ever such a coil!" she sighed. "Dear Pan, hast ever been my second brother, so do I forgive thee and, thus forgiving, bid thee go, thinking on me as kindly as thou may'st and believing that thine eyes do verily see visions." So the Viscount bowed and went, somewhat stiff in the back and making great play with his snuff-box. "Dear Pan!" she murmured as she watched him go, "I might have loved him had I any love to spare. And now—you, John—will you rail at me, too?"

"No, my lady," he answered dully, "never again!"

"Yet your voice is cold and hard! Did you think to see me too?"

"Aye, I saw—I saw," he answered wearily.

"And if I say you saw me not?"

"Then, my lady, I will say I saw you not."

Now at this she came near, so near that he was conscious of all her warm and fragrant loveliness and thrilled to the contact of her hand upon the sleeve of the war-worn Ramillie coat.

"And—wilt believe, John?" she questioned softly. The Major stood silent and with head averted. "This dear old coat!" she murmured. "Dost remember how I sewed these buttons on?"

"Aye, I remember!" he groaned.

"And—wilt believe, my John?" she questioned, and drew nearer yet, until despite her soft and even tone, he could feel against him the swell and tumult of her bosom; yet he stood with head still averted and arms, that yearned to clasp her, rigid at his sides. "Wilt believe, John?"

"Betty," he answered, "ask me to believe the sun will rise no more and I'll believe, but not—not this!"

"Yet, dost love me—still?" she whispered.

"Aye, my lady—through life to death and beyond. The love I bear you is a love stronger than death and the agony of heartbreak and dead hopes. Though you take my heart and trample it in the dust that heart shall love thee still—though you profane the worship that I bear you still shall that worship endure—though you strip me of fame and honour and rob me of my dearest ideals still, ah still shall I love you until—until——" His voice broke and he bowed his head. "O Betty!" he cried. "In God's name show me—a little mercy—let me go!"

And turning he limped away and left her standing alone.

IV

The Colonel's fierce eyes were transfigured with a radiant tenderness, his gruff voice was grown strangely soft and tender, his sinewy hand had sought and found at last those white and trembling fingers, while two soft eyes were looking up into his, eyes made young with love, and bright with happy tears.

Seeing all of which from without the casement, my lady Betty, choking back her own grief, smiled, sobbed and, stealing away, crept softly upstairs to her room, locked herself in and, lying face down upon her bed, wept tears more bitter than any she had ever known.

CHAPTER XL
OF THE ONSET AT THE HAUNTED MILL

A wild, black night full of wind and rain and mud—a raging, tearing wind with rain that hissed in every vicious gust—a wind that roared fiercely in swaying tree-tops and passing, moaned dismally afar; a wind that flapped the sodden skirts of the Major's heavy riding-coat, that whirled the Sergeant's hat away into the blackness and set him cursing in French and Dutch and English.

"What is't, Zeb?" enquired the Major during a momentary lull as they rode knee and knee in the gloom.

"My hat sir ... the wind with a cur——" The words were blown away and the Sergeant, swearing unheard, bent his head to the lashing rain.

"Are we ... right ... think you? ... long way ... very dark egad..."

"Dark sir, never knowed it darker and the rain—may the dev..."

"Are we nigh the place Zeb d'ye think, we should be ... by now——"

"Not so fur your hon ... a bye-road hereabouts if 'twarn't dark, with ten thousand..."

In a while as they splashed on through the gloom the Major felt a hand on his arm.

"By your left, sir ... bye-road ... can't see on account o' dark, may the foul fiend ... by your left, so!" Thus through mud and rain and buffeting wind they rode until at word of the Sergeant they dismounted.

"Must hide the horses, sir," said he in the Major's ear. "I know a snug place hard by, wait you here sir ... some shelter under the hedge ... never saw such a plaguy night, may all the foul——" And the Sergeant was gone, venting curses at every step. Very soon he was back again and the Major stumbled after him across an unseen, wind-swept expanse until looming blacker than the dark, they saw the ruin of the haunted mill. Inside, sheltered from rain and wind the Major unloosed his heavy coat and took from under his arm a certain knobby bludgeon and twirled it in the dark while Sergeant Zebedee, hard by, struck flint and steel, but the tinder was damp and refused to burn.

"Is a light necessary Zeb—if any should observe——"

"Why sir, like as not they'd think 'twas ghosts, d'ye see. And 'tis as well to survey field of operations, wherefore I brought a lanthorn and——" The Major reached out and caught his arm.

"Hark!" said he.

Above and around them were shrieks and howlings, timbers creaked and groaned and the whole ruined fabric quivered, ever and anon, to the fierce buffets of the wind, while faint and far was an ever-recurrent roll and rumble of thunder.

"Storm's a-waxing sir ... can't last, I..." Borne on the wind above the tempest came a faint hail. "Zounds, they're close on us!" exclaimed the Sergeant. "This way, sir, keep close, catch the tail o' my coat." Thus they stumbled on through the pitchy dark, found a wall, followed it, turned a corner, brought up against another wall and so stood waiting with ears on the stretch.

And soon amid this confusion of sounds was a stamping of horse, the tread of feet and presently voices within the mill itself; one in especial that poured out a flood of oaths and fierce invective upon rain and wind and all things in general.

"O burn me, and must we wait here, shivering in the darkness with a curse on't and me wet to the bone——"

"Content ye, my lushy cove, the others aren't far."

"The others, curse 'em! And what o' me shivering to the bones o' me as I'm a roaring lad——"

"What, Jerry," cried another voice, "is the Captain wi' you?"

"Aye, here I am—show a light!"

"Why so I will an ye gimme time. So we're all met, then—all here, Nick?" Followed the sound of flint on steel, a flash, a glow, a light dazzling in its suddenness, a light that revealed four masked men, mud-splashed and bedraggled, thronged about a lanthorn on the uneven floor.

"Now mark me all," said Joseph pushing up his vizard. "You, Jerry and the Captain will ride to the cross-roads, the finger-post a-top o' the hill. The coach should reach thereabouts in half an hour or so. Benno and I strike across the fields and join my gentleman's coach and come down upon you by the cross-roads. So soon as you've stopped the coach, do you hold 'em there till we come, then it's up wi' the lady and into my gentleman's coach wi' her. D'ye take me?"

"No we don't!" growled Jerry, shaking the rain from his hat, "how a plague are we t' know which is the right coach——"

"By stopping all as come your way——"

"Ged so—we will that!" nodded the Captain.

"And look'ee Jerry and be damned, if you——"

"Stand!" The four sprang apart and stood staring at the Major who stood, a pistol in each hand, blocking the doorway between them and the howling desolation outside. "Move so much as a finger either one of you and he's a dead man. Quick, Sergeant—their wrists—behind!" Thus while the Major stood covering the four with levelled weapons watchful and ready, Sergeant Zebedee stepped forward with several lengths of stout cord across his arm. Coming up to the Captain who chanced to be nearest, the Sergeant was in the act of securing him, when Jerry uttered a dreadful cry:

"God save us—look!" For an instant the Major's glance wavered and in that moment Joseph had kicked out the light and there and then befell a fierce struggle in the dark, a desperate smiting and grappling; no chance here for pistol-play, since friend and foe were inextricably mixed, a close-locked, reeling fray. So while the storm raged without, the fight raged within, above the howling of wind and lash of rain rose piercing cries, shouts, groans and hoarse-panted oaths. Smitten by a random blow the Major fell and was kicked and trampled upon by unseen feet; yet he staggered up in the dark, his long arms closed in relentless grip, his iron fingers sought and found a hold that never loosed even when he fell and rolled again beneath those unseen, trampling feet. Little by little the ghastly sounds of conflict died away and in their place was again the roar and shriek of wind.

"Zebedee—Sergeant Zeb!"

"Thank God!" a hoarse voice panted. "A moment sir—must have—light. Hot work your honour—never ask for warmer!" After some delay the Sergeant contrived to light his lanthorn; and the Major, looking into the face of the man he held, loosed his grip and got to his feet.

"'Tis him they call the Captain!" said the Sergeant, flashing his light.

"Pray God I haven't killed him!" the Major panted, clasping one hand to his side.

"'Twould but save the hangman a job, sir. Lord! but you're ripped and tore, sir!" The Major glanced from his disordered dress to the Sergeant's bloody face:

"Are you hurt, Zeb?" he questioned.

"Nought to matter, sir. Look'ee, here lies the rogue Jerry—zounds, and a-coming to already! Hold the light, sir—may as well tie him up nice and comfortable."

"And this other fellow too, Zeb—he's stirring, I'm glad to see——"

"Glad sir? Zooks, 'tis pity you didn't kill him——"

"Nay, I'll ha' no killing, Zebedee——"

"Zounds sir, why so queasy-stomached nowadays? 'Tain't as if you'd never——"

"Enough, Sergeant! I'm no longer a soldier and besides—things are—are different quite—nowadays."

"Why look'ee sir, where's t'others? Here be but two o' the rogues——"

"Only two, Zeb?—give me the lanthorn!" By its light they searched the mill inside and out; gruesome signs of the vicious struggle they found in plenty but, save themselves and their two groaning captives, the place was empty.

"'Tis mortal hard," mourned the Sergeant, "here's me i' the dark, seemingly a-knocking of 'em all down one arter t'other, continual. Yet, 'spite said zeal here's but two to show for same, sure enough."

"Why then we must after 'em, Zeb!" said the Major with a sudden sharp catch of the breath. "Go fetch the horses!" Forthwith Sergeant Zebedee hurried away and, left alone, the Major, leaning against the wall, set a hand to his side and kept it there until the Sergeant reappeared, leading their horses.

"You picked up my pistols, Zeb?"

"And put 'em back i' the holsters, sir. And the rogues are got away sure enough, their horses are gone, d'ye see."

"Then we must spur, Zebedee."

"Aye sir. And the rain's stopped, praise God!" quoth the Sergeant and blew out the lanthorn leaving their captives to groan in the dark.

"Take the lead, Zeb," said the Major as they reached the high-road— "the finger-post a-top the hill—and gallop."

CHAPTER XLI
CONCERNING HIGHWAYMEN AND THE ELEMENT OF SURPRISE

My lady Betty leaned back in the corner of her coach, gazed at her aunt's slumbering features dim-seen in the light of the flickering lamps, and yawned. The storm had abated, the rain had passed, but the darkness was around them, a darkness full of rioting wind, and mud was below them through which the heavy wheels splashed dismally as the great coach laboured on its way.

My lady Betty, stretching rounded limbs luxuriously, yawned again and having nothing particular to look at, closed her eyes; but, almost immediately she opened them rather wider than usual, and sat up suddenly as, from somewhere amid the gusty dark outside, a loud voice hailed, a pistol cracked and the coach pulled up with a jerk.

Instantly Lady Belinda awoke, screamed "Highwaymen!" and swooned. Next moment the coach door swung open and Lady Betty saw a sodden hat with a hideous, masked face below; she saw also two arms that seized her roughly, dragged her forward and whirled her out into the tempestuous darkness. Hereupon my lady struggled once, found it vain, screamed once, felt the cry blown away and lost in the wind and, resisting no more, reserved her forces for what might be. Next she was aware of a dim shape, was bundled through a narrow opening, was seized by hands that aided her to a cushioned seat, heard the slam of a door, a hoarse command, and was jolted fast over an uneven road.

Instinctively she reached out her hand, groping for the door, felt that hand clasped in smooth, strong fingers, and a voice spoke close beside her:

"That would be unwise, sweet Bet?"

Recognising that voice, she freed her hand and shrank back into her corner, shivering all at once; yet when she spoke her voice was almost casual.

"This is quite surprising, Mr. Dalroyd."

"But more delightful!" he retorted, and she was aware that his hand, in the darkness, was seeking hers again.

"Yet—how very foolish and—and unnecessary!" said she a little breathlessly.

"Unnecessary—ha, perhaps, dear Betty——"

"Had I not promised to fly with you, next week?"

"True, my Bet, true, but next week is—next week. And then besides though you would have run off with me in your own time yet I prefer to run off with you in my own time. Moreover——"

"Well, sir?"

"I love the unexpected! I want you, Betty, but I'd have you come a little unwilling to my embrace. Give me this pretty hand, suffer me to—what, no?—excellent! Presently, here in the dark, with unbridled tempest rioting about us, I shall kiss your lips and the more you struggle in my arms the sweeter I shall find you—so, dearest Bet, struggle and strive your best——"

But at this moment the coach slowed down, came to a standstill and a hand knocked at the window. Whispering fierce curses Mr. Dalroyd lowered it.

"Sir," said a voice humbly, "these bye-roads be evil going and in this dark hard to follow—shall we light the lamps?"

"Aye—if you must—light one—the off one."

Thus after some little delay the lamp was lighted and the coach lurched forward again. My lady sighed to find herself no longer in utter darkness, though the light was faint—scarcely more than a glow. Then dread seized her, for by this glow she saw her captor's eyes and, reading his sure and merciless purpose there, she grew suddenly and terribly afraid of him at last. Fronting that look she strove to hide her shame and terror but he, wise in the ways of proud and frightened beauty, laughed softly and leaned towards her. And in that moment, looking beyond him, she saw over his shoulder that which strung every quivering nerve of her, for in a sling, on Mr. Dalroyd's side of the coach, hung his travelling pistols; and now in her terror the one ambition of her life became narrowed down to this—to grasp sure fingers round the silver-mounted butt of one of these weapons.

"Betty," said he, "my beautiful Betty, which is it to be?"

"Pray sir," said she, striving to speak lightly, "pray be more explicit."

"Doth proud loveliness yield at last?" he questioned softly, "or shall it be forced?" Even as he spoke his arms were about her; for a moment she struggled wildly, then, as he crushed her to him, still struggling against his contact, she yielded suddenly and, bearing him backward, her white hand flashed out and, laughing hysterically, she wrenched herself away from him.

"Sir," she panted, "O dear sir, you love surprises, you tell me—look, look at this and beg your life of me!"

His arms fell from her and slowly, sullenly, he recoiled, watching her beneath drooping lids.

"Ah, Betty!" he sighed, "what an adorable woman you are!"

"Why then sir," said she a little tremulously but with hand and eyes steady, "you will obey me."

"'Twill be my joy, sweet Bet," he answered softly, "aye faith, my joy— when I have conquered thee——"

"Conquered?" she cried and gnashed white teeth. "No man shall do that—you least of——"

A hoarse command from the road in front, followed almost immediately by two pistol shots in rapid succession, and, lurching towards the hedge, the coach came to an abrupt standstill, ensued the stamp of horses, cries, fierce imprecations, the sounds of desperate struggling and a heavy fall. In an instant Mr. Dalroyd had snatched his other pistol, had jerked down the window and thrust out head and arms.

"What now?" he cried. "What the devil——" The words ended in a choking gasp, for the pistol was twisted from his hold and a strong hand was upon his throat; then the door was wrenched open and himself dragged into the road there to be caught and crushed in arms of steel while his hands were drawn swiftly behind him and dexterously trussed together, all in a moment.

"You!" he cried, staring into the pale, serene face of his captor and struggling against his bonds. "God, but you shall repent this outrage, I swear you——"

"The gag, Sergeant!"

"Here, sir!" And Mr. Dalroyd's vicious threats were choked to sudden silence.

"His ankles, Sergeant!"

"All secure, your honour!"

"Then mount and take him before you—so! Up with him—heave!"

Next moment Mr. Dalroyd lay bound, gagged and helpless across the withers of the Sergeant's horse.

"What's come of the coachman, Zebedee?"

"I' the ditch, sir."

"Hurt?"

"Lord love ye, just a rap o' the nob, sir."

It was now that my lady, crouched in the darkest corner of the chaise, fancied she heard shouts above the raving of the wind and, grasping the pistol in trembling fingers, ventured to look out. And thus she saw a face, pallid in the flickering light of the solitary lantern, a face streaked with mud and sweat, fierce-eyed and grim of mouth. She caught but a momentary glimpse as he swung to horse but, reading aright the determined purpose of that haggard face, she cried aloud and sprang out into the road, calling on his name.

"John—O John!" But her voice was lost in the rushing wind, and the Major, spurring his spirited horse, plunged into the dark, beyond the feeble light of the lamp, and was swallowed up in the whirling darkness.

Deafened and half-dazed by the buffeting wind and the suddenness of it all, she stood awhile, then, squaring her dimpled chin, set about freeing one of the horses.

CHAPTER XLII
WHICH DESCRIBES A DUEL

Colonel Lord George Cleeve, dozing over a bottle beside the hearth, stirred at the heavy tread of feet, unclosed slumberous eyes at the sudden opening of the door, glanced round sleepily, stared and sprang to his feet, broad awake in a moment, to see the Major and Sergeant Zebedee, wind-blown and mud-splashed, tramp heavily in bearing between them a shapeless bundle of sodden clothes and finery the which, propped upright in a chair, resolved itself into a human being, gagged and bound hand and foot.

"Jack!" he gasped, his eyes rolling. "Why, Jack—good Lord!" After which, finding no more to say he sank back into his armchair and swore feebly.

"Off with the gag, Sergeant," said the Major serenely as he laid by his own mud-spattered hat and riding-coat. The Sergeant obeyed; and now beholding the prisoner's pale, contorted features, the Colonel sprang to his feet again.

"Refuse me!" he gasped. "What the—Mr. Dalroyd!"

"Or Captain Effingham!" said the Major. "Loose his cravat and shirt, Sergeant, and let us be sure at last." Sergeant Zebedee's big fingers were nimble and the Major, taking one of the silver candlesticks, bent above the helpless man for a long moment; then, setting down the light, he bowed:

"Captain Effingham, I salute you!" said he. "To-night sir, here in this room, I propose that we finish, once and for all, what we left undone ten years ago, 'tis for this purpose I brought you hither, though a little roughly I fear. My Lord Cleeve will oblige me by acting as your second, I think. But first, take some refreshment, I beg. We have ample leisure, so pray compose yourself until you shall have recovered from the regrettable violence I have unavoidably occasioned you. Loose him, Zebedee!"

Freed of his bonds, Mr. Dalroyd stretched himself, re-settled his damp and rumpled garments, and lounged back in his chair.

"Sir," said he, viewing the Major with eyes that glittered between languid-drooping lids, "though my—enforced presence here runs counter to certain determined purposes of mine, yet I am so much of a philosopher as to recognise in this the hand of Fate and to find therein a very real satisfaction, for I have long been possessed of a most earnest desire to kill you—as indeed I think I should ha' done years ago but for a slip of the foot." The Major bowed:

"May I pour you a glass of wine, Captain Effingham? he enquired.

"Not now sir, I thank you," answered Mr. Dalroyd, languidly testing the play of right hand and wrist, "afterwards, perhaps!"

"You are without your sword, I perceive sir," said the Major.

"Gad, yes sir!" lisped Mr. Dalroyd, smiling, "in our hurry we left it behind in the coach."

"Still, you will prefer swords, of course?"

"Of course, sir."

"Go, bring the duelling-swords, Sergeant," said the Major and sitting down filled himself a glass of wine while Mr. Dalroyd gently smoothed and patted wrist and sword-hand with long, white fingers and the Colonel, standing on the hearth, his feet wide apart, stared from one serene, deadly face to the other.

"Ten years, sir, is a fair span of life," said Mr. Dalroyd musingly, "and in that time Fortune hath been kind to you, 'twould seem. You have here a noble heritage to—ah—leave behind you to some equally fortunate wight!" Here he turned to glance at the wicked-looking weapons Sergeant Zebedee had laid upon the table. "When you have finished your wine, sir, I will play Providence to that fortunate wight, whoever he may be, and put him in possession of his heritage as soon as possible." The Major bowed, emptied his glass and rising, proceeded to remove coat and waistcoat and, with the Sergeant's aid, to draw off his long riding-boots and rolled back snowy shirt from his broad chest while Mr. Dalroyd, having kicked off his buckled shoes, did the same.

"We have no surgeon here, I perceive," he smiled. "Ah well, so much the better." So saying, he took up the nearest sword haphazard, twirled it, made a rapid pass in the air and stood waiting.

"My Lord Cleeve," said the Major as the Colonel drew his weapon and stepped forward, "when once we engage you will on no account strike up our swords——"

"But damme, man Jack, how if you wound each other——"

"Why then sir," murmured Mr. Dalroyd quietly, testing the suppleness of his blade, "we shall proceed to—exterminate one another. This is to the death, my lord!"

The library was a long, spacious chamber with the broad fireplace at one end; moreover the Sergeant had already set back the furniture against the wall and rolled up the rugs out of the way. Lord Cleeve glanced round about him quick-eyed, ordered the candles to be disposed a little differently that there might be no advantage of light, then, folding his arms, glanced from the pale, serene face of the Major to the cold, smiling face of Mr. Dalroyd as they fronted each other sword in hand in the middle of the wide floor.

"Then, 'tis understood, I am not to part ya', not to interfere until——"

"Until one of us is dead, my lord!" said Mr. Dalroyd, his nostrils quivering.

"Exactly so!" said the Major. "Sergeant Zebedee—lock the door!"

Lord Cleeve shrugged his shoulders: "'Tis a damnably cold-blooded business altogether!" said he as the Sergeant turned key in lock.

"Agreed, sir!" smiled Mr. Dalroyd. "But pray be so obliging as to give the word."

The Colonel shrugged his shoulders again, cleared his throat and took a step backwards:

"Ready, sirs!" said he curtly. "On guard!"

The narrow blades glittered, crossed, kissed lightly together and remained for a moment rigidly motionless, then, quicker than eye could follow, flashed into swift and deadly action. Followed the soft thud of swift-moving feet, the quick, light beat of the blades, now ringing sharply, now clashing and grinding, now silent altogether. Mr. Dalroyd's white teeth were bared in a confident smile as, pressing in, he beset the Major with thrust on thrust, now in the high line, now in the low, constantly changing his attack, besetting him with cunning beats and skilful twists; but cunning was met with cunning and fierce attack with calm and unerring guard.

Thus as the moments sped, the fighting grew ever more close and deadly, the blades darted and writhed unceasingly, they flashed and flickered in narrow circles, while the Sergeant, leaning broad back against locked door, watched the rapid exchanges with a fencer's eye and the Colonel forgot all else in the world but the sublime skill of their play. But as the moments dragged by, the Colonel's fingers began to pull and twist irritably at one of the buttons of his coat, and about this time too, Sergeant

Zebedee's nonchalant attitude changed to one of rigid attention, his black brows twitched and in his look was dawning bewilderment; for while Mr. Dalroyd fought serene of face and tireless of arm the Major seemed to have become strangely languid and unaccountably slow, his pallid cheeks were lined with sweat and he laboured painfully in his breathing; noting all of which the Sergeant's bewilderment grew to anxiety, while Colonel Cleeve's fingers were twisting and wrenching at the button harder than ever.

Without the windows was the ceaseless rush of the wind, now rising to an angry roar, now dying to a mournful wail; within was a ceaseless tread of shoeless feet and ring of steel, now clashing fierce and loud, and always the Sergeant's anxiety increased, for the Major's parries seemed slower than ever; again and again his adversary's point, flashing perilously near, was turned only just in time, once ripping the cambric at his neck and again at shoulder; and ever Mr. Dalroyd's smile grew more confident and the spectators' anxious bewilderment the keener.

All at once the Sergeant uttered a gasp, the Colonel took a quick stride forward as Mr. Dalroyd, thrusting in tierce, flashed into carte and drove in a vicious lunge—was met by lightning riposte and flinging himself sideways sprang out of distance, a fleck of blood upon his shirt-sleeve.

"You are touched, I think, sir?" enquired the Colonel.

"Thank you, 'tis nought in the world," he answered, panting a little but with lips that curled and nostrils that quivered in his cold smile as he watched the Major who stood, haggard of face, one hand pressed to his side, his lips close-set, breathing hard through his nose.

"Art hurt, man Jack—art hurt?"

"Nay sir I—I am well enough!" he answered, forcing a ghastly smile— "when Captain Effingham is ready——"

"Nay sir," answered Mr. Dalroyd, bowing, "pray take your time—you are a little distressed I think, pray recover your breath——"

"I am quite ready, sir." So they bowed to each other, advanced upon each other and again their weapons crossed. And now as though they knew it was a matter of time they pressed each other more fiercely and with a new impetuosity, yet equally alert and wary—came a whirl and flurry of ringing steel drowned all at once in the crash of splintering glass at one of the windows—a frenzied hand that groped, then the casement swung wide with a rush of wind and, as though borne in upon the raging tempest, a figure sprang into the room, long hair flying, a cloud of tresses black as the night, silks and satins torn and mud-splashed, one white hand grasping a silver-mounted pistol, the other stretched out commandingly.

"Stop!" she panted. "Stop!"

At sight of her Mr. Dalroyd lowered his weapon and bowed; the Major, with head drooping, viewed her beneath his brows, then, crossing to the table leaned there with head averted, and Lord Cleeve, having opened his eyes to their widest, opened his mouth also—but said not a word and dropped a button from suddenly relaxed fingers; as for the Sergeant he unclenched his fists, breathed a deep sigh of thankfulness and murmured "Zounds!"

"My Lord Cleeve," said she at last, "when Mr. Dalroyd has taken his departure, I will beg you to escort me to my house."

Lord Cleeve bowed and sheathed his sword looking foolish the while.

"A—a happiness!" he stammered.

"Mr. Dalroyd," said my lady very proudly for all her torn and muddy gown, "I ask you to prove your manhood by setting by that sword and leaving the house—now! You will find one of your coach horses below the terrace. Your quicker way will be by the window yonder."

Mr. Dalroyd hesitated, his pale cheeks flushed suddenly, his sleepy eyes opened wide, then he smiled and bowing, reached for his coat and with the Colonel's assistance got into it, and he slipped on his shoes. Then, heedless of the others, he caught my lady's hand to his lips and bowing, kissed it.

"Ah, Betty," said he, "you are worth the winning—aye, upon my soul you are!"

"Take your pistol, sir!" He took it, turned it over and laughed gently.

"My dear lady," said he, "after your exploits this night I wouldn't forego you for any woman that ever tempted man. Your time shall be my time and my time is—soon, Betty—ah, soon!" And bowing again, he crossed to the open window, stepped out into the dark and was gone. For a moment none moved, then the Sergeant crossed the room and closed the shattered casement.

"Major d'Arcy," said my lady, and now there was a troubled quiver in the clear voice, "upon a night not long ago you made me a promise—nay, swore me an oath. Do you remember?" The Major was silent. "Sir," she continued, her voice growing more troubled, "you did not give me that oath easily and now—O is it thus you keep all your promises?" The Major made no answer, nor did he stir, nor even lift his head.

"John," she took a quick step toward the rigid figure. "O Jack—you are not hurt——"

"Thank you—I am—very well!" he answered, still without turning, and gripping the sword he still held in rigid fingers. After this there seemed a long silence filled with the rumble of wind in the wide chimney. Then my lady stirred, sighed, and stretched out her hand to Colonel Cleeve.

"O my lord," she said wearily, "prithee take me home." So the Colonel took her hand, drew it through his arm and led her towards the door, but ever as she went she gazed towards the Major's motionless back; reaching the door she paused, but still his head was averted; then she sighed, shivered and, despite her muddy and tattered gown, swept away upon Lord George's arm like a young, disdainful goddess.

The Major drew a quivering breath and his sword clattered upon the floor.

"God above!" exclaimed the Sergeant, clasping strong arms about that rigid form, "the Captain pinked you after all, sir."

"No, Zeb, no—but I fancy I've broke a—couple of ribs or so—as 'twere, d'ye see, Zeb——" And sighing, he fell forward with his head pillowed upon the Sergeant's shoulder.

CHAPTER XLIII
HOW THEY DRANK A NEW TOAST

"The Major's rib will do, sir," nodded Dr. Ponderby, "'tis doing well and will do better and better. A simple fracture, sir—'twill be sound in no time, it being a rib of health abounding, owing, if I may put it so, to an abstemious life, a past puritanic—a——"

"Abstemious, sir!" exclaimed Lord Cleeve, rolling his eyes, "abstemious d'ya' say? O begad, hark to that, Jack! Abstemious sir, abste——" The Colonel choked and rolled his eyes fiercer than ever.

"My lord," said portly Dr. Ponderby, patting his smooth wig, "I am no Puritan myself, nor do I look askance at a glass or so of wine, far from it——"

"The bottle is at your elbow, sir," said the Major from his cushioned chair.

"Abstemious—begad!" chuckled Lord Cleeve, snuffing fiercely.

"I thank you, Major," said Dr. Ponderby, leisurely filling his glass, "and my Lord Cleeve, coming back to my patient's rib, I repeat its abounding health is due entirely to a youthful and immensely robust constitution and——"

"Abstemious—ho!" chuckled the Colonel. "Given occasion sir, Jack can be as abstemious as Bacchus. I remember last time we made a night on't—aha! It being nigh dawn and we on our fifth bottle, or was it the seventh, Jack—not to mention Sir Benjamin's punch, begad, it being nigh dawn, I say, and I happening to glance about missed divers faces from the genial board. 'Where are they all, Jack?' says I. 'Under the table,' says he, sober as a judge, and damme sir, so they were and Jack as I say, sober as yourself sir, for all his abstemiousness!"

"Hem!" exclaimed Dr. Ponderby, gulping his wine and rising. "None the less, Major d'Arcy, my dear sir, you shall be abroad again in a week if—I say, and mark me sir, I say it with deepest emphasis—if you will brisk up, banish gloomy thought and melancholy, cultivate joy, sit i' the sun, eat well, drink moderately and sleep as much as possible."

"A copious prescription, sir!" sighed the Major wearily.

"Brisk?" snorted Lord Cleeve, "brisk, is it? Refuse me but he's as brisk and joyous as a gallows! Here he sits, hunched up in that old service coat and glooms and glowers all day, and when night draws on, damns his bed, curses himself, and wishes his oldest friend to the devil and that's me sir—his friend I mean."

"Stay, never that, George," smiled the Major, shaking protesting head.

"But ya' curst gloomy Jack, none the less."

"This won't do," smiled Dr. Ponderby, "won't do at all. Gloom must we dissipate——"

"Dissipate!" exclaimed the Colonel, "dissipate—aye man, but he won't drink and the Oporto's the right stuff you'll allow——"

"He must have company——"

"Well and aren't I company?"

"The very best, my lord——"

"Not to mention Viscount Tom and——"

"Very true sir," smiled the doctor, "only you don't either of you happen to wear petticoats——"

"Petticoats!" exclaimed the Colonel, rolling his eyes.

"Petticoats are my prescription, my lord—plenty of 'em and taken often. A house is a gloomy place without 'em——'

"Agad and ya' right there—ya' right there!" nodded the Colonel vehemently.

"No!" protested the Major.

"Yes!" cried the Colonel. "Look at my place in Surrey, the damndest, dreariest curst hole y'ever saw——"

"Nay George, when I saw it last it was——"

"A plaguy, dreary hole, Jack!" snapped the Colonel. "Used to wonder why I couldn't abide the place—reason perfectly plain to-day—lacks a petticoat, and Jack man, a petticoat I'm a-going to have soon, man, soon ha, and so shall you begad!"

"Never!" said the Major drearily.

"Now hark to the poor, curst wretch, 'tis the woefullest dog!" exclaimed the Colonel feelingly, "won't drink and no petticoats! Man Jack, I tell thee woman is to man his—his—well, she's a woman, and man without woman's gentle and purifying influence is—is only—only a—well, man. Look at me. After all these years, Jack 'tis a petticoat for me."

The Major murmured the old adage about one man's meat being another man's poison, whereon his lordship snarled and rolled his eyes as he rose to escort the doctor to the door.

"Petticoats quotha?" said he, "Petticoats it shall be."

"In large doses!" nodded Dr. Ponderby, "and repeated often." So saying, he shook the invalid's languid hand, smiled and bustled away.

"Ha!" exclaimed his lordship, "there's a man of stark common sense, Jack."

"Aye, aye," nodded the Major a little impatiently, "but what of Effingham, you say he has left Westerham?"

"He left at mid-day, Jack."

"For good?"

"'Twould seem so, he marched bag and baggage. The rascal fences purely well, I vow."

"Superlatively well," nodded the Major beginning to fill a much smoked clay pipe.

"Man Jack, I thought he had ya' there in carte."

"Nay I was expecting it and ready, George. I should have caught him on the riposte but I was short d'ye see——"

"Owing to ya' rib, Jack."

"Damn my rib!" exclaimed the Major. "'Tis pure folly I should be laid up and sit here like a lame dog for so small a matter as a rib, d'ye see——"

"'Tis more than ya' rib is wrong with ya', Jack!"

"A Gad's name, what?"

"A general gloom and debility induced by lack of and need for—a petticoat."

"Folly!" snorted the Major, but his pale cheek flushed none the less.

"Talking o' Dalroyd, ya' pinked his sword arm, Jack."

"But he's alive, alive George and now, now for all I know—where's Tom—where's Pancras? For all we know they may be fighting at this moment!" And the Major half rose from his elbow-chair.

"Content ya', Jack, content ya'!" said the Colonel, pressing him back with hands surprisingly gentle, "the lad's not fighting—nor likely to. I swear again, he shan't cross blades with Dalroyd or Effingham if I have to pistol the rogue myself, so ha' no worry on that score, Jack."

The Major sighed and leaned back in his chair while Lord Cleeve watched him and, snuffing copiously, sighed sympathetically.

"'Tis the woefullest figure ya' cut, Jack, wi' that long face and damned old service coat."

"'Tis the one I wore at Ramillies," said the Major, glancing down at faded cloth and tarnished lace.

"Is it, begad! I'd never ha' recognised it. Then 'tis time 'twas superannuated and retired from active service. You was wounded that day I remember, Jack."

"Yes."

"Twice."

"Yes."

"But ya' never wore look so doleful—never such a damned dumb-dog, suffer-and-smite me air—not then, Jack—not in those days and ya' were generally nursing some wound or other."

"I was younger then!" sighed the Major.

"Pah!" exclaimed the Colonel scattering a pinch of snuff in his vehemence, "I say pish, man—tush and the devil! Ya' younger these days than ever ya' were—all ya' need to become a very youth is a petticoat—take your old comrade's advice and marry one."

"Never!" exclaimed the Major, clenching his fists.

"Tush!" exclaimed the Colonel, snuffing. "As ya' friend, Jack, 'tis my duty to see ya' happily married and I'll be damned if I don't. Wedlock 'twixt man and woman is—is—ah, is well, marriage. There's little Mrs. Wadhurst over at Sevenoaks—a shape, Jack, an eye and a curst alluring nose. Hast ever noticed her nose?"

"No!" snarled the Major.

"Ha!" sighed the Colonel. "Not to ya' taste, belike. Why then there's Lady Lydia Flyte—a widow, Jack—another neighbour—a comely piece, man, bright eyes, wealthy and sufficiently plump——"

"Ha' done!" snapped the Major, puffing smoke.

"Dooce take ya'!" snarled the Colonel, scattering snuff. "Begad, man Jack, ya' damned peevish and contrary, y'are 'pon my life! If I wasn't the most patient, long-suffering, meek and mild soul i' the world I should be inclined to lose my temper over ya' damned stubbornness—rot me, I should!" At this the Major chuckled..

"Your meekness, George, hath ever been equalled only by your humility!" said he.

"Nay, but man Jack, look'ee now—'tis not that I would ram my own happiness down thy throat, but to see thee so glum and spiritless, damps my own joy doocedly. And the word glum brings us back to petticoats."

"Nay George, for mercy's sake no more——"

"But comrade, a petticoat should be—ah—should be, a petticoat is—is a—ha!"

At this moment was a knock and, the door opening, the Sergeant advanced two paces and stood at attention:

"Your honour," said he.

"Ha, Zeb," exclaimed the Colonel, fixing him with fierce, blue eye, "ho, Sergeant Zeb, what the dooce is a petticoat?"

The Sergeant stared at his lordship, stared at the ceiling, scratched smooth-shaven chin with thoughtful finger and spoke.

"A petticoat, m' lud, is a article as a woman can't very well go without and a man shouldn't—and won't!"

The Colonel set down his glass, threw back his head and roared with laughter till he stamped. "Aha—oho!" he cried at last, sprinkling snuff over himself and everything within reach. "O Gad, Zeb, ya' right, ya' right— must remember that. D'ya hear that, Jack—oho—aha!" And he roared again while the Major smiled, chuckled, and despite rib and bandages, laughed until Sergeant Zebedee anxiously bade him have a care, and announced that Sir Benjamin Tripp, Lord Alvaston, Mr. Marchdale, Sir Jasper and Captain West had ridden over to see him and enquire after his health.

"Why then let 'em in, Zeb—let 'em in," said the Major a little breathlessly, "and bring up a half-dozen or so of the yellow seal——"

"The yellow—ha!" sighed the Colonel, "if the same as last time 'tis bottled sunshine, 'twill warm the very cockles o' ya' heart, man——"

"Nay, George——"

"Tush, Jack—an you don't drink, I don't——"

"But George——"

"Pish, Jack! You'll never go for to deny ya' old friend?" Here the door opened and the company entered with a prodigious waving of hats, flirting of gold-mounted whips and jingling of spurs.

"Major d'Arcy, sir!" cried Sir Benjamin, "your very devoted, humble servant. My lord, yours! Ods my life, my dear Major d'Arcy, I joy to see you no worse, sir, after your desperate battle with nine bloodthirsty ruffians——"

"Four, Sir Benjamin——"

"Common report, sir, makes 'em twelve but I'm assured they were but nine——"

"Sir, they were but four," repeated the Major gently. "But gentlemen, you have lost one of your number—Mr. Dalroyd is gone, I understand?"

"Faith and so he has, sir," answered Mr. Marchdale petulantly, "clean gone and with eight hundred guineas o' mine and more of Alvaston's, not to mention——"

"But then we never had 'ny luck wi' th' cards, Tony," yawned his lordship.

"Luck!" spluttered Mr. Marchdale, "luck, d'ye call it——"

"Ahem!" exclaimed Sir Benjamin. "'Tis true Dalroyd is gone, sir, and suddenly, nor will I disguise the fact that his ahem!—his departure was in some sort a relief considering the deplorable scene 'twixt him and Viscount Merivale——"

"And his curst secret ways," added Mr. Marchdale, "and his treatment of that fellow of his—Dalroyd's room was next mine and I know he's beaten the poor rogue damnably more than once of late."

"Haw—that's true enough!" exclaimed Captain West, "heard the miserable dog myself. Dismally a-groaning a-nights. More than once, haw!"

"And yesterday, just as he mounts to ride away Dalroyd must fall a-kicking the fellow—in the open street and with us standing by! And kicked him, look you, not as a gentleman should but with such vicious pleasure in it—faith, 'twas positively indecent!"

"Od's life, sir, and that's true—indecent is the word!" nodded Sir Benjamin tapping his snuff-box, "and gentlemen, if the human optic, basilisk-like, could blast soul and wither flesh—Dalroyd would have hem! I say would have known—ha—would have made a sufficiently uncomfortable not to say painful exit—or setting forth the matter in plainer terms Dalroyd hem——"

"Hold hard, Ben!" yawned Alvaston. "Y' gettin' lost again. What our Ben wants t' say 's simply Dalroyd's f'low looked bloody murder 'n so he did."

"Ha—begad! He did so!"

"Dalroyd is well enough enjoyed now and then," said Mr. Marchdale sententiously, "but as a constant diet is apt to become devilish indigestible! And as regards his unfailing lack with the cards, I shouldn't wonder——"

"Then don't, Tony—don't!" murmured Lord Alvaston, crossing his slender legs. "Dalroyd may be this, that or t'other, but Dalroyd ain't here— enough of him."

"Aye, true," nodded Sir Benjamin, "true indeed, Dalroyd is gone and we, dear Major, like this year's roses, are going too. In a week sir, this fraternity amorous will suffer disruption, our lady hath so decreed, the fiat hath gone forth."

"Indeed sir, you surprise me!" said the Major, glancing from one to another, "whence comes this?"

Here Sir Benjamin shook his head and sighed, Sir Jasper stifled a groan, Mr. Marchdale swore beneath his breath, the Captain uttered a feeble "Haw" and Lord Alvaston whistled dolefully.

"Sir," sighed Sir Benjamin, "you behold in us a band of woeful wooers each alike condemned to sigh, and yet to sigh in unison and in this, the measure of our woe doth find some small abatement. Each hath wooed and each hath proved his wooing vain, his dreams, his visions must remain but—hem!—but dreams and——"

"Hold on, Ben," murmured Alvaston, "burn me but y're gettin' int' th' weeds again! What poor old Ben's strivin' t' say 's simply that——"

"Betty'll ha' none of us," scowled Mr. Marchdale, "though if I'd had more time——"

"None of us!" added the Captain, "er—haw! Not one!" Here Sir Jasper, trying to sip his wine and groan at the same time, choked.

"And yet—and yet," sighed Sir Benjamin, holding his glass between his eye and the light, "seeing that our ahem! our unspeakable grief is common to us, each and all, it shall, methinks, but knit closer the bonds of our fellowship and we should unite to wish her happiness with whatsoever unknown mortal she shall some day make blest. Regarding which I think a toast might be appropriate—pray charge your glasses and I——" Sir Benjamin paused and turned as with a perfunctory knock the Sergeant reappeared.

"Your honour," said he, "my Lady Belinda Damain with Lady Carlyon to see you."

The Major caught his breath, then sat upright his square chin showing a little grim.

"You will tell their ladyships that I present my humble respects and thanks but regret I am unable to see them."

"Sir?" said the Sergeant, staring.

"Go, Sergeant!"

"Jack!" exclaimed the Colonel as the door closed "why, Jack!"

"Sir!" answered the Major, his eyes very keen and bright.

"P-petticoats, man—two of 'em—doctor's orders! O rot me!" spluttered the Colonel.

"Gentlemen," said the Major, smiling wearily, "pray charge your glasses for Sir Benjamin's toast."

"Major d'Arcy, sir," said Sir Benjamin, bowing from his chair, "permit me to say that I applaud the delicacy of your feelings. We lovers who have wooed and lost, alas! Ods my life, sir, 'twas well done—honour me!" And he extended his snuff-box. "Sir," he continued, when they had bowed and snuffed together, "summer is on the wane and with the summer we, like the swallows, shall desert these rural solitudes. A week hence, instead of perambulating bosky Westerham we shall most of us be jolting over the cobblestones of London—but we shall one and all treasure a lively memory of your friendship and trust that it may be renewed from time to time. Meanwhile, ere we fly hence, it is our united hope that you, together with my Lord Cleeve will honour us again with your company to supper on an early date——"

"A Gad, sir, we will that!" nodded the Colonel. "Speaking for myself I thank you heartily, and speaking for Jack, I say he shall come if I have to carry him there and back again."

"And now, Sir Benjamin," said the Major, "pray give us your toast."

Sir Benjamin rose, glass in one hand, lace handkerchief in the other.

"We have all here, I think, with the exception of the gallant Colonel, essayed our fortune with my lady Betty, and with equal ahem! equally deplorable lack of success. 'Twould seem that she is determined on according to no one of us here that felicity we have, each one, dreamed of and sought for. But she is young and 'tis but to be expected that one day some happier man shall succeed where we have failed. Now sirs, as lovers, as gentlemen and sportsmen true, let us raise our glasses to that happy unknown whoever he be, let us drink health to him, joy to him, success and long life to him for the sake of Our Admirable Betty. Gentlemen 'The Unknown!'"

CHAPTER XLIV
SOME ACCOUNT OF A HIGHWAYMAN

Mr. Dalroyd was a man of habit and of late it had become his custom to take particular heed as to the lock and bolts of his chamber door of nights and to sleep with his pistol beneath his pillow.

He had formed another habit also, a strange, uncanny habit of pausing suddenly with head aslant like one hearkening for soft or distant sounds; though to be sure his eyes were as sleepy and himself as languid as usual.

But the stair leading to Mr. Dalroyd's bedchamber was narrow and extremely precipitous and, descending in the gloom one evening, he had tripped over some obstacle and only by his swordsman's quickness and bodily agility saved himself from plunging headlong to the bottom. He had wakened in the middle of the night for no seeming reason and, sitting up in that attitude of patient listening, had chanced to glance at the door lit by a shaft of moonlight and had watched the latch quiver, lift silently and as silently sink back in place.

He had moreover become cautious as to how he took up his pistols, having found them more than once mysteriously at full cock. So Mr. Dalroyd continued to lock and double-lock his door at night and, in the morning, seated before his mirror, to watch Joseph the obsequious therein: as he was doing now.

"Sir," said Joseph, eyes lowered yet perfectly aware of his master's watchful scrutiny, "everything is packed save your brushes and the gillyflower water."

"Why then, my snail, you may pack them also."

"I will, sir."

"It is now half after ten, Joseph—we ride at eleven."

"To London, sir?"

"Order the horses to the door at that hour, Object."

"Yes, sir. Pray, sir," said he humbly, head bowed and big hands twitching nervously, "regarding your promise of permitting me to—to— quit your service—pray when is it to be?"

"I don't know, Joseph, I can't say."

"Sir—sir—d'ye mean——"

"I mean that I don't feel I can endure to part with you, Joseph."

"You mean—you—won't?"

"You interest me, Joseph. Yes, you amuse me vastly, there is about you such infinite repression, Joseph, such latent ferocity. Yours is a nature of great and unexpected possibilities. Ferocity, duly in check, allures me, Joseph; so I shall continue to be your master and to—master you, Animal. Reach me my pistols."

Joseph crossed the room to where they lay beside the bed.

"Sir," said he, taking up the weapons, "you won't let me go, then?"

"Are they loaded, Joseph?"

"Yes, sir."

"Are they cocked?"

"No, sir."

"Which is just as well, Joseph. With your hands shaking like that you might have had the misfortune to shoot me and be infallibly hanged for a deplorable accident."

Joseph's eyes flickered and he stood, still grasping a pistol in either hand.

"Sir," said he thickly, "do you mean to let me go—yes or no?"

"Hanged, Joseph, for—knowing you as I do, Reptile, I am leaving behind me a letter to the effect that should I meet with any sudden or untoward misfortune on my journey, a knife in the back, say, or a bullet, Joseph, justice may be done on the body of one Joseph Appleby, alias Galloping Nick, already wanted for the murder of——"

The weapons thudded to the floor and Joseph cowered.

"For the love of God!" he whispered hoarsely. "Sir—sir——" And he clenched and wrung his hands together.

"Pick up the pistols, Worm, and handle them carefully, they've taken to cocking themselves of late, 'twould seem. And I, Joseph, I've taken to locking and bolting my door a-nights and being particular how I tread in the dark."

So saying, Mr. Dalroyd smiled and went downstairs humming softly, where the company were gathered to see him off.

In due time the horses were brought to the door and Mr. Dalroyd, pulling on his gauntlets, prepared to mount; but before doing so, drew his pistols from their holsters and found that their primings had been shaken out. Whereupon he beckoned Joseph smilingly—saw them re-primed and, smiling still, kicked Joseph viciously.

Then he mounted, watched Joseph do the same, waved an airy farewell to the company and rode gracefully away.

Reaching the open road, Mr. Dalroyd summoned his follower to ride beside him.

"On the whole, Joseph," said he, "I prefer to have a man of your— infinite possibilities beside me, at my elbow—within reach. Besides, I'm in the mood for conversation, let us talk, creature." Joseph's heavy brow grew rather more lowering and he kept his gaze bent obsequiously on the dust of the way as he drew level with his master, who had reined his horse to a gentle, ambling pace.

"You were educated above your station, Joseph—the law, I think?"

"Yes, sir."

"Owing to your mother's exertions—hence the extreme warmth of your—ah—filial regard."

"She also shielded me from a father's brutality, sir."

"Hence, Joseph, as I say, the ardour of your regard for her. 'Tis strange to find that even in the basest, most depraved natures the softer qualities of gratitude and love may occasionally be remarked by the philosophical observer, a fact sufficiently strange and interesting!" Joseph's wolverine mouth twitched and he lifted his gaze slowly as high as the top of the hedge and kept it there. "Your first noteworthy exploit," continued Mr. Dalroyd good-humouredly, "was the forgery of a bill——"

"Sir—sir," stammered Joseph, glance abased to the dust again, "pray why must you——"

"My good Object, I would see that I have the facts sufficiently clear. To begin again, you forged a bill on one Hilary Girard, he, discovering your criminality, taxed you with the fact, whereafter poor Mr. Girard suddenly died—misfortunate wight! Lead poisoning was it, or powdered glass?" Joseph uttered a sound between a choke and a groan. "Nay, after all, 'tis no matter which," continued Mr. Dalroyd, "suffice it—he died. Thereafter you took to the highway, became famous for your daring, were finally betrayed by a jealous beauty, were sentenced to hang, escaped on a legal quibble, and were cast for transportation, effected your escape and—Fortune sent you to me and I give you life, Joseph, and a certain amount of freedom so long as you are of use to me."

Joseph's mouth had become a twisted line and he moved in his saddle as if undergoing some sharp, physical discomfort, while Mr. Dalroyd lapsed into pleasant reverie as they rode on through the warm and fragrant air.

They held a course south-easterly staying only to change horses at the various stages where Joseph, acting on his master's instructions, ordered post-horses to be in readiness three nights hence. Towards late afternoon Mr. Dalroyd halted at Tenterden for refreshment; after an excellent meal he sauntered out into the yard and summoned Joseph, but without avail, the obsequious Joseph was not to be found. Mr. Dalroyd's modish languor changed to a sudden cold ferocity before which ostlers, post-boys and stablemen quailed; within five minutes he had roused the whole place and set everyone searching, from host to pot-boy. Every hiding-place, likely and unlikely, was ransacked, the inn, the stable and scattered outbuildings, but to no end, Joseph had vanished. Finally he ordered his horse to be saddled and while this was doing, stood, chin in hand, like one lost in vexed thought yet more than once fell into that attitude of strained attention as though listening for distant sounds. Roused by the clatter of his fresh horse's hoofs on the cobbles of the yard as it was led from the stables, he glanced up and surveyed the animal with quick, appraising eye and prepared to mount; but, before doing so, stayed to lift his holster-flaps and found that his pistols were gone. At this he laughed suddenly—a strange laugh, at sound of which the fellow holding the horse put up an elbow and cowered behind it as if expecting a blow; but Mr. Dalroyd, laughing still, turned and beckoned to the landlord with his gold-mounted riding-whip.

"Look'ee," said he, his mirth still distorting his features, "I've been robbed by the rascal and among other things, of my pistols. I must have another pair—at once!"

"Sir," began the landlord, bobbing apologetically, "there ain't a pair in the house Lord love me, no such thing except a blunderbuss — — "

"Blockhead!" exclaimed Mr. Dalroyd, pointing at the speaker with his whip, "I said a pair of pistols, go get 'em—how and where you will, but get them and bring 'em to me and don't keep me waiting, my good oaf." So saying, Mr. Dalroyd turned and sauntered up and down the shady side of the yard apparently lost in dreamy reverie. Very soon the landlord came hurrying back triumphantly bearing a long-barrelled weapon in either hand. Mr. Dalroyd took one, balanced it and cursed its weight and clumsiness.

"Careful, sir," warned the landlord, flinching, "they're loaded."

Mr. Dalroyd glanced around; overhead a crow flapped heavily on lazy wings. Mr. Dalroyd aimed the weapon and while the report still rang and echoed, the crow turned over and over, a shapeless bundle of ragged feathers and thudding down into the grassy ditch opposite the inn lay there struggling and croaking dismally.

"They'll serve!" nodded Mr. Dalroyd, "have the thing loaded again and hasten!" Watched by many awestruck eyes, Mr. Dalroyd crossed to his horse, mounted, and oblivious of the interest he caused, sat awhile with eyes half-shut and head aslant, listening, until the weapon was brought; then he examined each with care, flint, priming and charge, and thrust them into his holsters.

"Landlord," said he, as he put away his purse, "did you take any heed to the general appearance of that runaway rogue of mine?"

"Aye sir, a tall chap wi' big hands and a way o' lookin' down his nose and—come to think on't, a fresh-healed scar just over one eye-brow——"

"Caused by a cut-glass perfume bottle!" nodded Mr. Dalroyd. "A just and fair description, landlord. Should you ever chance on such a fellow anywhere at any time you will do well to apprehend him——"

"For robbery, sir——?"

"For murder, landlord!" As he spoke Mr. Dalroyd touched spurs to his horse and cantered away, leaving the landlord to stare open-mouthed and the crow to thrash broken wing and croak dismally in the ditch as, reaching the highway, he spurred to a gallop.

All the afternoon he kept the road, and as the day waned he became ever more alert, his quick eyes scanned the road before and behind and he rode for long stretches with his head leaned to that angle of patient listening for sounds afar. Now, as evening fell he had an unpleasant feeling that he was being followed, more than once he fancied he caught the faint throbbing of distant hoofs, now lost, now heard again, never any nearer yet never any further off. Once he reined up suddenly to hearken but heard nothing save the desolate sighing of wind in trees; yet when he went on again he could have sworn to the distant beat of galloping hoofs, wherefore, ears on the stretch, he loosed the flaps of his holsters.

So day drew to evening and evening to night and with every mile the fancy grew within him, little by little, until it became an obsession and he spurred fiercely uphill and down, often turning to glance back along the darkening road and with his pistols cocked and ready.

CHAPTER XLV
CERTAIN ADVENTURES OF
THE RAMILLIE COAT

The Major's rib mended apace; nevertheless his fits of gloom and depression seemed but to grow more pronounced, insomuch that he would seize any and every opportunity to escape from Colonel Cleeve's cheery presence or the Viscount's affectionate solicitude and, locking himself into his study, would strive feverishly to banish thought with his gabions, angles of fire, etc.

To-day the Viscount and Colonel Cleeve had ridden abroad together, and being alone, the Major had ventured forth into the orchard and now sat in the hutch-like sentry-box hard at work on his History of Fortification.

The afternoon was very still and very hot, so hot indeed that he had laid by coat and wig and sat in shirt-sleeves, his close-cropped, brown head bent above his manuscript, writing busily. But presently he set this aside and leaning head on hand wearily, became lost in troubled reverie, then, sighing deeply, took pen and paper and began to indite a letter. At first he paused often as if the composition were difficult, but, little by little, his thoughts seemed to flow more freely for his quill flew rapidly, never staying until the letter was finished. Having sanded it, he read over what he had written, folded it, paused, shook his head and tore it across and across in his sinewy fingers, made as if to throw the scraps aside, checked himself and crammed them into one of the yawning side-pockets of the Ramillie coat. Thereafter, he sat staring straight before him until, moved by sudden impulse, he drew to him a new sheet of paper and wrote again busily. Then, not staying this time to read over what he had set down, he sanded, folded, sealed it, and turning, thrust it carefully into a pocket of the Ramillie coat and so turned back to his history once more.

All at once he started, lifted his head and glanced across at a certain part of the old, red-brick wall and, dropping his pen, got stealthily to his feet.

"A young cavalier he rode on his way
Singing heigho, this loving is folly."

The singing voice on the opposite side of the wall was drawing nearer, wherefore the Major snatched up his wig, clapped it on anyhow and incontinent fled.

My lady Betty, having watched this hasty retreat, frowned, plucked a leaf, bit it with sharp, white teeth and—espied the Ramillie coat. The wall was rather high and there was no ladder this side, but my lady was of courageous temper and determined character, so——

The Major, turning a sharp corner of the yew walk, ran full tilt into Sergeant Zebedee.

"Ha, Zeb," said he, a little breathlessly, "I—I was looking for you——"

"Same likewise, sir," answered the Sergeant, standing at attention. "There's Colonel Cleeve, Sir Benjamin, and the Viscount a-waiting to play cards wi' you——"

"Excellent! I'll join 'em at once——"

"But your—your coat, sir?"

"Aye, to be sure! You'll find it in the arbour, Zeb, bring it to me in the library."

"Now, I wonder," murmured the Sergeant as the Major hastened away with long strides, "I wonder wherefore so rapid?"

So my lady jumped. She had just caught up the Ramillie coat when she heard the approach of heavy steps and, being as resourceful as she was determined, she folded the garment compactly and sat upon it.

The Sergeant, about to enter the arbour, paused, started and stood at attention.

"Good day, Sergeant Zebedee!" quoth she demurely.

"Same to you my lady and thank'ee."

"And pray how is the Major?"

"Ha'n't you just seen him mam?"

"Indeed, but he—he vanished before I could speak a word, Sergeant."

"Zounds!" murmured the Sergeant.

"What d'you say, Sergeant Zebedee?

"Why my lady, 'tis his coat I'm after——"

"Coat?" repeated my lady.

"Aye mam, his Ramillie coat, sent me here for same——"

"I don't see it, do you, Sergeant?"

"Why no, my lady, I don't! But he says he left same here and——"

"But it doesn't seem to be, does it?"

"No my lady, unless you——"

"And how is the Major, pray?"

Sergeant Zebedee sighed and shook his head.

"Lord, my lady, he is that gloomy, he do sigh continual—mopes in his study when he should be out i' the sun and wanders abroad when he should be snug abed——"

"But he sat out here to-day——"

"Aye, for a wonder! 'Twas Mrs. Agatha and me as coaxed him out."

"He seems to be a very—uncomfortably—moody kind of man, Sergeant."

"Aye—but only of late, my lady."

"I wonder why?" The Sergeant glanced down into her bright eyes, looked at earth, looked at sky, and scratched his chin.

"Why, since you put the point, my lady, I should say 'tis either on account o' petticoats or witchcraft or—maybe both. And talking o' witchcraft, there's his coat now, p'r'aps you might chance to be——"

"He seems mighty set on this coat," said she, deftly spreading out her voluminous petticoats, "and 'tis such a shabby, woeful old thing."

"True mam, but I follered that coat through the smoke and dust of Ramillies fight though 'twas gayer then, d'ye see, but even now it shows the rents in skirt and arm o' bullet and bagnet as he took that day. 'Tis a wonderful garment, my lady."

"It would irk him to lose it, belike?"

"Lose it! Mam, it aren't to be thought on!"

"Still I think 'twould do him a world of good if 'twere lost awhile, it seems to affect him so evilly."

"Nay, I think 'tis t'other way about, mam. Says I to him one day, 'Sir,' says I, 'when at all put out wherefore and why the Ramillie coat?' 'Because Zeb,' says he, 'when I put it on I seem to put on some of my lost youth also.' Still, there's limits, mam, there's limits, and for a gentleman o' his degree to go out in same, and among his tenants d'ye see, well, it aren't right—though I've darned same constant. No wonder Widow Weston, which same is a scold, my lady, but 'tis no wonder she contradictioned of his honour no later than yesterday arternoon towards four o' the clock as ever was——"

"Aye, I know Widow Weston!" smiled my lady. "Contradicted him—aye—she would."

"And did, my lady! Here's his honour in his old coat a-bowing to her and a-choking and coughing d'ye see, on account of her chimbley a-smoking woeful. 'Mam,' says he, 'I fear your chimbley smokes.' 'It don't!' she cries, 'it don't, and if it do 'tis no worse than it was in my husband's time and if it did for him 'twill do for me,' she says. Whereon his honour bows himself into the air and wipes the soot out of his eyes all the way home, mam."

"But referring to the coat, Sergeant——"

"Begad, yes mam, saving your presence. There's him a-waiting for same."

"You must insist on his leaving it off, Sergeant."

"Insist? Zounds, my lady, insist—to the Major. Couldn't nowise be done, mam."

"Why then he must lose same, Sergeant Zeb," said my lady roguishly.

"Lose it, mam! Lord mam, his honour would never forgive me."

"He would—O he would. Besides you didn't lose it. And it isn't here, is it?"

"Why it aren't apparent to human observation, my lady. But p'r'aps you might chance to be sit——"

"Hush!" cried my lady, white finger upraised. "Is someone coming?" The Sergeant stepped outside to glance about, listened dutifully and shook his head.

"No mam, but I must get back to the house, his honour will——"

"How is he progressing in health, Sergeant—his appetite—doth he eat well?

"Eat, my lady!" exclaimed the Sergeant dolefully, "he's forgot how."

"Truly I do begin to think he hath a soul after all, Sergeant."

"Soul, mam? The finest as ever was! He's all soul, my lady, 'tis his body as do worry me—vading mam it be, vading and a-languishing away. Aye, 'tis his body——"

"There seems plenty of it left, Sergeant, and it looks solid enough—O Lud!" she exclaimed all at once and clasped her hands, as from afar rose a hoarse, growl that swelled into a deep-lunged roar. "A mercy's sake, what is it?"

"My lady, 'tis the Colonel a-calling me. I must go, my lady, and consequently humbly request you to——"

"Stay, dear Sergeant Zeb, first pray go fetch me a ladder."

"Ladder, my lady?"

"How may I get back over the wall without it?"

The Sergeant turned and stared at the wall, shook his head and rubbed his chin:

"Question is, how did you get over, my lady?"

"'Tis no matter! Go—go fetch the ladder, I must not be seen here—go this instant!" The Sergeant went.

Once out of eyeshot my lady sprang up, sped across the orchard, hurled the Ramillie coat over the wall into her own garden and was back in the arbour a full half-minute before the Sergeant re-appeared, ladder on shoulder.

"You dear Sergeant Zeb!" she exclaimed, rising and crossing the orchard beside him. "The bravest soldiers and strongest men are always the kindest and gentlest to women, aren't they?"

"Are they, mam?" said the Sergeant flushing a little as he planted the ladder where she directed.

"To be sure they are," she sighed, gathering up her petticoats, "see how hard you kicked that hateful Jennings——"

"Shall I hold the ladder, my lady?" he enquired, flushing deeper.

"Thank you—no!" she answered and set a slender foot upon the lowest rung. "Sergeant Zebedee!"

"My lady?"

"Right about face!" The Sergeant turned automaton-like and stood so until a laughing voice cried, "Sergeant Zebedee—as you were!" And swinging round he beheld her smiling down at him from her own side of the wall. "Thank you, dear Sergeant Zeb, thank you!" she said, and nodding, vanished from sight.

The Sergeant, being orderly in all things, proceeded to set back the ladder in the tool-house, to dust his coat and re-settle his wig, then crossed to the arbour and stood there for a full minute staring at the empty bench.

"Zounds!" he exclaimed at last, and wheeling, marched very thoughtfully into the house.

"Eh—not there—not there, Zeb?" exclaimed the Major, laying down his cards and turning to glance at the Sergeant's expressionless face.

"Your honour, it are—not!"

"But—God bless my soul—it must be!"

"Why then sir, if 'tis it aren't apparent to human observation!"

"But I distinctly remember taking it off there!"

"Why then sir, it hath gone and vanished itself away!"

"Pish!" exclaimed the Major rising. "I'll fetch it myself."

"O rot me, Jack!" cried the Colonel, "here's a curst rampageous business over an old rag. 'Tis time 'twas lost——"

"Or burned, nunky!" added the Viscount.

"So let be, Jack—Sergeant Zeb shall bring you another!"

But the Major was determined, and presently sallied forth with Sir Benjamin, the Viscount, Colonel Cleeve and the Sergeant at his heels. Reaching the orchard, they searched the arbour within and without, they peered and prodded under bushes, they sought high and they sought low without avail.

"Very remarkable!" exclaimed the Major at last.

"Most extraordinary, od's my life!" assented Sir Benjamin, mopping heated brow. "Are you sure you had it on, sir?"

"Belike some stray cur hath taken a fancy to it and run off wi' it!" the Colonel suggested.

"Mistaking it for—er—something equally unpleasant, nunky!" added the Viscount.

"'Tis not so much the loss of the coat itself that gives me worry as—er—the contents of the pockets!" said the Major, wrinkling his brow.

"What, your purse, sir?" enquired Sir Benjamin.

"Nay that—would scarce ha' mattered."

"Ya' snuff-box, Jack?"

"Letters, uncle?"

"No, no, not—exactly letters as 'twere and yet—ah—O demme!" So the Major gave up the useless search. "Come, gentlemen—if 'tis gone, 'tis gone. Come, let us get back to our game."

CHAPTER XLVI
FURTHER INTIMATE ADVENTURES
OF THE RAMILLIE COAT

"Aunt Belinda," said my lady, pausing on the broad stair with lighted candle, "pray how do you refrain?"

"From what, dear Betty?"

"Sneezing, aunt!"

"O naughty puss!"

"All the evening by my reckoning you have sneezed but once. Sure you must be getting snuff-proof or——"

"O wicked, teasing baggage!"

"Art very happy, dear aunt?"

"Ah my sweet, so happy that I yearn to have thee happy too!"

"In two days, aunt, two little days! Charles will wait no longer and—I'm glad."

"Hast been up to wish him good-night, Bet?"

"Nay, he was asleep, dear boy, and looked so young, aunt, for all his trials."

"Trials do but better us, child—or should do. Good-night, my sweet, and pleasant dreams!" So they kissed each other and went their several ways.

Reaching her chamber my lady sent her maid to bed, locked the door, took a key from her bosom and, from its hiding-place among dainty, perfumed garments and laces, drew forth the Ramillie coat. Then she set it upon the back of a chair and, hanging thus, the well-worn garment fell into such natural folds and creases that its owner might almost have been inside it. The night was hot and still, and through the open lattice stole the languorous perfume of honeysuckle, and breathing in the sweetness my lady sighed as she began to undress; yet in the midst of this dainty business, chancing to glance at the Ramillie coat she blushed and started instinctively so lifelike was that broad back and the set of those square shoulders.

And now in dainty night-rail and be-ribanded cap she sat down and leaned near to snuff delicately at the worn and faded garment.

Tobacco! How coarse and hateful! And yet how vividly it brought his stately presence before her, his slow, grave smile, his clear, youthful eyes, his serene brow, and all his shy yet virile personality.

Tobacco! Him! O was there in all the world quite such another man, so brave, so chivalrous—and so unmodish?

Here in the sleeve was a rent, even as the Sergeant had said, and very featly mended by the Sergeant's own skilful fingers; a jagged rent it had been and even now she could see a faint stain—she shivered, for now she saw other like stains were here also. So my lady shuddered, yet, doing so, leaned nearer and drew the threadbare sleeve about her snowy neck and thus espied the yawning side-pocket. My lady peeped into it, hesitated, then plunged slim hand into those cavernous depths.

His clay pipe. His silver tobacco-box. A mass of torn paper. A letter sealed with his signet, and my lady sighed rapturously for it was addressed thus:

"To Lady Elizabeth Carlyon."

With this in one hand, the Ramillie coat in the other, she crossed to her great high bed and, seated there, the coat beside her on laced pillow, drew the candles a little nearer, broke the seals and read:

"DEAR LADY AND MY LOVE,

When you receive this I shall be beyond seas and 'tis like I shall not see you again for I leave suddenly and unknown to any.

All this summer afternoon I have sat here striving to tell you why this must be, and now my labour is lost for I have destroyed my letter since it doth seem that it might perchance have pained you to read it almost as much as me to write. So I have destroyed it since I would spare you pain now and ever. Of late I have been sick, not of body so much as mind, and mayhap once or twice have suffered harsh thoughts of thee, but to-day these are gone and out of mind, and love for thee burns within me true and steadfast as it shall do until I cease to be—aye, and beyond. For if I have grieved of late yet have I known joys undreamed and have looked and seen what Happiness is like unto, wherefore I do not repine that Happiness hath not stayed. Love and I have lived so long estranged that now methinks I am not fitted, so do I go back to the things I understand. But Happiness hath stooped to me a little while to brush me with his pinions ere he fled and hath left with me a glory shall never fade. So now, dear maid that I do love and ever shall beyond mine understanding, here do I take my leave of thee. I ride alone henceforth yet shall I not be solitary since thy sweet memory goeth beside me even unto my journey's end.

> JOHN D'ARCY."

And now my lady turned and looked upon that war-worn coat through a mist of tears and sinking down, laid soft cheek upon its tarnished braid and lay thus a long while, the letter clasped to swelling bosom. Then starting up she gathered those torn scraps of paper and strove to piece them together; but they were inextricably mixed, yet here and there the fragment of some sentence would leap to meet her.

"... my breaking heart ... ever doubted thine eyes so sweet and true ... joy for me is dead, the world a black nothingness ... O that night with thee in the dawn when earth touched heaven ... if Death should meet me in the field I'll meet him gladly ... my Love, my Betty, leaving thee I leave my very soul behind ... my farewell to thee and to love ... forget thee never..."

These she saw and many more. Every scrap of crumpled paper she smoothed with gentle fingers and every written word she read and laid tenderly aside.

And now, since she had pried thus far, she opened the other missive also, a folded sheet of paper, and saw this:

> "I, John d'Arcy of Shevening Manor, Westerham, Kent, in the event of my falling in action do will and bequeath as follows:
>
> To Zebedee Tring my servant late of His Majesty's Third Regiment of Foot the sum of Five Thousand Pounds and any cottage he may choose on my estate.
>
> To Mrs. Agatha Ridley the sum of One Thousand Pounds: But should she marry the aforesaid Zebedee Tring then I bequeath to them a marriage portion of Four Thousand Pounds making Ten Thousand Pounds in all.

And all the rest I die possessed of soever both land and monies I leave unconditionally to my dear Lady Elizabeth Carlyon.

JOHN D'ARCY."

Having folded this up again and laid it by, Lady Betty sat awhile very still, staring out into the fragrant, summer night. Then she blew out the candle and lying amid the gloom, fell to sudden, stifled sobbing and muffled, passionate whispers, her head pillowed upon a certain mended coat-sleeve; and when at last she fell asleep, that shabby, war-worn garment lay close about her loveliness.

CHAPTER XLVII
OF A FEMININE COUNCIL OF WAR

The Sergeant was at all times an early riser, but this morning he was abroad with the sun itself—a sun whose level beams wrought gloriously in dew-spangled grass underfoot, in scarlet, pink and flaming gold overhead and added fresh beauty to herb and leaf and flower; a fair, fragrant, golden morning where dismal Doubt had no place and Hope lilted in the joyous pipe of the birds, insomuch that the Sergeant paused to snuff the balmy air and to glance up at radiant sky and round about upon radiant earth feeling that life was sweet and held its best yet in store even for a battered sergeant of forty-three. And standing thus, his grim features relaxed, and for once in his busy life he fell to dreaming and forgot awhile the work that had lured him forth so very early; at length he roused himself and marched across wide lawns and along yew-bordered walks to his small tool-house, whistling softly as he went. And now, armed with nail-box, hammer, saw etc., he presently reached the work—a rustic pergola in course of construction; a very artful work this, in every respect, requiring many fierce contractions of the eyebrows, sudden fallings back two paces to the rear with head jerked suddenly left or right to judge of angle, alignment, nice proportion and the like.

The Sergeant, whistling still, had driven his first nail and had fallen back, eyebrows contracted, to judge the effect, when he wheeled suddenly about and dropped the hammer:

"Sergeant—O Sergeant Zebedee!"

Picking up the hammer, he set off at the double and reaching the orchard, halted at the foot of the wall, saluted and stared up wondering at my lady's lovely, anxious face.

"You be early abroad, mam."

"O I was here before dawn—waiting for you. Tell me, is—is the Major in?"

"The Major, mam? Aye, and sound asleep!"

"Are you sure—quite sure, Sergeant?"

"Sure, my lady. I went in but now to draw his curtains according to custom and found him sleeping soft as any child, God be thanked. But why— —"

"Because he intends to go away—soon."

"Where to, my lady?"

"Back to the wars."

The Sergeant swore, apologised immediately, and saluted.

"Be you sure, my lady?"

"Quite, O quite, Sergeant."

"But he would never go without me, mam, couldn't possibly—'twould be agin natur', d'ye see."

"But he will, Sergeant, he hath written me so—he will ride away—steal away at midnight—alone—to-night mayhap or to-morrow night—we must stay him."

The Sergeant stared grimly at a bold thrush that hopped upon the grass near by.

"Do you hear, Sergeant?"

"Aye, I hear, my lady, I hear!"

"Well—say something— —"

"Mam, there aren't no words as'll fit—not one!"

"Well, what can you do?"

"Pipeclay my cross-belts for one thing and then there's my spatterdashes— —"

"What do you mean?"

"I mean if he goes, my lady, I go— —"

"O folly, Sergeant, folly— —"

"Agreed mam, heartily, but dooty is dooty and when his honour commands, I obey—'tis become a matter o'— —"

"But he doesn't command—he means to ride without you."

"Same couldn't nowise be, my lady, consequently and therefore notwithstanding, if he goes—I go."

"And pray what of poor Mrs. Agatha?"

At this the Sergeant's grim mouth twitched and he turned to watch the thrush again.

"Dooty is dooty, my lady."

"Do you want to go fighting again?"

"No mam, I thought my soldiering was done, but if he goes, I——"

"And never try to stay him—you'll do nought——"

"Stay his honour the Major? My lady, if his mind's set on't, a whole troop o' cavalry couldn't stop him—no, not even a picked company o' the Third itself—earthquakes, fires, floods nor furies couldn't——"

"No, but I can, Sergeant, and I will!" said my lady setting her dimpled chin resolutely. "Lord!" she exclaimed fervently, "what troublesome, wayward children men are—and how helpless!"

"Children, my lady?"

"Aye—both of you! He so wilfully wayward and you so helpless. Prithee go fetch me Mrs. Agatha."

The Sergeant started. "Why mam—my lady, I——" he stammered, flushing, "'tis so early and she asleep and I—she being asleep, d'ye see, 'twouldn't be—that is I——"

"Sergeant," sighed my lady, "bring hither the ladder like a good child. I'll e'en wake her myself."

So the ladder was brought, the Sergeant turned his back and in the twinkling of an eye my lady was over the wall and walking across the dewy grass beside him; reaching the house he pointed to a latticed casement above their heads.

"'Tis rather high, Sergeant, but a handful of gravel——"

"Gravel, my lady?"

"Gravel, child—launched into the air and truly aimed——"

"But mam——" The Sergeant glanced from the loose gravel underfoot to the open lattice above and flushed. "Zounds mam, I—never did such a thing in all my days——"

"Then 'tis time you began, you're quite old enough—gravel, Sergeant—aimed carefully!"

The Sergeant obeyed and almost immediately out of the window came Mrs. Agatha's pretty face framed in a dainty, be-ribanded nightcap; at sight of the Sergeant, she flushed rosily, perceiving my lady, who beckoned imperiously, she smiled, nodded and vanished.

"Mrs. Agatha hath a pretty taste in nightcaps, Sergeant Zebedee!" said my lady demurely. The Sergeant looked sheepish, grew red, became exceedingly grim and finally answered:

"Aye, my lady."

"And a pretty face below, Sergeant!" said she, watching a lark that soared, carolling, against the blue.

"Aye, my lady!"

"And you will go a-marching to the wars, Sergeant!"

At this he uttered a sound between a sigh and a groan and thereafter looked grimmer than ever.

In surprisingly short time Mrs. Agatha appeared, as neat, demure and self-possessed as usual.

"Is aught amiss, my lady?" she enquired, dropping a curtsey.

"Only this, Mrs. Agatha, Major d'Arcy will away campaigning again and the Sergeant feels he must needs go too, so I have summoned you from bed that we together may end such folly."

The Sergeant stared.

"And end it once and for all!" added my lady firmly.

"Aye for sure, madam," said Mrs. Agatha, calmly.

The Sergeant gaped.

"Then come to the orchard and let us talk."

Seated in the arbour my lady beckoned Mrs. Agatha to sit beside her:

"I don't think we need the Sergeant, do we?" she enquired.

"I'm sure we don't, my lady."

"Then Sergeant, go and hammer!"

The Sergeant went like one in a dream.

CHAPTER XLVIII
OF THE INSUBORDINATION OF
SERGEANT ZEBEDEE TRING

"Man Jack," sighed the Colonel, ogling the wine in his glass, "now mark me, Jack, for pure Christian drink there's nought may compare with wine of Oporto, 'tis a heart-warmer, a soul-expander, a sharpener o' th' intellect, a loosener o' tongues. Moreover it doth beget good fellowship and love o' mankind in general. Begad sir, wine of Oporto is—is—I say Oporto wine is—is, well—wine. So give me Oporto——"

"And now and then a dish of tea, George!" added the Major solemnly. At this Colonel Cleeve might have been observed to quail slightly.

"You have acquired the taste—very lately, I think, sir?" enquired the Viscount.

"True, sir," answered the Colonel, rolling his eyes, "and on the whole ha' managed it very well. Tea is none so bad—once 'tis disposed of, I've drank worse stuff ere now—aye and so has Jack. Tea hath its virtues, sir, first 'tis soon over—a dish or so may be swallowed readily enough when cool by a determined effort——"

"Though," murmured the Viscount, "though 'tis better thrown out o' the window, 'twould seem, sir."

Colonel Cleeve rolled his fierce eyes again, sprinkled himself with snuff and finally laughed:

"Agad, Viscount, ya' ha' me there true enough. Look'ee now, one dish I can manage creditably enough, two at a pinch with my lady's eye on me, but three and with Belinda's eye off me—damme, no! So—out o' the window it went, aha! But how came ya' to spy me do't—eh?"

"I came to bring you news, sir, but seeing you so—ah—particularly engaged I let it wait."

"What news, lad—ha?"

"I am become a soldier, sir. I have secured a commission in His Majesty's Third Regiment of Foot."

"Ha, the old regiment—dooce take me, Viscount, but I rejoice to hear it!" exclaimed the Colonel and leapt to his feet with hand outstretched. "The 'Third' is the one and only—eh, Jack? And hath the noblest and highest traditions, yet—high and noble though they be, I'm bold to say you'll do 'em credit and be worthy of 'em, Viscount Tom—eh, man Jack?"

"Nay sir," answered the Viscount, clasping the proffered hand, "if I can but emulate in some small way nunky's and your achievements I shall be proud indeed."

"Whose company are ya' 'tached to—and when?"

"Ogilvie's sir—a fortnight hence."

"Begad, but Ogilvie's hath been cast for foreign service."

"'Tis why I chose it, sir."

"Aha!" exclaimed the Colonel, "Oho! Another case o' the heart, I judge. There was young Denholm talking but yesterday about a red coat, death and glory, or bleaching his dead bones on some foreign shore." The Viscount smiled serenely:

"I do confess love hath something to do with it, sir," said he, "though not altogether. I've had the project in mind for some time."

"Love—God bless it!" exclaimed the Colonel, "love hath made a many fine soldiers ere now, sir, and begad there's nought can cure a heartache like a brisk campaign. Come, a toast—and bumpers! Here's health and long life, honour and fortune to Ensign Viscount Merivale!" So my Lord Cleeve and the Major rose and drank the toast with hearty goodwill while the Viscount, his smooth cheek a little rosier than usual, bowed his acknowledgments.

"And now," quoth the Colonel, setting down his empty glass, "the bottle's out, 'tis near twelve and I'm for bed. To-morrow, Viscount, I'll give ya' certain advices may be of service to ya' in the regiment and write ya' a letter to Ogilvie. And so good-night, sir!"

"Good-night, George!" said the Major and reaching out suddenly he grasped Lord Cleeve's hand and wrung it hard.

"Why Jack!" said the Colonel, staring, "y'are dooced impressive, one would think ya' were going out to-night on a forlorn hope. Talking o' which, d'ya' remember the storming o' Douai, Jack? Aha, those were times—stirring times—but past and done, since, like you, I mean to quit the service for wedlock—'tis a great adventure that, Jack, belike the greatest of all, may we front it with a like resolution."

With which the Colonel bowed and betook himself to bed.

"Tom," said the Major, staring wistfully into the fire, "I'm glad you've chosen the old regiment—'ours'—very glad, because I know you will be worthy of it and this England of ours and help to add to the glory and honour of both. But Tom, as to your—your—er—love trouble, dear lad, I— trust 'tis no mistaken idea of self-sacrifice, no idea that—that she loveth— that she—I——"

"Nay sir, that you love her I do know right well, that she loveth you I cannot doubt, aye, despite the—despite the wall, with a curse on't! But that she loveth not me I am perfectly sure. So here is no self-sacrifice, nunky, never fear. And sir," continued the Viscount, taking out his snuff-box and tapping it with one delicate finger, "sir, I have a feeling, a premonition that, so far as you and she are concerned, matters will right themselves anon. For if—if she did sit on that—that curst wall, she is always her pure, sweet self and remember, sir, she kicked the damned fellow's hat off!" Here he opened his snuff-box and gazed into it abstractedly as he went on: "Sir, when love cometh to such as you and she, there are few things in earth may thwart or stay such a love, 'tis a fire consumeth all obstacles and pettiness. And indeed, in my mind I see her, in days to come, here beside you, filling this great house with gladness and laughter and, wherever I may be, you will know that in your happiness I am happy too. And sir, as she is the only woman i' the world, I do think you are the only man truly worthy of her and I—ha—I therefore—nunky—er——" Here the Viscount inadvertently took a pinch of snuff and immediately sneezed violently: "O Lard—O Lard!" he gasped. "'Tis the damndest stuff! Always catches me—vilely! A—a curse— on't and—goo'-night, sir!" And, turning abruptly away he sneezed himself out of the room.

For a long while the Major stood looking down into the dying fire, then he stirred, sighed, shook his head and, extinguishing the candles, tramped heavily upstairs, closing the door of his bedchamber a little louder than was necessary. Then, seated at his writing-table he fell to work and wrote so industriously that the clocks were striking the hour of one when at last he rose and stood listening intently. The house lay very still, not a sound reached him save the whisper of the night-wind beyond his open lattice. Treading softly, he crossed to the hearth, above which the Sergeant had hung his swords, half-a-dozen light, richly-hilted walking-swords and his heavier service blade, the colichemarde. This he reached down, drew it from shabby leathern scabbard and found the steel bright and glittering with the Sergeant's unremitting care; so he sheathed it, girded it to his side and, opening a tall, carved press, took thence his old campaign cloak, stained by much hard service, and a pair of long and heavy riding-boots. Kicking off buckled shoes he proceeded to don this cumbrous footgear but paused, and rising, took the spurred boots under his arm together with the cloak and crossing the wide room in stockinged feet, softly opened the door and stood again to listen; finally he took his candle, closed the door with infinite care and crept softly down the great, wide staircase. Reaching the foot he paused to look back up that noble stair and to glance round the spacious hall with its tapestries, its dim portraits, its gleaming arms and armour then, sighing, took his way to the library. Here he paused to shift the candle from one hand to the other; then he opened the door and fell back, staring.

The Sergeant advanced one pace and came to attention. Very upright he stood in ancient, buff-lined, service coat, in cross-belts and spatterdashes, his hat at its true regimental cock, his wig newly ironed and powdered—a soldier from the crown of his head to the lowest button of his long, white gaiters, a veteran grim and ineffably calm. The scarlet of his coat was a little faded, perhaps, but the sheen of broad white belts and the glitter of buckles and side-arms made up for that. His chin, high-poised above leathern stock, looked squarer than usual and his arm seemed a trifle stiffer as he saluted.

"Your honour," said he, "the horses are saddled and ready."

"Zeb—Zebedee!" exclaimed the Major, falling back another step. "A Gad's name what does this mean?"

"Sir," answered the Sergeant, staring stonily before him, "same do mean as I, like the horses, am ready and waiting to march so soon as you do give the word."

"Then, damme Zeb, I'll not permit it! I ride—alone. D'ye hear?"

"I hear, sir."

"You understand, Zebedee, alone!"

"Aye, sir."

"Consequently you will go back—back to bed, at once, d'ye hear?"

"Aye sir, I hear."

"Then begone."

"Axing your grace, your honour, but same can't nowise be, orders notwithstanding nevertheless—no!"

"Ha! D'ye mean you actually—refuse to obey?"

The Sergeant blinked, swallowed hard and saluted:

"Your honour—sir—I do!"

"God—bless—my—soul!" ejaculated the Major and stared wide-eyed at cross-belts, buckles and spatterdashes as if he had never seen such things in all his forty-one years. "Is it—insubordination, Sergeant Zebedee?" he demanded, his cheeks flushing.

"Your honour—it be. Same I do admit though same regretting. But sir, if you are for the wars it na't'rally do follow as I must be. Wheresoever you go—speaking as soldiers sir, I must go as by natur' so determined now and for ever, amen."

"And what o' the estate, ass? I ha' left you agent here in Mr. Jennings' room."

"Same is an honour, sir, but dooty demands——"

"And what of Mrs. Agatha, dolt?"

The Sergeant's broad shoulders drooped quite perceptibly for a moment, then grew rigid again:

"Dooty is—dooty, your honour!"

"And you are a damned obstinate fellow, Zebedee, d'ye hear?"

The Sergeant saluted.

"I say a dolt and a preposterous fool to boot—d'ye take me, Zeb?"

The Sergeant saluted.

"And you talk pure folly—curst folly, d'ye understand, Zebedee?"

"Folly as ever was sir, but—folly for you, folly for me, says I!"

Now at this the Major grew so angry that he dropped a riding-boot and, stooping for it at the same instant as the Sergeant they knocked their hats off and were groping for these when there came a soft rapping at the door and, starting erect, they beheld Mrs. Agatha, smiling and bright-eyed and across one arm she bore—the Ramillie coat.

"Your honour," said she, curtseying, "'tis very late, I know, but I'm here to bring your old battle-coat as I found to-day in the garden, knowing 'tis such a favourite with you. Good-night, sir!" So Mrs. Agatha dimpled, curtseyed and sped softly away, surreptitiously beckoning to the Sergeant.

Left alone, the Major let fall his boots and sinking into a chair sat staring at the Ramillie coat, chin on breast; then he leaned forward to take it up but paused suddenly arrested by a fragrance very faint and elusive yet vaguely familiar; he sighed and sinking deeper into his chair became lost awhile in reverie. At last he roused himself and reaching the garment from where Mrs. Agatha had set it on the table, drew it upon his knees, made as if to feel in the pockets and paused again for now the fragrance seemed all about him, faint but ineffably sweet, a sweetness breathing of—Her. And, inhaling this fragrance, the glamour of her presence was about him, he had but to close his eyes and she was there before him in all her warm and vivid beauty, now smiling in bewitching allurement, now plaintive and tender, now quick-breathing, blushing, trembling to his embrace—even as he was trembling.

So the Major sat grasping his old coat and sighed and yearned amain for the unattainable; imagination rioted and he saw visions and dreamed dreams of happiness as far beyond expression as they were beyond hope of realisation. Wherefore he groaned, cursed himself for a fool and casting the Ramillie coat to the floor, set his foot upon it; and frowning down at this worn-out garment, how should he guess of those bitter tears that had bedewed its tarnished braid, of the soft cheek that had pressed it, the white arms that had cradled it so recently? How indeed should Major d'Arcy as he scowled down at it know aught of this? Though to be sure there was that haunting fragrance, that sweetness that breathed of—Her. Suddenly he stooped and picking it up, raised it to his nostrils; yes it was here—particularly the right sleeve and shoulder. He closed his eyes again, then opening them very wide plunged a hand into the nearest pocket.

His pipe! His silver tobacco-box! In another pocket his purse and a few odds and ends but nothing more. He ransacked the garment feverishly but in place of will, torn paper and letter, he found only one other letter, sealed and addressed thus,

"To Major d'Arcy."

Letting the coat slip to the floor he sank back in the chair, staring long at superscription and seal; then he drew the candle nearer and opening the letter read as follows:

"DEAR SIR,

If this sorry coat looketh a little more creased and rumpled than it is wont to do, this is entirely my fault. And because I am as much a woman as our common mother Eve I have read every document in every pocket. And because every document was for me or of me I have kept them. Yet because, after all, I am truly a very honest person, I do return this your garment herewith together with all other articles soever herein contained, as namely and to wit: Item, one clay pipe and smells! Item, tobacco-box of silver, much scratched. Item, a tobacco-stopper of silver-gilt. Item, a silver sixpence with a hole in it. Item, one purse containing three guineas, one crown piece and a shilling. Item, a small knife for making pens and very blunt. O John, O Jack, great strong tender chivalrous man, and doth thy poor heart break? Stay then, my love shall make it whole again. And wilt thou to the cruel wars? Then will I after thee. And wilt thou die? Then will I die with thee. But O John if thou wilt live, then will I live to love thee better day by day for I am thine and thou art mine henceforth and for ever. But now do I lie here sleepless and grieving for thee and writing this do weep (see how my tears do blot the page) and none to comfort me save thine old coat. O John, John, how couldst have writ such things—to tear my heart and blind me with my tears—yet do I love thee. And thou didst break thine oath to me and yet do I love thee. And thou wouldst have left me—stolen away to give thy body unto cruel death and slay me with despair but still—still do I love thee dearest John. Shouldst thou steal away like a very coward I would be bold to follow thee—aye even into battle itself—so fly not John. And since thou didst break thine oath—thou shalt sue me an humble pardon. And since I do lie sleepless here and weep by reason of thee—so shalt thou make unto me a comfortable reparation. So dear John to-morrow night at nine-thirty of the clock thou shalt meet me at our stile—where we did watch the dawn—and there all thy doubts and fears shall be resolved and vanish utterly away for ever and ever and thou (as I do think) shalt learn to love me even a little better. So come my John at nine-thirty of the clock but not an instant sooner and fail not for my sake and thy sake and Love's sweet sake. O John my love 'tis nigh to dawn, art thou waking or asleep I wonder? Since I am thine so utterly, fain would I write that which I dare not write yet in these lines read all thou fain wouldst read. God keep thee my love and waking or sleeping thou hast the prayers and thoughts of thy Betty.

My poor eyes are all bleared with my weeping and my nose is woeful. And John dear take care of this dear old coat it shall be my comforter this night."

Having read to the end, the Major carefully re-folded the letter and thrust it into an inner pocket; took it out again, unfolded it and having re-read every word once more put it away. Then rising, he set the Ramillie coat upon a chair-back and taking out his handkerchief dusted it, touching its rumpled folds with hands grown almost reverent, which done he sat down and propping square chin on fist gazed at it with a new and wonderful interest. Then he took out the letter again, read it through again and pressed it to his lips; thus he sat, his attention divided between the letter and the coat, until the clock struck two. He was reading the letter for perhaps the sixth time when came a knock at the door and the Sergeant entered.

"Ax your pardon sir, but what o' the horses?" he enquired.

"Horses?" repeated the Major vacantly.

"Aye sir, they've been a-standing in their stalls saddled and bridled a hour or more."

"Have they, Zeb?"

"Aye sir, a-waiting for your honour to give the word to march."

"Why then Zeb," said the Major rising and taking the Ramillie coat over his arm, "you may unsaddle 'em, my honour has decided—not to march."

"Very good, sir!" The Sergeant blinked, saluted and wheeled about.

"Sergeant Zebedee!" The Sergeant wheeled back again.

"Sir?"

"I think—ha—I rather fancy I called you a damned obstinate fellow as 'twere and er—so forth."

"You did so, sir. Likewise 'ass' and 'dolt.'"

"Why if I said 'em, I meant 'em, Zebedee and——" The Major strode forward impulsively and grasped Sergeant Zebedee's hand. "'Twas true Zeb, 'twas true every word, so you are, but—God bless thee for't, Zeb!" Saying which the Major went upstairs to his chamber bearing the Ramillie coat much as if it had been some sacred relic rather than the rumpled, unlovely thing it was.

Being alone the Sergeant stared at his right hand, smiled, took it in his left and shook it heartily. "*Sapperment!*" he exclaimed, "All I says is, O woman!"

CHAPTER XLIX
OF A JOURNEY BY NIGHT

The Major stood chin in hand staring at the weather-beaten stile, set a little back from the road between high hedges and shaded by the spreading boughs of a great tree; its worn timbers were gnarled and twisted with years and the rigours of succeeding winters and, in its length of days, many were the lovers had sighed and kissed and plighted troth beside it; and yet of them all surely never a one had waited with more impatience or hearkened more eagerly for the quick, light tread of approaching feet than Major John d'Arcy, for all his quiescent attitude and apparent calm, as he stood in the light of the rising moon staring gravely at the rickety fabric.

It was here he had held her to his breast as night melted into day, it was here he had kissed her in the dawn—and to-night——The Major's big hand touched the warped crossbar and rested there a little tremulously. And standing thus he fell to thinking of love and the never-ceasing wonder of it and to-night——!

> "So dear John to-morrow at nine-thirty of the clock thou shalt meet me at our stile—where we did watch the dawn and there all thy doubts and fears shall be resolved and vanish utterly away for ever and ever, and thou (as I do think) shalt learn to love me even a little better. So come my John at nine-thirty of the clock but not an instant sooner and fail not for my sake and thy sake and Love's sweet sake."

How well he remembered those oft-read lines, he knew every twirl and flourish that her pen had made——

Soft with distance the church clock chimed the hour of nine. Half an hour to wait! He was earlier than he had thought. The Major sighed and leaning across the stile, stared away towards the rising moon. Half an hour and then——?

> "Come my John at nine-thirty of the clock but not an instant sooner."

And wherefore not? he wondered. Was it on his account or—? Here he fell to frowning thought and gradually a vague unease came upon him;

standing erect he half turned, meaning to walk awhile and return at the appointed time, then paused suddenly to listen.

The night was warm and so very still that sounds carried far and thus he heard a throb upon the air which his trained senses instantly recognised as the sound of horse-hoofs coming at a gallop. Wondering, he moved forward until, standing in the shadow of the high hedge, he could see the road stretching away white under the moon; and presently upon the road were two horsemen, travellers these who rode close side by side, despite their speed. Instinctively the Major stepped back into the shadow and had reached the stile again when he started and wheeled swiftly about—above the drumming of rapidly approaching hoofs he had caught the sound of a laugh, a lazy laugh full of languid amusement; the Major clenched his fists and standing in the shadow, watched the oncoming horsemen under knitted brows. Nearer they came until he could see that one of the riders was a woman; nearer yet until he could make out the pale, aquiline features of Mr. Dalroyd; on they came at speed until—the Major's breath caught suddenly for beneath the lady's riding-hood he saw a face framed in glossy, black curls—the delicate profile, the long-lashed eye, that sweet, proud, red-curving mouth—the face of my lady Betty herself.

'So 'twas thus she came to meet him! Well, even so—' he took an uncertain pace forward. 'But was she there to meet him?' She rode loose-reined at the same swift pace; twelve yards, six! 'Was she indeed coming to keep her appointment? No, by God!' For once in his life the Major's iron self-control was not, a wild rage possessed him; he wore no sword, but, acting upon blind impulse, unarmed as he was, he sprang for the head of Dalroyd's horse. A startled, breathless oath, a wild hurly-burly of stamping hoofs and rearing of frightened horses, then, whipping out one of his ever-ready pistols, Mr. Dalroyd levelled it point-blank at his dim-seen opponent, but as he pulled the trigger his arm was knocked up and the weapon exploded in the air. A desperate smiting in the shadow then, spurring his rearing horse, Mr. Dalroyd broke free and the Major, struck by the shoulder of the plunging animal, was hurled violently into the ditch. When at last he got to his feet, my lady and her escort were nearly out of sight.

"Ha—d'Arcy was it!" said Mr. Dalroyd a little breathlessly as he thrust discharged pistol into holster. "Egad, sweetheart, 'tis relief to know it, I thought 'twas—d'Arcy was it, poor devil. By heaven, Betty, since you are mine at last I can almost find pity for the poor devil, he loved you with a death-in-life adoration, sweet Bet, worshipped you with lowly fervour as you were a saint—you, all warmth and love and passion. O, 'tis a pitiful lover you'd ha' found him, sweetheart, 'tis a smug fool and would ha' driven you frantic with his grave and reverent homage. Now I on the other hand Bet——" Mr. Dalroyd paused suddenly to glance over his shoulder and rode on for a few moments, his head aslant in that attitude of patient listening.

"Didst hear aught, sweetheart? A horse galloping?"

"Nay indeed!" voice muffled in her cloak.

"Good!" Hereupon Mr. Dalroyd entered into a full and particular account of his own virtues as a lover, though more than once he paused in the recital to glance over his shoulder and to listen.

"Indeed, sweet Bet, 'tis as well you are set on Paris henceforth for 'tis necessary I should quit England for awhile. I had the misfortune to offend a gentleman some months since and last week the thoughtless fellow was so mistaken as to die—hence I must to France awhile—but with thee 'twill be a very paradise." Here Mr. Dalroyd reached out to touch his companion's hand but in the act of doing so, paused and glanced over his shoulder and immediately proceeded to change the pistols in his holsters.

"'Twas folly in my lord your brother to choose a different route, Bet, I have post-horses waiting all along the road and a lugger waiting in a certain snug cove. If he should be behind——"

"We must wait!" said my lady.

"Wait—aye Bet, we'll wait a reasonable while, though 'tis torment to an eager lover. To-morrow morning we should reach Boulogne and in Boulogne you shall wed me and——"

My lady turned and scanned the long road behind.

"Ha—d'ye hear hoofs, Bet—a horseman?" My lady shook her head, but now Mr. Dalroyd grew silent and rode alert and watchful.

So they rode, staying only to change horses and on again; even when they paused for refreshment, Mr. Dalroyd spoke little except to urge haste and often would cross to door or window and stand there, head aslant, listening.

It was after they had changed horses for the last time that Mr. Dalroyd lifted his head suddenly and glared back over his shoulder as, faint and far, but plain to hear, came the rhythmic throb of galloping hoofs.

"Ha!" he exclaimed in a long-drawn breath. "Dost hear aught, Bet?"

"One gallops behind us!" said my lady faintly.

"Art wearied, sweetheart?"

"Nay—not very."

"Then ride—spur!"

"Nay, 'tis Charles—my brother, perchance."

"'Tis not your brother!"

"How can you tell?"

"I know!" said he grimly and lifted his holster-flap. Thus, mile after mile they rode with never a word between them, yet, despite their speed, faint and far behind was that rhythmic beat of pursuing hoofs, now lost, now heard again, faint but persistent, never any nearer yet never any further off. And often Mr. Dalroyd glared back across his shoulder and spoke only to encourage his companion to faster pace.

Uphill and down they spurred and across wind-swept levels while the moon waned and the stars paled to the dawn; and with the first chill breath of coming day there reached them the sharp, salt tang of the sea. Mr. Dalroyd uttered a short, fierce laugh and, seizing his companion's rein, spurred his jaded animal to the hill before them. A sloping upland, wild and desolate, a treeless expanse clothed with bush and scrub, with beyond, at the top of the ascent, a little wood. Spurring still, they reached this wood at last and here Mr. Dalroyd drew rein, whipped pistols into pockets and dismounting, lifted my lady from the saddle; then he turned and looked back to see, far away upon the lonely road, a solitary horseman indistinct in the half-light.

"I can do it yet!" he laughed and, catching his companion's hand, hurried through the wood, across a short stretch of grass and so to the edge of a cliff with the sea beyond, where a two-masted vessel rode at her anchor close inshore, while immediately below them was a little bay where a boat had been drawn up. Mr. Dalroyd whistled shrilly, at which signal two men rose from where they had sprawled on the shingle and ran the boat to the edge of the tide.

Then Mr. Dalroyd turned and laughed again.

"Come Betty—my Betty!" he cried. "Yonder lies France and happiness."

"But Charles——"

"He's aboard like enough."

"But——"

"Come!" he cried, glancing toward the little wood.

But now my lady's petticoats must catch which caused much delay; free at length she, not troubling for Mr. Dalroyd's hand, went on down the precipitous path. The sailors, seeing her coming, launched their boat, and my lady, not waiting for their aid and heedless of wet ankles, sprang in, motioning them to do the same.

"But th' gentleman, mam—you'll never run off wi'out your fancy man, lady!" laughed one of the men and pointed to where Mr. Dalroyd yet stood upon the edge of the cliff, staring back towards the wood.

"Lady do be in a 'urry an' no mistake. Tom, give my lord a hail!"

The fellow Tom hailed lustily whereupon Mr. Dalroyd shook clenched fist at the little wood and turned to descend the cliff, but in that instant was a faint report; Mr. Dalroyd staggered, wheeled round, took a reeling pace towards that dark wood and fell.

"Lord—Lord love me, Tom!" gasped the sailor.

"Shove off!" cried my lady.

"But mam—your ladyship——"

"Shove off, I say." Almost instinctively the men obeyed, shipped the oars and sat waiting.

"Row!" cried my lady.

"But Lord—Lord love 'ee mam, what o'——"

"Row!" commanded my lady again, "Row and be damned!" And from under her cloak came a hand grasping a long-barrelled pistol. The little boat shot away from shore out towards the lugger.

Mr. Dalroyd lay motionless, outstretched upon the grass, one arm hidden beneath him and with blood welling between his parted lips; and presently, forth from the shadow of the little wood a masked figure crept, head out-thrust, shoulders bowed, big hand yet grasping the smoking pistol; cautiously and slowly the man drew near and stood looking down on his handiwork. Then Joseph, his obsequiousness gone for ever, laughed harshly and spurned that limp and motionless form with the toe of his heavy riding-boot.

With sudden, mighty effort the dying man struggled to his knees and glaring up into the masked face of his slayer, levelled the weapon he had drawn and cocked with so much agony and stealth.

"Ha, worm!" he groaned, "I waited and you—came. Die—vermin!" Steadying himself he pulled the trigger and Joseph, throwing up his arms, fell and lay staring up, unwinking and sightless, on the pallid dawn. Then Mr. Dalroyd laughed, choked and sinking slowly to the grass, moved no more. The death which had pursued him so relentlessly had caught up with him at last.

CHAPTER L
WHICH TELLS OF ANOTHER DAWN

By a kindly dispensation of Nature all great and sudden shocks are apt to deaden agony awhile. Thus, as the Major stared along the deserted road he was conscious only of a great and ever-growing wonder; his mind groped vainly and he stood, utterly still, long after the throb of horse-hoofs had died away.

At last he turned and fixed his gaze upon the weatherbeaten stile again.

It was here he had held her to his heart, had felt her kisses on his lips, had listened to her murmurs of love. It was here she had promised to meet him and resolve his doubts and fears once and for all. And now? She was away with Dalroyd of all men in the world—Dalroyd!

The Major stirred, sighed, and reaching out set his hand upon the warped timber of the old stile, a hand that twitched convulsively.

She was gone. She was off and away with Dalroyd of all men! Dalroyd—of course! Dalroyd had been the chosen man all along and he himself a blind, self-deluding fool.

The Major bowed his head, loathing his fatuous blindness and burning with self-contempt. Slowly those twitching fingers became a quivering fist as wonder and shame gave place to anger that blazed to a fury of passion, casting out gentle Reason and blinding calm judgment. Truly his doubts and fears were resolved for him at last—she was off and away with Dalroyd! So she had tricked—fooled—deceived from the very first!

The big fist smote down upon the stile and, spattering blood from broken knuckles, the Major leapt over and hasted wildly from the accursed place; and as he strode there burned within him an anger such as he had never known—fierce, unreasoning, merciless, all-consuming. Headlong he went, heedless of direction until at last, finding himself blundering among underbrush and trees, he stopped to glance about him. And now, moved by sudden impulse, he plunged fierce hand into bosom and plucked forth her letter, that close-written sheet he had cherished so reverently, and, holding it in griping fingers, smiled grimly to see it all blood-smeared from his torn knuckles; then he ripped it almost as though it had been a sentient thing, tore it across and across, and scattering the fragments broadcast, tramped on again. Thus in his going he came to the rustic bridge above the sleepy pool and paused there awhile to stare down into the stilly waters upon whose placid surface the moon seemed to float in glory.

And she had once stood beside him here and plied him with her woman's arts, tender sighs and pretty coquetry—and anon proud scorn as when he had vowed her unmaidenly and he, poor fool, had loved and worshipped her the while. And now? Now she was away with—Dalroyd of all men in the world, Dalroyd who, wiser in woman, loved many but worshipped never a one.

Borne to his ears on the quiet night air came the faint sound of the church clock chiming ten. The Major shivered forlornly and turning, tramped wearily homeward.

Sergeant Zebedee, opening to his knock, glanced at him keen-eyed, quick to notice lack-lustre eye, furrowed brow and down-trending mouth.

"Sir," he enquired anxiously, "your honour, is aught amiss?"

"Nought, Zeb," answered the Major heavily, "nought i' the world. Why?"

"Why sir, you do look uncommon—woeful."

"'Tis like enough, Zeb, like enough, for to-night I have—beheld myself. And I find, Zeb, yes, I find myself a pitiful failure as a—a county squire and man o' leisure. This *otium cum dignitate* is not for me so I'm done with it, Zeb, I'm done with it."

"Meaning how, sir, which and what, your honour?"

"Meaning that Nature made me a man of limitations, Zeb. I am a fair enough soldier but—in—in certain—other ways as 'twere I am woefully lacking. I'm a soldier now and always, Zeb, so a soldier I must live and a soldier, pray God, I'll die. Last night you were in a mind to follow me to the wars—doth the desire still hold?"

"Aye sir. Dooty is dooty. Where you go—I go."

"So be it, Zeb. We will ride to-morrow for Dover at five o' the clock."

"Very good, sir."

"Are the servants all abed?"

"Aye, sir, and so's the Colonel."

"Then lock up and go you likewise, I have certain writings to make. And mark this, Zebedee, 'tis better to die a man of limitations than to live on smug and assured the sport of coquette Fortune as—as 'twere and so forth. D'ye get me, Zeb?"

"No sir, I don't."

"Egad, 'tis none surprising Zeb," said the Major ruefully, "I express myself very ill, but I know what I mean. Good-night, Zeb—get ye to bed."

Reaching the library the Major crossed to the hearth and sinking down in a chair beside the fire, sat awhile staring into the fire, lost in wistful thought. At length he arose and taking one of the candles opened the door of that small, bare chamber he called his study; opened the door and stood there wide-eyed and with the heavy silver candlestick shaking in his grasp.

She sat crouched down in his great elbow-chair, fast asleep. And she was really asleep, there was no coquettish shamming about it since coquetry does not admit of snoring and my lady snored distinctly; true, it was a very small and quite inoffensive snore, induced by her somewhat unwonted posture, but a snore it was beyond all doubt.

The Major rid himself of the candle and closing the door softly behind him leaned there watching her.

She half sat, half lay, lovely head adroop upon her shoulder, one slender foot just kissing the floor, the other hidden beneath her petticoats; and as she lay thus in the soft abandonment of sleep he could not help but be struck anew by the compelling beauty of her: the proud swell of her bosom that rose and fell with her gentle breathing, the curves of hip and rounded limbs, the soft, white column of her throat. All this he saw and, because she lay so defenceless in her slumber, averted his gaze for perhaps thirty seconds then, yielding himself to this delight of the eyes, studied all her loveliness from dark, drooping lashes and rosy, parted lips down to that slender, dainty foot. And as he gazed his eyes grew tender, his fierce hands unclenched themselves and then my lady snored again unmistakably, stirred, sighed and opened her eyes.

"John!" she whispered, then, sitting up, uttered a shy gasp and ordered her draperies with quick, furtive hands, while the Major, eyes instantly averted, became his most stately self.

"O John are you come at last and I asleep? And I fear I snored John, did I? Did I indeed, John?"

The Major, gaze bent on the polished floor, bowed.

"I don't as a rule—I vow I don't! 'tis hateful to snore and I don't snore— ask Aunt Belinda. And O pray John don't be so grim and stately."

"So," said he gently but his voice a little hoarse, "so you have—have thought better of your bargain, it seems."

"Bargain, dear John?"

"Your—cavalier, madam. Mr. Dalroyd rides alone after all, 'twould appear."

"Mr. Dalroyd!" she repeated, busied with a lock of glossy hair that had escaped its bonds.

The Major bowed with his gravest and grandest air.

"Nay prithee John," she sighed, "beseech thee, don't be dignified. And the hour so late and I all alone here."

"And pray madam, why are you here?" he questioned. Now at this, meeting his cold, grey eye, she flushed and quailed slightly.

"Doth it—displease you, Major John?"

"Here is no place for you, madam, nor—nor ever can be, nor any woman henceforth."

At this she caught her breath, the rosy flush ebbed and left her pale.

"Must I go, sir?" she asked humbly, but with eyes very bright.

"When you are ready I will attend you as far as your own house."

"If I go, John," said she a little breathlessly, "if I go you will come to me to-morrow and plead forgiveness on your knees, and I am minded to let you."

"I think not, my lady—there is a limit I find even to such love as mine."

"Then is my love the greater, John, for now, rather than let you humble yourself to beg forgiveness for your evil thought of me, I will stoop to explain away your base suspicions. To-night you went to the stile before the time appointed and saw that hateful Dalroyd eloping with my brother Charles in my clothes as you saw him once before—upon the wall."

"Your brother!" cried the Major. "Dear God in heaven!"

"Is it so wonderful?" she sighed. "Had you been a woman you would have guessed ere now, I think. But a woman is so much quicker than a blind, blundering man. And you are very blind, John—and a prodigious blunderer."

The Major stood silent and with bowed head.

"So this was my scheme to save my dear Charles and avenge myself upon Mr. Dalroyd—and see how near you brought it to ruin, John, and your own life in jeopardy with your fighting. But men are so clumsy, alas! And you are vastly clumsy—aren't you, John?"

The Major did not answer: and now, seeing him so humbled, his grand manner quite forgotten, her look softened and her voice grew a little kinder.

"But you did save Charles from the soldiers, John. And after, did save me from Mr. Dalroyd's evil passion—wherefore, though I loved thee ere this, my love for thee grew mightily—O mightily, John. But now, alas! how should a poor maid wed and give herself into the power of a man—like thee, John? A man so passionate, so prone to cruel doubt, to jealousy, to evil and vain imaginings, to cruel fits of—of dignity—O John!"

The Major raised his head and saw her leaning towards him in the great chair, her hands outstretched to him, her eyes full of a yearning tenderness.

"Betty!" He was down before her on his knees, those gentle hands pressed to his brow, his cheek, his eager lips.

"I have been blind, blind—a blind fool!"

"But you were brave and generous also, dear John, though over-prone to cruel doubt of me from the first, John, the very first."

"Yes, my lady," he confessed, humbly.

"Though mayhap I did give thee some—some little cause, John, so now do I forgive thee!"

"This night," said he sighing, "I destroyed thy dear letter."

"Did you, John?"

"And thought to destroy my love for thee with it!"

"And—did you, John?"

"Nay, 'tis beyond my strength. O Betty—canst love me as I do thee—beyond all thought and reason?"

At this she looked down at him with smile ineffably tender and drew his head to her bosom and clasping it there stooped soft lips to cheek and brow and wistful eyes.

"Listen, dear foolish, doubting John, my love for thee is of this sort; if thou wert sick and feeble instead of strong, my strength should cherish thee; wert thou despised and outcast, these arms should shelter thee, hadst thou indeed ridden hence, then would I humbly have followed thee. And now, John—unless thou take and wed me—then solitary and loveless will I go all my days, dear John—since thou art indeed the only man——"

The soft voice faltered, died away, and sinking into his embrace she gave her lips to his.

"Betty!" he murmured. "Ah God—how I do worship thee!"

The hours sped by and rang their knell unheeded, for them time was not, until at last she stirred within his arms.

"O love," she sighed, "look, it is the dawn again—our dawn, John. But alas, I must away—let us go." And she shivered.

"Art cold, my Betty, and the air will chill thee——"

"Thy old coat, John, the dear old coat I stole away from thee." So he brought the Ramillie coat and girded it about her loveliness and she rubbed soft cheek against threadbare cuff. "Dear shabby old thing!" she sighed, "it brought to me thy letters—so shall I love it alway, John."

"But thy shoes!" said he. "Thy little shoes! And the dew so heavy!" My lady laughed and reached up to kiss his anxious brow.

"Nay," she murmured as he opened the door——

"'Tis dabbling in the dew that makes the milkmaids fair."

Hand in hand, and creeping stealthily as truant children, they came out upon the terrace.

"John," she whispered, "'tis a something grey dawn and yet methinks this bringeth us even more joy than the last."

"And Betty," said he a little unsteadily, "there will be—other dawns— an God be kind—soon, beloved—soon!"

"Yes, John," she answered, face hidden against his velvet coat, "God will be kind."

"And the dew, my Betty——"

"What of it, John?" she questioned, not moving.

"Is heavier than I thought. And thou'rt no milkmaid, and beyond all milkmaids fair."

"Dost think so, John dear?"

"Aye, I do!" he answered. "So, sweet woman of my dreams—come!"

Saying which he caught her in compelling arms and lifting her high ainst his heart, stood awhile to kiss hair and eyes and vivid mouth, then e her away through the dawn.

And thus it was that Sergeant Zebedee Tring, gloomy of brow, in faded, -lined service coat, in cross-belts and spatterdashes, paused on his stablewards and catching his breath, incontinent took cover behind venient bush; but finding himself wholly unobserved, stole forth to

watch them out of sight. Now though the dawn was grey, yet upon those two faces, so near together, he had seen a radiance far brighter than the day—wherefore his own gloom vanished and he turned to look up at Mrs. Agatha's open lattice-window. Then he stooped and very thoughtfully raked up a handful of small gravel and strode resolutely up the terrace steps.

Being there he paused to glance glad-eyed where, afar off, the Major bore my lady through the dawn, and, as the Sergeant watched, paused to stoop again and kiss her.

"Glory be!" exclaimed the Sergeant and instantly averted his head: "All I says is—Joy!"

Then, with unerring aim, he launched the gravel at Mrs. Agatha's window.